ADVANCE P

"*Silent Cries* is a must read for anyone who is in, has been, or knows someone in a domestic violence relationship. It addresses why women stay in violent relationships, the effects they have on children, and that there is hope for a full life after one chooses to leave."

—**Barbara Higgins, Law Enforcement Victim Advocate**

"*Silent Cries* is an authentic and true-to-life depiction of one woman's exodus from a life of psychological and physical servitude to one of empowerment and self-determination. This story captures the persistence and fortitude required to exit a life with an abuser without sacrificing gentleness and wisdom."

—**Donna R. B. Rogers, PhD, Licensed Psychologist, Founder, Sound for Healing Institute**

"Lisa J. Peck demonstrates that the advantages of education, economics, and faith are no guarantees for safety in a marriage. She offers a personal voice for the apprehensions, obstacles, and prejudices, as well as the victories, rewards, and fulfillment that accompany leaving an abusive relationship. [Many] will read *Silent Cries* and see their exact feelings mirrored and find validation, inspiration, and encouragement."

—**Staff members from No Shelter For Me, a nonprofit shelter for women of upper level income**

"Lisa J. Peck brings light to the corners of our suffering and shows a path to safety. Her triumphs and stories kindle the hope and promise in our faith and our lives. *Silent Cries* leads us to discover our own paths to safety for our families, and in safety is joy."

—**Michael Basile, Family Advocate Congregation Networks, Inc.**

Silent Cries

A Woman's Journey to Freedom

SILENT CRIES
A Woman's Journey to Freedom

Lisa J. Peck

SILENT CRIES: A WOMAN'S JOURNEY TO FREEDOM
PUBLISHED BY BRIDGEWAY BOOKS
P.O. BOX 80107
AUSTIN, TEXAS 78758

For more information about our books, please write to us, call 512.478.2028, or visit our website at www.bridgewaybooks.net.

Printed and bound in the United States of America. All rights reserved. No part of this book may be reproduced in any form or by any electronic or mechanical means including information storage and retrieval systems without permission in writing from the copyright holder, except by a reviewer, who may quote brief passages in review.

Library of Congress Control Number: 2007925645

ISBN-13: 978-1-933538-90-7
ISBN-10: 1-933538-90-2

Copyright© 2007 by Lisa J. Peck
Cover Concept by Priyanka Kodikal

This is a work of fiction. Names, characters, places and incidents either are the product of the author's imagination or are used fictitiously. Any resemblance to actual persons, living or dead, events, organizations, or locales is purely coincidental.

10 9 8 7 6 5 4 3 2 1

Thanks to those living angels who helped me and others through those dark times. A special thanks to my husband whose support allows me to soar.

Part One

Chapter 1

For three weeks, while her husband was at work, Charlene had been secretly e-mailing her friend, Judy, hoping he wouldn't find out. Opening Judy's return e-mails to discover what her friend had to say had been the highlight of her day. As long as Brad didn't learn she was doing it, she figured there was no harm in having an innocent friendship. It kept her connected to something besides drooling babies, loaded diapers, and burned dinners. But recently, Charlene hadn't felt as excited about pressing the open button. Maybe because Judy had started to pry, asking questions people weren't supposed to ask, like about her husband's temper. Charlene knew she had a good husband and didn't see any reason for her new friend to cast doubt.

Granted, Brad did get touchy about silly things, like when he saw Charlene eating anything with sugar in it. "Now, Charlene," he'd say, "You know I have your best welfare in mind by stopping you. You'd be miserable if you got fat. Chocolate really isn't worth it, is it?"

Charlene wanted to scream, "Yes! It is!" but after ten years of marriage, she knew better. She kept her protests to herself and hid the chocolates she wanted to eat. Every person had a few weaknesses, didn't they? Brad often searched the house for her hidden stash, and if he found it, there would be hell to pay. But sometimes, when the rich taste melted in her mouth, sending comfort and pure joy through her, Charlene thought it was worth the price of hell.

Another subject that tested Brad's patience was when she bought things without his permission. He insisted they stay on a budget—his budget. She agreed with him, of course. She didn't want to be like the many couples who ended up spending themselves into a huge pit of debt. After all, they had children to raise. A responsible, involved husband was a gift from God. Charlene did wonder if it was reasonable to get livid over buying a package of gum at the store, especially when the groceries got loaded into his new sport's car. Not everything made sense, but she was sure his temper was no worse than any other man's.

It bothered Charlene that her husband's qualifications were being called into question. She decided to focus on the parts of her friend's e-mails that she liked—the walks along the beach and how idyllic Seattle sounded. Charlene dreamed about flying up to Washington to visit Judy. She wanted to enjoy the white clouds hovering over the wild ocean. She longed to take those strolls and let the tension of motherhood ease away as the sand squished between her toes and the sun warmed her skin. That might just be the perfect escape from her humdrum existence.

Making a trip like that was impossible. Brad would never allow it. So instead of thinking about escaping her monotonous life, she worried about Brad discovering her e-mail account. Yes, he was a great husband. He just wouldn't like it if he knew she was on the computer instead of paying attention to the children. He believed being a full-time mother meant that was all the woman should do. He was right, of course. Guilt filled Charlene about writing Judy, but she'd go crazy without any outside contact. Maybe someday she would be the person she needed to be; the person Brad wanted.

For now, she gave in to her weakness and secretly wrote Judy, despite the negativity toward her husband. She didn't know how Brad would react if he found out. He'd probably break into the computer and read the e-mails—all of them. He used to search the whole house until he found her journal. The mental images of pillows, clothes, and dishes flying and breaking while he looked had not left her—or his anger after he read it.

"How dare you misrepresent me!" he'd shout. "You're nothing but a liar. And you're so negative. You're never grateful for all the good things I do for you. How come you can't see things the way they really are?" Charlene never wrote it right no matter how she tried. Eventually, it wasn't worth the fuss and she stopped writing altogether. Some things were just easier not to do. Besides, she hated to fight. Their conflicts had gotten ugly before, and she definitely didn't want to go there again. Every marriage had its problems. She needed to learn how to compromise and what to avoid doing. Unfortunately, sometimes her learning came at the price of experience.

But this time Charlene hoped he wouldn't find out about her e-mails. It had been years since the journal incidents, and her husband didn't even know she had a new friend who had recently moved to Seattle. She had told him about Judy and their trips together to the craft fairs, but he didn't know how close they'd gotten or how much they liked to chat. Brad was busier with work and surer of their marriage these days. Charlene hoped that by now he trusted her more and wouldn't mind her having a friend.

She had e-mailed Judy on the subject:

> If he does find out, it's on my head. Please don't stop writing me. Sometimes I feel like I'm silently crying out to you. I need someone to listen. I look forward to your news, and it's nice to have someone who cares. Brad knows very little about you, not even your last name. I won't mention that in the e-mails. He won't be able to trace you, only your e-mail address.

Charlene hoped Brad wouldn't trace other things she had done, like getting her own checking account to pay for the e-mail subscription. She had waited until Brad was caught up with a deadline at work that monopolized his attention. Then, she stopped at the bank. Unsure how to open an account, and worried her kids would unknowingly betray her to Brad, she used the drinking fountain in the front entry as a way to get a moment alone. "Sandra, can you get everyone a drink?" she asked her oldest, who was eleven and liked to be in charge. The kids scurried away, except for Nathan, who was two and too young to be out of her sight. He wouldn't talk.

She was quickly directed to the right spot. An older, silver-haired gentleman smiled at her. "What can I do for you?"

Paige, her six-year-old, ran up to her. "Mom, Sandra spit water on me."

Charlene looked at her daughter's tear-filled eyes and sighed. "Tell Sandra to stop that or she's going to get extra chores."

"But my shirt's wet," Paige insisted.

Clenching her hands tighter, Charlene said, "Go on and tell her." She heard her voice had gone up an octave.

Paige left, and Charlene turned back to the man. "I'd like to open a new account." She felt hot. Her heart raced as though she was doing something wrong. She looked over at her kids, made a quick mental count to make sure they were all still there, and then turned her attention back to the old man, who was getting forms.

"How much would you like to deposit?"

Charlene pulled out a check she'd received for wall hangings she'd made and sold at a local craft fair. She had created the arrangements when Brad was out of town and had carried the check around for over a month wondering what to do with it. If she kept it much longer, she risked Brad going through her purse and finding it. She didn't know what excuse she could come up with then. Brad had been okay with her going to the fair, but he wouldn't like her having a hobby when she should be taking care of the kids. He would also be enraged that she didn't immediately turn over the money to him.

"With this," she said, smoothing the crease in the paper. The check was made out for two hundred and thirty-two dollars and sixteen cents. It wasn't much, but it was more than she'd had in years.

"Fine," the man said, giving it a cursory glance. "Please fill out these forms." He slid some sheets over to her. The kids had joined her by now and were tugging on her pants. She tried to ignore them as she filled out each form.

Charlene stopped at the slot for her address. "What do you mail out to us with this account?" She knew this would seem like a strange question and hoped it wouldn't make him suspect she was up to something.

"An information letter and monthly statements."

Charlene had grown increasingly hot as she pondered what to do. Should she get this account? Should she go behind her husband's back? He would kill her if he ever found out. It had taken her quite awhile to decide to do this. Should she back out?

No. She'd get it. She knew it was risky, but she felt confident she could get the mail every day before Brad did. She'd have to make a point of it.

She looked up, watching her kids climb over everything. They were talking loud and laughing, obviously bothering many of the other bank customers. "Kids, come here." They obeyed their mother and came running.

"You defiantly have your hands full, don't you?" the banker asked.

Charlene gave a half nod. What the banker said was true.

"If you tell me your names and ages, I'll give them a sucker. Is that okay, Mom?"

Charlene nodded fully this time, relieved.

"Sandra," her eldest announced. "I'm eleven." Her short, brown curls shook as she spoke. "I want the green one."

The banker laughed and gave her the green sucker.

"Cameron," her second oldest said, head tipped down, and stuck out his hand.

"How old are you, little man?"

"Ten," Sandra answered for him. She put her arms around her little sister and pushed her forward. "This is Paige, who's eight." Then she pointed to next younger sister. "And that's Lorine. She's five, and the baby is Nathan, and he's only two. He doesn't talk much."

The banker laughed. "Well then, I guess that's everyone."

*

Charlene kept her new bank account a secret for several months. Then one day she came home from grocery shopping to find Brad's car parked in the driveway. What was he doing home so early? Charlene worried as she unbuckled Nathan from his car seat.

She hurried inside, taking a bag of groceries with her. She set it on the kitchen counter with a thump and walked quickly toward Brad's office. There he was, sorting through the mail.

A terrified lump rose in her throat. *Please don't let there be a bank statement,* she prayed, smiling at Brad. "Hello, what are you doing home?"

"I have to go back tonight for a big meeting, so I thought I'd spend a couple of hours at home before then."

"Oh," Charlene said. She glanced at the stack of mail. She'd have to look at it before he went through it—how? "Brad, will you help me bring the groceries in?"

"Yeah," he said, going back to sorting the envelopes.

She had to think fast. Throwing her arms around him, she gave him a long kiss. Then she grabbed his arms and coaxed them around her waist. "I've got some milk and other cold stuff out there. If you bring it in now, I'll cook your favorite meal." She batted her eyes to be silly.

He laughed. "Okay."

She walked with him to the doorway and waited until he went outside for the bags before she ran back. She sorted through the mail and, sure enough, spotted a bank statement. She grabbed it, folded it, and shoved it in her pocket before rushing to the kitchen. She waited until his second trip to the car to stash the envelope in her office.

*

Charlene knew she had to tell Judy about the risk she was taking, in case Brad made Judy pay for their friendship. Last year, Charlene had hung out with Kelly, a friend she'd made when taking the kids to the park. Whenever they met, Brad would greet her and then wait until she left to laugh about how "psycho," as he put it, she was.

"Anyone who believes the end of the world is just around the corner is cuckoo." Other times he would say, "I can't believe you're hanging out with that nutcase. She's not even in the real world. She's always quoting Revelations. That's not normal. She's going to end up in one of those cults, probably dead by a government raid, shot in the head."

Then he took to laughing at Kelly openly every time he saw her. "Had any more prophesies?" he'd ask, or, "How's Revelations? Any more six-headed monsters coming to swallow us all up?"

"Actually you don't understand Revelations at all. You're mistaken on thinking that a six-headed monster..." Kelly tried to explain at first, until she realized Brad was only mocking her. She became so angry and flustered she stopped coming over.

Another time she'd been on the phone talking to Nicol, another woman she'd grown friendly with while babysitting at Sunday school. Brad had called out, loud enough so Nicol could hear, "Is that your skinny, bean pole friend?" He made a habit of complaining to Charlene while she was chatting with her friend. "Why are you always on the phone? Why don't you ever make time for me?"

It was embarrassing, and her friends understandably didn't want to hang out long. For that reason, Charlene stopped inviting people over. This kept her more isolated, and sometimes the days of playing hide-and-seek and cleaning up spills became so tedious she wanted to scream. During those more boring hours, she'd remember with fondness when other mothers had visited when her kids were younger and Brad was away more. They'd sit in the backyard and talk under the shade tree, watching as the kids played and fought.

Charlene hoped her words of warning wouldn't scare Judy out of writing to her. Although Judy and Charlene hadn't known each other that well before Judy moved, Charlene didn't know what she would do if Judy thought their correspondence was too risky. Her life was already so lonely, and Judy seemed like her last lifeline.

*

Fortunately for Charlene, Judy didn't let the risk of getting caught by Brad stop her from e-mailing. She said she was willing to stand up to anyone for her. Charlene thought that was a little overdramatic but had a smile in her heart the whole day after she read the reassurance.

She immediately wrote and told her thank you. She also explained that she couldn't come to Washington with all her kids, even though Judy had offered to pay. The offer overwhelmed Charlene with its generosity. She thought about how wonderful it would be to sit on the beach, meditating away the afternoon. It sounded divine, but to have her friend pay for it? She couldn't do that. She and Brad had money. Why would Judy make such an offer? It was confusing, but Charlene decided not to make an issue out of it. Besides, Brad would *never* let her go anyway, no matter who paid for it.

As Charlene floated through her days, helping her children with their homework, cleaning house, and cooking, she thought often about the beach. Around noon, three days after Judy's offer, another e-mail dinged in. The contents took all of Charlene's focus.

Chapter 2

In the e-mail, Judy had brought up Brad's temper again and had since refused to let it go. She kept pressing, asking in as many ways possible in her next batch of e-mails what his temper was like. Charlene felt like a pit bull had a death grip on her throat. Charlene didn't want to ignore requests from her friend, especially since she feared if she didn't answer the questions she would lose her only contact with another adult. So she carefully explained that sometimes when Brad was having a tough day at work he would be grouchy. The kids and she would try to stay out of his way when he'd play that typical "hero comes home stressed" stuff.

When she wrote about her husband to Judy, an unsettled, guilty feeling fluttered in her chest. It was wrong to talk ill of one's spouse, and she knew she had sinned.

Guilt pricked at her until Judy's next e-mail. Again, she offered to have Charlene and the kids fly up to visit. Her friend was so insistent about her coming that Charlene actually considered it for quite some time, but she knew she couldn't. Asking Brad about something like that now was completely out of the question. He was so uptight about problems at work that his gray cloud of angst preceded him wherever he went. When Charlene gathered enough courage to ask what was ailing him, she learned his co-workers weren't treating him well. Immediately she was filled with sadness and empathy for the troubles her husband had to go through to provide for their family. She shouldn't be selfish and think about getting away when he was doing all this hard work and needed her at home to comfort him.

Charlene knew Brad's temper was caused by his continuous efforts to provide for his family and the pressure of all his obligations. Feeling confident that Judy, a smart woman, would see this as a normal reaction to a stressful situation, Charlene wrote her friend. She hoped that this would get Judy off her case, but the more she revealed, the more she realized she really did want to confide to her friend.

I wish you wouldn't ask me about Brad's temper. I know you say you feel inspired to, but this is really personal. Please don't be offended. I'm taking it under consideration. I know you care, and I think I can trust you. I'm not sure how to respond, though. I guess that's why I've waited a week to write back. I've been thinking about it a lot. I will tell you about it, but only if you promise not to talk to anyone else about this. I shouldn't complain about him. It's not what a good wife does, but I guess maybe I do want to. Maybe I need to. Maybe then I can find peace.

As Charlene tried to describe what had happened the night before with Brad, she felt herself begin to shake all over and had trouble typing.

She had gone to the grocery store and was running late because she'd had to stop three times for potty breaks. As soon as one child went, another needed to. When she pulled into her driveway, she saw Brad's new SUV parked next to their back door. She hurried the kids out of the van, thinking about the fastest dinner she could throw together. The minute Charlene saw his face, she knew something was terribly wrong. He had that look like he was on the warpath, his brows lowered ominously.

Gulping back a sudden attack of nerves, Charlene asked, "What's the matter?"

Brad set down his day planner. "My damn boss is at it again. He's so stupid. He thinks he knows how to market, and clearly he doesn't."

"Oh. Have you talked to him?"

"Yes," he said and stormed out of the room, slamming the side door on his way to get the groceries.

She flinched at the loud bang of the door. She had to get something for dinner fast. If she didn't, it would set him off more. She began digging through the cupboards, searching for an idea.

"Charlene," he said as he carried in the milk. "Why did you buy this brand of milk? You know it costs more."

"It tastes better than the others." She dug through the pots to find the right size to warm up canned stew.

"We've got to be careful," he said. "Money doesn't grow on trees."

She poured the stew into a large saucepan, hoping to get his focus changed to food, but that didn't work. It only made him madder.

"I can't believe how careless you are with my hard-earned money. It'll lead us to bankruptcy. Don't you remember what happened to my parents?"

"It's a twenty cent difference," Charlene protested, wrapping her arms around Nathan, who had suddenly raced into the room and clutched her legs. "Bankruptcy won't happen over twenty cents."

"What?" His expression turned dark. "You didn't earn that twenty cents. Obviously you don't care about how hard I work."

"I didn't say that." Charlene straightened and crossed her arms. Sometimes Brad could be so frustrating. She hated it when he took out his bad days on her. Tomorrow, when he calmed down, he would realize how ridiculous he was being.

Brad came up behind her, yelling, "Tell me! Does all my hard work mean nothing to you?"

"Would you stop it?" Charlene turned to face him. Feeling crowded and trapped, she side-stepped him to get away. "Sometimes you go over the top."

"You bitch," he yelled.

Charlene knew she had done it then. She had pressed his magical tick-off button. She needed to act now. "Kids," she said to Nathan and Paige, who were staring at their dad, "get down to the playroom, now." They continued to watch, not listening to her.

"Look at me when I'm talking to you." His breath was hot on her face. "You always try to pass off your mistakes onto others."

He hovered over her, and she tried stepping away from him, but he blocked her with the mass of his body. Desperate, she tried the other direction. She needed to get away from him. She needed to have space, breathing room.

He blocked her again. "Bitch. That's right, always creating a problem then trying to run from it."

"That's not true." Charlene tried to hold in her tears. "Stop swearing at me in front of the kids."

"Why? That's what you are." He stood right against her. All she could see was his chest. "Bitch, bitch, bitch."

Charlene began to shake. "What did I do wrong? I only—"

"Like you don't know. I can't believe you." He raised his arm as though he was going to hit her.

Charlene dropped to the floor and covered her head with her hands. She huddled into a ball, crying.

"Quit being dramatic. You're so manipulative." He started pacing.

The fear choking Charlene's throat rose, causing tears to fall.

"You're such a piece of work," he said, voice rising. Suddenly, he picked up the milk jug and threw it against the kitchen wall. It missed the children and Charlene, but broke when it hit the wall, splattering milk everywhere.

The violence broke through Charlene's fear. She had to get the children out of there. In the rage he was in, he could hurt anyone. "Come on, kids. Downstairs, *now*!" she yelled from her position on the floor.

Brad walked over to Charlene and grabbed her hand. "Let's talk about this upstairs."

As he was taking her up the stairs, she looked back at the kids, who stayed in the living room, watching them. They looked scared. She longed to reassure them and vowed to do so later that night when she had a chance.

Brad slammed the bedroom door shut and then locked it. "I can't believe you're so ungrateful."

Charlene knew it was worthless to try and argue back. She mentally drifted off as he ranted for the next hour. Finally he grew hungry and wound down so they could eat dinner. Charlene found the kids and talked to them until their fears were eased. She then read to them until everyone but Sandra had fallen asleep.

Later that night, as Charlene cleaned the milk off the counters, floor, and chairs, she noticed the splattered milk had stained the ceiling. How was she going to get to that? And how come she was always the one who had to clean up the messes he made?

The next morning the kids tried searching for designs in the patterns in the stains. Cameron saw a dinosaur ripping a tree out of the ground. It looked more like wind-blown clouds to Charlene.

*

A day later, an e-mail dinged in from Judy. What she wrote shocked Charlene. Judy was angry. She asked if Charlene really thought her husband's behavior was normal. *Yes,* Charlene had rapidly written back. *Everyone has his or her personality flaws. If you don't believe me, ask anyone, or get close enough to them and you will find this out.* Even as the words flowed from her fingers, something disturbed her. She didn't want to pay attention to it. Of course she would love it if Brad treated her better. She'd have to be crazy not to. But he was having a hard time at work, and she needed to be an understanding wife. After all, he only got mad every couple of months. Her father had been mad a whole lot more than that when he'd been around. Brad was so much better than her father. At least Brad cared about his family and loved them. Plus, he tried hard. That was what Charlene needed to focus on. Let go of the negative and acknowledge how good it was to be with a man who made an effort. Judy, though well-meaning, hadn't learned how to be as positive as Charlene. Perhaps that was why she wasn't married.

Charlene remembered her mother's constant admonition: "We're on this earth to endure trials, Charlene. That's our purpose." Charlene could think of no harder trial than trying to forge a union between a man and a woman. She related this belief to Judy, hoping it might help her understand the purpose and value of marriage more. Charlene did agree that maybe Brad should be treating her better, but the fact that he wasn't meant she had to put more effort into the relationship. If she could be more understanding, more loving, more patient, and a better mother, he would come around.

After she sent off her e-mail, Charlene focused on cleaning her office. While she'd been typing, the kids had found her full trash can, pushed it over, and giggled happily for the next eleven minutes as they played in the piles of papers, spreading them everywhere. Charlene shooed them out so she could clean, and they ran happily off to the next room and tore it apart. Then that wonderful chiming sound came, letting her know an e-mail had arrived. Charlene rushed to the computer. Her heart jumped in her throat when she saw Judy had responded to her post so quickly.

Brad had no right to treat you that way. Stop sucking up to him. It's unbecoming.

That was it; nothing else. Charlene felt like a knife had been thrust into her chest. If that was the way Judy was going to be, she didn't want to write her again. Tears surfaced, but before she could think much more about it, she heard splashing sounds coming from the bathroom.

She hoped Nathan wasn't playing in the toilet again.

Chapter 3

Fourteen days passed without any communication between Charlene and Judy. The days held nothing but an endless repetition of diaper changing, laundry, wiping tear-stained faces, and cooking. Although the June days were sunny outside, it felt like the overcast of winter to Charlene. Without writing her friend, there was nothing to look forward to. Charlene thought about reaching out to Judy, but then she would remember the sting of Judy's words and anger would swell in her. Then Charlene would tighten her hand into fists and resolve once again not to respond, no matter how lonely and miserable she felt.

She wasn't sure which was worse: the "no right to treat you that way," or "stop sucking up." Maybe it was the word "unbecoming." That echoed through her mind hundreds of times every day. How could a friend say something like that?

Finally, Judy wrote to Charlene to see if she had offended her—which, of course, she had. To Charlene, however, the fact that she reached out was enough to soothe all the rough feelings. Maybe she had overreacted and was being too sensitive. She did seem to take things more personally than others. Another thing to add to her self-improvement list—a "tougher skin." She eagerly wrote Judy back.

> Subject: Sorry
> Date: June 22
> From: "Charlene" <char@CharlenesWeb.net>
> To: "Judy" <bchcomber@yippee.com>
>
> Judy,
>
> Sorry. I know you were asking and saying those things because you care. I was totally surprised that you would see Brad as mean. Today somebody else commented to me, "How can you stand your husband talking to you that way?" I've thought about it since then, and I have no idea what they are talking about.
>
> I'm glad you see me as a daughter, because I see you as a mother.
>
> Still your e-mail friend,
>
> Charlene

After pushing the send button, relief washed through her. Things were better—back to normal—except that another comment had been made, this time by Sandy, a parishioner in her church. That morning, Sandy had called about a charity drive the women of the church were organizing. While they talked, Charlene scrubbed dishes and handed the kids Play-Doh—Cameron would make a meat-eating dinosaur, and Sandra would definitely create something that suggested she was the best.

The conversation went along smoothly, drifting from the charity drive to the children, then on to husbands and their inability to remember messages taken on the phone. Charlene laughed at a joke Sandy made about the reason men needed to get married. "It's so they would know that they aren't perfect," she said. Then she followed up with the shocking comment. "Now, seriously, Charlene, how can you stand your husband talking to you the way he did the other night? Does he treat you like that often?" And on she went about her concerns over Brad.

It was strange that people were complaining about Brad. Charlene had been happy with him on the night in question. She wanted to understand it. What could her husband have said that would cause Sandy to make a comment like that?

A week passed, and the question of what Brad had said kept popping into Charlene's mind. The more she tried to figure it out, the more confused she became. She had asked Sandy what she was talking about. Sandy wouldn't answer her. Instead she said, "Why don't you think about it?" That was all she was willing to say. She shouldn't let it bother her. It was just a remark. But two people commenting on Brad's behavior toward her? Did they see something she couldn't?

Judy didn't mention anything more about Brad or the marriage. Instead she wrote Charlene to inform her she'd injured her knee by tripping over a dress while trying to walk and hang it up at the same time.

Trying to be a good friend, Charlene pointed out the bright side—Judy could still meditate. In fact, that was about all she could do, Charlene couldn't help but add teasingly. Things needed to lighten up. She and Brad had been fighting all day. *Talk about living with pain*, she told Judy, and proceeded to share their latest disagreement.

They'd gone on a date the night before. Charlene was sick of the repetitive problem that occurred almost every time they went out, where he watched televisions the whole time and ignored her at the restaurant. So this time she brought a book to read. She had tucked it in her purse and waited, trying to talk to Brad several times.

"Brad, do you think that Sandra's anger is a problem?"

"Yeah."

"It's sure hot, isn't it?"

"Uh huh," he said as his gaze drifted over to the game. Then he began talking to the TV screen. "Ah, come on, that was a travel if I ever saw one."

Charlene gave up. She slipped her book out and began reading. The historical novel swept her away to another world.

"What are you doing?"

The sharpness of Brad's voice startled Charlene. "Um, reading."

"On our date?" Brad spat out.

She shifted uncomfortably in her seat. "You're watching TV."

"Can't you ever just be with me?" he asked. "Do you always have to be so boring?"

Those words bit into Charlene. Her husband thought she was boring. "I can put the book away if you'd like. Do you want to talk?"

Brad glared at her.

She slipped the book into her bag and turned to him, waiting for him to say something. He said nothing but continued to glare.

Charlene waited.

Still nothing. More glaring.

People in the restaurant cheered. Brad looked up at the television screen to catch the replay, and Charlene waited. He finally opened his mouth: "Nice rebound." Talking to the TV again.

Charlene knew from experience that if she said anything she'd be wasting her time. They wouldn't talk until he was ready to.

Eventually their food came. Still no talking. Not able to stand the silence any more, Charlene said, "Aren't you going to speak to me?"

"What do you want to talk about?" he snapped.

Charlene's pulse fluttered nervously at his tone. She didn't know what to say, so she asked the question on her heart. "Do you love me?"

"Why are you asking such a stupid question?" He popped broccoli in his mouth.

By the time they arrived home, Charlene was in tears.

"Would you quit crying?" He tossed the car keys onto the counter. "Sometimes you're so weird. You say you want to spend time with me, then you bring that dumb book. Maybe it's you that doesn't care."

"I do too," Charlene said, hearing the whine in her voice and hating it. Maybe that was the problem. Brad didn't understand how much she cared. She would be hurt too if she was in his position.

The next day, Charlene asked Brad to help her get the children ready for church. He stayed in bed and then half an hour later began yelling. "Why are we always late? Charlene, why didn't you get up earlier? It sucks that we have to be late."

"We're trying." Charlene hurried with her mascara. "Could you grab Lorine's shoes?"

Brad left and Charlene heard him screaming from the kitchen. "Can't anything be clean? We're white trash."

Charlene rolled her eyes. *Here we go again.* She was just putting her makeup away when Brad stormed in the room.

"The house is a pigsty. Why do we have to live this way?"

Charlene's hands tightened into fists. "Because we have a toddler. Have you ever tried keeping up with one? They're mess-makers on wheels."

"Maybe if you spent your time being a mom instead of reading all the time."

That did it. If he didn't recognize all the work she did around the house every day, then clearly he was clueless. She wasn't going to stand around listening to any more lies. Besides, if they kept this up, they really would be late for church. She marched out of the room.

"Where are you going?" Brad yelled.

"To make sure the kids are ready." She started down the stairs.

Brad crashed after her and grabbed her arm, jerking her back. "Don't ever walk out on me." His face turned an ash-gray and his eyes were fiery.

Charlene swallowed. She couldn't help whimpering from the pain caused by his fingers pinching her arm. "Sorry," she whispered, hoping to calm him.

"You're a mighty fine bitch. Let's go to church." He shoved her toward the garage door.

Charlene felt dizzy. There was no way out of this. Everything was too much.

*

Charlene should have known better than to tell Judy that she was fighting with Brad. Instantly Judy became overly concerned for her welfare, almost in a complete panic with her stream of questions: *Are you all right? Are you safe? Do you need to leave your home for a couple of days?*

At the end of the e-mail, almost as an afterthought, Judy mentioned that she had just lost her job. Charlene instantly felt guilty. Judy had enough to worry about. The loss of a job was much more important than a stupid fight with Brad. After getting Sandra, Cameron, and Paige off to school and the others down for naps,

Charlene sat at her computer to reassure her friend that things on her end were fine. Before doing so, she took a moment to check the brand-new e-mail account Brad had just set up for her so she could do bookwork for him. When she had told Judy about it, she explained that although this new event was contradictory to Brad's stance about only paying attention to the kids, he needed help, and this was part of being a helpmate.

To Charlene's surprise, an e-mail from her husband awaited her. She pressed the open key. He was apologizing for the pain he'd caused. He said he would strive to control his anger and to make things up to her. Relief cascaded through Charlene. This was more than she could have hoped for.

She read on. He told her of his love for her and how grateful he was that he had married her. She made him complete. He admitted he needed to work on his communication skills and was starting to understand that when he became mad, he was not thinking clearly. He promised he would work on stopping his floods of emotion by telling her when she was causing them. If she knew when she was driving him over the edge, maybe she could keep it from happening. This was better than she could have dreamed. They were going to overcome their problems. Brad loved and needed her. She happily logged out of that account and into the other one so she could update her friend with the good news.

He also wrote about his gratitude for my patience. I wanted to laugh. Me? Patient? I wish. Part of the problem is that I'm not patient. I don't want to have any more problems. I'm tired of handling them. I don't know how other people do it. Sometimes I wish I could walk out the door and not come back. Of course, I won't.

I'm feeling much better today since I received his e-mail. I do love him and want to make us work. I'm willing to do everything necessary to see that we succeed. I can't imagine not having a successful marriage.

After telling perhaps too much about her relationship, Charlene asked questions about Judy's job and life. She admitted that she guiltily hoped the job loss would mean Judy would move back. She joked about it and made light of it, but it really wasn't a laughing manner to her. Things would be so much better if she could have her friend back. They could go to craft fairs again and go shopping and out to lunch. Judy was one of those rare people who didn't care that Charlene had five children with her all the time. Her friend was patient and enjoyed the kids. They would joke back and forth as they shopped, ate, or wandered through the crowded aisles at the fairs. Once, while they were driving to the mall, Judy related an anti-Republican joke she'd heard.

Sandra, then nine, gasped. "You're not a Republican?"

Charlene, glancing in the rearview mirror, saw complete amazement on her daughter's face.

Brad was a fanatical Republican. He listened to AM talk radio every day and ranted about Democrats and how being one was a sin.

"Well of course I'm not a Republican," Judy laughed. She put a teasing note in her tone.

"But," Cameron's face turned red, "Democrats are evil."

Judy laughed hard at that. "Who have you been talking to? Republicans are the ones destroying the country."

"But Democrats pay people to not work," Sandra countered. "That's wrong." She jumped into one of her dad's favorite Democratic jokes.

Judy hollered with laughter then told a Republican joke, adding, "Why do you support a party who keeps raising taxes to spend on wars and cuts welfare, letting our own poor starve?"

"Democrats are wrong." Cameron's face turned pink.

Charlene and Judy laughed. "Someday they'll get you on that argument," Charlene promised. Those had been good times.

But it sounded like, from the next stream of e-mails Charlene received, Judy was not planning to move back. She talked about God guiding her to a place were she'd be happier, more fulfilled, possibly get paid more, and she talked a lot about loving being close to her children. Charlene did her best to offer support, although she kept the hope for the move tucked in her heart. Things would be better if Judy came back, even though she did intrude with her pointed, disquieting questions about Charlene's marriage. Charlene felt almost poetic, or at least philosophical, when she wrote:

Do you really think that others don't have my kind of problems in their marriages? Are you sure? I think they do. Of course, we're guessing—you're divorced and I only have my own marriage, and my parents', to go by. They divorced about five years ago. Brad's parents divorced around the same time. Maybe they aren't the most ideal people for me to use as examples for my marriage. "Are there any happy marriages?" I remember asking one of my professors when I was in college. He promised me there were. I didn't believe him. Still don't. But what if there are some? What are they doing that I'm not?

Charlene decided to get brave and describe her most recent experience with Brad. He had insisted she follow his wishes on this matter, and her agreement was the only way to stop their fighting.

Chapter 4

"I can't take this any more. You've got to get fixed," Brad said. He had asked Charlene to come and sit with him on the front porch. The sun was sinking in the sky, spreading coral pink across the horizon.

"What are you talking about?" Charlene hadn't heard Brad speak like this before.

"When I was engaged to Melissa and things broke down, my mom sent me to see a psychologist. I was mad at first, but then I realized it really helped me. Charlene, the problems you're having are beyond what I can help you with. You came from a rough home. I don't even know how you survived it, but it has messed you up. You need help. I made you an appointment for next Thursday morning. I'll babysit."

"A therapist? I don't need one of those." Charlene hugged herself, as though that could keep her safe.

"Yes, you do," Brad said. "I'd like you to give it a try for at least a month. It's that or I'm leaving you."

That made things very clear. Charlene remained silent, looking at the darkening sky. She could smell the neighbors' tangy barbecue and hear their children shouting and laughing. Was she so bad and messed up that she needed a therapist? Maybe it might help. She didn't know what to think about the whole thing.

*

Thursday morning arrived faster than Charlene wanted it to. It was time for her to visit the shrink so they could determine the extent of her mental illness.

Charlene checked in with the receptionist, wiped the palms of her hands on her pant legs, picked up a woman's magazine off the coffee table, and began flipping through it. She needed to go to the bathroom. She looked at the clock and decided she still had a couple of minutes. Most doctors were never on time. She dashed to the bathroom and came out to find a gray-haired lady waiting for her. "Are you Charlene?"

She nodded.

"I'm Mrs. Thomas. Call me Cindy. Shall we?" She led Charlene into a small office decorated with a blue couch, a chair facing the couch, a large oak desk, and a bookshelf filled with important-looking books. The room smelled of peach candles. "It's so nice to meet you," the lady began.

They shook hands and Charlene sat down. She put her purse on her lap and gulped. What was she going to say?

"So what has brought you here?" the lady asked with a smile.

Charlene cleared her throat and said, "My husband."

"Really," Cindy said, eyebrows raised. "How's that?"

She didn't want to answer. It was embarrassing. "He says I need to get fixed." Charlene knew her face was a deep red by now.

Cindy sat back in her chair, and the ticking of her clock filled the room. When she began talking, she said quietly, "Let's talk about your marriage, shall we?"

Charlene wrote Judy about it the next day.

When I first met my therapist, she asked me why I was there, and I truthfully told her that my husband sent me in to get fixed. I still can't believe he insisted that I go to therapy. I think he will live to regret it.

I don't like feeling. I don't like remembering. My counselor says I was abused. I can't believe she said that about my parents. I thought I came from the perfect family. My dad made good money. My parents were pillars of the community. People commented on how perfect our family was. Little did I know the price we paid for that perfection.

Charlene felt sweat break out all over as she admitted going to therapy. It was so embarrassing. She feared she might run into someone she knew in the waiting room. If that happened, what would they think? If they saw her there, would they assume she was crazy? That her marriage was struggling? In the waiting room, she felt as though she was wearing a branded tattoo on her forehead, almost like having to wear an *A* for adultery like the main character in the novel *The Scarlet Letter*. Charlene always brought something to read to bury herself in and hoped no one noticed her.

She had to tell someone about this. It would help her be okay with what she had committed to do. But not just anyone. People might look at her funny and perceive her as warped. She trusted Judy wouldn't say anything and would accept her in spite of her terrible flaws. Besides, Judy didn't live around anyone she knew.

Judy's reaction was unexpected. She was excited about Charlene's therapy and encouraged by it. She thought it might really help. *Hopefully that's true*, Charlene thought.

But therapy wasn't as easy or fun as Charlene thought it would be. It wasn't about just going some place and talking for an hour. Instead, her therapist kept digging deeper and deeper into her memories of her childhood. Those were awful. She didn't magically remember more or less than before therapy, but the newly dredged up emotions proved terrifying. When she first described what things had been like as a kid, she really didn't have any feelings, but now, as the weeks went by, she found herself feeling lonely, lost, and scared—so scared. This was surprising. She had thought she had the model family, but now she was beginning to realize her family lived a life of constant fear. Each of them hurried to make sure the house was spotless before her father arrived home. Her mom rushed to prepare dinner. If everything wasn't perfect, he might fly into a rage, yelling and hitting—especially Charlene, since she was the oldest child. But if they did everything right, it might be okay.

Charlene spoke of how she would pray her dad wouldn't come home. When he was there, she stayed out of his way, mostly in her room. If he saw her, he was critical and would get angry about everything. No matter what she did, she couldn't please him.

As weeks went by and the more her therapist wanted to know how she felt when the events happened, she started to re-live instances. When she was seven, her dad wanted her to drink a glass of orange juice. She refused, not liking it. The pulp made her gag. He wouldn't let her drink or eat anything else until she drank the whole glass. She obeyed, but threw up in the kitchen sink afterward, so he spanked her and sent her to her room, telling her if she was sick then she had to stay in her room all day. They went through this struggle many times. She often waited until he left the room and dumped the juice down the drain. One time he wasn't going to have that. He set up guards—her brothers—to watch and make sure she drank it. He cooked pancakes (her favorite), then wouldn't let her have any until she gave in and drank a glass of orange juice. Charlene refused that time and went hungry for two days before he gave up. He never made Charlene drink orange juice again and she hadn't since.

"What you learned from this situation," Cindy said, "is that if you stand up for your desires you will pay a heavy price, a life-threatening one. So you shut down don't ask for what you need or even know what it is anymore."

Those words haunted Charlene. She wondered why it took a professional therapist to help her see these things. The last time she visited with her minister, he promised that if she would "hang in there" she would achieve peace. But that was not enough.

"Do you want to push your children away?" Cindy asked.

She was taken back by the question. She'd never push her children away. "What do you mean?"

"If you don't learn how to feel, you will."

Charlene pursed her lips. This was utter nonsense. She was close to her children. That would never change. How would not feeling do that? But she couldn't help worrying. What if, by chance, Cindy's statement held a truth she didn't want to face? Charlene loved her kids and would do anything for them, so she decided to give this "feeling" crap a try. For them—her kids. She couldn't stand the idea of not being close to her children, and she'd rather die than ever hurt them.

When she arrived home, Charlene tried to explain what was happening to Judy:

I can't sleep at night. When I do sleep, I'm always being murdered in my dreams by someone I can't see but who has the ability to be everywhere. I feel like I'm losing control, and yet I'm getting stronger in my relationships by standing up more to Brad. It's weird. I'm saying things I would never have dared before. I'm taking risks, which doesn't always have pleasant results, but at least I'm not hiding as much anymore. Does any of this make sense? Can you relate to this? Have you ever had demons like mine?

Thank you for your vote of confidence that Brad and I will make it. I believe we will too. It's going to require a lot of hard work. Today I bought five books on how to improve your marriage. Brad probably won't go through them with me, but I'll do my part. I'm also getting up an hour earlier to study.

Judy's reply was filled with support and compassion for what Charlene was going through. She hardly ever mentioned her own life or problems, such as her continuing search for a new job, despite Charlene's repeated requests. Charlene felt bad for complaining when her friend had so many of her own struggles, but Judy didn't seem to mind, so Charlene wrote her about her ever-increasing health problems. Her stomach hurt constantly and her heart had developed jabbing, squeezing pains. Charlene wondered if she would die of a heart attack. She noticed more of her hair in the sink and on her comb. That made her worry. Would she end up bald before she was dead? If that was the case, she joked to Judy, *Hmm, closed casket for sure!*

She told Judy how tired she was and how most of the time all she thought about was taking naps, but if she slept the house would just fall even more apart around her.

Two weeks passed without her touching base with her friend. Judy had inquired how she was, but Charlene hadn't made time to respond. She explained that her life was a whirlwind. Things had not gotten any easier, just harder. Reluctantly, she confessed what weighed most heavily on her mind. Her therapist thought that Charlene's oldest daughter, Sandra, might be bipolar. This information had drained all the remaining energy out of Charlene. She wasn't keeping up with reading those parenting books or "How to be the perfect wife" or anything else. Every day had become a struggle just to hold on and not drown.

Judy's lengthy reply was full of references to medical research. It suggested that Charlene's poor physical health could be associated with her emotions. Charlene admitted in her response that she had always thought that idea hogwash. There couldn't really be any truth to that philosophy. Her life was not that rough, so she really didn't think there could be a connection.

*

"Charlene." Brad called out in a deep, sharp tone, instantly alarming Charlene. He came into the house and slammed the door behind him.

Charlene was in the laundry room. She thought about pretending she hadn't heard him but knew that would make things worse. "What?" she asked, stepping into the hallway with an armload of towels.

"I ran into Debra at the gas station. She says she wants to buy two more floral arrangements like the last ones she bought from you." His eyes peered accusingly into hers.

Great. He had found out about her earning money on the side. Not knowing the best way to handle this, she hurried past him to the kitchen, her mind racing. Getting a glass from the cupboard, she asked, "Do you want a drink?"

Not distracted in the slightest by her ploy, he said harshly, "I thought you wanted to be married to me."

Charlene felt the blood drain out of her face. "I do."

"Then why are you sneaking around doing things behind my back?" He banged his fist against the wall.

She looked down at the patterned tile. Maybe if she remained quiet and still, this storm would pass around her and leave no damage.

"Don't you care about our children? Our marriage? God? How dare you damn yourself like this and bring us along with you? What kind of woman are you? I thought you were God-fearing." With each question, his voice rose a little louder.

"I am," she said.

"Then why are you lying to me? What else are you hiding? Maybe you're having an affair too."

"No!" she said, grabbing his hands. How could he think such a horrible thing? She had to comfort him. "Please believe me. I would never do that."

He shoved her away roughly. "Why should I? You're lying to me, and you don't take care of the children."

"I do too." Charlene decided the safest position she could take would be to talk about the children. "I always take care of the kids. They never go without anything. They don't mind if I make floral arrangements while they play with their Play-Doh."

"It's the lying that makes me mad. I wonder what kind of person I'm really married to."

She knew she had done wrong. She wasn't even sure any longer why she had hidden the hobby from him. "I'm sorry," she said. "I'm sorry."

He looked down at her, his mouth twisted with disgust. "Why would you do that? I don't care if you make floral arrangements—but to lie to me? How the hell am I supposed to trust you now?" He walked into the kitchen, where a pot of beef stroganoff simmered on the stove.

Charlene went up to him and whispered, "I'm sorry. It won't happen again."

"It better not." He turned from her.

Charlene decided to initiate sex that night, knowing it would calm him down. Sometimes it was the only thing that did.

*

Charlene didn't often e-mail her husband. There was hardly ever any need—they saw each other every day—but today she thought it would be a good idea. Some things were easier and safer to say over the Internet waves than face-to-face. Plus, she could think about what she was wanted to communicate without any interruption.

Subject: I love you
Date: August 2
From: "Charlene" <char@Charlene.org>
To: "Brad" <brad@consult.com>

Brad,

You're not the only one who's confused in this relationship. You seemed to be much nicer, so I let the door open more to my heart. Then you kicked it down again, using the excuse that being minister of the house makes you the ruler who makes all decisions for the family. Yes, I made some floral arrangements for craft fairs. What's the big deal? The children helped. They weren't being neglected.
I don't feel like my money is only mine, but you can't be serious when you say I should give all of it to you so I can "know what it feels like to have my money spent." It's not that much, and I only used it to buy clothes for the kids.

My therapist says your behavior of insisting on knowing about every penny is controlling. Before you get all over her case, remember you are the one who sent me to her to get "fixed." She says part of me getting fixed is being able to make decisions on my own. She says I'll be much happier if I have some say in what I do. We both want me to be happy, don't we? If you would like me to achieve that, then it would be helpful if you let me buy some necessary items.

I guess I sound angry in this e-mail. Well, I am. I'll probably regret sending this to you. I love you.
Your wife,

Charlene

Besides the little relief that came from speaking her truth, the e-mail caused Charlene trouble. Brad called her on the phone, livid, demanding to know what she meant by calling him controlling. As he told her off, she had to excuse herself to run to the bathroom, which increased her husband's anger each time it happened, but she kept needing to go. She had defiantly developed a weak bladder from having so many kids. As she thought about it, she was convinced that her stomach problems and migraines were directly related to the stress of being yelled at by Brad. Later, she wrote Judy about it, wanting to know how she could end the health struggles.

My husband thinks I'm ill. He has reluctantly admitted that I'm not good at being a stay-at-home mom, so he consented to let me take a class at the local college. I don't care why he's supporting me in this, I'm just glad I get to take the class.

The bubbling tears that stubbornly refused to stop leaking from her eyes confused Charlene. She couldn't wait to go to class. It would be a wonderful escape from the boring life she had been enduring for what seemed like years. It had been a long time since she'd had something to look forward to, and she missed the feeling. Perhaps the tears were caused by the realization that her husband did care and was supporting things that would make her happy. She was truly blessed with Brad for a partner.

Another happy event sent her to the phone where she dialed Brad at work. "I received tickets in the mail for a week of lectures at our local church college. They were already paid for and everything."

"Where did they come from?" Brad asked.

Shrugging as though he was in the room with her, she said, "I don't know, but it must be a sign from God that I should attend some more lectures."

"A sign you need to be fixed," Brad said jokingly.

"Oh, stop that," Charlene said.

Since Brad had come to believe that Charlene getting out of the house was the secret to solving all their marriage problems, she wasn't going to miss out on this opportunity. "I'm calling a babysitter," she said, wishing Judy could go with her. There wasn't even a chance for her to fly down. She was still struggling with physical therapy over her injured knee. It was too bad because Judy would have really enjoyed it. Despite Charlene's skittish nerves, she had a feeling the classes would prove to be an important event in her life.

CHAPTER 5

Out of the hundreds of promising classes offered in the catalog, only one stood out when Charlene flipped through it: "Healing from Abuse."

Her attraction transformed to fright when she stepped into the classroom. Was she admitting something horrible just by attending the class? Her heart thundered more loudly than the toy drums her children loved to bang. Would others think she was one of *those* people? Fortunately for her, Brad could care less about what classes she was taking. If he did ask, she'd talk about the other, safer, classes she was attending.

She slipped into a seat in the back and buried herself in the notes from one of her other classes. As she tried to focus on what she had learned, she couldn't resist periodically darting glances around the room to see if she knew any of her classmates. As luck always had it, she did. Karla, her neighbor, sat a few seats away. Charlene ducked her head over her notes and pretended not to see her.

The instructor, a thirtysomething, slender female, began. "Trauma occurs when a person suffers an experience that has a lasting effect on his or her mental health. When a traumatic event occurs and the victim doesn't have a reasonable explanation for it, a chemical is released that floods the neurons like a river overflowing its banks. The force of the water makes its own pathways, causing destruction to the landscape. The surface damage is easy to detect, but deeper effects are harder to see. If a professional aids in the repair immediately, generally less harm is done. But if left undetected or unexamined, the damage can be much more devastating.

"This damage can result from being physically beaten, having something thrown at you, or witnessing another person's rage, whether it is directed at you or not."

Trauma can come from being physically beaten? Charlene had been beaten by her father and Brad many times. Could having things thrown at you have that kind of effect on the brain?

She started to feel queasy.

"There are many types of trauma," the instructor continued.

A lady sitting up front raised her hand and the instructor called on her. "Does the same thing happen to a person who's been raped?" she asked.

Charlene lowered her head. Why did a question like that have to be asked? The subject was already uncomfortable enough. Charlene didn't want to have to think about rape along with everything else.

"As much harm can happen to a person who experiences an attempted rape as to someone who is actually raped. A lot is determined by the individual's personality, how they perceive the event, and how soon after the incident there is intervention.

"If someone is raised with rigid religious views on sexuality and grows up in an environment that would make her believe she is shattered beyond repair if an immoral act happens, then the damage would be much greater than for a woman who has a more liberal mindset."

Oh, crap, Charlene thought. She must really be in trouble. She came from one of those upbringings. She'd had boyfriends who did things. She never wanted to think about it. The more the lady talked, the more uncomfortable Charlene became. What was being said hit home—her life, her experiences, what had happened to her.

As Charlene listened to the explanations of what constituted abuse, her head spun as though she were on a roller coaster being dumped upside down.

Suddenly, Karla's arms wrapped around her, anchoring her. Charlene allowed Karla to hold her, something she had never let another woman do. She needed the grounding sensation. The instructor called for a break and came to Charlene to help.

Later, after a break, the instructor described the symptoms of someone who has been through trauma. "Often, when people have been through trauma, they can't sleep well."

That had been true Charlene's entire life.

"They are irritable, angry, and hyper-vigilant—that means they are extra aware of their environment. Their antennas are up so they can detect who or what is going to hurt or reject them."

Duh. It would be totally stupid not to do that. Lots of people were out to get anyone dumb enough to let his or her guard down. What was wrong with doing that?

"They self-sabotage," the instructor said. "They are withdrawn, untrusting, overly busy, fearful, and often perfectionists. Some become promiscuous. Others get involved in substance abuse."

Charlene decided that none of those applied to her, except maybe the "untrusting" and the "overly busy." Before she could think more about it, the instructor continued.

"People who experience trauma have a high divorce rate, are more prone to marry into domestic violence, and have a low job success rate. Other signs are loneliness and emotional numbing. This means a lot of the time they don't feel anything, but other times they'll either over or under react to situations."

Charlene recalled Cindy telling her she needed to feel. That "feeling" word was being mentioned a lot lately. Why feel the pain if you didn't have to? Cindy said it was only for a while; then she would be free. Charlene thought she was a liar.

The instructor's lecture caught her attention again.

"Women who have experienced trauma normally sink into depression. Men often become angry. Feelings of hopelessness and helplessness are common with victims of trauma. They can be suicidal and confused. They can lack concentration, experience flashbacks, and block memories. The slightest thing—a smell, a sight, a word, a voice—can trigger the memory of a terrible event."

Maybe this stuff was why she had such horrible nightmares. Her therapist had defined this cluster of symptoms as PTSD—post-traumatic stress disorder—and said she had this also. Crap. What else? Would she ever be okay? It was beginning to feel like she had more wrong with her than she could ever "fix."

"Victims have a hard time having fun because it makes them feel vulnerable. They aren't willing to take that kind of risk. They have a lot of guilt and no sense of safety in their relationships. They are attracted to abusers because abuse is familiar to them. I hate to say it, but abuse is their comfort zone. They have problems in their relationship with God, and they struggle to trust in a higher power they believe has abandoned them. They also feel abandoned generally." The instructor made it very clear that this distrust was a natural reaction to the abuse.

"Abuse doesn't always consist of broken arms and the hospital trips you see on TV. Being hit or having things thrown at you aren't the only kinds of abuse. As I said before, just experiencing rage is traumatic."

Charlene shook. There was no doubt from what the instructor said that she had been abused.

Her father had abused her and so had past boyfriends. She could add her husband to the list sometimes too. She was one of those victimized people. She had a college degree, beautiful children, and an upper-middle-class life. How could she be an abused wife?

It took Charlene a couple of days to get her act together enough to jot a note to Judy about what had happened. Judy, being her typical self, was compassionate about the pain but insisted on knowing more. What had happened? What had been taught? Charlene, unable to explain it, wrote:

Subject: Off the edge
Date: August 27

From: "Charlene" <char@CharlenesWeb.net>
To: "Judy" <bchcomber@yippee.com>

Judy,

I'm struggling. I'm having a hard time not crying all day. I even had to have an emergency session with my therapist because I was falling off the edge. Many past issues bubbled up in that session, plus some focus on what the instructor had said at the college class. What an emotional trip!

Charlene

Fortunately, as she struggled with all of this, Brad was sympathetic and comforting. He held her as she sobbed. She didn't tell him about her realization of his abuse—only about her family and growing up.

"I'm sorry you had to go through that," he said. "Yeah, your dad wasn't a nice guy. If I had to live in your family, I would have run away. I don't know how you took it. You're better than me." Brad's understanding and willingness to help around the house and take the kids to the park really helped her out. She felt deep gratitude toward him.

A couple of days went by. Charlene felt better after shedding the host of tears generated by her past. She started to think of the hope the teacher had suggested could help a victim of abuse climb out of the quagmire of physical, emotional, and sexual abuse. Charlene began to wonder if she too could get out, be educated, and create a support system. With her family situation the way it was, her mother in a mental hospital and her father refusing to speak to her, help would have to come from the community.

She laughed through her tears when she remembered a quote the teacher had given: "I forgive the scorpion, but I don't put him down my shirt." She said one of the most important things a victim needed to do was to forgive. This was a process and could not occur by simply deciding one day that all was forgiven. The first step was to not hate the abuser, but to give the pain and damage to a higher power. Another step was to hold the abuser responsible for his actions.

Dr. Phil quoted the Bible, saying, "Mercy can't rob justice." And if Dr. Phil said it, well…Charlene would have to give it some thought.

*

She did a lot of thinking and praying, too. Her teacher had said, "Each person will know what he or she must do when it's time."

Charlene hoped that would be true for her. Would she really, *really*, know how to fix her marriage problems? Or maybe the right way to put it was: would she know how to protect herself and her children?

Things had gotten ugly again between Brad and her after a brief spell of courtesy. It wasn't right. Other husbands didn't treat their wives so badly. He had no right. But what made her really mad was when he turned his anger on their kids. This had rarely happened before, and she wasn't going to stand for it. She had promised herself long ago when she was still a child and suffering abuse at her parents' hands that her future children would never have to endure what she had. Well, now Brad had hurt her child, and she would not tolerate it. He had awakened Mother Bear, and he'd better watch out. The best way to get her message heard without him interrupting would be through e-mail.

Subject: Good Dad?
Date: September 3
From: "Charlene" <char@Charlene.org>
To: "Brad" <brad@consult.com>
Brad,

You were looking for reassurance last night that you were a good father. After I saw the terror on our Sandra's face when you ripped her shirt and yelled at her, how can I say you're a good dad? She's endured a lot of fear in our home. Are you asking me to support the fact that you have frightened our daughter? Impossible. If you hurt her physically again, I'm calling the cops.

You keep mentioning couples' therapy, but the two appointments I set up, you cancelled. And you're not going to your personal counselor. How am I supposed to believe you're serious about your promises when your actions speak so loudly?

Love,

Charlene

Charlene received an angry e-mail in response. She thought about calling Brad but disliked the sinking feeling in her stomach that always came when they didn't get along. She knew a phone call would set him off. She was too afraid to do it.

She busied herself with household chores. Twenty minutes later, the phone rang. It was Brad. "What was that e-mail all about? I didn't hit Sandra."

"I didn't say you did," Charlene snapped back. "I said you ripped her shirt and frightened her, which by law is still considered abusive."

"I did not."

Charlene wasn't going to put up with his denial this time. It wasn't okay for him to be messing with her baby. "You can deny it all you want, but it doesn't change the facts."

"What's next? You're going to accuse me of sexual abuse?" he yelled into her ear.

"Diversion," Charlene said calmly but firmly. "Why don't you ask our daughter if you scared her? I'm not making things up."

The fight over the ripped shirt started a string of bad events.

"Charlene," Brad said one day after she just arrived home from her college class. Brad had been babysitting. "You need to stop going to these classes. It wasn't such a good idea." His jaw was tight and his eyes narrowed with repressed anger.

A knot of nerves rose in her throat. "Why?" She tried to sound casual, giving no hint that what he was threatening to do would hurt as much as it would. Her classes were a breath of fresh air, her freedom, her way of coping with stress. If they were taken from her, she wasn't sure what she would do, but thoughts of not living shot through her.

Paige raced into the kitchen, wrapping her arms around Charlene's legs. "Mom, Mom, I fell off the monkey bars." Her eyes had turned sea green, which happened when she was in true pain.

Charlene examined her daughter's small arm. Paige had broken her arm before, and this looked and felt the same.

"Are you okay?" she asked, stroking Paige's hair.

Her daughter nodded.

"Why didn't you take her to the doctor?" Charlene asked Brad accusingly.

"She doesn't need one."

"She has to go." Charlene gathered her purse off the counter.

"You're making a big deal out of nothing," Brad said.

"It's broken."

"You're always so hysterical. It's fine. Paige hasn't been crying or anything. Look at it." He walked over to Paige and examined the arm. "There's no swelling or bones poking out or anything."

"I'm taking her to the doctor." Charlene pressed her lips together, preparing for what he would do next. She didn't care if he tried to stop her. She would get her daughter the medical treatment she needed. She pushed gently on Paige's shoulder, urging her toward the door.

"Yep, always anxious to waste our money."

Charlene held her tongue and walked out to the car. She asked Paige on the way how it happened to make sure Brad wasn't responsible. According to Paige, her dad hadn't touched her. She had fallen off the monkey bars.

When she returned home, it was late. The kids were still running around making messes while Brad sat in front of the television. "It's about time you got home," he said.

"Her arm was broken."

He shrugged and returned his attention to the game. Not wanting to get into it or talk about quitting her classes, she simply put the children to bed, cleaned the house, and had just started on her homework when Brad called, "Aren't you going to spend any time with me? Or are you too good for me now?"

Charlene closed her books and hid them in the lower cabinet below the counter. If he decided to explode tonight, she didn't want her homework ripped up again.

*

A week later, angry and cussing, Brad called on his cell. He had gotten into a car wreck. He said the accident was her fault because he had to race around like a crazy man to get everything done to make up for the time she was gone at her classes. Now he would have to pay higher insurance. "Doesn't anyone care about money around here but me?"

Charlene was stressed. She still worked to keep her house hospital clean in addition to doing her schoolwork and tending to the kids. Her therapist pointed out that she kept herself insanely busy. Charlene had tried to learn how to slow down—which she did by signing up for an independent study class. Brad didn't know. She thought it was best not to tell him yet. Would she ever be content and not involve herself in five million things at once? With a mixture of pride and sadness, she admitted her kids were like her. They wore her out with piano lessons, soccer, baseball, playing with friends, making craft projects, and a variety of other things.

She still couldn't believe she had five of them. Brad wanted more and more. After Sandra she'd thought, "Who am I to deny him a son if he wants one? I'll pray not to get pregnant. God will manifest His will by what happens." That was how the first two got to share the same due date a year apart. She didn't see things that way any more. Bringing the fourth into the world almost took her life. The pregnancy had been high risk, and she had struggled to stay conscious at the birth. Afterward she wouldn't stop bleeding and struggled with blood clots.

"It would be best," the doctor had said in the hospital, "considering how hard this child was to get here and all your complicated health issues, that you don't have any more children."

Brad had picked up the orange juice off Charlene's tray. He downed it in two huge gulps.

Charlene looked over at him. "Did you hear that?"

He shrugged. He waited until the doctor left, and Charlene questioned him about it further. Then he said, "The doctor was just making a suggestion. He doesn't know anything." He ate the cookie off her tray before adding, "Look at the baby. You can't honestly tell me you don't want another one, can you? They're so cute. Come on, don't you want a little Nathan? Wouldn't another boy be so fun?"

Brad saw to it that Charlene became pregnant again a mere six months later.

She thought about getting on birth control secretly but knew their marriage would be over if she did something like that. It didn't feel morally right to go behind her husband's back like that. Her fifth pregnancy was life threatening too, with all the difficulties—like blood sugar problems, anemia, and fibrocystic tissue growth—that came with the process. The doctors told her again that she shouldn't have any more children. Brad finally agreed because the nurses saw to it that he did. "No more children. Do you understand?" They kept rehashing it until he said, "Okay, okay. I got it."

Charlene was all right with that. Truthfully, she was relieved. Most of the time five seemed more than she could handle and definitely more than Brad could cope with. To solve the problem, Brad hired a maid to come clean the house once a week. When Charlene protested, he said, "You work so hard to keep everything so nice. You deserve it. I want to help you out and help you be happy.'" He also mentioned that he wanted to quit his job and assist Charlene with the kids more while working from home. Charlene had said, "Yeah, right, that's crazy," but from the look on his face she worried that he just might do it.

Chapter 6

Subject: Silent Treatment
Date: September 5
From: "Charlene" < char@Charlene.org>
To: "Brad" <brad@consult.com>

No, Brad, I'm not giving you the silent treatment. I'm trying to work through a lot of issues, which does not give you an excuse to be aggressive. I know you don't like hearing about your behaviors in our home, but it needs to be addressed if we're going to get the problems fixed.

I'm sorry it hurts that I don't trust you, but I can't. You have done too many things, and trust isn't earned overnight. You wonder why I don't divorce you? (1) I love you, and (2) I believe we can work it out. I'm glad you want to stay married too and that you want something better. That will take work on both our parts. I'm sorry for criticizing you about our daughter, but I don't know how we're going to fix the problems if I don't express what's bothering me. Your idea of only criticizing in marriage therapy is an interesting one. Of course, that would only work if we go. We could give it a try.

Love,

Charlene

Brad's idea of saving his criticisms for therapy turned out to mean he wasn't going to talk to her. He kept himself busy at work and rushed home only to eat, play with the kids, and leave again. He was getting even with her. She knew it, and it hurt. She longed to be with him and to have fun like they'd had in the past. She wanted him to hold her and take away all her stress. Days went by with him hardly saying anything to her until she couldn't take it any longer. It was one in the morning and Brad was in the bathroom preparing to go to bed.

She walked in, looked at him, and crossed her arms.

"What?" he asked.

"I hate it when I'm not important to you." Her voice shook as she spoke. She had waited for hours to go on their supposed date. She had gotten ready and had the babysitter lined up and everything. Brad kept calling, saying he was going to be later and later. They ended up not going anywhere at all. This was the second time he'd done that in a month.

"What are you talking about?" He turned around to look at her with his toothbrush in hand.

"You never take me out anymore on our couple's date. You're always too busy."

His eyebrow rose as she spoke. "We could go now."

Charlene gave a sarcastic laugh. "Yeah, right. It's too late and there's no babysitter."

He put his toothbrush down on the counter. "I don't know why you're making such a big deal about it."

That was it. She cared about him, wanted to be with him, and he'd promised time with her. Not only was he not honoring his promise, but he was laughing at her and dismissing her. "Has it ever occurred to you," she said in a heated tone, "that I need to get out of the house? I can't change diapers, stop the children's fights, and clean all the time. I feel trapped." She secretly thought if she had to give up her school classes too, she'd never make it.

"I'm not going anywhere. I'm tired."

"But we haven't gone anywhere in weeks," Charlene said.

"Whatever." Brad walked out of the room.

Charlene called after him. "If you have needs, they get met. If I have needs, I have to wait and wait and wait and listen to all these great excuses. I expressed my need to go out and spend time with you on Wednesday, and I'm still waiting four days later to see if that time will ever get scheduled. I'm getting the message that my needs aren't important."

"What am I supposed to do?" Brad asked, eyes narrowing.

"You could move your workouts at the gym to early mornings. That would leave an evening or two open for us."

He shrugged and climbed in bed, pulling her near him.

*

Brad came home the next night with two dozen roses and a kiss. "I'll do better," he promised. "It's just been extra stressful at work. To prove it to you, I lined up a babysitter and made a reservation at your favorite restaurant tonight."

Charlene let out a deep breath. Things were back to normal. Everything was going to be okay, or even better. She had been suffering from headaches, weakness, and chronic stomachaches. She suspected her hormones were having a field day, and no, she wasn't pregnant—thank heavens. She had taken the test to be doubly sure. She had been *real* firm with Brad on that issue. She was going to make sure she didn't have any more slipups. Sometimes Brad hassled her to "take a risk, lighten up," asking, "Where's your sense of adventure?" Then one of the children would start wailing. Reality must be destroying her adventurous side, Charlene thought. Brad would be angry at her refusal to go unprotected, pull away from her, and turn up his sports show. Let him, she thought. At least she could get some sleep—*and* she wouldn't have another person to take care of.

*

Judy had been writing and asking Charlene if she ever thought about leaving Brad. Charlene thought about it and wrote back:

Brad told me that if I ever left him, no one else would want me. That's true. Who would want a woman with five kids? That's a truckload of babies. I wouldn't be interested in me if the roles were reversed. If I were to ever leave Brad because things didn't work out (and I'm not saying that they're not, but just "*if*"), I'd be stuck single with five kids dependent on me. Brad already told me he'd make sure I didn't get any money. I have no choice but to make it work.*

Charlene couldn't understand why Judy was so worried about her marital status when she still didn't have a job. Things were getting down to the wire for her friend. Charlene had made it a ritual to pray for her every night. She was the one in need of help. Reading between the lines, Charlene decided that Judy's tone sounded down. In an effort to cheer her friend up, she wrote to her: *The cliché is true that it's darkest before the dawn. It's pretty dark. The dawn must be coming.*

Hoping God would help her friend, Charlene acknowledged that He had helped Charlene by showing her that others loved and felt concern for her. Her church minister had called to make sure she was handling things okay. Karla had called the day after. God was watching.

Two days later a blessing was poured onto Judy. Charlene received an e-mail from Judy telling her she had received a call back on one of her applications. Charlene was happy about the news; the job was high paying.

The other part of the e-mail caused Charlene to think a lot. Her friend assured her that many guys would want her if she was single. She didn't know how to respond to that. The idea was too shocking. So she said, *Judy, you're too funny. That's not even possible, but it's kind of you to say. I don't think Brad was saying that to trap me in the relationship. He was telling the truth.*

She quickly went on to write about how stressed she was and how she was the cause of her own stress. She had picked up extra classes in psychology. She admitted only to Judy that if she ever did leave Brad, she would need to support the children somehow, and therapists didn't do too badly. She felt guilty for even thinking about leaving Brad but chose to push that guilt aside. She was incredibly interested in psychology. What could it hurt to learn things that would make her a better parent and friend—or a better person for that matter? There was a master's degree program she had learned of that would allow her to take a couple of classes at a time at night. She thought about it often. A master's degree. It would be perfect for her situation.

She also asked Judy to stop nagging at her about going to the doctor. She had gone just two days ago. He wanted her to get blood work done. Charlene had honestly tried but couldn't find the lab listed on her insurance. Why did the medical world have to be so complicated? She gave up searching. It was so stupid. There was a lab in the doctor's office, but she couldn't use that one because her insurance wouldn't pay. She had been so exhausted and shaky; she just couldn't find the strength to search for the other place. She was so desperate to not have to do more, she even asked how much it would cost her out of pocket. They wouldn't even let her do that. Guess she wasn't in the right clique to get her blood drawn.

The doctor said he thought she had an ulcer and gave her a prescription for an acid-eater pill. She was also told to de-stress. Now that was funny. Charlene had laughed hard, and when she was done the doctor said, "This is serious. You need to get this under control." No sense of humor, she guessed.

When Brad found out, he gave her five hundred dollars to go on a shopping spree. Charlene, shocked, thought about questioning him about their money situation, but decided not to. Instead she had a great time spending the money at the mall while Brad babysat.

Six days later, she had more to tell to Judy about her health condition:

Subject: Stop nagging!
Date: September 20
From: "Charlene" <char@CharlenesWeb.net>
To: "Judy" <bchcomber@yippee.com>

Judy,

Stop nagging already! I'll find the lab. I don't want to be afraid to check my e-mail because I'll find another inquiry from you. They ran tests on me while I was in the office. One was to see if I had an infection, and that was ruled out. I decided last week it was a yeast infection, so I have gone through a gross treatment prescribed by the doctor. I won't go into details. I have to admit that my stomach isn't bothering me anymore. Only my head! I'm going to go to an alternative doctor to see what he thinks.

Believe it or not, Brad came to see our marriage therapist with me. It went well. I was relieved, because frankly, I'm too tired to put up with much.

Charlene then admitted that Brad did need to take some responsibly for the relationship, too. The fact that he came to therapy seemed like a good sign, and he appeared willing to do his part. Gratitude welled up in Charlene; her husband was willing to make changes. She knew so many wouldn't.

They needed to go easier on themselves for having struggles. They were faced with some heavy issues. Charlene's mom had checked into the mental hospital for her disillusions, and Brad's father deserted his family right after. Also the "no contact" rule with Charlene's father because of his toxic nature and the "too much involvement" with Brad's mother added to the weight of difficulty they needed to overcome. On top of that were her struggles with her oldest child, who kept throwing anger fits. All of it added to being hard, hard, hard on their marriage.

Charlene summarized it for Judy:

I feel confident we'll stick it out. He's not a quitter, and I love him. So we're stuck.

I do realize God may have given me challenges but not in every area. He never challenges anyone in every area. I don't have my mother in my life anymore, but He gave me you. I get the comfort and support from you that I never received from my mom. What a blessing. I get lonely and isolated sometimes. I can't tell you what it means to be able to communicate with someone.

Basically, Judy, you're my family. You're my support. Thank you for being there.

Classes were hard, kids cranky, and Charlene was put on a special diet to see if what she ate caused her headaches. But there was some good news. Judy got her job. Charlene teased her about it:

Congrats on the job! I think "I told you so" is in order. I told you so. I told you so. I told you so. I told you so. Okay enough gloating for now. I told you so!

Happy for her friend, Charlene had turned up her *Les Misérables* CD and was passionately singing with her kids, "Look down, look down, don't look them in the eye," when Brad walked in the side door.

"I quit my job," he said. "I'm going to stay at home from now on."

"Why?" Charlene asked weakly, not feeling like singing and dancing any more. They already had problems. Now she would get no space away from him at all.

"I can get plenty of jobs using my computer skills," he said with a smile. "I can help out with the kids and you more."

If you tell me how to parent, I'll scream, Charlene thought, but knew better than to say it out loud. "But what about the money?"

"I already told you not to worry about that. Don't you trust me?"

*

Brad did become heavily involved in her parenting. "Why are you doing this? Why aren't you doing that?" Plus, anytime Charlene said, "No," the kids would run to Dad, and he would say, "Yes." Charlene was almost sure there was a twinkle in Brad's eye when he did it.

To make matters worse, Brad timed her trips to the doctor. "No more than an hour," he said.

Subject: Crappy diet
Date: September 27
From: "Charlene" <char@CharlenesWeb.net>
To: "Judy" <bchcomber@yippee.com>

Judy,

I just got back from the doctor. I guess I'm allergic to milk and cheese. No more for me. My headaches should go away. But that's not the only problem. They tested my immune system. It's really weak. I also have an extremely low white blood cell count. The doctor says I will get cancer in some form within a year if I don't make some drastic changes. No cheese, I believe, is a drastic change.

Your new job sounds so cool. Sometimes I long to go out into the workforce to do something that is appreciated and to have a break from diapers, fighting children, and the drudgery of cooking and cleaning.

I'm so busy with my classes, but I suppose I'm grateful for the time to work on my studies. I'm learning cool stuff. I really like the application part. Too much theory, though. Some of the theories on how to raise children sound like "to do" lists and parent guilt trips. Not to mention they don't really work! Some nineteen-year-old instructor stands there lecturing on what it is like to be a parent and what the children should be doing and how to handle them. I laugh to myself. I'm in the trenches. Half their stuff sounds nice on paper but is really completely useless.

Charlene

P.S. I'm sick of people telling me to de-stress and stop going to school. It's like they want to cut off my lifeline. I'm thinking about picking up yoga. How about you doing yoga in Seattle and I will do it here? We can be the most peaceful, centered ladies in the world.

P.P.S. It's really helpful for me to vent. I apologize if I'm overusing you, but my husband's always stressed and caught up in his own worries.

*

More problems with Brad. What could she expect with him working in her home? Things had gotten ugly, and according to her therapist, she needed to say no and clearly tell him what she wanted in the relationship. She read over her e-mail to Brad one more time, checking to make sure she had kissed up enough so that when she wove in the truth it wouldn't set him off into another rage.

Subject: With all my love

Date: September 27
From: "Charlene" <char@Charlene.org>
To: "Brad" <brad@consult.com>

My Dearest Brad,

I can't tell you how much I love you. There's so much inside me that I long to encircle you with and give you. I believe this is what you long for from me. But there's one thing I need from you: safety and security. I knew it would hurt you if I told you I wasn't happy, and I wanted to protect you. I have wept many times after we fought, because I knew you were hurting inside and were ashamed of what you had done.

Brad, you're such a great person. You have passion, intelligence, feeling, and the desire to do what's right. There is no other person who I could love like I do you. Please help me trust you. I must have it in this relationship or I'll never be happy. If I could feel safe with you, I would feel safe in God's love, and then I could start trusting you and God.

You say I betrayed you by talking to others about your anger problems. Before I went to counseling, I would've agreed. But I have learned that dysfunctional situations rely on staying isolated. It's best to get problems out in the open and to fix them. If I'm offensive, remember it's not you, but my failure to be warm. I'd really like it if you'd join me in the pursuit of making this marriage successful.

I believe in you. I have faith that you'll make the necessary changes so our family can be happy.

Please love me, love our family, and love yourself.

With my love, your wife,

Charlene

*

Charlene hadn't kissed up enough. Brad read the e-mail, charged into her office, and said, "What is with all this dramatic crap? I'm a great husband. Maybe I should divorce you if you aren't happy with all I do for you. I quit work so I could stay home and help you with the kids. I'm constantly doing things for you, and I get an e-mail like this? Most women would be happy, but you always have to find something to complain about."

Brad accused Charlene of being up to more of her "dramatics" when she passed out in her college study group. "Always looking for attention, aren't you?"

Charlene didn't answer him. He was well into his typical lecture about how good she had it when the phone rang. It was JoAnn from the study group asking how she was doing. "Don't worry about not following me home." Charlene tried to sound reassuring. "I turned on the air conditioning full blast and froze all the way. I was dizzy the rest of the night, but I have been feeling much better. Thanks for asking."

"Tell your friend that you do that kind of stuff for attention," Brad said loudly, coming up close to Charlene's ear.

She walked away from him. He followed. She quickly got off the phone and asked, "What do you want?"

"For you to tell the truth," he said. "But that's too much for you to do. I don't have time for this. I need to go to work on the Norwood account." He went downstairs. A door banged shut.

Charlene cried, not sure why.

Chapter 7

"Are you okay?"

Charlene glanced at Peggy's worried expression, then away. She brushed away the hair the wind had just blown into her eyes. "Yeah."

"Are you sure?"

Charlene finished putting her bag and books into the car and turned around to face her classmate. "I'm fine. Feeling much better, thanks." She was lying. Her head still spun. Her stomach tightened, creating a nauseated feeling. But if she admitted how she felt, Peggy probably wouldn't let her drive home. People acted funny when a person passed out, even though it was only once. All Charlene wanted to do was get away from everyone's prying eyes and just vanish.

"You don't think reading my essay on abuse had anything to do with it, do you?"

Charlene shifted her weight. "No. It was beautifully written. Wow, you had to go through some horrible things."

"Yeah, well…It was hard to write."

"I bet." Charlene was trying to be nice, but she really didn't want to talk about the essay anymore or think about all the horrible things her friend had gone through. The essay had gone into explicit detail about the cruelty her classmate had suffered. Somewhere in the middle of it, everything went blank for Charlene. She had awakened lying on the floor with the entire class staring at her.

"I had an ear infection once that caused me to be extremely dizzy. Maybe that's your problem," Peggy said.

Charlene waved at the other classmates who were leaving campus. She knew she didn't have an ear infection. "I think it's from all the meds. I react strongly to drugs. When I get home, I'm going to call my doctor and ask about it."

"Is everything all right?"

"I just don't feel well. I have a weak immune system. They're running tests, but I should be fine."

A blast of air blew against them and Peggy shivered. "Oh, it's cold. I should be going. I just wanted to make sure you're doing okay."

"Fine, thanks." Charlene climbed into the car. She waited until Peggy drove away before she rested her spinning head on the steering wheel and let the tears flow.

*

With school in full swing, Charlene struggled to help her kids with their homework and keep up with her own. Because of this, she didn't find the time to write Judy as often. The delays made her confused about what she'd already told her friend and what she hadn't. Had she mentioned finding out that she had tendonitis and tennis elbow, probably from carrying babies all the time? She couldn't even remember if she'd told Judy that the doctors had lowered her med dosage and she was feeling less dizzy. And had she mentioned that the doctors were running more tests relating to her irregular cell count? They said if the tests came back negative again they were going to do a biopsy on her uterus and test thoroughly for cancer. A family friend who was a doctor told her that it probably wasn't cancer, but they'd more than likely have to perform a hysterectomy. He said she'd had too many babies too fast and had worn out her machinery. Lovely. But probably true.

Fear twisted Charlene's stomach. Cancer. Hysterectomy in her late twenties. What was she going to do? When she tried to talk about it with Brad, he told her to stop being so dramatic. She was making a big thing out of nothing. At first she was mad at him for dismissing her, but later she wondered if he was right. Maybe she shouldn't think about all the things that could be wrong. She would wait until she learned more information. That decision was easier to declare than to do. She caught herself twisting her fingers, wondering what kind of pain was in store for her. Would she leave her children motherless? Would they be okay? If it was going to happen, how could she make it easier on them?

Judy kept pressing her with intimacy questions. "How can you make love to a man who has hit you? Do you guys feel very close? Is it fun for you?" etc. Fed up with questions that Charlene didn't want to answer, she wrote:

I'm ignoring your question about problems with wanting to be intimate. I don't even know what to say. A wife has to make a man happy no matter what she feels. At least, that's what I was taught. I don't think I can keep it up, though. I wish I could trust Brad more. Sometimes I have a hard time with him even touching me. Other times there doesn't seem to be an issue. I don't want to talk about it any more than that.

Charlene thought that would stop Judy's questions, but instead it opened up a lot more about love. The questions stayed with Charlene. She was unable to blow them off, and she didn't know the answers, so she took them to her therapist.

"Um, Brad and I got into it again. He hit me in the arm."

"Are you okay?" Cindy asked, leaning in and looking concerned.

"Yeah, fine." Charlene laughed. She felt herself growing really hot.

"Why are you laughing? It's not funny."

Charlene shrugged. "Oh, I don't know. But since then it's got me wondering…" She stopped talking. How could she express what he was doing? She looked at her therapist, who waited patiently. She cleared her throat. "How can he do that kind of stuff and love me?"

Her voice broke and tears surfaced. She tried to fight them back. How come she was being such a baby lately? "Why don't I want to be around him anymore? I'm avoiding him. He's becoming more demanding, wanting hugs, kisses, and especially to hold hands. My hands ache when he holds them. I don't want to touch him."

"That seems normal, don't you think?"

Charlene looked up, surprised. "What do you mean? I should want to be with my husband."

"After he broke your trust? It's hard to want to be with someone who breaks your trust."

"But why at other times, like last week, I felt so much love for him?"

"The word 'love' has so many different meanings," her therapist said. "It's a very individualized concept. What love means comes from a person's experience, history, and beliefs."

"My friend, Judy—you know, the one I write to?" Her therapist nodded. "Well, she's having a hard time understanding how I could love my husband after what he has done to me. How do I answer her? I don't know what to say." Charlene pulled a couch pillow closer to her stomach.

"It's not that unusual for you to feel love toward your husband for many different reasons. First off, from your experience, you have only had love given to you in a hostile environment. Therefore, to you, it doesn't seem so strange that someone who loves you can also hurt you.

"Another thing to consider is that you might be more in love with the ideal, the fantasy. Many domestic violence victims believe their love is so powerful it can change the bad parts of their spouse."

Charlene knew she couldn't change Brad. It was his choice. But she did believe God could change him, work miracles with them both.

"Abusers aren't always all bad," Cindy said. "They're charming, loving, and nice. This keeps the victim waiting for or thinking that the good stuff will start to happen all the time and the other stuff will disappear."

After a moment of reflection she said, "It's really a Dr. Jekyll and Mr. Hyde situation. Another thing to consider, Charlene, is that the way a person interprets love is directly related to the degree of love and respect the individual has for herself. This self-respect determines what she will and won't put up with from others. A perpetrator plays on the victim's poor self-esteem or begins to wear down the individual's self-confidence by constantly putting her down, keeping her in a state of fear, and making her believe she can't ever find a better situation than the one she is in. He also convinces her she doesn't deserve better."

Charlene cleared her throat. "Brad often tells me no one would want me, that I'm used goods. I have five children. Who would take that on? He's right. I know that. Brad is a great guy most of the time and, heck, he's sure a lot better than my dad."

"Many victims have a lot invested in making their relationship work. They have children, finances, religion, and cultural issues. With religious people there's often a marriage covenant they don't break lightly. Divorce is often looked upon as a sign of personal, even spiritual, failure.

"These issues can be so overwhelming the victim will deny her own experience and what she is feeling so she doesn't have to confront these problems. The victim blocks the seriousness of the abuse—downplays it so she can stay and make the situation work."

"What about the fact that, if the victim left, she could end up dead?" Charlene asked. This was another fear she had.

Her therapist nodded. "That's a huge factor. Most of the deaths resulting from an abusive relationship occur when women try to leave. It's not something to treat casually. Leaving safely takes lots of preparation and support."

Charlene shifted her weight. "I was told once by a friend to stand up to my husband and say I wasn't going to put up with him treating me in such a way. 'Yeah, sure, and get my face banged in,' is what I thought. I'm trapped. If I stay, my health goes bad. If I stand up to him, I could get killed. If I call the police, I get beaten worse after they leave. If I go to my minister, I'm afraid he'll quote the Bible about being subject to my husband. Even if he agrees that my husband is wrong, he won't do anything about it. Then I'll get stalked by Brad, who'll try to find out what I said to the minister. Then I'll get beaten for that. But if I don't stand up, I risk losing my kids to the State because I'm failing to protect them, even if I'm the only one being hit." Charlene wiped at her tears. Once she felt that she could go on, she asked from the wounded depths inside of her, "If it's this bad, then why, why, why do I feel so much love for him?"

"He's not always that bad. You love the good parts of him," Cindy said. "There's also this thing called Stockholm syndrome. That's where the victim becomes so afraid of her perpetrator, afraid there's no way out, that she aligns with him to stay safe. The abuser uses brainwashing that, in many cases, is similar to what the victim experienced for years when she was young. The messages of being 'no good,' 'less than,' 'incompetent,' and so on, resonates with the victim."

"I'm going to have to give all this more thought," Charlene whispered.

*

Charlene did give it more thought. In fact, that was what she was thinking about when the doctor's office called her several days later. "We have good news for you. Your cell count is back to normal."

"Thank you." Charlene was tired and could hardly muster any relief. She lay down on her bed. She was so hot. All she wanted to do was maintain her relationship with her cozy pillow. Whenever she lifted her head, it spun.

Later that day, she hired a babysitter and went to the family doctor, where she discovered she had contracted strep. Her temperature soared to 105 degrees for three days and nothing she tried, sponge baths, medication, or rest, could get it to come down. When her husband finally arrived home from California and found her, he asked if he should take her to the hospital. He'd never done that before, except when she was in labor with their first baby. Charlene said, "No," and closed her eyes.

Her fever did go down the day after he returned, and her throat quit hurting, but the dehydration hung on. Charlene's skin shriveled up, giving her a wrinkly little old woman appearance. But on the positive side, she dropped five pounds, although she was sure it would hop back on when she recovered.

"What's this mess in the kitchen?" Brad yelled.

Charlene lay on the bed groaning. He had been yelling since he returned. He always became angry when she was sick. Her dad had been like that too. Her mom had acted like she wasn't ill when she was. Charlene refused to do that. Besides, she didn't feel well enough to pretend.

"Why do you have to have so many problems? You're no fun. Can't you ever be well?" he often asked her, like she had control over being sick.

Her husband didn't think she was good enough. He was right. She was always sick. She wanted to be healthy, and she had to do something to change things. She wasn't going to live the next thirty years like this. She planned it all as she lay on her bed, the outline of her body impressed in the sheets from the sweat. She was going to eat better, exercise, and de-stress. She would do anything to feel good again, except maybe getting rid of her germ-carrying children. Her children she'd keep no matter the price she paid personally.

She gave her complaints to Judy and finished by saying: *I hope your week is going better than mine. I didn't mean to give you an eyeful. I haven't been able to talk for several days either. I guess I'm busting with things to say.*

Judy's e-mail response was quick and full of worry for the kids. Did they get the strep that almost took Charlene out? Charlene wrote back that they hadn't. Everyone in her family seemed healthy and happy—just extra-demanding because Mom hadn't been giving them as much attention lately, although she tried. Charlene had tried to be very cautious. Four out of the five times she had strep, she had been the only one in the family to get it. No, Brad didn't come home from California early to take care of her. When he did get there, he'd pretty much left her alone and concentrated on his work.

The other concern Judy had felt strongly enough about to address was if Charlene was alone the whole time she'd had the fever. The answer was "No." She had begged her sister-in-law to come and watch the kids so she could go to the doctor.

She didn't tell Judy how much it really bothered her that her husband hadn't come home to help her when she was so sick and had all those young kids to take care of. It bugged her so much that she took it up with him as he ate his late-night snack in the kitchen the night he arrived home.

Still weak, she slumped into the first chair she came to and looked over at her husband, who leaned against the kitchen sink, eating ice cream.

"Why didn't you come home when you found out I was so sick?"

"I wanted to get my project done."

Charlene laid her head on the counter, still boiling with heat. "You could have taken time away. You have to go on another trip there anyway."

"You were fine."

"No, I wasn't," Charlene said, her head pounding. "I couldn't get out of bed, and the kids had to fend for themselves."

"They survived." He dug deeper into the ice cream carton. "Do we have any more chocolate ice cream?"

She didn't have the strength to hold it all together. "Don't you care about me?" She knew asking would make him angry, but she couldn't help it.

Brad rolled his eyes. "I'm so sick of everything always being about you. You're so selfish." He pointed his spoon at her angrily. "Don't you ever worry about how my work is going and how hard it is to get everything done when I have a wife always complaining that I'm not doing enough for her? You never appreciate me."

"Of course I appreciate all the hard work you do," Charlene said. "It's just you knew that I was seriously sick. You know, this time I almost ended up in the hospital. Don't you care?"

"You're a mighty fine piece of work, aren't you?" He glared at her.

This should have stopped Charlene, but it didn't. She had to know. "Why, Brad? Why didn't you come home when I was so sick? Don't I matter to you?"

"That's it," he said, throwing his spoon in the sink. He went over to her, grabbed her arm, and jerked her off the chair. He began shaking her. "I'm sick of you turning everything around so it's always about you. I want you to think about me and what I'm going through sometimes. Got it? Why do I have to have a wife that complains all the time?"

Charlene shook under his grip. Her head was already hurting. Would he make her sicker? Would he smack her over the head like that time, years ago, when she passed out and came to with him weeping over her? He had promised never to do that again, but what if he did? He was strong enough to cause serious damage or even kill her. He of course wouldn't do it on purpose, but if he got into one of his rages, there was no telling.

She looked into his small hazel eyes that seemed to have no light in them and yanked her arm, trying to get it out of his grip. "Please, let me go."

He released her and went back to the freezer to see if he could find more ice cream.

She looked at her arm. No bruise, yet, but she was sure that tomorrow there would be a big one. He had almost yanked it out of its socket.

*

Still weak, Charlene returned to school. She didn't want her grade to suffer too much from her absence. She was on her way to her car after class when her classmate ran up to her.

"Char, wait up."

Charlene turned to see that it was Peggy and smiled. "Hi. How did you like the lecture tonight?"

"It was long," she said, stifling a yawn. "I have a personal question for you, if you don't mind me asking?"

They had stopped walking. Charlene could tell from the way that Peggy was looking at her it was going to be serious. Pushing down the nervous, fluttering feeling in her stomach, she smiled and said, "Okay, shoot."

"Has Brad hit you recently?"

Maybe Peggy had noticed how Charlene had been favoring her injured arm. She thought back to what her therapist had warned her about. Cindy had a client who lost her kids because she exposed them to the violence in her home, which included yelling, items being thrown, hair pulling, spitting, kicking, restraining, breaking personal items, and punching doors. Cindy had explained it was a state law. She warned Charlene that she could lose her children if anything abusive happened in her home.

On the other hand, her friend said the law also stated that she'd lose her children and the house if she left when the fights raged. She couldn't call the police because, again, she risked losing her children. She couldn't live without them. No matter how she looked at it, she was stuck.

How could she explain this to Peggy? Would Peggy judge her and call the authorities? "Naw," Charlene said.

"Good to hear," Peggy said. "I'm here for you." She carefully placed a hand on Charlene's uninjured left shoulder and peered into her eyes. "For anything. I'm on your side, and you got to believe me that I wouldn't do anything that wouldn't be in your favor. You can always call me. You know that, don't you?"

Charlene looked away from her probing eyes, not wanting to admit that she trusted no one.

The next day, Charlene thought about Peggy's kindness; her concern appeared sincere. There was power and relief in being understood, and it seemed that Peggy really wanted to be there for Charlene. There were not many people Charlene could talk to candidly. She decided to risk it and share a little of what she was going through. She did desperately need someone to listen. She couldn't always be bothering Judy.

Subject: *Understanding*
Date: *October 18*
From: *"Charlene"* <char@CharlenesWeb.net>
To: *"Peggy"* <tentpeg@yippee.com>

Last night you asked me if I had been hurt by Brad recently. I've been thinking about your class report about what your father did to you. You seem understanding and have been through a lot. The other day Brad didn't hit me in the face, but he bruised my arm. It's hard to know what the right thing to do is. I want peace desperately. If I don't let this out, my shrink says I'll never be able to grow or have the peace I long for.

I can't tell you how much I appreciate your support.
Please don't share this e-mail with anyone. If you would erase it when you're done reading it, I'd much appreciate it.

Charlene

Chapter 8

The relief Charlene felt after talking to Peggy was short-lived, which was strange. Brad had already hurt her, and she was still nursing both an emotional and physical wound. Normally when that happened, things would settle down for awhile, but not this time. They were getting worse. Brad woke with a blackness about him and his jaw drawn tight. He'd snap at her over the smallest thing, like the toothpaste being left out. When he started a sentence with, "Charlene, why…" Charlene began to jump and gasp.

"Why do you do that?" he asked. "Geez, what's wrong with you?"

Telling him that *he* was the problem would only set him off more. Since her therapist had warned her that she could lose her children, she now looked at her relationship with Brad in a completely different light. When she had to hide from him to avoid being hit, when his anger exploded and he threw things, she thought about divorce and what a major battle it would be. She wished she knew the right thing to do. Her minister had reassured her that if she did get a divorce, the congregation would support her. God didn't want her to live in fear. Was this his way of telling her to go? Many church leaders were hesitant to come right out and say "leave." Several years back, Charlene's previous minister had told Charlene that "God wanted her to work out her marriage to Brad." He promised she would find the happiness she wanted in her marriage if she stayed faithful. His assurance was one reason why she had never considered divorce before. But now, she was becoming more desperate and confused.

Unsure what to do, Charlene reached out to the only person she could trust with this kind of problem. Judy told her how strong she was and that she was capable of handling it. She knew Charlene would know what to do. Feeling like she could trust Judy more and valuing her past compassion and insight, Charlene revealed more of what concerned her.

Subject: Danger
Date: October 21
From: "Charlene" <char@CharlenesWeb.net>
To: "Judy" <mailto:bchcomber@yippee.com>

Judy,

I'm still stressed. I'm still thinking about the fact that I could lose my kids by staying with Brad if he continues to act out. No man is worth losing my children to the State. No man. If the State thinks what's going on here is bad enough to take my kids, what am I subjecting them to?

Charlene

Days were passing and her situation still wasn't improving. She kept her e-mails going to her friend, and Judy replied faithfully. Maybe through writing them Charlene would be able to sort out her thoughts, fears, and everything else that she needed to get through so she would know what to do and how to get out of this pressure cooker she seemed to be doomed to remain in.

Judy's replies were helpful. In one, Judy asked Charlene why she was giving so much power to Brad and allowing him to make her life miserable. Why *was* she doing that? Charlene wondered for days.

Subject: Tiptoeing
Date: October 24
From: "Charlene" <char@CharlenesWeb.net>
To: "Judy" <bchcomber@yippee.com>

Judy,

I'm still doing a lot of thinking. Brad seems like he's going to explode soon, so I am tiptoeing around. And yes, you're right. I shouldn't give him that kind of power. Every time he leaves, though, I'm working on things in case I decide to divorce him. It's better to "be prepared," as the Boy Scouts say.

Charlene

Charlene went to the police station and got the papers that she needed to fill out a protective order. They wanted to know all the past incidents of abuse that had happened. *Ha! That would be one long book,* Charlene thought. She worked on it diligently. It took several days. When she wasn't working on her plan of escape—just in case—she was thinking about it as she did household chores and helped the kids with reading and spelling. There wasn't much time while Brad was away. She didn't get many opportunities like this, and she needed to take advantage of every moment. She went over her plan repeatedly in hopes that she would come up with ways to improve it. It was imperative that she had every contingency worked out. If she overlooked anything, Brad was sure to find it. He had a special talent for discovering her weaknesses and using them against her in the worst ways.

*

Charlene spent a lot of time cruising the Internet, searching for information for victims. There were many sites that outlined specifically what to do to prepare to leave. Following the advice, she put together a grab bag and hid it in the garage, prepared with an outfit for each child and herself. It was in a place she didn't think Brad would look, and she could easily snatch and go. She also kept her cell phone with her at all times when Brad was home. It was a pain, but a necessary precaution. She wasn't going to lose her kids, no matter what.

She set up secret passwords with three different friends and neighbors so she could call for help without Brad knowing what she was doing. She also hid important information at her friends' houses. She made records of finances and copies of birth certificates and social security numbers and other important documents. She hid a list of essential numbers in her purse: the women's shelter and a place where she could drop off the kids if she got in a jam. She included her minister's number and a list of friends who had volunteered to help if she needed it, including Karla, her friend from the neighborhood, and Peggy from her psychology class. She wasn't going to be caught unprepared the next time he came after her.

*

Brad was out of town.

Taking advantage of the time, Charlene called Peggy and asked her to come over. Peggy brought a book on domestic violence she thought would be helpful and the two women spent the afternoon going over the information.

About six o'clock, Brad unexpectedly walked in the front door. Charlene looked up from her notes and took in his reddening face.

"Oh, Brad, what are you doing home?" She shoved the book under a pile of papers on her office desk. Before he could answer, she turned to Peggy to explain and hopefully ebb his anger. "My husband was away on a business trip. We didn't expect him home until tomorrow night." Charlene spoke quickly, hoping to prevent her husband from being rude like he so often was whenever she had a friend over. She didn't want to lose Peggy, too.

Brad put down his suitcase and slapped his folders onto the counter. "While the cat is away, the mice will play."

"Hi, I'm Peggy." Peggy rose from her chair, hand extended to shake his.

His focus zoomed onto her. "Here to corrupt my wife, I see." He brushed past her to kiss Charlene. His lips met hers, hard and demanding. His fingers dug into her shoulders as he held her to him. Charlene struggled out of his embrace, embarrassed he was treating her like this in front of her friend.

Peggy crossed her arms.

"We're working on our class assignment," Charlene quickly said.

"So you're into the hocus pocus, mind reading stuff, too?" he asked Peggy. "I guess that makes you no smarter than my wife." He laughed at his own joke and continued to tease them about studying psychology until Peggy left.

Later that night, after Brad fell fast asleep, Charlene crept out of bed. She had to be careful because if her husband by chance woke, he'd ask, "Where are you going?" then demand she stay in bed with him. Brad didn't wake this time. She hurried to her office to write Peggy an apology and to thank her for the book. As she wrote, she felt like telling Peggy how she had talked to her minister yesterday about her marriage. Reverend Sinclair had said the Lord didn't want her to stay in an abusive relationship. She thought about that for a long time. She thought about how the minister said she deserved to be treated well. On the flip side, Brad had informed her while on the trip if she ever left he would get the house and all five kids. Her minister, too, warned her that if she divorced, she'd have a major battle. She agreed with that one.

*

The days passed and the decision about whether to stay in the marriage or go pressed on Charlene to the point she dropped seven pounds. She slipped into a pair of jeans that normally were too tight and spun around, feeling the fabric fitting nicely against her. If only she didn't have to feel so sick to lose weight.

She didn't know if she had the strength to get a divorce. Plus, she was scared of what Brad would do. She was also concerned about being alone and responsible for five young children. To add to her worries, Brad had started saying things like, "I don't know if that Peggy person is a good friend for you."

Her heart seemed to flop in her chest. Here they go again. Quietly she asked, "Why would you say that?"

He refused to answer. If he was going to stop her from seeing her friends, he needed to have a good reason. She pressed him, but the most she could get was that he had "a weird feeling around her" and didn't like how she looked at him. He didn't think it was good for Charlene to be with someone he felt was threatening their marriage.

Charlene's anger got the better of her. "Stop trying to control me and who I see. You're such a control freak." This led to a back and forth fight until Brad went after her again.

He twisted her arm, shaking her, telling her that she wasn't listening. When all was said and done, a sobbing Charlene locked herself into her bathroom and checked her arms. There were no bruises. If there were, she could show them to the police and get them on record. It would make her position stronger.

Brad didn't like her running from him. He banged on the door, demanding to be let in.

She ignored him until the door began to splinter. Then she opened it, not wanting to live without a bathroom door. He never replaced what he busted. She rushed past him while he swore at her.

"Charlene, stop your nonsense."

She kept going, not knowing where she was headed, but knowing she needed to get away.

"You're being a bitch," he called after her.

He was trying to lure her back into the argument. Why? So he could beat her up? Twist her arm? Spit on her? She didn't care to find out. She wanted to get away from the beast. She shouldn't leave her children, but she sensed he wouldn't touch them. She prayed for them to be protected.

She slipped out the back door, not noticing she was in her nightgown until the cold wrapped around her like a crude blanket. She gasped for air, wondering where to go. She saw the swing set and figured that was a good place as any. She nestled herself underneath the slide, hoping it would block the wind. It didn't work. She huddled in a ball. A memory flashed over her…another time, another fight, a fist pounding down onto her head, blackness coming over…Charlene sadly wished she could just black out again to get away from the fear, the chaos, and this cold. Last year, the doctor had taken x-rays of her head. He'd said it looked like she had some brain stem damage. She knew that injury had happened the night Brad had pounded her in the head.

Brad had never knocked her out cold again, but there had been fat lips, black eyes, bruised arms, bruised, swollen legs, and many cuts from things being thrown at her. Judy was right. Why was she giving this man so much power?

When she slipped inside an hour later, she discovered that he had left the children alone. They were still sleeping in their beds. That was a big relief, but somehow it was not enough to settle the nausea in the pit of her stomach. The rage that Brad seemed to be feeling hadn't completely dissipated. She found him in a deep sleep. It was only a matter of time before it would erupt again.

CHAPTER 9

The eruption came full-force. Brad said one night, "You need to quit school. You're not being a good enough mother. The kids are suffering."

"What are you talking about?" she asked, dropping her book bag on the kitchen counter.

"Look at this place." He extended his arms. "It's a mess. We're white trash. It looks like we're living in a trailer. We didn't have a good dinner tonight, and Paige has this huge project due tomorrow. She's done nothing on it."

"But I cleaned the house and cooked dinner before I left for class. All you had to do was heat it up. The house got messed up when you watched the kids."

"Dinner burned."

"But—"

"Charlene, I'm tired of your excuses for neglecting the family."

"I'm not. I'm a good mom. I spent most of the day taking care of the kids, playing with them, and cleaning. I did four loads of laundry today, cleaned the bathrooms, and picked up the toys. Plus I made chicken casserole and salad." How dare he say she wasn't doing enough or wasn't a good mom?

"Charlene, this isn't working."

"I'm not quitting school."

"What are you telling me? That your little classes are more important than your children?"

"I'm not saying that," Charlene stuttered.

"Yes, you are, by your actions."

"How—" Charlene started.

Brad loudly cut her off. "Why is doing your own thing so much more important than your family? That saddens me. My priorities aren't like that. My children are a lot more important to me than pursuing my own selfish interests."

Charlene bit her lip. "How dare you say that my schooling is selfish? It will only benefit this family. I'm learning better ways to raise the children and to be a better mother, and besides, I only go once a week at night with their dad watching them."

Brad shook his head, black disgust etched all over his face. "You can stick by your illusions all you want. Maybe when you're taking all those classes you can take some basic classes on logic. It would really help you out."

Anger flared. How dare he say that about her? He had no right, and she wasn't going to stand here and listen to any more of it. Besides, she needed to check on the kids and get to work helping Paige on this supposed project that she hadn't heard anything about until this minute. Why hadn't Paige mention it when she asked her about her homework earlier today? She started to walk out of the kitchen, when her school book whizzed past her head and crashed against the wall.

"You chicken. You're always running from your responsibilities," he called after her.

She ducked in order to avoid whatever he decided to throw next and headed toward the phone. She might need to call for help. It looked like he was flipping out again.

A fork soared past her ear. It clattered against the gravy bowl in the china cabinet.

She needed to take cover. She squatted behind the living room couch. Next she heard a big bang. She peeked over the armrest and saw he had thrown her backpack. She hoped her makeup case hadn't broken. If it had and the powder spilled, that could mess up her homework.

Charlene ran for the phone, ducking as a shoe whirled by her head.

The instant he saw what she was doing, he charged after her and ripped it from her hand. "Who are you calling?"

"I need to put the kids to bed," she said.

"Fine." He crossed his arms over his chest. "You do that."

Charlene hurriedly left the room. She collected the kids and got them to bed, giving each one a kiss as she tucked them in.

Cameron looked up at her, his eyebrows knitted together. "Is Daddy going to hurt you?"

Deep sadness shot through Charlene. How could she keep their problems away from the kids? "Don't you worry about that," she said, then ran her hands through his thick hair. "Mommy is fine."

"I hate it when you fight." His lip quivered.

"I know," Charlene whispered. "I do too."

She dreaded that Brad would go into a rage after she was done putting the kids down.

When Paige asked her, tears in her eyes, for help with her project, Charlene quickly agreed. Normally she would have said that Paige should have told her sooner and then work out some accountability plan, but tonight she was glad for her daughter's procrastination.

At ten o'clock, Brad came into the kitchen and glared at Charlene. "What you have done needs to be good enough. It's past bedtime."

They were almost finished with the project, so Paige sighed and left for her room.

Charlene began picking up the markers they'd used as she waited for the blast from Brad to begin.

"So you think this is going to make up for the whole evening you were gone?" Brad's voice reeked with ridicule.

"No," Charlene said, searching for a way to get out of this. "It—"

"Exactly. That's my point. So when are you going to quit these classes?"

"I'm not. It's not hurting the kids." No way was she going to stop going to her one place of relief.

"Look," Brad said, slapping his hand on the counter. "This is costing me money. I have to pay for things you're supposed to do and for your classes. I could just stop paying for them."

"What?" she asked, confused by his new line of argument. "You told me to take a class, and you were the one who wanted me to get the maid."

"Yeah, but I'm feeling taken advantage of. I see that I set a bad precedent, and I don't like it." His jaw drew tight.

"What? How am I taking advantage of you?" Charlene didn't understand this accusation at all.

"I give you an inch, and you take a mile. I meant for you to take 'a' class, not become a student again. It was for a break not a lifestyle."

"You can't tell me what I can and can't do."

"This is the problem. You're getting real mouthy."

She crossed her arms. "I'm not quitting, no matter what."

"This is the very problem I was afraid of. You defiant bitch."

He ran after her.

She took off, trying to get away.

He tackled her onto the living room floor.

Brad grabbed Charlene's favorite statue, a carving in wood of a mother holding a child that was mounted on a marble base. He held it above her head. He was yelling in her face, but she couldn't make out what he was saying. She couldn't pay attention except to struggle, to try and wrestle free. As she fought him, Brad swung the carving toward her head. Terrified, she closed her eyes, bracing for the blow, only to hear it splinter inches from her skull.

She gasped. Her uncle had made the figurine for her right before he died. Now it was gone, but more sobering was that it could've been her skull shattering.

"Get off me, you jerk," she screamed. "You could've killed me."

Brad climbed off her, looking pale and startled. "I need to go to the bathroom," he muttered.

Using this unexpected moment of freedom, Charlene rushed to the library and slid under the table. Soon she heard Brad looking for her. She listened. "Charlene. Charlene, where are you? Come on, I want to talk to you. Stop this silliness."

She clutched her hands to her chest, eyes closed, choking back her heavy breathing. His footsteps sounded down the stairs. "Where are you? Stop this game. I just want to talk to you."

Yeah, right. Charlene strained to hear, trying to make sure he was going the opposite direction from where she hid. She heard nothing. She slipped from under the table and into his office.

The clock showed 12:17 a.m. Maybe she shouldn't call her minister. It was so late. He'd be asleep, and he was a busy man. Shaking, she closed her eyes. Brad would find her soon enough. What would he do if he saw her calling someone? Memories of the time he had smashed her in the head came to her. She was lucky to have survived that. What if the next time he hit her extra hard and she wasn't so lucky?

She shivered. What would happen then to her children? Would they be left to him to be raised? Would he abuse them the way he did her? She didn't want to think about that. She remembered Reverend Johnson had told her to call no matter the time. She hoped he meant it. She dialed the number and was in tears when he answered.

"It's going to be all right," he reassured her in a calm voice. "I'll be right over."

Five minutes later the doorbell rang.

"Who's that?" Brad ran down the stairs.

"Um," Charlene looked away from his glare, "I think it might be Reverend Johnson."

"You called him? Damn it. I'm going downstairs. You handle it, and no, I'm not talking to him."

Charlene straightened her shirt before opening the door to the elderly, stout man dressed in a suit.

He didn't have to dress up, Charlene thought. "Thanks for coming." She pushed the door open for him.

"Is everything all right?" he asked, taking in the room.

"Brad went downstairs. He says he won't come up."

Charlene gestured to their front room couches. Reverend Johnson took her cue and sat on the edge of the cushion. He slipped off his trench coat before asking, "What happened?"

"Oh," Charlene said, trying to put it all together in her mind. "Brad is having a hard time at work. He's just lost an important account. It's making him a bit ornery. He wants me to quit my college classes. I told him no. Maybe I should just quit."

"Did he hurt you?"

"He pinned me to ground and broke a mother and child figurine over my head. He barely missed my skull." Charlene hoped she was talking soft enough so Brad couldn't overhear.

"Do you have any bruises?"

This question took Charlene by surprise. "Ah." She examined at her arm. "Probably, from when he held me down."

Reverend Johnson fell silent for a long time. Charlene could tell he was in deep thought. She gave him time to sort it out. "Would you consider going to a shelter tonight and taking the kids with you?"

"I heard if I do that I will lose possession of the house, which will make it easy for him to get the kids," Charlene whispered. "I can't do that."

They discussed her options a little longer before Brad came in and shook the minister's hands. "It's been great having you here, but it's getting really late," Brad said. "It's time for you to leave. Everything's fine. There's no need to worry." He gave one of his dashing smiles.

The minister gulped. He looked at Charlene and then back to Brad. "Um."

"It'll be fine, really," Brad said. "Nothing will happen."

"Ahh." Reverend Johnson glanced back and forth between them.

"Really," Brad said, taking him by his arm and escorting him out.

Charlene stared at the closing front door, her stomach sick. Reverend Johnson had deserted her.

Now she was alone with him.

Brad turned to her. "You're just as abusive as me. I can't believe you won't admit it."

Charlene clutched her shirt to her throat, waiting for the blows to begin again. He stepped to her. She flinched. He reached out and jerked her to him. He kissed her roughly then yanked her up the stairs into the bed. Once in bed he pulled her into his arms. As Charlene lay there waiting to hear his snores, she wondered, *I'm abusive? When did I ever strike back? He's twice my size!*

The next morning, Brad woke her by kissing her forehead. "Hi, my dear, would you like breakfast in bed?"

"Ah," she said, feeling heavy with fatigue. She tried to clear her thoughts from the fog of sleep. "No."

She closed her eyes, hoping he'd let her sleep. Thankfully, he was leaving town for five days this morning. He didn't have time to bother her much. He crawled into bed with her, pulled her into his arms and whispered, "I love you. Things will get better. I'll take the kids to school."

*

Charlene woke an hour later to the sound of the phone. It was the female leader, Samantha, from the church calling to talk. She told Charlene, "You might actually have to go through with a separation and be *extremely* loving if you want the marriage to work." She also said, "You need to let Brad have space and he'll return."

Why should she have to do all the work and have all the faith if it was Brad who was scaring and hurting her? Something didn't seem right with that logic.

Over the next few days, Charlene knelt in prayer a lot. Finally, as she prayed, for the first time she felt leaving Brad wouldn't be against God's will. But, oh, she had so much pain at the thought of losing her marriage. It felt like it would destroy her. She couldn't think of the overall picture of what it would be like. How would she survive? What would happen to the children? What about money?

She decided to take small baby steps while her husband was away. Peggy gave her a list of the best divorce lawyers in the area. The first attorney was booked, but she set up a meeting with the second on the list for the next day to learn what she needed to know and do if she chose to separate rather than divorce.

She couldn't get the images of the beating out of her mind—the pure blackness in his face as he raised the statue, the disgust in his voice, and the filthy names he called her, his own wife. Maybe she should go ahead and separate when Brad returned. Things were nicer with him gone. She could breathe, sleep, and play with the kids. Time would pass. Yet as she helped the kids with their homework assignments and cooked dinner, she began to feel guilty. What if she quit on this marriage too soon? What if she gave up when they were just months away from everything turning around and getting better? What if she was close to having everything she always wanted—a loving, doting husband, a *Leave it to Beaver* existence for her and her family?

It was so hard to know what to do.

As the days passed and it came time for Brad to return, she resolved that she couldn't go ahead with the separation plans. Despite everything, she loved him, and she wanted to do what was best for her and the kids, no matter how hard.

*

While Brad was in Virginia, Charlene had to act fast. She'd rather work out their marriage difficulties, but if things continued to go sour and she couldn't fix them, she needed to be prepared. She wasn't about to lose her children or end up on the street.

That afternoon, she met with a lawyer for the free consultation of her case. It was nerve wracking and complicated with all the legal terms. As he talked, Charlene found that she had a hard time concentrating or understanding what he was saying. There was so much at risk. She kept trying to force herself to pay attention, but her thoughts kept wandering. She did learn it was true that she couldn't leave her home when Brad became violent.

"Possession is nine-tenths of the law. If you leave the home, your husband has a better chance of getting the house, and the person who gets the house is more likely than not to get the children—even if it's proven he's an abuser."

Charlene had a hard time believing what she was hearing. Brad was the one hitting her and traumatizing the kids, and if she ran out of the house—even if it was to save herself from getting killed—she risked losing the children. It didn't seem fair.

The lawyer gave her a lot of reading to go over so she would know what to look at in a custody case. She needed to fully arm herself. He also gave her another protective order application. "You'll want to fill that out right away. You don't want to wait until you're in a desperate situation. It would be best to have it done ahead of time."

At the end of the meeting, the lawyer asked Charlene if she had any questions.

"Yes, if we by chance get divorced, would I get any money?"

"The law requires that you get half."

"Brad swears he'll leave me penniless."

"Did you sign a prenup?"

"No."

"Then the law says that you're entitled to half." Charlene nodded now for the more important question. "And is there a chance he'll get the kids from me?"

"Very unlikely."

As Charlene drove home thinking about the whole situation, she decided it would be a good idea to store some stuff at her friend Karla's house. She'd pack emergency clothes and toiletries for herself and the kids to keep over there.

*

"Hi, darling. How's your trip going?"

"I'm making a lot of deals. It's intense, but going well…" Brad then proceeded to tell her over the phone a long story about how he closed deals with everyone he talked to.

When he finally settled down, Charlene said softly, "I've been thinking about us."

"What about?" Brad asked.

"You know how we have been having our problems lately and…" She wasn't sure how to put it. No matter what she said he would be angry, but a small hope rose in her, and she thought that maybe, just maybe, he would see the reason in what she was about to suggest.

"What about the problems?" Brad asked.

"I thought it might be a good idea if we got a trial separation."

"Either married or divorced. There's no other choice." His voice was harsh and matter of fact.

"But—"

"There's no buts."

*

Time felt like it was closing in on Charlene. She only had a little left before Brad returned home and so much that she wanted to have prepared. The first thing on her list besides taking care of her kids, the house, and her homework was to read the really *boring* legal papers her lawyer had given her. She knew it was important to understand what they said and be prepared. The text was difficult to pay attention to, and she was college educated. She wondered what it would be like for a woman in a similar situation who lacked the education. How would she manage to get through the maze?

Not only did Charlene have to comprehend it, but she also needed to collect a lot of information. She was tired as she worked and didn't feel well, but she kept going. These things were too important to not get done. She could sleep when Brad returned.

Doing all the things that she felt were necessary to prepare for the "maybe" event in the future scared her. Was she betraying him? What would happen if Brad found out what she was up to? Would he kill her? Was he capable of that? She didn't think he would intentionally set out to end her life, but sometimes when he was flipping out in his rages, she wondered if it would happen accidentally. It would only take one wrong hard blow to her small frame and she would be gone. To help relieve the stress, she wrote to Judy.

Subject: Stealing?
Date: November 20
From: "Charlene" <char@CharlenesWeb.net>
To: "Judy" <bchcomber@yippee.com>

Judy,

I hope all is well for you. I think I'm prepared for whatever happens. I even transferred some of "our" money into my own account. Is this dishonest? I felt like I was stealing, but then I thought about what would happen if the kids and I were left with no money if I did decide to divorce Brad. Transferring the money became a whole lot easier after that.

Charlene

*

Judy confirmed that the money transfer was the smart thing to do. Charlene's intent was to protect her children, and besides, it was her money too. This calmed Charlene's guilt.

*

When Brad came home, Charlene noticed she held her breath whenever he came near. He had a quizzical expression. She believed he had a radar on top of his head that alerted him any time something was up. This was no exception. After kissing her hello, he started in. "What's going on?" Charlene's answers must not have been satisfying, because it didn't take him long to ask her when she planned on leaving him. At first Charlene thought she would choke on the nerves that rose in her throat. Had he found out about what she had been doing while he was gone? He didn't say anything. She waited and waited for him to use some proof against her, but he didn't. She made sure that she got the bank statements for the next couple of months. Charlene had been really bugged that Brad would never balance the checkbook. It was always off thousands of dollars, and he refused to let her do it. Right now, she was grateful for his laziness.

*

Part of planning ahead "just in case," Charlene was counseled to take some domestic violence classes offered by the city. The lawyer said they would help familiarize her with the different terminologies, plus help with her situation. Going to classes and doing other things in a proactive way would also reflect well on her if she ever had to go to court. It showed that she was taking steps to fix her situation.

The weeks slipped by quickly with pressure from the kids, school demands, and going to the government classes. Before Charlene knew it, the calendar had flipped over into the month of December. The hustle and bustle of the holidays brought enough stress, but Brad's foul mood added an extra challenge. Charlene tried to cope by avoiding him. When she couldn't do that, she was stuck listening to him go on and on about how great he was doing in business. After hearing all the detailed plans for the thousandth time, it grew boring. Although Charlene liked being bored far better than enduring the fight that erupted when Brad found out she was taking a class with the State. She attended it for over a month before she got caught. She had told him she was going to a support group to help her with her childhood trauma, which was partially the truth. Actually, it was geared to victims of abuse and what the law does in different situations.

Brad had found a paper that had slipped out of Charlene's notebook. When he read it, he started yelling, "What is this? What is this, you liar?"

Charlene knew he was right in being mad at her. She had misled him and been dishonest. What could she say to that? She didn't know what else to do. There should be loyalty and honesty between husband and wife. She tried to make excuses to calm him, but it didn't work. He screamed and kicked a few shoes the kids had left out before storming out of the house.

Charlene waited to make sure he was gone before calling her minister to confess. Reverend Johnson said she had done nothing to be forgiven for and talked to her more about her situation with Brad. They never talked about the night he had come over and then left so abruptly. Charlene was glad. She didn't know what she would say about that if she was pressed. He mentioned that maybe if she separated from Brad, even if he didn't agree to a separation, he would get a clue.

Charlene was unsure how to take that counsel. It didn't sound too bad, taking a break from Brad. She surely needed one, but getting there was what she feared.

*

Charlene read and reread an article about abuse. There was no doubt from the way the author described it that she was being victimized. The writer made it very clear that throwing things, putting down a person, and causing someone to fear for his or her life were all unacceptable behaviors. She knew she needed to tell Brad about this. He surely had no idea that his behavior was abusive. When she talked to him about it, she was sure he'd stop. Since he was clear across the country on business again, now would be a good time to tell him. Much safer.

When he called, Charlene said, "I've been reading this article today. Listen to this…" She then read parts from the article.

"I'm not guilty of that stuff," Brad said.

"Yes, you are. You throw things."

"But they're talking about throwing things at a person. I never do that."

And so the argument continued, with Brad pointing out emphatically how he wasn't guilty of anything bad.

"Brad," Charlene butted into his sentence. "If you hit me again, I'll leave you." She couldn't stop shaking as she said those words. She had never spoken them before. She wasn't going to say that unless she meant it. Now, she meant it. She wasn't going to live her life being beaten.

"Why would you say that? I'm not saying it's okay to hit, but isn't it a bit dramatic to ruin a whole relationship over? I can't believe you would do such a thing. Obviously our relationship means nothing to you. Maybe we should end it now. I don't want to talk to you anymore." He slammed the phone down.

Charlene called her friend, crying. "Peggy, can you come help me?"

"Are you okay?"

Charlene went on to say, "Yeah," but couldn't hold back the tears. "It's Brad," she said.

"I'll be right over."

After Charlene explained her story, Peggy helped Charlene make copies of important financial records.

Brad called again.

Charlene looked at Peggy then decided to answer on the speaker phone. She really needed to know if Brad was being abusive or if she was being too sensitive.

"Charlene," he said, his voice filled with anger, "I don't appreciate the threats. If you ask me, that's considered abusive, and if you don't stop threatening to leave me, I'll end our marriage." His voice grew louder as he spoke until he was yelling. "Your jerking me around is worse than anything I've done to you. Think about what you're doing. You're threatening the lives of our children, your life, and my life. Sure, I get upset sometimes, but you can't in good conscience dump a whole relationship over that. I can find some articles on how women can please their husbands. You want to read those? Then maybe you wouldn't provoke me so much."

"But Brad, I was just trying to tell you what I would put up with and won't. I don't mean it as a threat."

"Who do you think you are, Queen Elizabeth? Telling me what you'll put up with and what you won't. Life doesn't work that way. I'm not going to tell my clients I'm not going to deliver half the goods and I want twice the price. Dream on. What an ungrateful, self-centered attitude you have."

"Selfish? 'Cause I told you that I don't want to be hit again?" Charlene said, desperately, wishing he would calm down and stop yelling. His anger made her head spin.

"You are selfish. I'm not claiming to be perfect, and you certainly aren't. You have no idea how much crap I put up with from you. And now your latest move—threatening to destroy our children's lives."

"What are you talking about?" She pressed her lips together to hold back harsher words.

"Only people who don't love their kids would consider putting them through such a painful thing as divorce," Brad said. "I don't care for myself, but I hope you would start thinking about the children and not put them through such misery. I know when my parents got divorced it was one of the worst things they could have done. We shouldn't put our kids through that."

He was screaming so loud, Charlene's stomach turned. She needed to calm him down. "I'm sorry," she said, not knowing what else she could possibly do or say to appease him.

"Why would you even threaten it, Charlene? You know if you keep saying that and get used to it, one of these days it'll happen just because you're always thinking about it."

"Stop yelling," she said. She feared getting hit even though he was clear across the country.

"I wouldn't be yelling if you weren't screaming 'fire' in a theater. You're not comfortable with things going well, so you always have to stir things up. You're a mighty fine piece of work."

When Charlene finally hung up the phone, she looked up at Peggy. "What am I doing wrong?"

"Nothing," Peggy said. Tears welled up in her eyes. "I can't believe someone could be so mean to his wife."

CHAPTER 10

Brad came home on schedule. Charlene worked hard to compliment him. The moment the door opened, she ran up to him and threw her arms around him. "I missed you so much," she said, giving him a big kiss even before he could get his suitcase out of his hands. Once he put his bags down, she opened the refrigerator and pulled out dinner. "I cooked your favorite, roast beef and potatoes. Would you like me to warm it for you?"

When he started eating, she asked softly, "How was your trip?" She pulled up a chair next to him and listened. She threw in a few questions to let him know that she was paying attention with interest.

This started to ease the tension and soon he was taking her in his arms to love her. Charlene figured this was the best thing for her to do. Christmas was only a few days away and she didn't want her problems with her husband to boil over now. That would not be good for the kids. She could ignore his poor treatment of her and he could ignore his frustration with her until the holidays were over.

Doing the ignoring didn't mean that the tension magically disappeared. It was still there, but there were no explosions. They made it successfully through the parties, dinners, and opening of gifts without any scenes. They even made it to the day after when Brad left for an emergency meeting in Philadelphia. *Whew!* Charlene thought. *We got through it.* That was the Christmas miracle she'd prayed for.

But the silence couldn't last forever, and things started sparking again. Two weeks after Christmas, Brad barely stopped himself from slugging her with his fist when she still refused to quit school.

Charlene decided another e-mail was necessary. She needed to stand up to him and warn him. If she did end up leaving him, she had to know for herself that she had given him every chance possible.

Subject: It's your choice.
Date: January 3
From: "Charlene" <char@Charlene.org>
To: "Brad" <brad@consult.com>

Dear Brad,

First off, I love you and it's my hope and dream to live a happy life with you forever. You're a good man and have many great things to offer. Christmas slipped by so quickly, and you don't seem to be home long enough for us to resolve things before you're away on business again.

The underlying problem is that I do not feel safe in our relationship. My counselor said if a person doesn't have safety then there isn't much chance of improving anything else. If that isn't fixed, it's impossible for me to have a relationship with you. I have been doing my part to solve the problem by trying to be attentive to you and give you all the love you ask for.

I was guilty of not having enough self-respect to stand up to you and say that the way you treat me is wrong. For the past two years I have been working on that. I am of worth. God does love me, and I don't need to allow disrespect to be directed toward me. Over and over, I have gotten the answer that God doesn't want me to be scared and hurt all the time. Ten years of this is enough. Our relationship could become everything we've dreamed if you decided to fix the problems you have. I love you so much, and I don't want to leave, but if I get scared again, I won't have a choice. You'll have to choose your relationship with me or your anger.

You have done much better about not hitting me, and I'm happy for that. But you have done it out of fear that I would leave—

which I will. What needs to happen and must take place so I can truly feel safe is a change in your heart. It's pride that says, "I will fix it myself." It has been at least two years since you began trying to fix it yourself. When are you going to admit you can't get the assistance you need all by yourself?

Because of what you have done, you could be asked to leave our church. A therapist, who is also a church minister, told me this. If you don't make the changes you need to make, I'm afraid you'll have to go through that humiliation. Brad, please, I'm begging you to take control of your life before people start intervening. We love you. We want you to be happy. It does no good to force you to do something I know you need to do, because the change would not be real.

People tell me to leave you because you will never change. People who have your problem usually don't. I don't believe that. I believe you're a good person. I believe you can make the transition. I hope that's true. I can't live under even the threat of violence. I won't. I love the kids, and I love you. I don't think living in a house where violence is a problem is best for our children. I'll never forgive myself if our daughters grow up and marry men who hit them. I would never forgive myself if our boys grow up and think it is okay to hit their wives. No. The chain of abuse must stop, even if it means I must leave you.

My heart is breaking. I pray you will fight for us, your family, and yourself. May God bless you to be your best self.

Charlene

    Brad wrote her back. Charlene was glad. She didn't want to talk to him. She didn't feel like that would help. It would cloud the issue, and she wanted to maintain her boundaries here and not get softened out of fear by hearing anger in his voice. She didn't want to have to worry even though he was so far away. She hated how she got scared. Hated what a chicken she had become. Maybe someday she could overcome that.

    His e-mail made her mad. It was filled with victim talk and how he wasn't responsible for anything. If she could just get him to see that he did have control and he could claim it and turn everything around, then she'd know their relationship would work. Maybe if she was bold with him, he'd get the message. He had to. If he didn't, well, if he didn't, their lives, their marriage, and their children would be changed forever.

> Subject: Doormat—NOT!
> Date: January 4
> From: "Charlene" <char@Charlene.org>
> To: "Brad" <brad@consult.com>
>
> Brad,
>
> I agree that writing e-mails helps each of us get our thoughts out better than talking on the phone. Blaming our marital problems and the reason you have hit me on our abusive childhoods is not going to work. I'm sorry, but you aren't going to convince me our problems are beyond our control. There are reasons I feel you are out to get me—following me around the house and keeping me up until 4:00 a.m. while you try to talk me into seeing things your way. These techniques are ways of bullying a person.
>
> You have repeatedly told me that if I'd quit believing you're out to get me, my pain will go away. I can't believe this, no matter how many times you restate it. It seems to me you're trying to convince me that my reality is a fantasy, trying to get me to admit I'm crazy for seeing things the way I do so that I will give into your views—the "right ones." You ignore my pain as though it were an imaginary spin-off from paranoia. How painful for you to tell me I'm becoming just like my crazy mother. How can you tell me I should ignore my own experience and go on believing "things are not that bad," as I've been doing my whole life? What do you mean by telling me, "You weren't really knocked out that long"? Do you want me to get used to being scared all the time? Is it normal for me to be hit every once in a while, when I least expect it? Do you think knocking me unconscious is nothing?!
>
> Charlene, your wife, not your doormat.

*

To Charlene's shock, when Brad came home, he was full of tenderness, kind words, and apologies. He even thanked her for being such a caring and thoughtful wife and a wonderful mother to the kids. He knew how much work she put into it and was grateful.

To add to Charlene's surprise, Brad was up and ready early to go to marriage therapy and willing to work on their "issues" while in session. *I'm glad that I held on and waited*, Charlene wrote to Judy when an e-mail came in. Charlene, caught up in happiness of the way things were going, had forgotten to write her friend. Judy had written her in panic wanting to know if she was okay.

Things were going so well, in fact, that Charlene wrote of her true feelings about Brad and didn't hesitate to let them bubble forth: *I think we're going to make it. He's such a great guy. I really do love him. It's weird to have the fear and the tension so high, and then to have it vanish all of a sudden.*

Charlene sensed that her friend had grown tired of their ups and downs. She hoped Judy would hang in there. She knew it hurt Judy to see or hear about her suffering, but that was all in the past. All she had to do to get things fixed was to make a stand with Brad. Now he knew exactly what her position was. Since he cared, he would honor that. Plus, he was sincerely making efforts. They hadn't had another episode for over two weeks, which was building her trust.

Yes, Brad had made some mistakes in the past, but he didn't realize that what he was saying and doing was threatening her life. He would never purposely do that. Now that he knew, he wouldn't go there. He wouldn't hit her again. She prayed. She believed. A person had to have faith.

Chapter 11

Subject: Quick change
Date: January 21
From: "Charlene" <char@CharlenesWeb.net>
To: "Judy" <bchcomber@yippee.com>

Dear Judy,

Things can change quickly. Brad was being so nice and kind, and then boom, he was angry. The dramatic shift almost gave me whiplash. He's so mad. I'm worried.

Thanks for your support and concern. He's angry this time because we got a new minister, Reverend Sinclair. Reverend Johnson was forced to move because of health reasons. We aren't sure what happened to him. He wouldn't say, but we suspect it was advanced cancer. I knew I needed to talk to the new minister to ensure the safety net with the church still existed. I met with him. I told Brad I needed to know how this would affect my church responsibilities. Brad thought I wanted to tell on him. He was right, but if I admit it, it'll set him off. I'm frightened. Thank you for your prayers and e-mails of support.

Charlene

Charlene pressed the send button before jumping from her desk and running to her door in her office. She did not want Brad to suspect what she was doing. He was calling throughout the house for her.

"Yes," she yelled.

"Where are you?"

Charlene left her office as she answered, "Living room." She looked at the scattered toys, books, and clothes the kids had left out. She busied herself tidying up.

Her arms were full with stuff to put away when Brad found her. "I want to talk to you," he said.

"Okay." She bent over to pick up Cameron's baseball cap.

"What did you talk to Reverend Sinclair about?"

"My new position in the church."

"And?"

"He wanted to know how we were doing as a family." She walked over to the white cabinet to put the loose books away—anything to avoid his glare.

"What did you say?"

Charlene paused at the bookshelf to avoid turning around.

"I said we were fine." She didn't want to go into the fact that Reverend Sinclair had been apprised of their situation by Reverend Johnson. She started to leave the room.

Brad followed her. "What else did you tell him?"

"What do you mean?" She forced herself to sound normal and not reveal the fear that consumed her.

The kids' voices came from downstairs. "We need to get the children to bed," Charlene said, hoping to distract him.

When all the kids were quiet and in their beds, Brad came up to her and wrapped his arms around her. "Let's go on a walk."

She looked up at him, searching for his motive. He smiled and squeezed her tight.

"Okay."

She got her coat out of the closet. Thinking that it might be wise to bring her cell phone, she hurried to her office to get it. She had unhooked the phone from the charger and was about to slip it into her pocket when Brad came up behind her and wrapped his hand around hers and the phone. "You don't need to bring that."

"But—"

"Nothing is going to happen. Leave it here. I hate it that you always have that thing around. I feel like a prisoner."

There wasn't a way out of it. If she protested, her resistance would set him off. He was already edgy. She released the phone into his hands. Moments later he came back to her and helped zip up her coat. "It's cold out there. We don't want you to freeze. Do you have your walking shoes on?" He bent down and saw her tennis shoes. "Good."

He opened the door for her. As she stepped outside, the bitter wind wrapped around them, dusting them with snow. Charlene flipped her scarf around her mouth and nose. They were silent as they walked under the moonless sky. Brad reached out and took her hand, leading the way.

Her hand ached from his touch. She wished to pull it out of his, but knew he would be hurt and then enraged. She didn't want him to be any more upset than he was. As they waited to cross the street at the light, he turned to her. "Why did you have to go talk to the minister? Are you trying to set me up?" He spoke with fire in his eyes and ice in his voice.

Panic filled her. She felt naked without her phone. If only she hadn't let him talk her out of bringing it. He was mad. Real mad. She might need to get away. How was she going to get out of this? What was he going to do to her? Was he taking her on a walk to beat her? Her heart felt like it twisted in her chest. Why did her heart keep hurting? Was she going to die of a heart attack?

Before she said anything, the light turned red and he was jerking and pulling her arm to cross the street. When they reached the other side, he glared at her. Charlene had seen that look before—right before he'd hit her. She flinched.

"Tell me why you're betraying me. You're such a piece of work." On and on he went. His broad chest seemed to puff out as he hovered over her. His voice grew into shouts. "You dumb ass bitch. How dare you treat our marriage so lightly?"

He pounded on a trash can they walked by, leaving a dent.

Charlene jumped, startled.

"Stop jumping," he yelled and then went on with more swearing about what she was. As he was cussing, he let go of her hand to retie his shoe. Now was her chance. She had to get away or soon he'd be hitting her again.

She ran into the bitter stinging wind. She gasped for air, trying desperately to find a place to get away from him.

He took off after her, calling, "Charlene, come back here. Charlene, what are you doing?"

She wished he'd stop yelling her name. Others would hear. She had to go, go, go. He came closer. What would he do if he caught her? She had to get away from him. Her foot slipped on the concrete. She struggled to continue, tears escaping.

He caught her. "What did you do that for? What have you done? What did you say to the minister? Tell me."

Charlene shook, tears slipping from her eyes. How was she going to get out of this?

The anger, the demands continued until four in the morning. Charlene was exhausted and wanted more than anything for him to go away. She knew that he had to leave in the morning to catch a plane. This knowledge kept her hanging on and helped her keep quiet about her decision. Reverend Sinclair had said Brad would most likely be asked to leave the congregation. It depended on how he responded when he was confronted by the church leaders. When Reverend Sinclair learned of Brad's behavior from his predecessor, he was shocked and outraged that nothing had been done about it before. What was Charlene going to do when her husband found out? Would he kill her over her betrayal?

*

The doorbell rang. *It's time*, Charlene thought, wiping her hands on a dish towel before going to answer. "Time for truth," she reminded herself. "The whole truth." When her mom had been asked about the truth of her relationship when she was divorcing, she refused to say anything. She protected her husband to the very end, thinking she had promised to honor him and she wouldn't betray that. Look at her father now, still causing pain wherever he went. Of course, someday he might change. If her mom would have spoken up, if he had been held accountable, maybe things would have been different. Charlene was glad that Brad was gone again on another business trip. The timing was perfect.

She opened the door. The minister's wife was standing next to her husband. Surprise. Embarrassed, Charlene looked at the woman. Why was she here?

Reverend Sinclair cleared his throat. "My wife's here to watch the children so we aren't disturbed."

When Charlene sat in the front room to answer Reverend Sinclair's questions, she wished she could vanish. "We need to know what he did to you for the court."

Charlene nodded.

As Charlene spoke, she tried not to think about what this would do to Brad and what consequences her actions would all mean. The one thing she knew now, but didn't before, was that she wasn't going to go on pretending there was no problem.

"Here's all the evidence I have collected for my lawyer against Brad," she said. She showed him the busted statue, ripped book pages, angry notes, and the police reports, etc. Reverend Sinclair's matter-of-fact attitude made things easier when she explained why she'd had so many kids so close together. "He wanted them and did anything to get them," she said, wondering if a person could die of humiliation.

*

Everything had settled down between Charlene and Brad by the time Brad returned home from Maryland. Knowing what was going to happen some time in the future, Charlene made extra efforts to be kind to him. Maybe that would prevent him from being as explosive when he discovered what she had done. Her stomach knotted every time she thought about Brad being called in and being told that she had revealed their secrets.

Other times, when she held him in her arms, she lingered, thinking this may be the last time that they held each other, kissed each other. She didn't want it to end, but if he flipped out, she might have to run for her life. It would be all over then. She couldn't keep going through these cycles, for her children's sake. They deserved peace. One more time she promised herself that she'd leave for them.

Once, Brad pulled away from her. "What are the tears for? It's not that time of month is it?"

Charlene shrugged and felt fortunate that was enough of an answer for him.

Time passed like this until one day, while she was doing dishes, the phone rang. Desperate, frightened, Charlene handed the phone over to Brad. The church was calling to inform him that they wanted to consider disciplinary action and wanted to hear his side of it.

"Hello?" she heard him say as she left the room.

It would be best to get the kids out of the way just in case…She hurried them downstairs. "Time for a movie."

She had barely started the DVD when she heard Brad calling her, his tone brisk, harsh. Oh, how she wished she could just melt into the carpet and disappear, but knowing that she didn't have the skills to do that, she answered, "Yeah," hurrying up the stairs, hoping that she could keep the upcoming scene from the kids.

When she reached the top of the stairs, Brad immediately asked, "What was that call all about?"

"What do you mean?" she asked. She pressed against the wall for support. "How would I know? It was for you."

He stood in front of her, peering down, his hazel eyes flashing. "What did you do?"

Charlene squeezed away from the wall, searching for an escape route. Once again, she had to escape. He was going to hit her. She scurried up the stairs, him chasing after her. She headed into the bathroom, not knowing where else to go.

She slammed the door and locked it, praying. She pulled her portable phone out of her sweater pocket, dialed Peggy, and whispered their password. Brad banged on the door so hard it splintered. She left the phone on and hid it behind the toilet. If her friend stayed on, at least she would be able to tell what was happening. If things became deadly, her friend could call for help. She hoped.

Brad had gotten the spare key and unlocked the bathroom door just as she put the phone down. Charlene ran over to him. "What do you want?"

"You're such a—"

The doorbell rang. Both Brad and Charlene stopped arguing long enough to listen to the pattering of feet running toward the front entry. "Don't answer it," Brad called to the kids.

But whichever child was on the way to the door either ignored him or didn't hear him, because next thing they knew, Lorine was calling for Brad. "Door."

Brad glared at Charlene then left the room.

Timidly, Charlene followed, praying this would be one of those "saved by the bell" incidents.

Charlene's breathing returned to normal when she heard Peggy and her husband laughing. Hearing that, she had enough confidence to enter the room. Her friend said that she and her husband "happened" to stop by.

Peggy's husband talked to Brad for hours about sports. Brad was obviously agitated, but his efforts to get rid of them failed. "Well, it was sure nice talking to you," he tried.

Trent slapped his knee. "It was. Did you happen to watch the big game yesterday? What did you think?"

Brad gave a quick response.

"Those referees were something. What did you think about the call when…"

The conversation went on that way until Brad couldn't keep from yawning and his eyelids sagged. The couple left after midnight.

Brad and Charlene immediately retired to bed and fell asleep. Brad didn't mention anything about the incident afterward, but there was a stony coldness between them that lasted for days. Charlene was scared about what it all meant, but she wasn't about to bring up the subject. That would definitely wake his monster.

CHAPTER 12

Charlene answered the phone timidly.

"This is Minister Sinclair. How are you doing?"

"All right," Charlene lied. What was she supposed to say? That she was scared out of her mind? That she was so frightened she couldn't even function?

"I slipped out of the church meeting to give you warning about what's going to happen so you can be prepared."

His voice sounded distant as she struggled to hear through the pounding of her heart. "What did they decide?" she said, sitting down on the couch.

"He confessed to most of your accusations against him, except about you being forced to have babies. I was disappointed he didn't clear his conscience of that too while he was at it. He seemed mad when we asked about that, but to give him credit, he did admit he smashed you on the top of the head years ago and that could have caused you brain damage."

"What's going to happen now?" Charlene whispered, knowing the harder they came down on him the angrier he would become and the more danger she'd likely be in.

"They've decided to give him a warning."

Charlene's head began to spin as she heard the verdict. He'd hit her for years and caused permanent brain stem damage, which she'd always have to live with. He put their children's lives and her own in danger—put them through all sorts of hell. And he got a slap on the wrist. She didn't get it.

"Charlene." Her leader's voice drew her attention back. "Let me give you my private cell number. Call me if you're in any danger."

"Okay."

She hung up the phone and went to the computer to tell Judy as she waited for her husband to come home.

I guess it isn't my place to question the leadership. I will accept what is and trust that there must be a good reason. If not, it still isn't my problem. The Lord's servants are accountable to Him. I trust God will take care of all this in the end. Sometimes it's just hard, though. You know what I mean?

Although grateful for the warning, Charlene didn't know what she could do. If she took off, that would only enrage him more. Eventually she'd have to come back. And the lawyer had said she mustn't do that, anyway. If she hid the kids, then he would surely blow. Any steps she took to protect herself and the children would most likely set him off.

She did hurry the kids to bed, though. Plus, she slipped the portable phone into the pocket of her sweater and attached her cell phone to the top of her jeans waistband. She pulled her shirt over the phone then slumped to bended knee to pray.

*

Subject: The police
Date: February 10
From: "Charlene" <char@CharlenesWeb.net>
To: "Judy" <bchcomber@yippee.com>

Judy,

I know I wrote you earlier this evening, but I have to write you again. An hour after the church review, Brad came home very upset. He started hovering over me, spitting on me, demanding to know how I could say those things about him to the church council. He took a tennis racket to our furniture, shattering things. I became so scared that I pushed the panic button on our alarm system when he wasn't looking. I kept Brad busy chasing me around until the police arrived. Because of prior incidents, they removed him from the house.

Brad called later that night from his mom's house, demanding to know what we should do. I said, "Separate," and hung up. So many things are happening so fast.

Charlene

Charlene cried as though her heart had split into a thousand pieces. She would have to leave him now. It was clear that he was no longer safe to live with and probably never would be.

If she allowed this abuse to continue, their kids would think it was normal and put up with it or dish it out. Either way, she would fail as a mother. If it was going to be a choice between her children's best interests and her love for Brad, then there was no choice at all. Her children were helpless. They had nowhere else to go or anyone else to take care of them. Whether right or wrong, she knew deep down inside that if she had to pick, it would be her children. They deserved a better life. Although it was going to break her heart, she was going to see to their safety or die trying to give it to them.

Subject: More trouble with Brad
Date: February 11
From: "Charlene" <char@CharlenesWeb.net>
To: "Judy" <bchcomber@yippee.com>

Judy,

Thanks for the worry and concern you shared in the last e-mail. I'm having more trouble with Brad. He came over late tonight. I wouldn't let him in the house. We got in a fight over the children. When I tried to go back inside, he grabbed me and ripped my pajamas. I don't know how much longer I can put up with him.

I appreciate your ever-faithful support.

Charlene

When Brad ripped her clothes and the cold night air struck her, so did a cold chill toward Brad. What had she ever seen in him? He was a bully. He would resort to any tactic to get his way. Why hadn't she seen that before?

He was scary and mean, and all she wanted to do was to be away from him. It was so nice to be able to say "No," then close the door and lock it. She had the locksmith come over the first day Brad was out. They changed all the locks. She also figured out how to reprogram the alarm. She wasn't going to allow him to come into her home unannounced.

Although it was better having him gone, she still feared what he would do. How far would his anger take him? She learned from the past it could take him into violence, and she definitely didn't want either herself or the kids to be on the receiving end. She slept with the phone under her pillow just in case.

Brad called hundreds of times a day. Peggy was over to make sure Charlene was all right. When she heard the constant ringing, she went around the house and turned off the ringers. Charlene wondered why she hadn't thought of that.

When the phone method didn't work, he started e-mailing. Charlene, unsure what she wanted in the relationship, felt it was only decent to respond with the truth. She answered:

Subject: I am not wrong
Date: February 12
From: "Charlene" <char@Charlene.org>
To: "Brad" <brad@consult.com>
Brad,

I do not have an open-door policy for you to freely criticize my parenting, especially in front of the children. I will not have you nit-picking me to death. It's called "water torture." You do not know what you're talking about. I take excellent care of the kids. I feed them healthy food. If they are ill, I immediately get the help they need. If they are sad or scared, I work through their feelings with them. I'm constantly researching the best ways to parent and how to help them deal with their problems in healthy ways. I play with them, and I spend hours talking to them. Do you make this much effort? I AM NOT A BAD MOM. I'm sick of you doubting me. I never bruised them or threw anything at them. I don't scare them, and when I make a mistake I talk to them about it.

Your efforts to make me out to be a bad mother aren't going to work. I'm not! There's not a soul who loves their kids more than me or who tries harder. I'm doing what I believe is for their best mental health, whether you agree or not. Since the children are getting better, I have the results to prove it.

Saying the "F" word to me is SOOOOOOO upsetting and wrong. It opens up many wounds. It's not acceptable, and I will not wait for you to get your act together while treating me like dirt. This is not a threat. This is a boundary. I don't appreciate you ripping my pj's, either. How dare you? You have no right to treat me that way. I am your wife. You owe me new pj's. I don't want to see you again until you replace them and you are ready to apologize and promise never to treat me like that again. EVER.

Brad, I love you. I really do, but I won't wait for you if you continue to treat me like dirt. If you're not going to go the whole distance and change, we might as well call it quits. I'm willing to risk being on my own. Being alone has got to be better than playing mind games and living in constant fear of your explosions. It will be better for the kids for us to separate than to have a mother growing more ill from living like a terrified rabbit.

I feel you aren't really changing when you make statements like: "Our problems aren't all my fault. Tell me what you did wrong. You were at least fifty percent responsible." That's part of the blame I have continually lived under. For ten years, I accepted that I was the reason you got mad, the reason you broke phones, smashed holes in the walls, physically bruised me. I did everything you asked me to do to make it so you wouldn't get mad. For example, I didn't buy milk that was twenty cents more expensive than other brands in order to be sensitive about the money. In fact, I never overspent. I went without clothes that fit so as to be careful with the bottom line. I begged for forgiveness when you pointed out what you believed were my wrongdoings, I tried my best not to be negative or critical, etc. This is just the tip of the iceberg when it comes to things I have done to conform so you wouldn't get angry. None of it did any good. It never will.

Charlene

Part Two

CHAPTER 13

Larry Greene, her neighbor, stood straight on Charlene's porch, showing his full six foot, four inch height.

"Hi," she said, gripping her phone. Ever since separating from Brad, she felt increasingly vulnerable.

"Stay away from my wife." Larry glared down at her.

"What?"

"I got your number. I know what you did to poor Brad, and I'm not going to have you giving any more radical ideas to my wife." He stepped closer. "If I see you anywhere near her, I'm calling DCFS on how you mistreat your children."

"What?" she stuttered. "What am I doing?"

"I know you make them sit in time-out an awful lot."

"Only when they misbehave. That's what their therapist recommends."

"That's what you say. Watch it."

Charlene watched him leave, shaking. How dare he threaten her by using her kids? Naturally she'd stop talking to his wife.

These kind of hostile events from her neighbors were becoming more common. She'd been called a "feminist," "home breaker," "unforgiving," and her favorite, "unrighteous." These unjust reactions were unnerving Charlene. She couldn't stop shaking. It was hard enough to get through the day, but with such harsh judgments, she struggled to go on.

Then Chris came to tell her the neighbors were concerned about how messy her front yard looked with the toys and bikes left out. There was a standard in the neighborhood and they hoped she would do something about it.

Charlene just nodded, and then muttered that she'd fix the problem.

*

Valentine's Day, and Brad stood on her front porch holding a dozen red roses. Charlene wasn't sure what she should do. Talk to him? What would she say? He'd want to know if they were getting back together. Pretend she wasn't here and wait for him to go? Today was a day of supposed love. He'd gone to the effort to remember her.

Her decision was made when Sandra answered the door. "Dad's here for you," she said flatly. "Can I go play?"

"Yes." Charlene looked for the phone. When she found it, she slipped it on top of her waistband. She went to the front door to find Brad shifting his weight.

"Can I come in?"

A cold gush of wind blew against her as she tried to decide if that would be safe. "I guess." She opened the door a crack.

When he came in, he looked around as though to see if anything had been changed. "Have you decided when you're going to let me come back?" He handed her the flowers.

Sandra peered around the door frame. Charlene, not wanting her daughter to witness anything that might happen, said, "Sandra, please put these flowers in some water."

"But, Mom…"

"Do as I say," Charlene said, sharply. After Sandra had gone, she turned to Brad. "I don't know about that," she said.

"Why not? We can't stay separated forever."

Charlene took a step back. Things, although still hard, were so much easier with him gone. Her therapist had talked to her a lot about standing up for herself and believing she could do better. She decided that she wanted better. She wanted her children raised right and not in violence. She wanted empathy. Someone to understand her pain, her sorrows, her wishes. She thought hard about it. Brad would never be able to get past thinking about how everything affected him and what was going on for him. He didn't think of others.

"I've decided a divorce might not be such a bad idea," she said.

"What?" he screamed. "You can't do that."

She took several steps backward, her heart twisting. "I just can't go on like this."

"Yes, you can." He took another step toward her. "Why would you break us up?"

Charlene started crying as he kicked the office door. His foot broke the wood. "Brad, stop," she pleaded.

"Don't ruin this marriage." He threw a book he picked up off the floor.

She ducked. "Stop!" she screamed, covering her head.

He didn't. Instead he kicked the French doors. The glass shattered then he stormed upstairs.

She dialed 9-1-1 as she grabbed Nathan, resting him on her hip to stop him from walking in the glass.

"State your emergency."

She heard Brad's heavy steps upstairs. "I'd like police assistance," she said.

*

The police came and watched Brad pack his bags—while he cried. They escorted him to his Jeep. He peeled away.

Shaking, Charlene thanked the cops and called Karla, who immediately came over. She cried to her friend. The older children arrived home from school. Charlene gathered them in her arms and talked to them as Karla cleaned up the broken glass. The kids handled the news better than they had at other times. Of course, those other times Brad would make a dramatic exit. "I'm leaving, and don't count on me coming back." The worst line he told the kids was, "Your mother wants me to leave, so I must honor her wish." That one always caused instant anger directed at Charlene from the kids.

Brad asked to come back to get more of his stuff. Charlene planned ahead on that one. She made sure the kids were visiting friends, plus she decided to have the cops there to "keep the peace." Brad would probably flip, but she didn't care. She wasn't taking any more chances. Charlene called her therapist and left a message detailing what had happened on Valentine's Day. The therapist called back and told her to review some of the information she had given her a few months ago—a list of ten characteristics of men who kill their spouses. She said getting out of their relationships was when abused women were at greatest risk. Brad had eight of the ten traits. Charlene shuddered.

"Buy a gun," her therapist said.

Guns scared her. She didn't know how to shoot, and now wasn't the time to learn. Besides, what if one of the kids found it? Her minister had promised she would be protected by angels. She'd put her faith in the angels instead of a gun. That was right for her, but maybe some women should get a gun.

Once she made the decision to divorce, Charlene became swamped with things to do. She needed to contact her lawyer and figure out the finances. Brad hadn't let her near their finances during their entire marriage. The children had so many needs that she spent most her time trying to meet them. She couldn't think about it all. It was too much. She doubted she could sleep, but she was afraid her health would plummet if she didn't rest.

Charlene breathed deeply. That was how she would get through this. She couldn't think about everything all at once. Breathe. It was too much. Breathe. She had a roof over her head today and food in her cupboard. Breathe. She knew where her children were. Breathe. She was okay.

She just couldn't believe she actually called the police on him and he was gone!

*

Charlene rolled over in her bed and woke. She opened her eyes to find the other side of the mattress empty again. She rolled onto her back and took a deep breath. Having Brad gone—out of the house and not coming back any time in the near future—would to take a lot of getting used to.

When it came down to it, Charlene wasn't sure how she felt. Pressure was squeezing in on her to make a decision about whether or not to divorce Brad. Weighing out that choice kept her awake and restless most of the night. Her head throbbed, which didn't make her position any easier.

When she wasn't trying to decide what to do with her marital status, she worried about him coming back and attacking the family. She had pushed him hard by calling the police and having him removed in full daylight. It was possible the neighbors had seen that happen. He said he would never put up with separation. How much of this could he handle without getting even? That she didn't know. In the past, getting even was his pattern, and in this situation she wasn't sure what that would look like. She did know from the past he always upped the ante when it came to revenge. She wrote Judy about her situation, telling her friend that she was on high alert, and that was the truth.

Judy wrote back in a panic. *Are you all right? I'm so worried about you. Please write me back even if it's every few hours. I want to know that you're okay. You are going through a difficult time, but remember you will get through this. You're a strong and brave woman.*

Charlene didn't feel strong and brave and was taken aback that her friend saw her that way, but it helped. Her friend believed in her and thought she could make it. She must see things that Charlene didn't. To ease Judy's fears, Charlene wrote her again several times, updating her on the situation.

Subject: Still here
Date: February 15
From: "Charlene" <char@CharlenesWeb.net>
To: "Judy" <bchcomber@yippee.com>

Judy,

Today is so long and still here. I'm finding it hard to get out of bed. I'm actually e-mailing from my laptop in bed. My kids are trashing the place, and I can't seem to move. I haven't done my hair, makeup—what a joke—not even a bath. One of my children has a high fever and it looks like it could be an ear infection. I don't have the strength to go to the doctor. My car has two flat tires. I don't know how to fix them.

I'm going to bury my head in the first sandbox I see and not come out. My doorbell is ringing. Oh, no, one of my children answered...

Cameron called up to Charlene. "Mom, door."

Charlene rushed into her closet to throw on sweats. She definitely didn't want to be caught in her silky nightgown. She also ran a comb threw her hair and brushed her teeth.

"Mom, they're waiting."

"All right," she mumbled. She peered at herself in the mirror and saw a worn-out, tired person who seemed frightened. Well, she was frightened, so she might as well look it. She didn't want to talk to anyone, but apparently there wasn't a choice. If she didn't hurry down the stairs, her kids would drag whoever it was up.

Later that night, she wrote to Judy about what happened.

Subject: Still here—sorta
Date: February 15
From: "Charlene" <char@CharlenesWeb.net>
To: "Judy" <bchcomber@yippee.com>

Judy,

It's about 11:30 in the evening. Sorry I left you hanging. It was our minister at the door. He took over the job recently. "Welcome," I wanted to say. "What a great way to start out, with a problem like mine." He seemed overwhelmed with my situation. I would be. I am.

I cried. Told him my tires were flat and I didn't know how to fix them. One of my children needed to go to the doctor. I didn't know what to do and I was scared.

He called people in the church. They fixed my tires within the hour. He made more calls and some young women from church came over and cleaned my house (sooooo embarrassing) and tended the kids while I took Nathan to the doctor after hours and went to the grocery store.
Today is over. Thank heaven.

Charlene

Charlene meant every bit of the thank heaven part of her e-mail. She didn't want the day to continue anymore. As she climbed the stairs to go check on Nathan and his fever, her thoughts jumped to Brad. What was he doing right now? Did he miss her? The family? Was he angry? Would he forgive her? Was he the one who had flattened her tires? Would he try to sabotage her so she couldn't make it on her own? Could she make it on her own?

She wished she could call her family. Their help and support would mean everything to her right now, but she couldn't. Maybe she would find the courage to call her dad. Maybe he would realize her desperation and be willing to help. It had been so long since she'd talked to him. Would he reject her? Or would he be angry at Brad for putting her in this situation?

The more she thought about it, the more Charlene believed her father would help. He wouldn't know how to do the "feeling stuff," but he was smart about money. He could give her direction on what to do with that and help her know how she could support herself and her kids. He loved her underneath all their issues. Surely he would be there for her since things were so bad.

The next day, after Charlene saw to it that her kids were busy, she sat on the couch in her office, day planner open, and her heart thumping wildly. It felt like she had a jackhammer in her chest chipping away. "Dear God, help me," she whispered as she rested her forehead in the palm of her hand.

Taking a breath to try to clear her dizziness, she dialed her dad's number. The phone rang three times before he answered.

"Hi, Dad," she said, her voice shaking and emotion filling her.

"Charlene. What's going on?"

She spilled out to him the details of the past few days. "Dad," she choked out, "Brad sometimes beats me."

"What do you want?" he asked.

"I don't know what to do about money and how to make ends meet," Charlene said. She had stood during the conversation and now was pacing the floor.

"That's what you get and have to deal with if you leave your husband," her dad said. "That's what you're choosing."

"But what should I do?" Charlene hated the desperation she heard in her voice. Her father had helped her in the past. In fact when she didn't know whether to marry Brad or not she had called him. She had asked him, "How does a person know when it is right?"

Her father drove up to her college, went out to dinner with the two of them, and said, "Marry him."

He had been there for her then. Granted, she could think of hardly any other times, but the marriage choice mattered. Just as supporting her five children and deciding whether to leave Brad and the abuse counted.

Her father's voice cut into her thoughts. "If you choose to leave, then you'll have to figure it out."

"But he beats me," Charlene cried, hoping to appeal to his sympathy. She could feel heat burn off her chest and neck.

"How come I haven't heard about that until now?"

Charlene couldn't find her voice but thought, "Because I was too embarrassed."

Her father didn't wait for her to answer. Instead, he said in his critical father voice, "Charlene, I don't believe you. You need to get back together with him and cook for him more. It'll all work out then."

When she hung up the phone, she burst into tears. Her hands shook. Her head spun. She felt as though she might pass out.

"Mommy, Lorine hit me," Paige said, coming into the room.

Charlene couldn't find the strength to look up at her child.

Chapter 14

Charlene learned that the only way to get through the days was not to take it in one big chunk. She needed to focus on it minute-to-minute. She found herself saying repeatedly, "I have a roof over my head, food in the cupboard, and I know where my children are. I might not later, but at this moment I do. I can go on for another minute." A few minutes later, when panic filled her and the recurring thoughts—*How am I going to pay the bills? Brad left me with nothing. Will he steal my kids and leave the country? He told me I will never get the kids from him. Will he kill me?*—raced through her mind again, she repeated, "I have a roof over my head, food in the cupboard, and I know where my children are. I might not later, but at this moment I do. I can go on for another minute." Days passed and that mantra got her through them.

This method worked for her every day except Sunday. On Sabbath mornings she dressed, got her kids ready for church, and hurried up the stairs for extra diapers. Each step forced her to move through her exhaustion.

There was no way to hide the circles under her eyes, and she was on show at church. The breakup of her marriage was the latest thing.

People watched and they were passing judgment. Some came up to her and openly chewed her out for leaving her marriage. Told her she was not a good Christian. Told her that she was at fault. Told her that she didn't try hard enough. Or told her how much they missed and liked Brad. Charlene's head began to swirl whenever she thought about it. The congregation loved Brad for some reason. She guessed it was the charisma he could turn on and off at will. People were too dense to see through the games he played. Many of them thought this whole problem was her fault. Could she go on enduring the looks, the sneers, the whispers? It seemed as though those thoughts drained every last bit of strength out of her. She lowered herself onto the staircase and closed her eyes. She didn't want to go to church anymore. For that matter, she didn't want to get out of bed. She longed to climb back on her mattress and pull the blanket over her head.

But Sunday after Sunday, Sandra called up to her, "Mom, we got to go. We're going to be late," in an anxious, tense voice.

Sunday after Sunday, Charlene breathed deep. She knew she had to attend church despite everything. She had to for her kids. They had already endured enough changes. They didn't need change with their church and their friends also. She pulled herself up and went.

Walking in with five little children on her own, all the eyes of the congregation on them, was the hardest part. Let them stare, Charlene decided early on. She made a habit of strolling to her pew with her head held high. She heard whispers as she passed, but didn't let that stop her.

Nathan invariably fussed. She would look down at him and think about taking him outside, but then she'd be leaving Paige alone, and Paige was too young to be left alone. Charlene would sometimes glance hopefully at Sandra, but her nine-year-old's arms remained crossed week after week, and she kept her face screwed up like she was about to explode. Charlene realized Sandra couldn't be left in charge. There was always a lady or two sitting in front of Charlene who would turn around and eye Nathan with an irritated expression.

Go ahead and stare, Charlene thought, squaring her shoulders. If nobody was going to step up and help, she was going have to make do. She wasn't going to be chased out of church. She of all people needed it.

After dragging herself home from that ordeal, Charlene often found that making peanut butter sandwiches for the children sapped the final reserves of her strength. She would suggest they watch videos and wend her way up the stairs to her room. Once in the bedroom, she would take in the empty, still-made side of the bed and cry.

*

Sundays passed into history and so did the difficulty of having Brad gone. Overall, it was easier. There was no one standing behind her telling her all the things that she did wrong, expect when she talked with her neighbors. No one calling her a loser. Actually, several of her girlfriends called and told her how strong and brave she was. She found herself laughing and having more fun. She would crank up her music—early 80's or New Age, and dance for long periods. It felt so good to relax.

When Brad wrote wanting to get back with her, she thought about how much nicer it was with him gone. The kids had stopped fighting, the tension and drama had lessened, and she gradually began sleeping more peacefully without someone waking her to tell her what a lowlife she was. It was also nice to be able to go to classes and not worry that her homework would be ripped up. Karla had taken over watching the kids when she was gone. When she returned, the kids were in bed and the house was as clean as or cleaner than she'd left it. Karla was a good friend, and Charlene often bought her little gifts of chocolate, trinkets, or flowers.

Charlene thought about the day Brad had told her she was fat. He wanted to know if that was her sneaky way of being less attractive to him. She'd had five kids in nine years, and he had the gall to call her fat. That memory did it for her.

"Not yet," she wrote to his request for reconciliation.

She should have been prepared for the backlash those words would cause but she wasn't. Brad sent angry e-mails and the phone began ringing incessantly again. She read his e-mails just long enough to realize that she was in trouble from his wrath. *I will not allow you* to take the kids away for me nor let you destroy this family. Rest assured that will not happen. Watch out, you—

Charlene called Karla, and after reading the e-mail together, they both got ready for Charlene to flee with her children.

Subject: Hiding
Date: February 21
From: "Charlene" <char@CharlenesWeb.net>
To: "Judy" <bchcomber@yippee.com>

Judy,

I'm disappearing this week, so I won't be responding to your e-mails. I have to go into hiding. I'll write you when I get back. Don't worry about me. I'm taking extra precautions. I never know how Brad will respond when he finds out I'm not letting him back into the house. I had to take the phone off the hook last night because it kept ringing and ringing and ringing. I would have answered it eventually, and it was driving me crazy. Luckily, my neighbor Karla was here with me. She unplugged the phones so we didn't have to listen to them. There were fifteen messages on the answering machine this morning, and the caller ID said they were all from Brad. I'm going to wait until I'm in hiding with Karla to listen to them. I don't know if I can handle it otherwise. I don't want to make a stupid decision, like getting soft and going back to him.

Hope all is well for you. Thank you for praying for us. Your support means so much.

Charlene

Charlene, the kids, Karla, and Karla's husband, Harold, drove out to the desert, where they were surrounded by juniper trees and sagebrush. The air was clean and they could see for what seemed a hundred miles. Karla loved being away from the city and camping. She laughed a lot. Charlene took in the dust, sagebrush, and rolling hills and didn't quite feel the same appreciation as her friend. Plus, she suffered a bit from allergies. But she was away from Brad, and the kids enjoyed playing in the dirt. They made no demands on her and they appeared to be happy. That was really all she cared about.

After Harold helped Charlene erect her pop-up trailer, she crawled onto her bed and laid there for the next couple of days. She came out to help with dinner and clean up, double-check on the kids, kiss them, tell them she loved them, look at the stars, which were definitely bigger and brighter than they were in the city, and then crawl back to bed. Karla and Harold were excited to look after and play with the children on what for them was a family camping vacation. Karla, who could not have children of her own, told Charlene often how much she cherished this time.

Late at night, when everyone else was asleep, Charlene unzipped the tarp and peered out at the sea of stars to think about what waited for her. Could love be possible with someone who treated her decently? As she gazed at the navy sea, it seemed anything could happen.

*

When Charlene arrived home from her trip, she had two items of business she needed to accomplish right away. First was to listen to the floods of calls Brad had left on the home phone and her cell. Initially, the calls were angry and threatening, "You can't do this to me." "Charlene, you need to answer the phone. Where are you? Where are my children?" "This is wrong what you are doing. How dare you destroy our family." But as the days went by his tone calmed down.

He launched into the nice approach. "Charlene, I'm sorry for what I've done. It was wrong. There was no excuse. Can't we give it one more try? I now understand why you left. I'm starting therapy. I've changed." Then more messages. "If you want to separate for awhile so you can feel safer, I can understand that. I do have an idea how we can make the separation work out with the least amount of stress on the kids. We can share the house. When I have the kids, I live there. When you have the kids, you live at the house. We could buy a condo over by that shopping center you like. We could switch back and forth depending on the visitation schedule. We'd just do this until you let me come back home."

By the time Charlene listened to all thirty-two messages, her stomach was hurting and she felt shaky.

"Mom, can I go play?" Sandra popped in and asked.

Charlene sighed as she looked up at her oldest child's beautiful face. All Sandra seemed to care about was her friends. She acted as though the separation wasn't happening. "Come here," Charlene said, extending her arms.

"What do you want?"

"I want to hug you."

Sandra rolled her eyes.

"Please come here."

Sandra stomped her foot, but came.

Charlene pulled her in and gave her a kiss on her forehead, which Sandra immediately wiped away. "Uck. Can I go, Mom?" She pulled out of Charlene's embrace.

Charlene put her hands on her daughter's shoulders and looked her in the eyes. "Are you doing okay with…everything?"

"Yes, Mom," Sandra snapped. "Can I play now?"

Unsure how to help her daughter, Charlene sighed. "I guess."

Sandra tore off as though she was afraid of getting called back and stopped from being with her friends. All Sandra wanted lately was to play and be with her friends. Paige sat around crying, and Cameron consoled himself with computer games and fidgeting. Since the separation, Charlene had gone easy on them. She allowed them to sleep in her bedroom at night. At first, she brought them into bed with her, but Sandra kicked so much and so hard, that Charlene sent them all to the floor with pillows and blankets, except for the baby, Nathan. He didn't kick, plus his snuggles were divine.

Once things got settled, she planned to load them up in the car and buy them their own computer so they could play educational programs, and then take them out for pizza. Maybe that would ease things a little.

It was time to e-mail Judy and let her know everything was all right. Charlene picked up Nathan, who was crying, and put him on her lap.

I still haven't decided if I'm divorcing him. It's such a big decision. It affects our lives so much. It affects our kids. I will be choosing to be alone the rest of my life. Then there's the responsibility. I don't know if

I can meet the expense of raising these kids. So far, Brad has given me nothing. Thank heavens I transferred that money into my own checking account before this happened, just in case. That's what we're living on. I'm glad I took so much.

Things started to fall into a pattern. Brad called often enough, but Charlene learned to not answer the phone. The kids went to school and Charlene worked on putting her life back together, from figuring out the finances, keeping the house filled with food—she had gotten a check from Brad—and visiting her lawyer.

The only thing that didn't improve was church. What a shock it was that one of the hardest things about getting separated was attending church. She didn't blame church, per se, but the members didn't seem to know what to do, so they basically avoided her. Perhaps they were embarrassed about the Sunday morning Brad confessed to the entire congregation in the sanctuary that he'd been hitting her. He cried and said he was so, so sorry.

Several of the men weren't too happy with Charlene. In their opinion, she had driven her husband to leave. They became upset if they saw their wives talking to her. "Dear, we have to go, *now*," they would say, grabbing their spouse's arm, and would give Charlene disgruntled sideways glares.

She felt the heat of peoples' stares, overheard the gossiping. "Brad is such a great guy. She must have deserved what he did to her." That statement left her in a puddle of tears. How could people say she deserved that? How could Christians ever think anyone deserved to be beaten?

*

Brad called Charlene in one of his tempers. He was rude, demanding she do this and that. He called her stupid and told her she was packing on the fat.

"*Fat?*" Charlene screamed. "You're calling me fat? You're fifty pounds overweight and you're calling me fat?"

That was the breaking point. She decided it was all over. Brad hadn't changed and wouldn't. She was tired of waiting for him to get a clue. It was a fantasy. The fat comment proved it. It was ironic that such a small thing served to be her breaking point. She must have been tipping that way for a long time.

She got on the phone and talked to her friends, who helped her keep her courage up. She even told her doctor during her regular appointment that she was thinking about divorcing her husband. Immediately, he closed the door. "Charlene," he said, "we're going to talk as friends, because we are friends. I left my doctor's hat in the other room. That man has caused you nothing but pain. I keep putting you back together, but truthfully, I don't know how much longer you're going to be able to handle it. If you stay with Brad, I promise it'll kill you. You'll be dead within the year. Then your goal to save your children from abuse will not happen. You'll be leaving your children to him. What will happen to them?"

He spoke the truth. She knew it. She had to leave for her children's sake. Right then and there she made the "divorce" call to her lawyer. Then her doctor made sure that she called Karla. Her friend came, took the children, and told Charlene to go visit the Domestic Violence Advocates at the police department. She did. The ladies there helped her. When she left their office, she knew she wasn't going to change her mind about the divorce.

*

The following Sunday, Brad came over. He brought an entire dinner he had cooked himself for the family: roast beef, potatoes, corn, and pie. Unbelievable. After he dropped it off he wanted to talk to Charlene privately. They went out on the deck. The children pressed their noses against the windowpane, watching.

Charlene looked from the kids to Brad. The wind twisted around them, blowing her hair onto her face and into her mouth. She swiped at the strands as Brad said, "Thanks for letting me talk to you."

"Yeah, and thanks for the roast beef."

"I've been doing a lot of thinking, and I realize you might be right. I might have a problem. I want to get help." He stopped talking.

She looked at him, pressing her lips together. "That would be a good thing for you."

"Will you wait a year for me without getting a divorce while I go on medication and to therapy? Will you wait for me to get my act together? I love you, and I want to make up for the things I have done wrong."

Charlene felt her limbs going weak. How many times over the years had she wanted to hear those lines? She wished she could believe him. She knew he meant it honestly right now, but she had enough experience to know that once he was back in her life and felt comfortable, he'd revert to his old behavior.

"I need to get a divorce." She crossed her arms over her chest.

"A year is not long to wait for a decision that affects our entire family."

Charlene shifted in silence. She wanted to run to him and be held by him. She wanted everything to be all better, but something deep inside her knew that it would never be better. It hadn't been yet and she had given it years and years—ten, to be exact. No matter what he promised, he always slipped back into his rages. The therapy and drugs might improve things, but she just couldn't take the ride anymore. Her children deserved better.

Brad interrupted her thoughts. "I know what I did was wrong. I hurt you. I don't blame you for wanting to divorce me." Charlene could see his whole being was filled with pain and remorse. His heart was breaking. He wanted her. He loved her.

She curled her hands into fists.

"Why?" Brad asked, his voice choked up. "Don't you want to keep us a family? Is there someone else?"

"No. There's no one else. It's just I need the freedom to be my own person."

"I don't understand this." He scratched his head. "There must be someone else or you would be okay with the separation."

"Brad, I was faithful to you. You know that." She bit her tongue to keep from saying, *You broke the promise to "love and cherish" the first time you hit me. Those vows are no longer valid.*

"Then why are you giving up so easy? I love you. It's killing me to be away from you. I've missed you. I'm going to work to get us back together."

His words ripped into Charlene. She felt herself wanting to run to him, throw her arms around him, and tell him that she would stay. She had wanted to hear what he was finally saying for so long. She was so lonely, stressed, overwhelmed, and there he was chipping at her resolve.

"I'm sorry I called you stupid and fat. I don't think you're stupid or fat."

"Thanks for saying you're sorry," Charlene said. She wanted to add, *But that apology doesn't change the damage that has been done.*

"So will you give it a year?" Brad asked.

"I'm too tired and worn out to fix our relationship right now." How was she going to get out of this without setting him off? She couldn't go back to him, but if she rejected him he could easily flare into a rage. "Maybe in a year we can try it again. We'll see."

He walked up to her, kissed her on the lips, released her, and said, "In a year, I will have you back." Then he left.

Charlene stood there blinking, unsure what had happened. Maybe in a year. Hmm. She hoped Brad would make good on his promises, that he would go on meds and visit a therapist. He just might fix the problem.

She thought about the kiss and had to force herself to not run after him and return to him. She needed help. She called her neighbor friend Vickie. She, her husband, and all their children came over within a half hour. They prayed with Charlene. The deep darkness, the torment that wracked her soul, lifted during the prayer.

It was taking every ounce of faith to believe that God was carrying her through. She kept praying that she was making the right decision. Sometimes she was okay and even felt happy. Then she'd see Brad or talk to him on the phone and everything became muddled again.

Brad continued to talk and talk and talk, coming up with plans. Then when Charlene didn't answer the phone, he began e-mailing, which at last she responded to.

Subject: Visits
Date: March 9
From: "Charlene" <char@Charlene.org>
To: "Brad" <brad@consult.com>

Brad,

If you do not stop calling, I'm going to be forced to get a restraining order against you. You're not welcome at the house.

As far as visitations, of course I'm going to allow you to see the children. I believe that if at all possible, children should have a relationship with their father.
If you would like to see them tomorrow, that will be fine. I'm glad you were willing to sign another contract saying you would not do certain things. You say that should be proof enough that you're not going to be abusive. Sorry, I'm going to need to see that you don't mistreat the children. I promise if you do mistreat them, I will press charges and you will lose your visitation rights.

Charlene

She was finally standing up for herself and making her own decisions, not caving in because somebody else wanted something or out of fear. She felt strong.

The next day she rose early. Her lawyer wanted her to investigate how much money Brad and she had. As she dug through more of the papers she found and asked for current balances at the bank, her jaw fell open. Brad had been such a miser, making her think they were bad off!

After her anger at all the misleading and deception faded, relief flooded her. Her problems were solved. She would get enough to put herself through school and support the children for the three years it would take to get a master's degree.

*

One evening, Charlene and Brad tried to work out visitation on the phone. "I think it would be a good idea to go as a family to Sandra's and Cameron's piano concert," Brad said. "It would be nice to show the kids that we can still be civil."

"Um," Charlene said, trying to think this offer through in her mind. "How would that work with Sandra? You know she's mad at you right now and doesn't want to have anything to do with you. The therapist recommended that we don't push that issue."

"What did you do or say? You must have said something, because she liked being with me before."

"Nothing." Charlene bent over and picked a crying Nathan off the kitchen floor. She rocked him back and forth. "I don't think that we are at that point, yet. I don't think it would be a good idea for all of us to go together."

"Then when do I get to see the kids?"

He had panic in his voice. Charlene could understand that. If she wasn't seeing the kids, she'd be pretty freaked out too. "If you feel you can handle their situations appropriately, then I think it would be good for Lorine, Paige, Cameron, and Nathan to go to McDonald's with you."

"What do you mean appropriately?" he snapped.

"I mean not talking to them about our problems. Come on, Brad, they're kids. They don't need to be dragged into this."

"What's wrong with telling them that I don't want this divorce and you're the one insisting on it? It's the truth."

Charlene bit her lip. He could be so ridiculous at times. "The kids don't need to be involved in our problems."

"What am I supposed to say to them? They keep asking me when I'm going to come home and live with their mommy. I'm going to tell them the truth even if you don't like it."

Charlene rolled her eyes. There was no stopping him. Reason and a sense of what was best for the kids didn't work with him.

"So when can I see them?"

"Why don't you pick them up in front of the house at 1:30 and have them back here no later than 4:00, say, tomorrow?"

*

The e-mail response that arrived was filled with how much Brad still loved her and how they could make it work if only Charlene was willing. It would be so much better for the children. They didn't need to know the pain that he had been forced to endure when his parents divorced. Why didn't they at least go on some dates and try it out? There was no need for a divorce. This kind of talk went on for pages and pages. Charlene had never seen her husband write so much and was surprised that he had the time. It seemed like he wasn't working anymore, just focusing on their plight.

Charlene tried to get right to the point in her response.

Subject: If you love me
Date: March 13
From: "Charlene" <char@Charlene.org>
To: "Brad" <brad@consult.com>

Dear Brad,

If you love me like you keep saying you do, let me go. Divorce me. If our marriage is "meant to be," we'll get back together. I'll consider dating you in a year if everything is on the up and up.

Charlene

P.S. Thank you for the check. I got it just in time.

Charlene was grateful for the money. She wasn't sure what she was going to do about all the mounting bills, especially since she was getting down to the final pennies in her checking account.

She hadn't written Judy in awhile. She'd been so caught up in the work that a divorce entailed, keeping up with the children and their heartaches, and her schoolwork. She decided it was past time to give her friend a brief update.

Subject: Bomb deactivation
Date: March 13
From: "Charlene" <char@CharlenesWeb.net>
To: "Judy" <bchcomber@yippee.com>

Judy,

I'm trying to keep Brad from exploding. If he still thinks he has a chance, then he won't blow up. I promised him I'd date him in a year maybe, if he gets his act together. Why not? I doubt he can do it. I need to keep him hopeful enough to cooperate in working through a divorce, but the truth is, I need out of our entanglements. The domestic advocates I have spoken to have warned me,

and my experienced agrees, that so long as you stay married to an abuser there will always be cycles of fear and enticement to stay. As long as one falls for the game, one can never be free. I have got to escape this trap, however difficult. I remind myself if I go back, eventually he'll start abusing me again. He always does. Then it'll be twice as hard to leave the second time around. It's been hard enough the first. Thank you.
Thanks for all your wonderful support. How are you?

Charlene

Charlene found some notes Brad had written to the children. He wrote about how much he still wanted to be a family and "if" their mother let them get back together, how wonderful things would be, and other such nonsense. She figured the best way to handle it was to write him an e-mail. The kids had to be kept out of their mess, and Brad had to respect that. She would not let this continue.

She warned him to stop writing notes that dragged the kids into adult issues. The children didn't belong in parents' problems. It wouldn't be fair to them and would harm them. She also asked him to stop asking the kids to tell her things for him. She did have voice mail and e-mail. He could give her his messages without putting their children in the middle.

Brad asked Charlene to come to couple's therapy. "A little too late," Charlene told him.

He continued to beg her.

"Since you've been in therapy with this therapist, your behavior has been increasingly difficult and aggressive. It would put me on unsafe ground," she said.

Brad used paying her any more money as bait. He said he wouldn't pay a dime unless she agreed to come back. Charlene realized she would have to stop therapy for the kids soon if he kept it up. "Just when they need it the most," she complained to anyone who'd listen. How was she supposed to get the kids the help they needed?

Here he was, extremely well off, and she had to worry about getting an income because he was refusing to take care of not only her, but also his children. This money situation had to get worked out or her plans to become a therapist would slip from her. Supporting five children was no easy thing, and with her present qualifications she was in no position to do so. She would probably have to take on several jobs with no time to even see the kids. If she was gone all the time, she heard from other victims that Brad could use that against her in court to get the kids from her.

Of course, money wasn't the only problem. She wrote to Judy about the increasingly frustrating problems Brad was stirring up.

Subject: Still alive
Date: March 15
From: "Charlene" <char@CharlenesWeb.net>
To: "Judy" <bchcomber@yippee.com>

Judy,

Sorry, I haven't written back sooner. I don't mean to scare you. I'm still alive. Brad hasn't tried anything violent lately. I think that scare is over. He still continues to drive by my house. Yesterday he visited the neighbor to play tennis when I was trying to put the kids to bed. One child looked out the window, saw him, and they all ran over to the neighbors' to see their daddy.

After I got most of them back in, Brad carried our youngest in his arms to go say hi to a different neighbor. I had to call Karla and ask her to go the neighbor's to get my son back. I didn't want to deal with him. After my son was returned, Brad asked if he could talk to me alone. Karla watched us from a distance the whole time. Brad told me he had been to the parenting class that we legally have to attend in order to get divorced. He has this bright idea from the class that he should buy the property three houses down from me. That way, if the kids ever miss him they can run down the street to see him. He could also be more available to babysit if I needed him and all sorts of other fun things. Grr! I'm talking to my lawyer about it. He must be stopped. That would be worse than being married to him. I would have no control over disciplining the children, and he would watch my house like a hawk. It's just another way to control me all over again. What a nightmare.

This legal stuff is sure a pain. It's taking up all my time. I'm not responding to anyone or anything right now. So if I don't write for a while please don't get offended. I will write you when I get a chance. I enjoy that. I'm so overwhelmed with everything that I don't want—or know how—to write it all down. I'm really tight on money, so I can't call.

Sorry to hear that you re-injured your knee. Do you think you're going to need surgery? You need to be taking it easy! I wish I could get away and visit you to give the kind of support to you I feel in your concern for me.

Charlene

Charlene faithfully attended her domestic violence group. It was great. In it they educated victims. They met once a week. A different expert in the various fields came and taught how to best deal with their situations. The class was free and they provided babysitters. Charlene liked to hear the other women's stories. It helped to see others in similar situations. They understood what she was going through. Some of them had it much worse than she. She liked talking with them, seeing how they handled things.

Although she did have to admit she was the only one in the group who leaped around her house when the kids were gone doing a freedom dance. It just felt so good to be rid of the stress that came from her husband. She didn't want her kids to know how happy she was to be away from their dad. It wouldn't be good for them. Too many of the women had sad, drawn faces, but Charlene was happy. Much happier than she had been in years. Yes, it was hard being a single mother and all she had to deal with, but at last she was free—free to think, be, and make decisions.

She wasn't divorced yet, but soon would be. Her lawyer was pushing it through fast before Brad changed his mind about letting her go. She figured the time was ripe, while he was in the "honeymoon" stage. Charlene had begged for urgent handling of her case, fearing that if and when Brad switched mental states, she'd be endangered again. She explained it to her lawyer. "An abuser goes through cycles: honeymoon, tension building, and rage. In the honeymoon, they'll do anything to sweet-talk you. They're nice and they tell you about all the great stuff that will happen. They tell you how much they love you and they're really, really, really kind to you and so sorry for what they have done. Then they get more irritated, the tension-building stage. Here they tell you how things are going to be and get a bit snappy. Then at some unpredictable point—*boom*! They explode into rage. Over and over we have gone through this cycle."

Charlene wanted the divorce papers delivered to Brad while he was still trying to do everything he could possibly think of to show her how wonderful he was and how much he loved her. Charlene worried that she was being a shrew, but she was fighting for her life, and more importantly the lives of her children. She meant to do whatever she had to.

*

At last the news came that she had been waiting for. Charlene jumped around her room, unable to hold back her excitement. When she calmed down, she sat at her office computer to write Judy with the great news.

She was soon to be officially divorced.

CHAPTER 15

Charlene stepped into her lawyer's office. He sat behind a shiny, cherry wood desk, which rested on thick carpet. There were expensive tapestries and portraits on the walls. He looked up from his folder as she crossed to a plump leather chair. "Charlene," he said, standing and extending his hand. "Come in."

When they were settled, he continued. "I've been over the paperwork and in contact with Brad's lawyer. It seems like we're nearly there. There are just a few more things we'll need to battle over. Please read these papers and tell me if you have any more concerns."

Charlene went through the points. She asked her lawyer various questions, then her lawyer said, "Things are good. We only disagree on a few points. For one, you most definitely need to get more child support...." Then off her lawyer went strategizing.

After they had their plan was set up, her lawyer called Brad's lawyer. They argued and argued, and Charlene's stomach twisted. She hoped she could get through this. At last her lawyer smiled. "Thanks Fred, it looks like we have a deal." Hanging up the phone, he looked up at Charlene and asked if she was okay with everything.

She nodded, just wanting the whole thing over.

"Do you have any questions?"

"Yes. How long is it going to take before I am divorced?"

"We're rushing this one to the judge because of your physical safety concerns. I'd say no more than a couple of weeks."

*

Subject: FREEDOM!
Date: March 21
From: *"Charlene"* <char@CharlenesWeb.net>
To: *"Judy"* <bchcomber@yippee.com>

Judy!

I'm divorced! Yes! I'm so happy. I'm finally free!
I'M FREEEEEEE!!!

No more man dictating his law to me. No more fear. I can learn who I am meant to be and work to develop that. I'm so happy. If I knew how to do flips, I'm sure I'd be doing a whole series of them right now.

By the way, best of luck in your surgery. What day? I guess if it'll get you out of pain, it'll be worth it. I wish I could give you some of the energy I feel flooded with right now, to help you through. Is your health insurance going to cover most of it?

Charlene

*

It had taken a year to build the dream house Charlene and Brad had shared. But now that he was gone, it was becoming impossible for her to physically and emotionally handle. When she went downstairs, she'd see the dent in the wall and remember a full suitcase thrown, along with a stream of cussing from Brad. Sometimes in her bed, a chill would shoot through her when she recalled waking up to him holding a pillow over her face trying to suffocate her.

One chilly morning, Charlene went outside to get the newspaper and found herself pausing. She remembered wanting to kiss the cold hard surface of the concrete driveway because standing on it meant she had returned home alive. Three years ago, still pregnant with Nathan, her youngest, she had gone on a simple trip to the grocery store with Brad. On the way home, they got into another fight over who knows what. His rage burst. He swung at her, hitting her arms and chest as they drove. At a stop sign, Charlene launched herself out of the cab of their pickup and jumped into the back, hoping the physical distance and window between them would stop the fighting and hitting.

Sticking to quiet back roads, Brad took off from the stop sign with a lurch. She gripped the edge of the pickup bed, squeezing her eyes shut with a prayer for the safety of the child still two months from birth. "Oh God, please help me." He jerked hard, left and right, throwing Charlene around the back like a rag doll amongst spilling bags of groceries.

Finally stopping in the driveway with a conclusive lurch, Brad got out of the truck and stormed into the house like nothing had happened. Charlene crawled out of the back and fell to the concrete. Bruised, her child fluttered within her and piercing contractions raced through her womb. She wept upon the dry cement, grateful she was alive. This ride was over.

But the ride wasn't over.

"Mommy, Mommy, what's wrong?" Now three years old, Nathan came toddling out of the open front door and to Charlene's side. She turned and looked at him, somewhat bewildered, taking a minute to land in the present.

"Oh, Nathan, my baby, you're all right. Thank God you're all right." She took her son in her arms and cried on his shoulder as she sat in front of the garage. Nathan was silent as though he somehow knew what Mommy was going through. He put his little arms around Charlene's neck.

"Mommy loves you," Charlene whispered. "Things will be all right." She kissed his forehead and ran her hand through his blond hair before picking him up to go on with the day.

It seemed as if Brad's ghost was everywhere, and she wanted to leave him in the past. Her neighbors didn't let her forget her condition either with the funny way they acted around her. Either they avoided her or tried to dig for dirt, often in a hostile way. Charlene knew divorce made everyone uncomfortable. It didn't fit into their perfect picture of fairytale happily ever after. Divorce was real and statistically affected half of adults, something that people needed to realize.

The gossip, the snide remarks, and the house that was too big and full of bad memories was becoming more than Charlene could stand. She looked at the endless messy rooms. She was exhausted, and the never-ending tasks seemed overwhelming, not to mention her children's needs.

When Charlene wrote Judy about her struggles with the way people were treating her, her friend e-mailed her back wanting to know how she wanted to be treated. Judy wanted to know what it would look like and how someone could support a person in Charlene's position.

To answer your question, I'd like people to treat me better; you know what I mean, like a friend. Ask me how I'm doing and really care when they ask. Maybe say that they are sorry I'm having such a hard time. To push it, I'd like to hear things from them like I hear from you constantly, "I believe in you." "I know that you can do it." "You're strong enough to do this." Or, if they don't know very much about my situation, talk to me about anything they would talk to a "normal" person about. Talk to me! Acknowledge my existence! And yes, if people offered to help out with the children at church that would be a welcome relief.

*

Cameron struggled to breathe. He sat on the couch, his fingernails digging into the cushions.

Charlene knelt on the floor against the couch, peering into his big brown eyes. "What's the matter?"

He was unable to put words to it.

Charlene felt his suffering. It was as though her heart was being stabbed. She slipped onto the couch and lifted him into her lap. He continued to shake and scratch. Any time she tried to get information, he'd tear up and said, "I don't know."

She prayed silently for the answer. Then she looked into his panic-filled eyes and did the only thing she knew to do.

"Dear God." She began praying out loud, holding her son close to her heart. "I love my son so much and he's hurting. Please fill him with your comfort and ease his worry."

She continued to pray until his breathing returned to normal and his shaking had ceased.

For the next couple of weeks, Charlene checked on him daily with conversations and prayer to make sure he was all right.

She'd often take him in her bedroom, sit with him on her lap on the couch, and ask him how things were going. He responded well to this and he no longer had such violent panic attacks.

*

When Charlene could put off lawn mowing no longer, she went outside and started up the tractor. She had cut about half the lawn before her machine died. She tried to start it again. It sputtered. Again and again, the sputtering sound. She felt like scratching her head and saying, "We'll I be darned," like an old-fashioned farmer. That was until she looked at the lawn she already cut.

Big piles of brown cut grass trimmings sat on top of the grass. She had lowered the blade too far. These piles of dying grass would suffocate the "struggling to go green" grass below. It all needed to be raked. She'd never get to the other household chores at this rate.

She wished her children were home to help, but it was Brad's weekend. As she raked, she watched the way her neighbors would drive by in their cars and slow down to see what she was doing.

The frustration of being single, being away from her children, having the house falling apart (two broken toilets, a busted dishwasher, and counting), and bearing social stigma, all came to a head as she raked. She had always hated this neighborhood—never feeling accepted by the strangers who lived right next to her. The only person she liked was Vickie. It was too bad Karla and Harold didn't live closer so they would be her next-door neighbors. She didn't want to live here anymore. At least new neighbors in a new neighborhood wouldn't know Brad and have such mixed loyalties.

Besides, the expenses of maintaining such a large home were eating up her financial reserves. In addition, the neighbors kept inviting Brad over to visit. Thanks to legal prevention, Brad was barred from taking up residence any closer than one mile, so he bought a house exactly one mile away. Too close, especially with the way he liked to take walks. She could picture him on her front doorstep too often. If she moved, maybe the old adage "out of sight, out of mind" would kick in. Surely he wouldn't sell and follow her. She hoped.

As she raked and raked, she complained in her thoughts. *This was going to take forever. Why did she have to have such a big place? It had been Brad's idea. He didn't listen to her desires.* The more she raked the more realization settled in—she didn't have to listen to him anymore. She was single. She was free.

She had always dreamed of a much simpler life. She stopped raking. Now, she could do what she wanted. She could get the life she wanted.

Glenna, a neighbor who was driving by, saw Charlene struggling in the hot sun. She parked her car and walked over. Charlene shielded her eyes with a cupped hand and watched Glenna approach, her young kids straggling behind. They had barely ever talked. Charlene wondered what she wanted.

"Are you okay?" Glenna asked.

Charlene thought about putting on the fake smile, but then wondered, why should she? "No," she said. "I cut the grass too short. Now I'm stuck raking, and my lawn mower isn't working."

"Kids, grab a rake," Glenna said, then smiled at Charlene. "Don't worry."

Soon Glenna's husband, Randal, came over. He worked on the lawnmower, but failed to get it running. That made Charlene feel somewhat better. She couldn't be a complete failure if a full-grown, competent, mechanically minded family man couldn't start it. Fortunately, Randal knew just who to call. Within an hour, a guy who knew a guy who was a genius mechanic had come by and the lawnmower was fixed.

Charlene thanked the couple for helping. She felt relieved and grateful, but also awkward. She hated depending on others so much.

"Are you all right?" Glenna asked again, coming up and putting her arm around Charlene.

The sympathy was too much and she cried on the lady's shoulder. "I'm moving," she said, surprised at her own words.

"What? Where?"

"I don't know yet. I just made the decision."

"Are you sure?" Glenna asked, her eyes worried.

"Yes."

Glenna grew silent and reflective. After giving the situation a lot of thought, she asked, "Is it because of the way you've been treated by the neighbors?"

Charlene thought about trying to make it all rosy by denying that possibility, but then something broke inside. She wasn't going to lie to make it more comfortable for others. "Yes," she said. "These people have caused a lot of pain for me. It's also because I can't keep up with this house."

Glenna's face filled with sorrow. "I'm sorry. They really have treated you bad." She spoke softly. "I'm at fault, too. I'm sure going to miss you."

"I'll miss you too."

*

When Charlene set out house hunting, she had hopes that things would be more manageable if she bought a house a couple of sizes smaller. Not knowing how to go about it, she searched with a real estate agent. It was a bit daunting. Throughout her entire marriage, she had never spent more than $300.00. Now she was dealing with much bigger numbers. Because of Brad, she had to be careful how she did this. He was nearly ready to close on his new house. Once he was securely in, it would not be easy for him to follow her somewhere else. She hoped if she could get out of his sight, she'd get out of his thoughts. He would be upset, and some of her children would be upset about moving away from their best friends, but she didn't see any other way. If she stayed, her kids would be labeled as the "children of the man who hit his wife." She didn't want that put on them. Who knew what people would do with that information, especially the kids at school? She was also careful not to confide in her children about the plan. They might tell Brad.

*

Two days later, Brad came over to visit with the kids. Charlene looked at him, dressed up in a dress shirt and pants. His hair was done, and he was actually clean-shaven. She had no feelings for him. Gone. Nothing. No hate, no love, nothing. It had all disappeared. It was almost as if he was a stranger. They had spent ten years together, supposedly as lovers, and yet there was nothing there.

When his SUV pulled out of the driveway, Charlene's neighbor ran across her lawn. "Charlene. Charlene," she called, arms waving.

Charlene waited for her, her thoughts still on the funny, empty exchange with Brad. "Is it true?" Mara gasped out once she reached Charlene.

"Are you really moving?"

"Yeah," Charlene said. She still had to find the right house to buy, and there was all the packing to do, but she'd decided this was what was going to happen.

"I've come to ask you not to. Please give the area one more chance. You make a big difference and help people to broaden their minds."

Too many decisions, Charlene concluded.

Chapter 16

"Kids, we're moving," Charlene said. She had all of them gathered in the living room for a family council. It was as if from the moment those words slipped from her lips, a microburst was triggered. "What?" "Moving?" "Where?" "Why?"

After she explained the details, the kids demanded to go house shopping with her. "But don't you want to play with your friends?" she asked.

"No, we want to help pick our house."

"But it's going to be boring and long."

"We don't care."

Charlene shrugged. She didn't have enough energy to fight them, even though five kids was a lot to be dragging around looking at homes.

They saw so many houses, none of them thought they could stand much more of it. Either they weren't big enough for her family or they needed too many repairs—which she couldn't do or afford to have fixed. They were too expensive, too close to a busy road, or "too" something. By the end of the day, she doubted she would ever find a house that would work.

That night Charlene wrote to Judy about Brad.

He isn't paying attention to MY feelings even when he claims to want to "work things out." Aaaarghhh. Then she wrote the bare truth of what her heart was going through. *I'm lonely. I miss him—but I'm frustrated with him at the same time. Does that make sense? Weird, I know, but it wasn't all bad. When he was good, he was very good. We use to sit and talk for hours.*

The next day's incoming e-mail from Judy was comforting. Her friend told Charlene that what she was feeling was normal. Then Judy disclosed that her ex-husband, Sterling, had left her. She also revealed that it was ten years before she saw him again. Judy had no feelings for him either. Charlene hoped this lack of feeling would last. She didn't want to get sucked back into this and then have to go through all the heartache again.

Not only did Charlene have a comforting e-mail, but she had good news that she couldn't wait to write Judy about.

Subject: Perfect home, perfect haircut
Date: April 19
From: "Charlene" <char@CharlenesWeb.net>
To: "Judy" <bchcomber@yippee.com>

Judy,

Omigosh, Judy! I found the perfect home! The master bedroom overlooks the lake and mountains. I can't think of anything more fitting or more grounding. I'm worried that it's too close to Brad's sister's home. I sure hope it's not. That would be awkward. Sandra is the one who was doing an Internet search with me on homes. Since she's the oldest, she feels like she should be involved. She found this one, took a couple of minutes to study it, and said, "This is the one." On the way over, we were following the realtor and Sandra talked on and on about how great the house was. Before going into the house, she kept saying things like, "Look, it has a small yard, but a fun hill for the kids to play on." I turned to the realtor and said, "She's making your job real easy." All the kids loved the house and begged me to get it. It wasn't a hard sale.

I'm still thinking about when your husband left you. He left with no explanation, and you never heard from him again except for the divorce papers? How awful. I can understand why you had a difficult time. I'm having a hard time too, and the divorce was my decision. You said you stayed in your house for six months and didn't go anywhere. That sounds tempting. Maybe I will follow your example. The kids are with their dad, and I'm enjoying the time off. Funny, I longed for more time for years, and here I am all of the sudden having extra time. Who'd have thought?

Lorine, my fourth child, cut her hair off with a pair of kitchen scissors. She looks like a miniature Edward Scissorhands. In therapy she said she did it because she was mad at her father and didn't like being with him because he was angry all the time. I wonder if it has something to do with her being a middle child. "Hello, Mom. Pay attention. I'm hurting too." There are so many things to pay attention to. It is such a balancing act.

Charlene

*

The phone kept ringing and ringing and there was always an angry intense Brad on the other end. He had the kids for the weekend, and he was in such a fret, mostly angry at Sandra for her temper. He kept calling to ask what to do. At least he wasn't hurting their daughter. Instead, he was trying to figure out new ways to deal with her problems. Charlene worried about how her other kids were handling the tension.

Saturday afternoon Brad showed up on her doorstep.

"What?" Charlene asked.

"Moving, huh? If I had known you were planning to abandon our dream home and move farther away, I would not have let you have the house in the divorce, and I wouldn't have hurried to buy the house I just moved into." Brad stood there fuming and struggling to keep from erupting. Thank goodness there were neighbors nearby.

"I want the paintings we got for the kids."

His presence looked dark, menacing. Charlene wondered if he would dare try to hit her. She doubted it. He'd get in a lot of trouble if he did. She thought about her paintings on the walls then looked at the flushed man standing on her porch, shifting his weight back and forth. "Fine, have them. Come and get them."

He brushed past her. He went into the house and walked to the stairwell and proceeded to remove the pictures from the wall. When he was done, he slammed the front door and left.

How could he be so charming one day about wanting to work things out and the next day act like such a jerk? Where did he think that would get him?

The next day she went to what she thought would be her new church if she purchased the house she wanted, which was in a different city. It was calm, peaceful, and had tons of friendly people. She felt she was supposed to be there. Legally she had to stay within shuttling distance of her ex to facilitate his visitation nights. The new home was in the same county, but a determined drive away, thankfully.

In the afternoon, as the quiet of the old house wrapped around her, she thought she would do the assignment that Judy had requested. Make a list of the problems she had with Brad. Once she got started it began to flow from her pen.

1) I lose a sense of identity with him around.
2) He often engages in revenge, going for where it hurts.
3) Physical Abuse—hitting, throwing things, breaking things.
4) Verbal Abuse—name calling—sometimes really crude ones.
5) Spiritual Abuse—"I am the man and the leader of the home, therefore you will do as I say."
6) Crazy Making—He says something then denies saying it.
7) No Empathy—even in the process of trying to get back together with me, he does not consider my feelings or my concerns, much less my fears.
8) Controlling—I've never known how much money we have. I can't do anything without his permission. I can't even choose what kind of milk to buy.
9) Involves the children with our problems.
10) Doesn't take ownership for his mistakes or issues.

11) Blames me for all our problems.
12) Drains my spirit when I'm around him.
13) Doesn't trust me—constantly accuses me of having affairs, etc.
14) Doesn't see me for who I am.
15) He often changes the "rules" of our relationship.
16) Chauvinistic—thinking a man should be served by women.
17) Image focused, so worried how he appears to others.
18) Has to get his way in everything all the time no matter how small. It is as though "getting his way" is more important than the issue itself.
19) Unable to bond. He has never connected emotionally with me.
20) He is not safe to be around. I never know what he will do or when. Very unpredictable.

Why in the heck had she stayed with that man!? By leaving him, she had chosen happiness. It had to be her choice, and she had made it. Now she was on her own. If she turned back, then she'd be returning to where she'd been. She had heard that most women who leave their abusive husbands go back. She prayed not to be one of them. She couldn't do this alone with five kids, but with God, maybe she would be successful—one moment at a time.

She walked over to her window and looked out at the swing set. As she watched the swing move slightly in the wind, she thought that maybe with the knowledge she had gained, she could go out and serve others. Now if she could get over the next couple of hurdles, she'd be ready.

*

Monday morning, the phone rang right after Charlene got back from getting her older children off to school. It was her real estate agent. "You got it. The owners accepted your offer. You're getting the house."

"Incredible," Charlene said. This was the first big purchase she'd ever made on her own. Amazing. She'd done it. Wow.

When she told the kids the news, instead of, "Yes," they said, "Do we have to move? Why are we moving?"

Charlene paid them little attention. She needed to worry about packing. It wasn't going to be long before the new home would be vacant.

Packing became more emotional than Charlene expected. One night she sat down and grieved by writing her dear home, which she'd just received an offer on, a letter.

Goodbye,

Goodbye, dear house that I never wanted to move into. I was so scared the first night behind your curtainless windows feeling everyone was peeking in. But I learned to love you, to make you my own. I spent hours decorating and recreating so I would find my own identity and I could settle in.

I loved my sitting room with my beautiful couch and elegant wall hanging, my office with a view of the mountains and the playground where I played with my baby. I never made you complete, but I was on my way.

Goodbye dear house with the memories. The holes in the walls, the busted doors, the roof I escaped to while eight-and-a-half months pregnant. Goodbye to the spot where the TV sat and where he once threw the remote control at me and bruised my womb that carried our youngest son. Goodbye to the bedroom where I tried for hours to wake my husband up to go to the hospital because my water broke with my last baby. He wouldn't take me for hours. Goodbye to the bed where I was attacked in my sleep physically and sexually.

Goodbye to my library lined with books, one of the places I would flee to, to hide from him; to my office where I called out for help so many times while he banged on the door or went searching for the key.

Goodbye to my bathroom, which I made my "mini-Hawaii." He intruded onto my sanctuary and busted the door. Goodbye to him owning me. Goodbye to the sweet words "my husband," and the feeling I belonged to someone and was wanted. Goodbye to the hope that he'd make good on all his promises, the promises that said he was there for me and cared for me. Goodbye to the promise that he'd love me. Goodbye to the belief that he'd ever give empathy.

Goodbye to his malicious verbal attacks, to his physical abuse, to objects flying at me, especially in the middle of the night when he'd keep me up with long lectures. Goodbye to the hours of intense ridicule. Goodbye to the triangulation with the kids that left me exhausted and defenseless. Goodbye to being talked out of trusting my instincts. Goodbye to fear. Goodbye to never being good enough. Goodbye to an unhappy marriage and to the constant effort of trying to be better and thinking something is wrong with me. Goodbye to poor health, because now I am free to be myself and to do my emotional work.

Goodbye to the neighbors who were never my friends and who never accepted me. Goodbye to the gym three minutes away, to Karla so close and therapy around the corner.

Goodbye to Brad's broad chest that I always believed would protect me and keep me safe. Goodbye to his unendurable intensity. Goodbye to his talk-it-to-death antics. Goodbye to his cruel comparisons between me and my parents. Goodbye to his beliefs that my thoughts and feelings weren't valid. Goodbye to my efforts in helping him heal.

Goodbye to not having friends because he chased them away. Goodbye to my anger that kept me safe from him because it helped me have the courage to say no.

Goodbye.

Hello, freedom!

CHAPTER 17

Subject: Children Trauma
Date: May 7
From: "Charlene" <char@CharlenesWeb.net>
To: "Judy" <bchcomber@yippee.com>

Dear Judy,

You're one of the few people that I can talk to about my problems with my children. I hope you don't mind me dumping on you. I need a fresh perspective, and writing it out helps me see things more clearly.

Sandra, as is typical of the oldest, is really upset with me because we're moving, even though she picked the house. Natural, I suppose. She's angry that she'll be in a smaller room. She says I'm ruining her life and she hates me. It's my prayer she will someday understand and realize this is the best thing for her. She says I don't care and I don't think of her. Oh, if she only knew. If she only knew how hard it is to disrupt our whole life, and how much I hate doing this—how much my heart is breaking. If she knew how much criticism I'm getting for this. If she only knew how unsafe it is here in this house for me, or her for that matter.

I feel like we're pilgrims, moving away to some unknown adventure. I don't know if I can stand up alone against the wrath of my children, the wrath of my X, plus the change and loss.

Am I doing the right thing? This is so hard. I feel like I'm the one responsible for breaking up the family, although I know its Brad's fault. I have placed heavy responsibilities on my shoulders. There are so many questions and decisions to make.

Charlene

P.S. I know that referring to one's former husband should be spelled ex, but I just love how the big solid X looks. I earned the X, so that's how I'm going to spell it.

*

Charlene continued to pack and pack and pack. The daunting task that lay before her depressed her. She was exhausted and ached as she moved. She didn't want to do anything but sleep. The move had become overwhelming. When had they gotten so much stuff?

Brad called in the middle of this. "Can you help me with a business proposal?"

In the past, Charlene had often gone over them for him. She wasn't sure if she should help him or not. "Are you paying me?"

"Why would I have to pay you? Can't you just help me out?"

Charlene looked at the pile of toys that she needed to go through and then thought of the endless other rooms that still waited. "No," she said.

"Why not?"

"Brad, I have a lot on my plate right now."

"But—" On he went trying to convince her that she was bad for not helping him out.

Charlene wanted to help him but then gave it more thought. If she gave in to him and did this, then he would take that as a sign and want her to do more things. He wouldn't take their divorce seriously unless she drew some boundaries. He definitely wasn't getting the divorce concept on his own.

At the end of the phone call, Brad said, "Charlene, you are seriously making a mistake."

When the neighbors came over to help her pack, thank heavens, they told her to completely cut him off, to not let him have any contact with the children. She disagreed. The kids needed their father. Besides, she couldn't legally do that.

Charlene wondered why the neighbors never talked to her or helped her before this. Why would they be so cold before and complain about the toys out on her lawn and then all the sudden act like they cared and start helping her? It was confusing. Maybe she had misjudged them. Maybe they were nice because she was moving. It was hard to tell.

One of the ladies asked, "Why did you marry Brad?"

Charlene took a moment to collect her thoughts and said, "I thought I loved him, and I probably still do, but how did I get so entangled with him?"

The lady shrugged. "How did it begin? What were your circumstances when you met him?"

"I wanted to get away from my parents, so I rushed right into Brad's strong, comforting arms, believing in the Cinderella fairytale. That must've been where I went wrong."

After the ladies left, Charlene wrote Judy. Judy wrote back immediately with the insight that this too would pass. Change was hard. Moving and divorce together would be a lot for anyone. Charlene appreciated the new perceptive. She leaned back in her desk chair and reflected. The impulse to run back to Brad was sometimes strong. She longed to be held in his arms. Was that sick and wrong? She missed his familiarity, the connection they shared, the Brad she had known who was tender yet strong. She didn't miss the abuse.

She must focus on the positive. She loved her new house. Yes, it was small and much less, as far as living standards went, but it was hers. She would live close to the mountains. They were visible through her bedroom windows. She imagined that the sight of the grand mountains rising to touch the night sky would settle her as she tried to go to sleep.

*

Charlene gathered around the television with the kids to watch a show with them. She had a child on both sides and one plopped on her lap. She hoped the extra attention would help ease their anxiety. The phone rang. She looked at the television, at the kids on her lap, and decided not to get it. "Ignore that," she said, not wanting the phone to take time away from her kids. It was nine at night on Friday. Surely the call couldn't be important.

Five minutes later, the show cut to commercial break and the phone rang again. "Stay here," she said to Lorine, who was jumping out of her lap to answer the phone.

"Phone, Mommy. Phone," Nathan said.

"I know, dear," Charlene said, and bent down to kiss his fluffy cheeks.

Two minutes later, it started ringing again. Paige dashed off. "It's got to be important," she said before answering. She carried the phone into the room. "Mom, Dad wants to talk to you."

Charlene was about to say, "Well, I don't want to talk to him," but looking at all the faces watching her, she held that comment. It would disturb her kids if she didn't talk to their father. She felt trapped into talking to him.

She stood and went into another room to get out of the kids ear shot. "I just thought I'd call and see how you were doing," he said. He sounded happy.

"I'm fine." Charlene tried to hold back her anger. Why was he constantly bothering her?

"Do you want to go out on a date?" he asked. "I want you to know that it's not too late."

"I'd rather not right now," she said.

"Then I guess I'll go on the date that I have set up for tomorrow."

Charlene didn't understand why she burst into tears once she got off the phone. Maybe, she thought, she was upset that he was trying out his new skills on someone else. Maybe she was crying because he never loved or respected her like he promised. Brad with his golden tongue. A part of Charlene wanted to be loved by him, but a bigger part demanded to be free.

*

Charlene worked and worked, packing item after item. She also created a charity pile of things she didn't want any longer. She was moving into a place much smaller and had to de-junk. Despite all the labor she put into it, it seemed like she wasn't making any progress. She looked at the endless rooms and wondered how she was going to get through them.

"Mom, Sandra won't stop hitting me."

"Mom, how come we have to move?"

"Mom, I want Daddy."

"Mom, I don't want to see Dad. Why do I have to?"

"Mom, the computer won't work."

Mom. Mom. Mom. There was an endless stream of demands from the kids. Charlene stayed up until midnight every night packing. Her arms and back throbbed. It was an extra struggle to get up on Sunday mornings. Church was hard.

Charlene was preparing a chicken lunch when the phone rang. On the other end of the line was Vickie. "What can I do for you? I felt I was supposed to call." After a few minutes of taking in the situation, she said, "I'm putting together a team of helpers."

Angels must have stirred peoples' hearts because on Monday people started showing up to help. When one group had to go, another came.

Right in the middle of the move, Brad came over. Charlene answered the door with a box in hand. "Yes?" she asked.

"I've come to get more of my things I left downstairs. Do you care if I get them?"

"No," Charlene said, opening the door.

Brad brushed past her as the children ran up to him. He hugged them and asked how they were. They chatted idly with Charlene hanging back. She wanted to make sure he didn't steal any of her stuff.

As he rounded the staircase, he stopped and looked at the hole he'd made in the hall wall. There had been a painting there to cover it, but now that it was gone, so it caught his attention. "See that hole?" he asked Paige and Lorine.

They looked at it.

"I made that hole when I was mad at your mom."

How could he talk that way in front of her children? Did he not care about the messages he sent them? "Brad, what are you here for?" Charlene snapped.

"My gun."

This stopped Charlene cold. A deadly chill tore through her. She wondered if that was Brad's subtle way of threatening to kill her. That worry kept her on edge for days.

*

Moving was exhausting. Junk constantly materialized as if from nowhere. The kids were somewhat helpful. Sandra copped an attitude and was angry at everything. "Why do I have to do that?" "You're ruining my life." "I don't have to listen to you." "Mom, all you care about is yourself."

Unable to deal with that and the daunting task of moving, Charlene let Sandra spend the final days before they were totally moved over at her friend's house even though her help was very much needed. Maybe this would help calm her down.

Kitty from church asked Charlene while they packed what Charlene was going to do to support her family.

"I'm going to apply for the counseling program at the University of Phoenix. The course is one night a week and I meet with a study group another day. I will have to be in a group that can meet when my kids are in school. In three years, I'll be a therapist! I've secretly—okay, as a child my stuffed animals knew—always wanted to be a therapist."

Kitty laughed. "You go, girl," she said. Those words stayed with Charlene for many hours as she packed. She felt good and like she was on a mission. She clung to that as she continued to shove things into boxes.

The work seemed endless. She lifted box after box when the neighbor church group came with the moving truck. She felt like she could never pause from working. What right did she have to stop and rest when everyone was here to help her? That would be lazy and unappreciative to all these people who were coming to her assistance. When they arrived at the new house, her new neighbors, a group of middle-aged ladies, cooked lasagna dinner for the crew.

Tears brimmed in Charlene's eyes when she saw the food on the counter and the ladies unpacking supplies for the kitchen. Little miracles kept surfacing, letting her know God's hand was in her life.

The day after they were finally in the new house, she found herself making an emergency trip to the chiropractor's office.

"One of the discs in your back is about ready to rupture," he diagnosed. "You pushed yourself too hard. You are to stay down for the next couple of days and not lift anything or it will go."

Charlene told Judy about her concerns. *I'm glad school just finished and my kids don't have that to deal with right now. I'm tired, in pain, and everything is new. I worry too much. I want my house put together now and it's not happening. Why am I so impatient? So people won't think I'm a slob? Don't say it, I can hear it—I'm being co-dependent, caring about what other people think. Don't run faster than I have strength to run. Geez.*

After complaining about her plight, she focused on what was happening to Judy. Her friend had said she was staying up for days until two in the morning trying to complete business assignments and then she'd worked all day on Sunday to straighten her house and do church work. Charlene knew she wasn't the only one heading for burnout.

CHAPTER 18

Getting into the counseling program consumed Charlene. She didn't have to take any tests, but there was a requirement of eighteen credit hours in psychology and an undergraduate degree, which she already had in Secondary Ed. Thankfully, Brad's "solution" to their earlier problems—that she should get out of the house and do something—had paid off. Attending those classes had given her the credits she needed.

To get into the program she had to obtain several professional references, which was a harder task. It took a while for her to think of anyone who could do that for her. Finally she thought about the craft fairs. She had made friends there. After having her stomach tie up in triple knots, she called them up to ask if they would give her references. "Sure," all of them said. "It's good to hear from you," or, "A therapist, huh? You'll make a great one."

The next thing on Charlene's list was to take two classes at the University of Phoenix campus. Basically they took the place of advanced testing, which appealed greatly to Charlene. The professors would evaluate her and decide if she fit into their program. Not everyone made it. The thought of not knowing whether she would fail or succeed made her want to visit the ladies' room. What would she and her family do if she didn't get in? How would she support them? Would she be stuck in a job she hated for the rest of her life? Would she and her kids be forced to scrimp? And would Brad use that against her, running up legal bills to take the children? How would she live if he tried that? He had threatened many times that he would sue her to get the kids if she didn't do what he wanted. One of these days he just might follow through on his threat.

Charlene's first class would start on the nineteenth of June. That was only two weeks away. After she went through the classes and got by the professors, she would find out if she'd made it for the September start. To prepare, she read as many psychology books as she could find in the midst of unpacking and watching kids.

Taking a break from the unpacking and books, she decided to give Judy a quick update.

Subject: Shifting
Date: June 8
From: "Charlene" <char@CharlenesWeb.net>
To: "Judy" <bchcomber@yippee.com>

Dear Judy,

Hello again my dear friend. Things are really shifting in my life. I'm now realizing I can do anything I want. I don't have to ask permission or even tell anyone what I am up to. I decided I would take a huge risk and sign up with a dating service. Can you believe it? But it's just an adventure. I won't be dating anyone. I just want to see what it's like. There's a couple in my church who seem perfect for each other, and they met through one of those services. They say it's pretty safe if you use common sense. It's crazy, I know, but I signed up today between unpacking boxes and taking care of the kids. What can I say? I needed a break and adventure in my life.

You're welcome for the flowers. I'm glad to hear you finally had your surgery and that everything was successful. I'm also glad your daughter and son-in-law live next to you so they can take good care of you, since I can't.

Charlene

P.S. Have you ever used one of those Internet dating services?

Charlene had to laugh at the e-mail response she received back. Internet dating service? It sounded like her friend was dying of shock and worry.

The Internet dating service wasn't as bad as everyone thought. Charlene had already received two hits. That meant an icon popped up and said people had sent a "flirt" or the message that they were interested in her profile. Charlene hadn't even put her picture up yet, but she did write a bio that she thought would keep most abusers away.

After she signed up, creating an Internet name of Misty, she curiously began browsing and discovered some really hot-looking men. It made her blush, feel guilty, and excited all at once. The attraction of looking and thinking about what could be caught her attention. She felt drawn to the computer in between her work to add spice to the day.

The first night she was doing a search on the guys, her kids caught her. Her son came into the room and said, "Oh, Mommy's husband shopping. Oh, yeah." Before she could stop him or say anything, he called the other kids into the room. She covered the screen to keep them from seeing, but they begged for a peek. Although it was a bit embarrassing and she felt somewhat uncomfortable with what they were doing, they spent the evening looking at men. The kids were funny about it, making their list of favorites and groaned at some of Charlene's. They laughed a lot.

The next morning, to Charlene's surprise, she received an e-mail from a guy. Flustered and excited she hurriedly wrote him back.

Subject: Hi back
Date: June 11
From: "Charlene" <char@CharlenesWeb.net>
To: "Richard" <richardb@ripples.com>

Dear Richard,

Thank you for sending your note. I'm new to this Internet singles thing. Total greenie. As you can tell from my profile, I have a lot of children. They keep me busy, but I love them. Looks like you have a lot of children, too. Five also? Wow. From the pictures you have on the profile, it appears that most of them are out on their own. Mine are at the opposite end of the spectrum, 11 to 3 years old. Three girls and two boys. It's too bad you have no boys. They're a lot of fun. Girls, I believe, are much harder to raise—moody. Of course I was raised with, or should I say, I raised five brothers. So maybe that's what I'm used to.

You teach self-improvement courses? Sounds fascinating. What kind of subjects do you teach, and what service projects have you been involved in?

Misty

A few hours after sending off that e-mail, another e-mail made its way into Charlene's inbox. This was a thirty-year-old man who claimed he was a beautician. He asked Misty if she would like to meet.

Fingernails jumping into her mouth, Charlene paced her office. Meet? A guy wanted to meet her? How did this happen? It was unreal. Didn't he read how many kids she had? Hadn't he read her profile about how scary she was? Why would he want to meet her? It would be a blind date. Was that safe? Was it a set up? Was he one of those nasty married men trying to pick up vulnerable single women on the side? How would she know? Maybe he was one of those dreaded polygamists disguising himself as a beautician.

She had to laugh at that conclusion. A beautician would be a lousy career choice if you wanted to attract women.

Charlene tried to put the e-mail aside and read her psychology book while her younger kids napped, but she couldn't get it out of her system. She had to do something. She couldn't just jump in and go out with someone, knowing so little about them. She had kids to think of. She decided she would play therapist by confronting him with his issues and seeing what he would do. She wrote to him. *Meet? Well, maybe; but first I would like to know why you got divorced and why you picked the career you did?* After she pushed send, she was satisfied. If he was the cause of the divorce, that would be one uncomfortable question to answer. Let's see if he was comfortable with his profession and his divorce.

She just had to tell Judy about this.

Subject: No picture?
Date: June 12
From: "Charlene" <char@CharlenesWeb.net>
To: "Judy" <kenk@ripples.com>

Judy,

Now what? My picture is not even up on the Internet dating thing and I already got asked out! What is going on? I can't believe this. I never, in a million years, thought I would be asked out, and here I'm getting asked without even a picture! There's something wrong here. The guy isn't bad looking, either. Is he desperate? Maybe he likes kids! Or maybe he's a pedophile. Jeepers, this is a whole new world for me.

I don't actually want to meet any men. I want to write guys and get to know them. I asked the guy who asked me out why he got divorced. I figure if he can't come up with a good answer then I don't want anything to do with him. I wouldn't want to fall for another Brad. Heck, I just got free. I need to live it up. Besides, if I make a mistake in the relationship department, it'll hurt my kids.

I've realized something in the past couple of days as I continue to unpack and study. Being single could be a lot of fun. I can go play. I'm missing Brad a bit. I don't miss the suppression or the abuse, but I miss him as a friend. Isn't that confusing? I love being single, but it causes me and my children a lot of pain. There's a lot of freedom and fun, awkwardness and feeling stupid.

You took your granddaughter on a walk on the beach? That sounds so perfect. When my frequent flier miles I got in the divorce settlement transfer to my account, I'll have to fly out to Washington and see you.

Charlene

E-mails from potentials began pouring in, especially after her picture was posted. She wrote back a guy named Ken, who was in his early thirties and also had a lot of kids. At least they had that in common. He wrote her and told her that she didn't look old enough to have as many kids as she claimed. He wanted to know if she used an old picture. *Not!* Charlene wanted to scream. Who did he think she was? Ken said he wasn't going to be perfect any time soon. Charlene responded to that: *Too bad, because I will.*☺

As she thought about it, Charlene concluded that unpacking all these boxes must have done something to her brain because when she grew tired of working, she'd stop and check in on the kids, kiss them, then rush to her computer to see if she'd received any flirts on the dating service.

Days passed and she didn't hear from the guy who wanted to go out. Maybe he was scared to tell her why he got divorced. Warning sign? Or maybe he just got distracted by another raving beauty with five little kids. Hmm. She wondered how many single women out there were her age and with her number of children.

Some of the men were older and a bit preachy. She started writing a guy named Richard who was twelve years older than she, and whom she had written to when she first signed up. He kept reminding her as she spilled her aspirations for her life that she needed to focus on her children. She explained that she intended to do that. That was why she was planning to go to night school. It was slower-paced and she was able to be there for her children when they needed her.

Richard wanted to move from Wyoming to Mississippi. Why Mississippi? She did get brave enough to ask, "What are you doing in Wyoming if your heart is across the country and that's where you want to be?"

Since Richard seemed more like a father image to her than anything, she told him more than she would normally tell anyone. One day they were talking about their church experiences. She explained how much she loved her new congregation and how she felt she had stepped into heaven. People were kind and friendly.

*

Judy wrote to tell Charlene about being the new choir director for her church, and Charlene wrote about attending her first class at the University of Phoenix. Although nerve-wracking, Charlene slipped into her seat next to a nice, older-looking man named Tony and felt a flutter of excitement go through her.

She took notes on everything the professor said. They would be evaluated by paper, oral presentation, and therapy skills, where they would pretend to be therapists. The judges would watch them through a one-way mirror.

"What is this?" she said to Tony during break. "I thought we were being sent to school to learn those skills, not to be tested to see if we have them."

He agreed.

Charlene asked him what he wanted to do with this program. He told her how he had been working with at-risk youth for years and the degree would help him move up the chain, get paid more, and be more effective.

The lady on her other side talked about how she worked in a care center and wanted to be able to connect with the elderly better. The lady next to her had just graduated from college and was interning at a clinic.

As these people spoke, Charlene's stomach knotted. She didn't belong here. She didn't have the experience. How could she compete? She thought about running for the bathroom when the internship lady asked Charlene what her children thought about her trying to become a therapist.

"They don't say too much," she said. "The older kids don't like the idea. They said, "It'd be weird."

"I asked them, 'What would be the worst part?' They said therapists turn mean and always want to know your feelings. My oldest is afraid I'll dissect her. I think eventually she'll become more comfortable with the idea. Hopefully, by the time I become a therapist, she'll see how it could be a benefit and blessing in her life."

The group around Charlene laughed at her story. She immediately felt better.

"Oh, they'll be grateful," the older woman said, and went off in her nurturing way. Charlene wanted to talk to her and hear that she was doing her kids a great service that they would one day thank her for. Somehow hearing it even from a complete stranger felt good.

*

On the weekend Charlene got brave. She just had to tell Judy her crazy experiences.

Subject: Oh my heck!
Date: June 22
From: "Charlene" <char@CharlenesWeb.net>
To: "Judy" <bchcomber@yippee.com>

Judy,

I went to my first singles' dance! Oh my heck! is about all I can say. I walked in, and this guy grabbed my hand and asked me to dance. I stumbled all over him. They do ballroom dancing. It has been years! I felt like I was a foreign exchange student on the first day in a strange land. Plus, I felt awkward being in the arms of someone other than my X husband. Totally different. When the song ended, he held onto my hand and wouldn't let me go. I didn't know what to do, so I kept dancing with him. After four dances, I really wanted to get away. So I pretended I needed to go the bathroom and ran out to the hall.

When I came back, I hurried over to the older ladies I had come to the dance with and started to tell them about my experience. Another guy interrupted to ask me to dance. Let me explain: these guys are older—like twenty to thirty years. One was nice. He started teaching me how to do the steps and asked if I was new. I told him I had only been divorced for three months, and this was my first dance. He patted me on the back and said, "It's going to be okay. It's overwhelming at first. But you are 'normal' and you will do really well." He was nice and funny and wasn't pushy at all, and I felt better.

After we parted, the first guy came snooping around. Judy, he begged for my phone number. He took my hand, pranced me around the room, and I didn't know how to escape. I can't believe I did this, but I gave in and gave him my cell number. I really wish I hadn't done that. He's been calling all day. I turned off my phone.

This single stuff is crazy.

Charlene

The single dance was so overwhelming to Charlene that she had to write Richard. She started the letter talking to him about the woman he had recently started dating, then she went for the advice. She told him that she went to her first dance and how scary being a single woman was, especially when guys were so pushy. *I felt trapped by one of them and had no way of getting out. Do you know what I should do?*

Trying to forget about aggressive men, Charlene busied herself keeping up with the kids, household, and attending another training class at University of Phoenix. Again she was overwhelmed by everyone's qualifications and the lack of her own. How would she support her family if she didn't make it? She tried to keep that thought away and put her trust in God.

When she got out of class and was driving home through the dark stillness of the night, Brad called. He was having a horrible problem with Sandra.

Charlene kept her eyes on the road, taking this all in. First thing she did was to check to make sure her children were safe and Brad wasn't going to hurt them. After she felt her kids were safe and Brad was more annoyed than out of control, she thought about how Brad was becoming extremely dependant on her. "What do you want me to do?" she asked.

"What?"

"You heard me. Why are you calling me? What can I do about it?"

"Well, I, um, well she isn't listening to what I have to say."

"You already said that." Charlene tried to keep emotion out of her voice. "What do you want me to do about it? I'm not there." He'd use any trick as an excuse to have contact with her. She'd have to write Richard about Brad's behavior and see if he had any good ideas on dealing with that. She liked that idea. She liked thinking that she had friends all over the USA to whom she could reach out.

Brad whined a little longer. Charlene used the broken record technique she'd learned in therapy.

"What do you want me to do about it?" she asked, over and over.

Finally he said he had to go. She pulled up to her dark house. Once inside, she put her book bag on the empty couch and wrapped her arms across her chest as she wandered through the house flipping on lights. She didn't like being the only one home. She couldn't help worrying about her kids. She wished she was with them. Trying to shake the feeling, she hurried to the computer.

Richard had responded with a list of "un-pick-up" lines. Charlene printed off the e-mail just in case she ever got crazy enough to go to another dance. She would have to review the list. "No thanks," and, "I'll pass this time."

Richard wrote about how hard it was to keep one's boundaries and not offend someone and how, in the singles' world, people's feelings got hurt all the time.

Charlene was amazed at what a big subculture the singles' world was and how she knew nothing about it. What was she getting herself into?

CHAPTER 19

Charlene had often heard that life was happier without a man, but she had never believed it. Yet one morning as she sang to the radio as she got ready for the day, she figured out that she was *a lot* happier without one. Life was so much easier, even though she was a single mother.

That day, she received a call from a friend she hadn't heard from in a long while. Dawn was seeking help with her marriage.

"I shouldn't say anything against him, though," she said after complaining that her husband was on the computer all the time chatting to other women.

Charlene didn't want her friend feeling like she was the guilty one because she had reached out for help with her problem. She said, "There's nothing wrong with talking to someone and getting the support you need. Some people think talking about marital problems is a betrayal, but it isn't. Betrayal is when someone takes your trust and shreds it to bits. That's betrayal! And oh, poor them if they don't like you talking about it. What are you supposed to do? Suffer in silence, letting things eat you up until they kill you or you develop a life-threatening disease? Of course you shouldn't blab it all over the world and defame him, but you have every right to talk to a trusted friend. If your husband doesn't want you to discuss it, then he should stop giving you reasons to blab.

"You love him. You don't want to hurt him. But you do have a right to take care of yourself. You'll be no good to him, your kids, or yourself if you don't take care of your pain."

"You're making a lot of sense," she said. "I'll give it thought."

"I'd like to be a support to you whatever you decide," Charlene offered. "I know how painful it is to hear, 'Leave the jerk.' The situation you're in is difficult. It'll take staying close to God to navigate successfully. Yes, your husband has a lot of pain from the past, and he's trying to avoid it through his bad behavior, which leaves him feeling more ashamed and unloved. He needs to realize he's of worth despite his mistakes. Jesus sacrificed His life for him. He needs to deal with his past by letting God heal him and creating a complete change of heart. People don't understand that religion can sometimes be a great source of healing. The scriptures call Christ 'counselor,' and it's really true.

"I hate what you're involved in. He destroyed your trust by going behind your back. The lady might be a manipulative person—she sounds bad—but he's the one choosing their relationship. If you haven't already, you need to find out what you can do to protect yourself and your kids in case you decide to leave. You need to know what you can do about finances, since he might lose his job."

That led to a half hour of problem solving while Dawn pondered what she could do to support her family if she had to.

When Charlene hung up the phone, she felt she did in fact have something to offer. Maybe she would make a good therapist. She had certainly been through enough things to understand others' problems even though they weren't the same as her own.

*

Having the children leave to visit Brad every other weekend grew unnerving. No one talking endlessly at her. No crying. No complaining, no whining, no blares from the TV. The phone didn't ring. No computer noises. No one to love, to focus on, to help.

Nothing. Charlene used the time to keep up with her schooling. Sometimes she'd take a break when it felt like her head was about to erupt from so much information, and then she'd clean house.

She also checked her e-mails. She'd received some saying: "You're real cute and I would look you up, but too many kids. Sorry." Things like that. She wasn't sure how she should respond. She had a friend tell her she was lucky. The kids served as a protection and kept her away from a lot of creepy guys. That might be the truth. If they couldn't handle children, it didn't matter how cool they were. She was a mother. She had heard stories about people who hid that fact and once the person was head-over-heels, they would spring one child at a time on the love interest. That seemed so dishonest.

At the dances, she learned that saying "No" in a non-conflictive way was really empowering, and it was surprising how most people were okay with it. One guy she said "No" to when he asked for her phone number didn't just walk away; he sat for a minute or two and chatted before he left. It was really nice of him—or maybe he didn't want others to see that he'd been turned down. Charlene preferred to think he was being nice.

The hardest time was when the children were gone on Sundays. The day was so quiet. Charlene slept as much as she could and then forced herself to eat. She attended church. The people were really nice when she needed help, but socially she felt like a ghost. It was like she didn't exist. She'd sit on a bench alone. It was strange to not worry if her children were being noisy. It was also strange to not worry about which child needed extra attention. When she had her kids, the one that seemed to be struggling the most would be picked to sit by her. With the kids gone, she had no excuses to leave the meeting.

Charlene thought about extending herself and making more friends, but she couldn't seem to do it. She didn't know what to say. "Hi, I'm the weird one who doesn't have a spouse. Ladies, please don't fear me. I'm not going to steal your husbands. And men, don't fear me, I'm not going to talk too much to your wives about how wonderful the single life is. No, I didn't commit some great sin. No, that 'single reject' label you're plastering across my forehead shouldn't be there. No, I don't want to tell you why I'm divorced, but I do know what's going on in your minds. 'There must be something wrong with her. She must be impossible to live with.' She wanted to scream, 'It's not true! He abused me because of his own problems with rage, not because of me. I wasn't wrong in leaving him.' Of course, if she said this, they would still think she was after their husbands; a bad influence on their wives; and in either case a huge sinner that would somehow pollute them. Maybe she was being dramatic, but it felt like people were thinking those things from the way they looked at her.

There was a kind, motherly woman who came up to Charlene after service and put her arm around her. She told Charlene, "I have a special love for single women, especially since my daughter is one." Charlene cried and wasn't even sure why.

She opened up and said, "Brad won't leave me alone. He keeps calling late into the night. He tells the kids I'm coming back. He plays games with my child support. He holds it back enough to keep me dependent and guessing but not enough to get in legal trouble. And he *still* wants to get back together." Charlene burst into tears, wiped at them and said, "Like I would do that after the way he treats me? Give me a break."

Charlene came home and told Judy of her misery.

Subject: Sundays
Date: June 24
From: "Charlene" <char@CharlenesWeb.net>
To: "Judy" <bchcomber@yippee.com>

After church on the weekends Brad has the kids, I drive home to the still, quiet house. I wander around, wishing it was a different day and I could use the time playing with the kids or doing my homework. I don't do the homework because I feel that it is not right to do that on the Sabbath. I write in my journal. I cry. I read. The silence drags out and somewhere in the midst of that I fall asleep, normally after a real hard cry. Then noise. Fighting, crying, "I want Dad." I wake to see my children—all wanting something, all needing something, and anxious. I need to normalize and make the transition back to me as smooth as possible. I'm off to take care of them. So and so forgot about doing a project that's due tomorrow and another one is begging for attention by their actions—hitting, fighting, being grouchy—they want me to hold them and reassure them everything is okay. One child is hungry and claims, "Dad didn't feed us. Where's dinner?" Another one is still out on the porch talking to Dad. The last one is saying, "Dad wants to talk to you." All or nothing is what my life is. Silence or utter chaos. No in-betweens. As soon as I start adjusting to one lifestyle, it flips.

It's interesting to learn about how others' lives are. Mine has always been filled with children, noise, needs, and meeting needs. There must be many who live a quiet, less stressful existence, but they also have struggles. I much prefer it with the children. I'm happier when a child climbs into my arms. I find myself playing with them and smiling. When I'm alone there's no smiles, no laughter, no playing—just existing.

How do you do it?
Charlene

P.S. My last training class at University of Phoenix is tonight. We get a week break and then I'll be into the testing and observation phase. This is happening so quickly.

*

Monday morning the phone rang. "Hi, Dawn," Charlene said. She kissed Nathan on the cheek, lifted him off her lap where she had been reading to him. As she talked on the phone, she prepared him a peanut butter sandwich. "Are things any better?"

"We had a big, long talk, and he agreed that he needs help. He even asked me to forgive him."

"I'm glad things are looking better," Charlene said.

"I am too. I'm so relieved. I think we're going make it."

"That's great." Charlene wiped her counter, hoping that the goodness with Dawn's husband would continue, but she knew that the chances for a relapse were highly probable. "Men can sometimes be stubborn and the walls can go up fast. Does George know you want to put money away? Is he okay with that?"

"He doesn't know. I just didn't have the guts to tell him."

"I can understand that," Charlene said. "You do need to do things to take care of yourself. Be careful. He could revert."

"How are things going with Brad?" Dawn asked.

Charlene sighed. "Ongoing. Sometimes it becomes critical and stops everything in my world, and other times it's more manageable. Brad is always going to be part of my life. I doubt he'll ever leave me alone. He keeps calling. He wants to talk about our marriage and how I shouldn't have left him."

"That's hard," Dawn said.

After they hung up, Charlene clicked onto the dating site. She had an e-mail from a guy named Adam who was the primary caregiver of two children, one four and the other five. Charlene wrote back that she had five. *Crazy, huh? 12, 10, 8, 5, and 3.* That would probably scare off any more e-mail exchanges.

Charlene became so absorbed with school, her lawyer, the kids, taking kids to therapy, and house cleaning that it startled her that another Friday had come. The days had become monotonous and the stress mounting.

Taking a deep breath for her assertiveness training, she went to another singles' dance after she had put the kids to bed and they were asleep. She left Sandra, who just turned twelve, to babysit. Sandra was glad to get paid to stay up and watch TV.

When Charlene stepped into the college gym, the lights were dim and the music thumped. She smiled at people as they glided past her and looked for a familiar face or a girl standing alone looking as uncomfortable as she felt—someone she could go talk to until and if she was asked to dance.

It wasn't long before men were leading her out to the dance floor asking her what she did. As she looked at their curious eyes, she feared that they would ask her out and she would have the awkward moment of telling them no. She learned to quickly tell them the truth. Her first line, "I have five kids," didn't have the shock value that she expected. Only a few of the men choked on that. Others were strangely more interested, which confused Charlene, but didn't discourage her from trying another scare tactic. So she said, "I have a BA and I'm working on a master's degree in counseling." Or "For free time I enjoy yoga and meditation." And the ultimate: "Yes, I'm considering becoming a vegetarian." And to the question, "Do you like watching movies?" she'd answer, "No, I'd rather read an academic book." Who'd have thought that her real interests would be so threatening? She laughed at their expressions. It was great.

The next morning, after sleeping in till nine, Charlene cooked for her children a big stack of pancakes. As she did, she thought about how she was going to find friends her own age. Where could she find them? It wasn't so fun hanging out with people her mother's age, especially when it was clear they didn't want her around.

Flipping on cartoons for the kids, she went on the Internet dating service to search for online social groups to join. She browsed through the various offerings until she stumbled on one that sounded like so much fun she couldn't resist. It was called "Successful Singles." It looked like they gathered and talked about how to be a successful single. She would have a lot to say and learn from that. She clicked the button to join.

Her thoughts turned to her children. Was she adequately helping them through their grief process? She wrote Judy to see what she thought of Charlene's efforts. She went down through her list of kids starting with the oldest.

My friend, Karla, who acts like an adopted grandmother, takes Sandra once a week and gives her sewing lessons. After the lessons, Harold, Karla's husband, and Sandra go for Taco Tuesdays. So far she seems happy with this. She and Harold tease each other until I can get over there to pick her up. Harold took Cameron, my second child, under his wing and is showing him how to cut rocks. Harold loves it. I saw his eyes brighten up when he heard Cameron was coming. He is a good male role model for my son. With Paige, the middle child, Karla has started cooking lessons. Paige asked for sewing lessons like Sandra, but I thought the sibling rivalry wouldn't be good—let them each have their own thing. For Lorine, I have her pick a book to read at bedtime. I start with her, but then the other kids catch wind of what's going on and I end up reading to all of them. Nathan is home with me all day and gets lots of extra time. I'm keeping him out of preschool because I feel he needs to be with me and feel more secure after the divorce. Harold watches him when I absolutely need a babysitter. Those two are cute together. It's like they are talking the same language. Karla and I often laugh about it.

I also take the kids to the park a lot. I have a theory that play can be very healing. They like going, and when we aren't at the park, sometimes I give them finger paints and paper to draw out their feelings. They, especially the younger ones, like doing this. I let them hang up their paintings all over the house.

Chapter 20

Later on Saturday, Charlene rushed to her e-mail after getting home from a grocery shopping trip. The kids continued to unload the car as she read a greeting from the group leader of "Successful Singles." He told her a little bit about their get-togethers and the discussions sounded like a blast. Charlene planned on attending to get a better idea what all the craziness was about.

She checked out the leader profile. He had thick, black and gray hair, a friendly smile, and a square-shaped face. He was divorced with four children, only one living with him. There were pictures of his home, him hiking, and his Cadillac. He wrote about his adventures in life and his pursuit of the truth. This piqued Charlene's interest, because she too had written about pursuing truth.

In the e-mail, Dave, the leader, wrote, *I find your profile intriguing. You seem like an interesting soul.* Dave wanted to know how long she had been divorced.

Charlene wondered why he would want to know that. She helped the kids put away the groceries and returned to the computer as her children got on the phone searching for kids to play with.

I'm a Greenie, four months out. I thought about divorcing for years, so I feel I got a head start on my grieving.

Misty

*

The doctor had her open her jaw several times before saying, "It's TMJ." He wrote on his chart, flipped through the papers she had filled up, and then looked up with eyebrows raised. "It looks like you're clenching and grinding your teeth a lot, which wears out the joint. Given your history, I think these are bad habits caused by stress—perhaps you aren't saying things that need to be said. I recommend journaling on top of a basic pain reliever. See how that works and we'll reevaluate."

Charlene shifted on the exam table. If she did that, she would have to explore all the things that she was avoiding feeling. She didn't want to look at her situation too closely. What if she couldn't handle it? Her therapist had told her last week that she was looking at life through a microscopic view of her future. She needed to look through a more hopeful and wider lens.

Her jaw throbbed, sending piercing pain up her skull and down her neck. Her head throbbed, and aspirin wasn't taking away the edge. It was getting to the point that she couldn't eat anything but soft foods, and sometimes when she opened her jaw, it stuck in that position, refusing to close or open, just stuck there mid-way between the two. She had to get rid of some of the pain in her jaw.

The pen glided over the paper slowly at first. "I don't know what to write about…" But then she wrote about Brad and how sad she was that things didn't work out with him. "If only he didn't…" The pain welled up in her chest, pushing out tears. She didn't understand why she had such a powerful conviction when she married her ex that she was doing the right thing. She didn't understand how she got here: single, alone, so many kids, and wanting and needing so much. With so many phone calls from her ex, it was worse than being married. How could she have had such a powerful conviction that what she had done was right, when things turned out so wrong? What did she do to deserve this?

She kept praying to God through her writing to love her, protect her, take her up in His arms and comfort her. She wrestled on paper with the idea that she was single and on her own. She had never been truly on her own before.

After writing about those things, she turned to write about the mundane, everyday occurrences like when the vacuum broke. She had knelt down with the children gathering around her looking at the switches and screws. She flipped knobs for about twenty minutes. Then she pronounced it dead. Others could have easily fixed it, but she couldn't, so she gave up. She hustled all the kids into the car, drove to the store, and found a sale on vacuums. She bought the cheapest one, since every time they break she'd be purchasing a new one. One problem down, five thousand to go.

Did she have what it would take? How was she going to do these "guy" things around the house when her father never let her anywhere near them and her husband followed suit? She had no skills, none, zilch, zip. The toilet and dishwasher were broken, and the grass always needed mowing. Earlier that week she had met with a financial planner to come to grips with money. At the end of the journaling, she declared that she felt like an avalanche had buried her alive.

Subject: Evaluations
Date: July 16
From: "Charlene" <char@CharlenesWeb.net>
To: "Judy" <bchcomber@yippee.com>

Judy,

My official evaluations for school start tomorrow. First on the list is to hand in a paper stating why I would be good in the counseling program and what qualifications I have.

The paper required a lot of research, which I found fun and fascinating. I read a whole bunch of articles—more than the ones required for class. This therapy stuff is incredibly interesting.

My paper is completed. I've written and rewritten it. I've had several friends look it over. I feel confident that what I hand in won't be trashed. I'm being very honest as to why I want to do this program and why I feel I fit in. Hopefully, they like honesty.

Charlene

*

Charlene woke up with a start. Today was speech day, and she had a dramatic one prepared. The subject was on why she wanted to be a therapist. She was going to talk about the chains of abuse and how she wanted to be part of the crusade of not only breaking them in her own family, but also in the lives of as many others as she could. She made up red and black construction paper chains and wrapped them around a volunteer. When she ended her presentation, she said, "I am going to break," she ripped the chains off the volunteer, "the chains of abuse."

The audience gasped and she knew she had them. She smiled and returned to her seat to watch the next presenter. She had done all she could. Now the fate of her future waited for her.

The next person stood there, petrified. He mumbled. Charlene had to strain to hear him. As he muttered on, Charlene's mind wandered. It was so great not to fight with Brad about everything in the marriage. Now that it was just her, she could get up and do her thing, like this presentation, without worry that he would somehow sabotage her. Brad didn't know what she was doing; she didn't tell her kids, therefore there were no surprise flat tires, ripped up notes, or any other suspicious events.

In fact, most things were getting easier. Sandra was making friends, which made everything smoother. Cameron hadn't been successful with that. He was stressed and anxious. Last night Charlene had prayed with him over the dilemma. Charlene really hoped that his prayers would be answered. The other kids, except Paige, the middle child, seemed happy. Paige found a picture of Brad and her together. She stared at it, crying. This was how she went to bed at night—every night. She wanted her parents together, a natural feeling. That was hard. Charlene couldn't think of anything she could do to help her. She put her faith in what she was told by a lady in her church, who said that she had a dream where she saw the planet Earth with tiny lights radiating from it.

"What are those lights?" she asked an angel.

"Those are prayers."

She also saw large brighter light beams. "What are those?" she asked.

"Those are mothers' prayers. They're answered first."

Charlene made a wish that this was the case as she looked over at the judges who were rating the mumbling speaker.

*

Sunday was beautiful, with the sun kissing the earth and radiating a comfortable, pleasing heat. Charlene couldn't resist enjoying the weather as she read. The sweetness of the day soothed her soul as she spread herself across the lush grass (okay, spotty with lots of rocks). Today she studied the power of God and His many miracles. He could make the mountains move or raise valleys. If He could do that, then surely He could make order out of her chaos.

As Charlene read and wrote, she decided she would avoid the meat market aspect of the singles' world. God could send Mr. Right—the man who'd be her equal. Not one that would make her happy, but one she could be happy with. She would choose happiness, and God would grant it to her. He would grant her desires.

She felt as though God smiled down on her as He said, "At last. Charlene, I've been waiting so long for you to choose happiness. At last."

*

July 23rd finally arrived. It was the day Charlene was supposed to attend the "Successful Singles" group. Charlene wanted to go, but she had called everyone she knew who could attend with her as support, and everyone was busy. Should she go alone? It was at this guy's home. The multitude of stories of girls getting raped from the dating services and some even murdered plagued her. No matter how she looked at it, and no matter how tempted she was, it wasn't safe for her. She wrote her regrets to Dave and hoped that she could make it next month.

Instead of spending the evening talking psychology with a group of single strangers, Charlene retired to bed early. She had been getting up early to do yoga tapes with her kids. It had a calming influence on all of them.

The next morning, Charlene did make the effort to get up. Of course she went straight to her computer and right into panic after reading the e-mail that awaited her.

Chapter 21

Subject: Totally Your Fault
Date: July 28
From: "Charlene" <char@CharlenesWeb.net>
To: "Judy" <bchcomber@yippee.com>

Judy,

Okay, this is your fault. I'm freaking out right now. I just agreed to go on a date, like you suggested. And Dave, the "Successful Singles" guy, wants to go on a walk tonight to enjoy this pleasant summer eve. This doesn't sound so safe.

Charlene

Darn that Judy. She had written and written Charlene, encouraging her to go out on a date. Get it over with, so she wouldn't be so scared. That had sounded like good advice until Charlene received the invitation from Dave. Then suddenly fear had gripped her. She didn't need to date. Life was fine without men. Simpler. Easier. Why mess with it?

Charlene fluttered from one thing in her house to the next, unable to land or focus. When Brad came and picked up all the children after school, the silence tortured her. She opened the refrigerator to get something to eat before the walk so she wouldn't get light-headed. There was nothing in there that she wanted. She closed the door and grabbed a broom to sweep up the mess the kids had left on the floor.

Her stomach tightened. Two hours until she had to leave. How should she dress? Was she going to primp or go looking less than her best? What would they talk about? Was walking with a strange fellow in the mountains really a good idea?

The phone rang. Charlene shrieked, startled by the sudden noise. "Hello?"

"Charlene, this is Dave. Are you ready for tonight?"

Charlene tipped the speaker part of the phone away from her mouth to take a deep breath. "Um, I'm not so sure about going on a walk."

"Why?" His voice was calm, smoothing.

"Um, I'd feel more comfortable if it was a public place with lots of people." Her grip on the broom tightened.

He laughed. "All right, we can meet in front of the police department."

Charlene couldn't help but laugh at that. "Maybe not that extreme."

They settled on Denny's, the restaurant. "A high-class date," Charlene said to Karla, who she just had to call after the conversation. "Don't worry, I'm bringing my cell phone and will have it hooked on my waist at all times. Maybe I could get a tool belt and have my cell phone, mace, pepper spray, and Taser. What a stunning array."

Karla volunteered to plant herself at the restaurant with her husband to watch for any signs of trouble. Charlene knew that all these precautions weren't going to make Judy happy when she found out. Her friend did want her to date, but *not* people on the Internet. She believed Internet dating was too scary.

Charlene continued to talk on the phone to Karla while she got ready. To keep her mind off the upcoming date, she started in on a "mother complaint."

"Nathan is still not potty trained. I try to introduce the idea to him, and he's not interested at all. In fact, I think he's regressing a bit. I heard that's normal in a divorce. He's gone through a divorce and a move. That's gotta be rough on a kid. I feel it would be wise not to push potty training on him, but oh, it sure would be nice if he were trained."

Karla joked, "Tell Brad that is his responsibility to train him since he's the guy."

Charlene laughed. "That'll be the day."

*

Subject: Cute
Date: July 30
From: "Charlene" <char@CharlenesWeb.net>
To: "Judy" <bchcomber@yippee.com>

Judy,

Dave was cuter than his picture and really personable. He had me laughing within the first thirty seconds. He was really interesting to talk to. He checked me out to see if what I said in my profile was the truth. I couldn't remember what I wrote, but I figured I passed the test since I don't lie. I have nothing to hide.

As we talked, I got the sense that he understood me better than I have been understood in a long time. I felt he saw who I really am. I liked him more than I wanted to. I felt this incredible connection. He is a thinker. I miss that. He cares about God, plus he was funny. We talked late into the night, even though he had to get home and do work for the next day.

He asked for a hug at the end of the date, and I about jumped out of my body. That was awkward. He said he would be considerate about my time with my children. I took that as a sign he wants to spend more time with me. What do you think?

Charlene

*

Charlene went from stressing about her date to the next day stressing about her final tryout for the master's in therapy program.

She had to play therapist, using reflective language and other psychological techniques. She'd been practicing a lot with fellow classmates, doing more visualizing and praying. In the end she hoped that would be enough.

When she went into the therapy room, there was a mirror on the wall where people from behind would be observing her. A young, blonde girl came in the office.

"Hello," Charlene said cheerfully. She could feel a plastic smile go across her face. *Relax*, she thought to herself. *Be normal. They can tell if you are stressed.* "Come in and sit down. It's so nice to meet you. What's your name?" She had gotten the order wrong. Would they notice that? Knock her grade down? She took a deep breath and focused on the girl. She had come to her to get help. Her life was troubled. How could Charlene help her?

*

Charlene wasn't sure what she worried about more through the remainder of the week. How she did playing a therapist or the fact that Dave hadn't called her. He wanted to go out this weekend, but then didn't call to schedule. By Friday afternoon, Charlene wondered what she was going to do. The kids were at her ex's. She had promised herself that she wasn't going to be like those ladies she had seen at the dances. They didn't know if they were going to the dance until they found out if their guy was going to ask them out. They sat by the phone and waited!

To keep true to her resolve, she packed her stuff to go to an evening lecture and then arranged to go to the dance with friends.

In the middle of the seminar, Dave called. She couldn't keep from smiling when she slipped into the hallway to talk to him. He wanted to know if she wanted to go to dinner.

"Oh, I'm sorry. I already have plans tonight."

"Hmm, it is kind of late to be asking, isn't it?"

There was a long drawn out silence. He was waiting for her to fill in the space. She didn't. Maybe he would ask her out for Saturday. She hadn't arranged anything yet for that.

"Let's see, where are you now?"

"At a seminar on healthy eating. Do you want to come?"

"I'd be really late. How about we get together on Monday?"

"Sounds great," Charlene said, wondering why he wasn't asking her to go out on Saturday or Sunday. Maybe he already had another date lined up? She didn't like thinking about that.

"All right then," he said.

Charlene smiled. It was going to be hard to wait for Monday.

*

Subject: No accident?
Date: August 6
From: "Charlene" <char@CharlenesWeb.net>
To: "Dave" <allaroundman@yesterday.com>

Dave,

Thanks for coming by Monday evening. Glad to hear you had no accidents looking at my yard in the dark after we said good night. My lawyer will be disappointed. ☺ *I like your ideas on where to plant trees. The yard needs work, but has a good start. Maybe next spring I will put in a few trees. I'm definitely going to take out the plants in front and replace them with white roses. I had white roses at my last house and just loved them. They're my favorite. I believe in surrounding myself with things I love so they'll feed my soul.*

I'd love to play a game of croquet with you. I have to admit I'm not very good. I've only played it once or twice.

I'll drive to your house early Thursday evening, six-ish, and we can leave for the lecture together. It sounds fascinating. I'll see you then.

Charlene

*

Charlene woke up thinking about her evening with Dave. There was something about him. It was more than the fact that he was good-looking, made great conversation, and made her feel like a princess around him.

When he first entered the home, he looked around with intensity. "Nice. I like the way you keep it up. Everything is in its place and with five kids. How do you do it? I'm a bachelor, and I can't keep my place this nice."

As soon as those words were out of his mouth, Charlene spotted some kids peeking at them around corners.

"Nathan, come here. Come say hi to Dave."

Nathan's large blue eyes peeked shyly around the wall.

"Sandra, you too."

With the invitation, all the children started giggling and gazing at Dave curiously over the banister.

Dave started joking with them and headed up the stairs to shake their hands.

Sandra glared and refused to offer a hand.

"Sandra," Charlene said in her mother tone that meant she'd better straighten up.

Dave turned to Charlene. "That's okay. She doesn't have to."

"All right. You need to finish the dishes then get to bed. You have to visit your father early in the morning."

The kids moaned.

"I'll help," Dave volunteered.

"No, that's okay." Charlene wished she had gotten the dishes done before he arrived.

"I don't mind." Dave slipped off his jacket, rolled up his sleeves, and began washing.

After they finished, Dave wanted to play with them, but Charlene put her foot down. "Sorry, they have to get up early tomorrow. Come on kids, go hop in bed."

The kids stomped their feet moaning all the way to their bedrooms.

"Good night," Dave called, a smile on his face. Turning to Charlene, he said, "Nice children."

Charlene waited for Dave to make a signal that they should leave. Although she'd rather stay—not wanting to leave her kids home alone even though they were old enough to watch themselves—Dave had suggested that they go on a walk or out to eat. She wasn't sure which one he had in mind. Instead of the signal, he wandered into the library that overlooked the mountains and the lake. "Do you have many problems with your children?"

Charlene launched into a long discussion of the problems she had, her worries, and what she was trying to do to help them. When she was wrapping up explaining her parenting style and philosophy, Dave said, "I love your parenting skills. They show such conscientious intelligence. I admire your dedication and the higher purpose it reflects. I find that very attractive."

Charlene shifted in her seat, not knowing how to respond to that. She was sure she was blushing.

Dave went on to explain how he shared similar parenting philosophies and some of the things he'd done with his own children, who were all raised and out on their own except for one. As he spoke, he took her hand in his and began to stroke it.

At first, Charlene thought about pulling her hand away, but then she let go and let him hold it. He eventually wove the conversation back to her again. This time he wanted to know why she was divorced and how that came about. As she spoke about the beatings and the disrespect, her fear for her children, tears surfaced. He pulled her to his chest. An overwhelming peaceful comfort washed over her. She rested her head on his strong chest. He stroked her hair before saying, "Not only are you beautiful on the outside, my dear, but the trials you're overcoming and truths you're seeking create a beauty within you that can endure forever."

That night, about midnight, an e-mail arrived from Dave. He wrote: *I enjoyed being with you last night very much. You're a very dear soul that I can't help but feel affection for.* At the end of his e-mail he called her sweetheart.

Was it too early in their relationship for him to call her that? Charlene wondered. There was no way she was going to say that to him. He was jumping into terms of endearment quite early. Maybe he was playing her.

Subject: Teenager again?
Date: August 9

From: "Charlene" <char@CharlenesWeb.net>
To: "Judy" <bchcomber@yippee.com>

Judy,

I went to a fun lecture with Dave last night. Afterward, we went out for a bite to eat. We talked at length about our families and past experiences. It would seem that his first wife is a lot like my mother. It was strange to meet someone who knows what it's like to live with that sort of person. I felt very connected to him. We went back to his house and talked. I can't believe I stayed up so late. I feel like a teenager who is sneaking around, hiding from my parents. Who would have ever thought I would feel like a teenager at my age?

We're going on our first family outing this weekend—a hike in the mountains. It'll be nice to take the kids out. I don't do much with them except take them to the movies. It's overwhelming to do things with them by myself. I run out of energy.

In his e-mail to me he said, "My regard for you is offered freely, with no expectation of an outcome or return, and this is how I honor God who is 'our' Father." There you have it in his words, at least how he's presenting himself, and why he treats me kindly.

You're probably right about time being the only way I can tell what his true motives are. I hope he's not a player. I like him. We can talk about spiritual concepts. He's so different from Brad. He's so much nicer. He seems to have depth that is refreshing and intriguing to me. Of course, he is a few years older than Brad, who is a few years older than me.

I would try for that promotion if I were you. You can do it. The sky's the limit.

Charlene

P.S. You won't believe this, but Nathan came home potty-trained. His dad said he'd had enough and it was time. I don't know what he did to get Nathan trained, but I'm grateful. Yahoo!

*

Charlene folded laundry with the phone set on top of the dryer so she wouldn't miss hearing it ring. Today the school was supposed to call her and tell her fate. *August 12, August 12, August 12, I have to wait until August 12.* This had been her mantra. She had, in her child-like way, thought the day would never arrive, and now here it was.

She grabbed the towels out of the stack to fold. She couldn't work on the computer or do anything that required concentration, to her children's frustration. Lorine and Nathan wanted her to read a book, which she tried to do, but then her thoughts wandered and the kids grew impatient.

Her nerves might explain why their arguing had increased. The last thing she wanted was for the school to call and have to deal with her children bursting into a fight.

Her stomach twisted. "Kids, please go outside to play," she called to them when they were screaming at one another, "She did…" "Mom, he…"

"But, Mom…"

The phone rang. Charlene's heart thundered. "Outside now," she snapped, grabbing the phone and darting into Sandra's room, locking the door.

"Hello."

It was a telemarketer. "Argh," Charlene yelled at the phone. "I can't take much more of this."

The phone rang again. This time she checked the caller ID. Her ex. The last thing she wanted was to talk to him. He would have to wait. That call had to be coming in any time now. She hoped him calling wouldn't interfere with the phone lines somehow.

By the time she was putting the clothes away, the phone rang again. "Is Charlene there?"

"Speaking."

"We're calling to inform you that you have been accepted into our master's degree program."

"I have?" Charlene said. She realized then that she hadn't expected it.

After she hung up the phone, she wondered if she had made up the whole acceptance thing. She sat on the couch. She was going to school. Graduate school. Her stomach twisted. She could do it. It seemed like it would be hard but she could do it.

Wow, she made it in. She had to tell someone.

Chapter 22

Judy's last e-mail was reassuring. She said she had also spun out of control when she was first divorced. The Judy Charlene knew was so calm, wise, and self-confident. It was weird to think that once she was acting as lost as Charlene knew she acted. It was almost like she was reliving her teenage years. Maybe everyone acted weird for awhile after a divorce. Judy promised Charlene that she would calm down on the dating thing.

For now, though, it was all she could do to try to focus on the upcoming school and her children. Dave and her interactions with him had a way of taking over her thoughts. They were asking each other questions that caused Charlene to think a great deal. E-mail did allow a person to know each other in a better way.

Subject: Your questions
Date: August 18
From: "Charlene" <char@CharlenesWeb.net>
To: "Dave" <allaroundman@yesterday.com>

Dear Dave,

I have some time on this quiet Sunday, so I thought I'd respond to your last e-mail. I definitely have things to say. Thank you for explaining yourself. I find the reason you chose real estate interesting and admirable.

You asked me about my father. I will tell you, although I don't talk about him much with anyone. I want to honor my father because he was the man who helped give me life, provided for me, and gave me an education. I do, in fact, love him and have done much on my journey to forgive him. I used to think he was a good man, and I wanted to marry someone like him. (Turned out, sadly, that in many ways I did.)

There was a time in my adolescence when I felt things were not right, and I remember questioning my mom. "How do you know we can trust Dad?" I asked. Mom talked me out of my negative feelings by telling me she had "searched the whole world and found the most righteous man there was."

Later we found out he had been seeing other women—about the time I had questioned things and yet been assured all was well. My father held fairly high positions in our church. People almost worshipped him. He taught intellectually and informatively. It was all a lie. Denials and cover-ups. As long as things looked good, they were good. This made it very difficult for me to discern the difference between truth and falsehood.

My parents did eventually go through a nasty divorce several years after I was married. Realizing these things causes me to wonder: was I deceived by my X? I thought he was good. He was a God-fearing, church-going man before we married, and then after the "I do," everything fell apart. He harassed me for my devotion. On Sunday, when I'd get out my books to study, he'd accuse me of trying to make him feel guilty for watching football on the Sabbath. My actions had nothing to do with him.

I knew I was supposed to marry him. I have learned and grown and had my faith tested. Was I deceived? Or was it God's will? Hard questions that perhaps you have asked about your divorces. All these things have given me experience. I trust God will bring understanding.

Dave, I know we have different backgrounds—your parents were together until your father passed away, and you have only two siblings. Yet you've had your share of trials with two divorces. I admit I have concerns about you, along with concerns about my ability to succeed in realizing our high ideals.

We are only as strong as the weakest link. People like my father and my X need help and support, not condemnation and shame, I agree. Right now I can't help my father or X. I have too many emotional issues with both of them. I put their progress in God's hands and the responsibility to deal with them in their leader's stewardship.

Yes, I believe it when you say I can learn a lot from you, but don't underestimate me. There's much you can learn from me too. I have been well seasoned.

Looking forward to going to the canyon with you and my kids this weekend. I'll wait for your phone call about the timing.

Charlene

*

August 20th was Charlene's first official night class for her master's. A buzz of nervous excitement pulsed through her as she entered the classroom. Her classmates were friendly, and each person came into the room giving each other high fives for making it to this point. There were a few shockers of people who hadn't made it, but thoughts of that faded when the professor started the class by jumping into lecture mode. The first session was called "Life Span." They would be studying different stages of life. It sounded interesting, and Charlene thought she would like it, although she was worried about the amount of homework involved.

When she arrived home, she was tired, hungry, and still uneasy with the silence of the house. She popped a burrito into the microwave, and while it sizzled she scanned her inbox for new e-mails. She sighed when she saw what was there. Yet another "flirt" from a guy who called himself Snuggles. They clearly had different values. She had made it plain on her profile, yet several times a week he shot her flirts. She had to put an end to this. She quickly typed: *Thanks for the e-mail. You sound like a very interesting man and one who likes to talk straight with people, so I will get to the point. Although I understand why you wouldn't want to go to church (believe me, I really understand), your zero church attendance is a problem for me. I'm the type of person who, despite my issues, attends faithfully and can't imagine being with anyone who is different in this area. I hope you don't feel "judged," because you are not. Best wishes in your search.*

She hesitated before hitting the send button. She didn't want to be rude or to hurt his feelings, but hopefully this would stop his endless solicitations. If relationships didn't begin with the same foundation values, there was absolutely no reason to waste time on them. From the amount of homework she'd been given tonight, time wasn't going to be something she had plenty of.

Charlene, yawning, studied the calendar. Her children would be going back to school in six days. It would be easier for her to get her schoolwork done with most of her children gone during the day. She loved her kids and hated not having them around, but staying up late every night to complete her homework was difficult. Granted, she would have two kids at home half a day. Lorine was now going to kindergarten the other half. As she'd told Judy before, Charlene had decided not to put Nathan in preschool. Hopefully this decision would help with his insecure feelings of being tossed back and forth been parents. It was too bad he had to start his life this way.

*

The days passed quickly with the mounting pressure of homework. Dave offered a nice break by arranging to pick her up with the children for a hike in the mountains on Saturday. Charlene thought it would do her good to spend time on something other than study. Her children did need family time, and hiking with five wasn't something she would ever do on her own. With Dave helping, they would have a good time.

And they did. The day was a bit nippy, which they prepared for with flannel shirts and jackets. Charlene had packed a lot of water and snacks, knowing how her children would get. The food became necessary. The kids grew tired and didn't want to walk anymore.

"If you make it to the next bench to sit on, I'll give you a granola bar," Charlene would say, and the children would drag themselves onward.

Dave laughed. He picked up Nathan and carried him. He teased the kids that they were too little to make it. This flared their determination and they walked faster. By the end, Lorine and Nathan were both in Dave's arms, which he grinned about. Paige wanted to join, but Charlene said no. She wasn't going to have Dave packed down like a mule. Dave said he could do it.

She laughed. "Do you want to travel the world with me and carry my children as you do?"

Dave said, "Of course. Where would be the first place we would go?"

This launched a conversation about where they wanted to travel and why, what they liked about various places, and what they wanted to do.

All of the kids, except Sandra, laughed and laughed at Dave's jokes. Sandra sneered and criticized. *What can you do?* Charlene thought. She was a budding teenager.

Dave dropped them off and the kids begged him to come in. Charlene nodded in agreement. She offered everyone another snack, which everyone gobbled up, especially Dave. Then she decided to make dinner. When Dave got wind that more food was coming, he took the kids into the family room and began playing horsey until it was ready.

The kids laughed and fought. "My turn, my turn."

Charlene looked at Sandra, who was now a big twelve-year-old. She smiled and called out, "It's Sandra's turn."

Sandra crinkled her face then suddenly a spark of understanding hit her. "Move over," she said, pushing Paige off Dave's back.

Dave grunted but started neighing and bucking on all fours as Sandra clung to him. Sandra set her jaw firm and managed to stay on the horse while Dave continued to buck.

Charlene laughed. Yes, Dave did seem good-natured and did handle the kids well. The kids loved him and seemed to forget their troubles when they were around him.

When it became apparent that Dave was going to stay for the evening, Charlene ran upstairs, called her dancing friends, and told them not to pick her up tonight because something had come up. As she hung up the phone, she was glad for the family time.

*

Two days later, an e-mail arrived from Snuggles thanking her for her honesty. Charlene smiled. She was handling things better.

The phone rang.

"Hello."

"I need to have the kids tonight." It was Brad. Lately he had been giving her almost constant pressure to take the children on visits. If she gave in to him, she would never see them and wouldn't be able to teach them character-building values. Besides, it set precedent. If he could establish he had the children all the time, he could get the visitation schedule changed to favor him. She had to stand strong.

"No, it's my time and I have plans."

"Come on, I have tickets to the basketball game. They've been dying to go."

"Sorry. We have plans." Worry filled her. The kids would love the game. Was she doing the right thing? The extra time would help her get her homework done, but no, she had to be in their lives. If she was going to be a good mother, she had to spend time with them.

"What plans?"

Uh oh, a trap. He was going to argue the importance of the plans. "It doesn't matter what they are," Charlene said. "It's my visitation."

"Man, I just ask for this one time and you won't even let me take them to the game. I can't believe you can be like this. I'm going to take you to court and force you to let me have more visitations."

"Oh, come on," Charlene said, "I give them to you plenty. If you had your way, I would never see them at all."

"Whatever. The kids would really like the game, and you won't even let them go. I don't understand why you're being this way."

And on he went with his argument and put downs. By the time Charlene hung up the phone, she was sick to her stomach. Would he really take her to court? How could she afford that plus school, plus the kids' therapy, plus everything else? Would he *really* try to take her children from her?

She was having a hard time keeping up with the kids' activities. Four of them were gone most of the day, which gave her time to spend on her schoolwork and tending the two youngest. When the older children arrived home, she had little time to get everything accomplished. She ran, ran, ran, dragging five kids to the grocery store, five kids to the craft store to get supplies for a science project, and on and on it went. By the time she pulled up to her garage, she was exhausted. She rarely cooked a full-fledged dinner. She found that cutting up fruit and vegetables, and having sliced meat, plus ice cream for dessert worked well and was fast and healthy.

The children's homework was a bear. Charlene felt like she was going to school twice. She often wondered why teachers made parents do so much. If they had to volunteer the parent, then maybe they should consult with them about whether Wednesday night was good for them to do the five-hour project, or do they by chance have to go to school themselves, or perhaps by some weird coincidence they might have something else to do—like have a life?

*

Saturday rolled around again and Charlene looked forward to de-stressing on the dance floor. Forget the undone, pressing homework, the angry threatening ex, the livid daughter who claimed Charlene had destroyed her life. Forget the housework she had fallen helplessly behind on, and forget the chirping smoke alarm she didn't know how to fix. Tonight would be about falling into the hypnotic rhythm of the music, having her body spin and sway, listening to a few jokes, and receiving a compliment or two. She decided to dive into the experience, slipping on her black dress.

She could hear the beat thumping and vibrating before she walked into the dark auditorium. She began swaying to the music.

Guys approached her. She danced with a few then slipped to the sidelines when she saw guys lining up, apparently to dance with her. She glanced at each of them rapidly, trying to figure out who she should go with. Some of them were scary looking and had an expression that made her want to run the other way. It didn't take long to figure out that the increased attention was due to how she looked physically.

Feeling twinges of panic, Charlene eyed the group to determine who might be the safest. The guy that Charlene chose was almost bald, short, and had a puppy dog expression. They danced several dances then he suddenly pulled her in and said, "You have such a sexy ear." Before she could do anything, he licked it!

Charlene decided she would *never* go to another dance again. She didn't want to have another ear-licking experience! She was so disgusted at what had happened that she came home and wrote her dear friend about her misery. Tomorrow she would have an e-mail filled with compassion and understanding of what she was going through. Judy wouldn't laugh at her as her dance friends had. She would understand Charlene's horror and have some type of wise counsel. Hopefully, some explanation on how to get that wet tongue image out of her mind. Ooh, it made Charlene's skin crawl just thinking about it.

*

Subject: Not funny!
Date: September 7
From: "Charlene" <char@CharlenesWeb.net>
To: "Judy" <bchcomber@yippee.com>

Judy,

Ear licking is not funny. Stop laughing. Stop it right now. I mean it. It was awful. I felt violated.

Charlene

Memories of the icky tongue remained with Charlene through Sunday. On Monday, as she took a break from her studies, she was grateful to receive an e-mail from Dave. She stayed up to talk to him on the phone. Since he'd written her, she thought writing him back would serve as a great distraction.

They had debated for hours about the role of God in peoples' lives. She needed to tell Dave about the role God played in her becoming a therapist. She wanted Dave to understand that God was indeed important to her. She wrote: *An effective therapist is merely a guide for others, someone to help the client learn to trust God and find the answers for themselves. The therapist's job is to mourn with those who mourn, to be of comfort, and to help fill in gaps of knowledge, but mostly, someone who encourages and testifies in God, and teaches others how to tap into that source. This isn't the typical ideal for a therapist, I'm sure, but it is how I feel. Some think it's unscientific, but if it is true that God exists and will help, then how is that unscientific? I understand even Einstein believed in God, and who is more scientific than that guy?*

Dave wrote that people's "wagonload of traditions" blind them to their relationship with God. Charlene thought about that. She liked the sound bite "wagonload of traditions."

Dave didn't talk about the same things other men talked about. He thought about higher-level things that caused her to think and ponder. She liked that. She felt like she could share deep experiences with him and he would appreciate and understand her. She felt she could open up and tell him things and he wouldn't think she was crazy. This being the case, she wrote about an experience she'd had while she was praying for something. *It was given to me that I wasn't yet ready for that blessing and to stop worrying about it. God will give it to me as soon as I am ready. Instead, I should focus on what God is trying to teach me. I had to trust Him and do my part. As soon as I was ready, joy would come into my life.*

Seems like it always goes back to trust—well, at least for me. I want to learn to completely trust God in all things. But so often I catch myself turning to human wisdom. I hope that's a habit I'll learn to break. I believe relying on a mate instead of God is one of the big reasons for many failed marriages. Between God and me, we can fix the problem. A mate can be a support, but "making it all better" is the wrong role to obligate him with.

After she shared this with him, she knew that Dave could teach her many things. Since becoming single, she had learned that much of her thinking had been wrong. She had thought that when she chose to be single, she was choosing to be alone the rest of her life. She remembered that people, like Judy, had said there would be guys, but she didn't believe them. She honestly thought she was too old, and with as many kids as she had, no way would she ever have a relationship again. But there were many guys who showed an interest. Some even hinted about marriage. Some of those were even serious. She'd already had to refuse marriage proposals from two men she barely knew. Crazy. Her dance friends had told her that happens a lot in the singles' world. Scary.

When Charlene thought about marriage, her thoughts always ended up in worry that she'd be stuck with another abuser. She knew she'd rather be single forever, even though it became lonely. Of course, now she had developed a great coping method to deal with the isolation—she looked up many different online single sites to see what interesting events were going on. She'd investigate more of them and attend at least once if she could find a girlfriend to go with her. So far, the single women she had met who were around her age didn't want to attend the events. They weren't ready to try again. She definitely understood that. It had taken her forever to get out of her relationship with Brad. She had left him mentally long before she actually left physically. Unlike those other women, she was ready to move on.

CHAPTER 23

Charlene couldn't help putting on another coat of lipstick, preparing to go to class. Randal would be there. He was in her study program. Moreover, he was tall, buff, single, smart, and religious. They had fallen into a habit of lingering in the parking lot after class let out. He had told her about his ex-wife and the sadness of the divorce. Maybe tonight he would stay after and talk to her again. She wanted to help him with his pain—plus he was cute.

When Randal entered the classroom, Charlene noticed right away how pale he looked. He came in late and his shirt, which was normally pressed, was wrinkled. Charlene raced up to him during the break to see if he was all right. He said, "I'm fine. Just some problems at work. If you'll excuse me, I need to use the restroom."

Since their break was only five minutes, Charlene didn't take his rush personally. Whenever the lecture waned in the interest level, she planned out what she'd say to him in the parking lot. "How can I help you?" "What went on?" "Have you seen your ex recently?" etc. But when the professor dismissed them, she gathered her belongings, eyed the room, and didn't see him anywhere.

The fall evening chilled her when she went to look for him in the parking lot. He was gone. Depressed by his quick exit, she rushed to her computer when she arrived home and wrote Dave. Dave had wanted to know about her feelings about money. She wrote: *I didn't have any control over the finances at all in my marriage. I don't choose to do that again. Brad used the cloak of having a vision and a mission that he believed God wanted him to accomplish in order to justify his controlling the funds. I believed God wanted him to fulfill that mission too, but not at the expense of his wife and children, which is what happened. It becomes dangerous when someone's vision morphs into a misuse of power.*

After writing to Dave, Charlene warmed up frozen french fries and sat to think about relationships and what she wanted in one. She had read author Scott Peck defining love as two birds in the air kissing. Each person remained independent, but would not have that experience without each other. That was the type of relationship she would look for if and when she wanted one. She would only go into a relationship because she chose to be there, not out of need.

What would that look like? She thought about Dave's spontaneous acts of kindness, getting her a cold glass of water, offering to change her child's diaper, changing her light bulbs when they went out, and fixing the beeping smoke alarm. He wasn't into the "wife as a servant" thing that she feared. Were those acts showing someone that you loved them? Or did they show a kind heart willing to help out? Or both?

*

Subject: The Wyoming Move
Date: September 22
From: "Charlene" <char@CharlenesWeb.net>
To: "Richard" <richardb@ripples.com>

Richard,

Sorry to hear things didn't work out with your girlfriend. That has got to be disappointing. If it's important for you to move away from Wyoming when your kids are grown, I can understand your breakup. Never move out of Wyoming? Craziness. I say follow your heart and the Lord will bless you.

What's new with me? Hmm. I've gone on another couple of dates with Dave. He's forty-four, like you. He seems very mature and healthy. I like that. He opens doors for me. He asks questions about me and talks about God and showing our love to Him—all good things.

My children are having various reactions. My oldest, Sandra, isn't happy about it at all and says so, but likes the babysitting money. My second child, Cameron, told me he wants me to get married and to hurry up about it. He doesn't care if I get divorced. He likes weddings. I think what he's saying is he'd feel more secure with a man around. Paige, my third child, responds a lot like the first. The rest of the children just want horsey and piggyback rides when they see Dave. He's a good sport and gives them wild rides as they screech with laughter.

Charlene

*

The weather had turned chilly, but that did nothing to calm Charlene's temper at church. A mother started slapping her child in the hallway. Then she swore and jerked on the daughter's arm, talking in a harsh whisper. "You get control of yourself or else." It wasn't hard to guess what the "or else" would be from the fire that could be seen in the mother's eyes. Charlene watched, speechless, not knowing what to do until she raced to the bathroom to dry heave.

Things didn't get better when she arrived home. The kids were grouchy and complaining about the other sibling stealing this, saying that, and looking at them that way. Rubbing her forehead, Charlene picked up the phone to listen to her messages to find five of them from Brad. "I've been thinking about it and decided you're right about the problems with our marriage." "I came on too aggressive and I should've listened." "Can't we try again?" "I'm not going to talk you out of your decision, but..." "I have improved so much, and I can do more..."

As Charlene listened, Cameron ran in. "Mom, these roses were by the front door." Charlene didn't have to open the note to know who they were from. She sighed. It was too bad Brad didn't bring flowers like that when they were married. That would have really helped.

As Charlene prepared lunch for the kids, the phone rang again. She checked caller ID. Brad. She told the kids to let the phone ring. She didn't have the energy for him right now. When lunch was over, she checked her messages. On this one he admitted that he hadn't been sensitive enough. He couldn't be the perfect husband with so many kids. He was in so much pain. Was there someone else? Was that why she'd insisted such a hurried divorce?

She sighed heavily. "Why can't he leave me alone?" she whispered. They had been divorced for over six months. The decision was made. They had to have contact because of the kids, but did they have to constantly talk about the condition of their relationship? The condition was all summed up in the word "divorce."

Later that night, Brad called to talk to the kids about the same issues. Charlene had begged him not to countless times for the kids' sake, but so far he hadn't listened to her. She took the phone from the kids and told Brad they had to go. She wasn't going to allow talking if it was going to be only about whether their mommy and daddy should get remarried.

But the day wasn't a complete loss. She had arranged two dates for the next week through the Internet dating service while all the kids were at school. Charlene knew Nathan would have a blast with Harold while she was away from him for an hour or two. One guy, Brent, seemed like he would be kind. She thought Duane might be a poet. She would see.

After taking care of her e-mail messages, she put that aside and gathered her children to her. "Let's go to the park," she said.

Most of them cheered.

Sandra moaned.

Charlene looked at her beautiful, growing daughter with her perfect, flawless skin and grouchy manner and decided that she would give Sandra the most attention at the park. While the other kids took to the slide and swings, Charlene talked to Sandra about her friends, school, and generally how she was doing.

Sandra still flinched when Charlene put her arm around her that night to tuck her in, but Charlene felt good that she had made an extra effort to reach out to her.

*

The lunch date with Brent was set for a Mexican restaurant. The place was colorful, decorated with bright reds, oranges, greens, and black. Cheery, wide windows overlooked large, hanging trees. Sunlight slipped through the green leaves. The atmosphere was divine, but Brent turned out to not be.

"Howdy," he said, stomping through the doorway. "You must be Charlene."

"I am," she said, shaking his hand.

"Great. Let's get some grub, shall we?" He led her to a nice table overlooking the leafy trees then proceeded to describe how he got fired from most of his jobs, was married for awhile, but liked being alone. He decided a couple of months ago that he was lonely. He didn't have any children and didn't know what to do with them, but was sure that Charlene could easily teach him all that stuff. After that, he talked about his mounting debt and how it was all Uncle Sam's fault.

Within the first five minutes, Charlene concluded it would be best to keep this relationship strictly on a friendly level, and no more. It was surprising that she didn't find out this information before. She'd have to be better at getting information out of the potential meetings so she wouldn't be a way from her kids for no good reason.

Two days later, she put down the books, took Nathan to a sitter, and met with Duane. Duane was tall and slender with thinning hair. He dressed like a traditional businessman. They met at a restaurant with a great salad bar. Charlene focused on salad, because Duane turned out to be incredibly intellectual but couldn't get out of his own wise musings and ruminations long enough to see that she existed. At the end of the date, Charlene concluded he wanted a dummy doll that just nodded her head and seemed interested. Oh well, two strikes in a week was not the worst record a person could have.

The lousy dates got her to thinking about Dave. She hadn't heard from him in a couple of days and found herself missing their interaction. She e-mailed him to make sure he was doing all right. In the e-mail, she informed him that she had just finished the final in her Life Span class, and in hopes of sparking a dialogue, she told him about her favorite topic in the class, which involved the issues that come with aging.

Charlene was surprised that she found aging so interesting. Who'd have thought? She was glad that the final was over and she could enjoy a week of down time.

Most of the time she spent playing with the kids—cooking huge breakfasts for them, taking them to the park, baking cookies, which she froze for treats when they came home from school, taking them to movies, and to the local museum. She also took Sandra to therapy like she had been doing every week. Sandra was so angry. The therapist had recommended some books for Charlene to read to get a better understanding how to help her daughter. She read them, practiced them, and scheduled an additional appointment with Sandra's therapist for just Charlene so she could understand better how to help her daughter.

Despite doing all that, Dave's silence bother her enough that she wrote Judy about it and asked for her advice.

Subject: Silence
Date: October 11
From: "Charlene" <char@CharlenesWeb.net>
To: "Judy" <bchcomber@yippee.com>

Dear Judy,

Dave isn't writing or calling me. It's been days. It's really getting to me. One night he's telling me how much he appreciates me, then the next three days, nothing! It's absolutely driving me crazy. I got brave and asked when I would hear from him again. Do you think he's distancing himself? It doesn't make sense.

Charlene

P.S. I keep thinking about how you told me a while back that remaining single and standing on your own all these years has made you strong and self-confident. Maybe the distance from Dave will be better for me in the long run.

Charlene busied herself with helping the kids de-junk their rooms. Things had gotten messy over the past hectic weeks. A few hours after loading a whole garbage can with junk, she allowed herself to check her e-mails again. Dave had written.

The next morning, Charlene wrote her friend to inform her that her worries were over. Dave had e-mailed back and even signed it "with love." He said he'd been busy writing his thoughts. This Charlene didn't understand. He'd chosen writing thoughts over being with her? Shouldn't he want to be with her instead of obsessing over it?

The next day she shook off her frustration at Dave and wrote to him about her exhausting day.

Subject: Stitches
Date: October 13
From: "Charlene" <char@CharlenesWeb.net>
To: "Dave" <allaroundman@yesterday.com>

Dave,

Been writing all day on the concept of love? Hmm. No, love doesn't scare me, at least not right now. Maybe that's because I feel a sense of freedom in our relationship. I'm not being controlled by you, and I don't sense any underlying feelings of servitude. (If I even sense a hint of control, I become a fireball.) I appreciate your affection. It amazes me how I feel so "myself" with you. It seems it's all right that I'm not perfect. I don't feel compelled to become something I'm not.

I have to go, but I wanted to acknowledge your e-mail. The kids are demanding today. It's a day "off" for them, which means a day "on" for me. This morning I've worked hard with the kids, getting them to do chores and trying to have family time. I experienced some drama. My daughter was dancing in the bathroom right after taking a bath. She did a big twirl, slipped, and plowed into a mirror I haven't hung on the wall yet. It shattered on top of her. I took her to the emergency room and she got five stitches in her hand. I had a hard time with the squirting blood, but I managed to stay conscious. When I was younger, I would have fainted. It seems my ability to cope has become better over the years. Thank heaven for bedtime. I feel incredibly guilty about Lorine's hand.

Hope to hear from you soon.

Love,

Charlene

*

In no time at all Charlene had hit the schooling treadmill again. The second class of her master's program started. It was called "Counseling Models and Theories." Charlene anxiously reviewed the schedule and outline to see what was in store. This course was going to be cool. They were going to study some of the main theories of psychology and analyze which methods were best for which circumstances and with which types of people. They would also get into the complexity of issues that arose from culture and gender. The teacher appeared to be gung-ho about giving lots of assignments, so Charlene would be extremely busy the next couple of months. Her next break wouldn't be until the 20th of December.

On the weekends she often saw Dave. He came over and ate dinner with them. The kids, of course, screamed for horsey rides as Charlene cooked. He became a bucking bronco, and the kids timed how long they could hang on.

Charlene loved the fact that he would clean up after the meal as she read to the children. She laughed because she knew he was listening, too, but trying not to be obvious about it. He turned off the water during the good parts. Lorine insisted on him tucking her in. He gladly did so. She was sure taking to him. Dave appeared to enjoy the hubbub of the all the kids. "Oh, they're fun," he'd often say, laughing over their latest thing.

By October, Dave had started inviting Charlene to join him at church meetings when her kids were with their dad. They would attend the meeting then go to his place, where Charlene would whip up a lunch from the skimpy pickings that a bachelor had in his fridge and cupboards. They would laugh and talk the Sunday afternoons away until Charlene would need to leave because her kids were coming home.

> Subject: Baby, Baby
> Date: November 1
> From: "Charlene" <char@CharlenesWeb.net>
> To: "Dave" <allaroundman@yesterday.com>
>
> Hey Babe (Dave)
>
> Does that expression work for you? Or am I showing how young I really am? I'm still thinking about you, you busy man, you. You know, you're a rare man who's been through much and yet is still willing to be vulnerable and show your heart. That's truly impressive.
> The kids asked when you are going to swing them by their feet.
> Looking forward to the light to come.
>
> Love,
>
> Charlene

*

As the days went by and the homework piled up, it became harder and harder for Charlene to keep up with her other e-mailing correspondents. She decided it would be flat out rude if she didn't respond to Richard's e-mail, so she wrote to him about his career. Richard had landed a big job. He'd said he was a jack-of-all-trades, so Charlene told him how Dave was a real estate agent for now and how he also worked in construction and was involved in scientific research before that.

In his last e-mail, Richard wanted to know if Dave had children. She explained that Dave had raised three stepchildren with his first wife and then had three more with her. His youngest was eighteen and still living with him. She also confessed that Dave's two former marriages worried her, and so did the amount of time he spent thinking about concepts instead of doing things.

After she listed all the reasons Dave worried her, she went on to list all the reasons why she worried about herself. Was she on the rebound, or did she have her wits about her? How could she tell? How would she know if she was getting into the wrong relationship? Sometimes she wanted to pull out to protect herself from more hurt. Right now it amazed her how anyone got remarried. She then turned her attention to Richard's love life and asked how things were going in that department.

A few days later, Richard wrote back describing how great his love life was. Charlene was happy and wished she could think about hers instead of being worried that she would flop at presenting her huge project at school.

She also worried because Randal would be there. She felt stupid about last week and didn't know what he was thinking or what he would think of her after she finished her presentation. They'd had fun flirting when he came over to her home with the study group. Charlene had liked being around him. He was kind, funny, and thought a lot about self-improvement, which she adored. A few weeks ago, he had told Sandra he admired how Charlene never gave up and had the courage to face life head-on. How did he know this about her? She couldn't get Randal out of her mind, so she wrote to Judy about it.

Subject: To Be Someone
Date: November 7
From: "Charlene" <char@CharlenesWeb.net>
To: "Judy" <bchcomber@yippee.com>

Dear Judy,

You don't seem to be worried about guys and you're single. How do you do that? Besides school and kids, I think of them a lot. I need your secret. I've been sweating all day over Randal in my class—does he like me? Will I be embarrassed talking to him? How stupid is that! He should be worried if I like him! Ha.

This single stuff has put me right back into my teenage dysfunction. I look at it as an opportunity. I can redo the crazy ways I thought and acted as a kid. Truthfully, so far I don't know if I'm doing much better. But here are my ideas. Tell me what you think.

I've realized I have a bias about being single. I've had it as long as I can remember. If a girl is alone, doesn't have a boyfriend, *doesn't have dates, then she's a nobody. There must be something wrong with her. No one wants her. That's why she's alone. We need somebody to be somebody. We need a significant other to validate us. Not true. So why have I thought that for so very long? Hmm. Maybe this fear of being alone, of being a nobody, kept me in my marriage so long. What do you think?*

Charlene

P.S. I've had someone tell me that I seem insecure in all my flutter. I have this to say to that comment: I've thought about it, and I feel more secure now then ever before. I'm like a kid in a candy shop for the first time. So many choices and I want to try them all.

After sending the e-mail, Charlene felt much better. She glanced at the clock and realized it was time for her to get the children to their dad's. She hurried them, her homework, and presentation material into the car. Once it was all in, she double-checked to make sure that she looked okay then sped out of the driveway.

When she made it to her class, she pulled out her notes for her presentation and was going over them again when Randal came up to her. She glanced up and smiled at him. He looked better today. There was more color in his face and he returned her smile.

"Hi," she said.

He sat down. "Did you know that I will never date anyone who has children?"

What? Charlene thought. She gave a fake laugh. "Why are you saying that?"

He shrugged. "I thought you should know." He then stood and left the room to go get a drink of water.

Charlene watched him go. He had gelled his hair into small, darling curls and his pants were pressed and clean. He looked so… *Oh, ouch,* she thought. She was rejected because she had children? She felt like she had the plague. She wiped at her eyes, not appreciating his message. She would have to present despite what he'd just done. Well, she would just have to show him, and getting an A was as good a way as any. She knew he probably wouldn't pull that. It was good he had shown his true colors now so she would not have to waste any more time on him.

Days like that put her in the mood for the weekend. So when an e-mail came in from her friend Amy, who asked her if she wanted to go to the single dance together on Friday night, she was thrilled. What better way than to go dancing to put her in a better mood? It had been a while since she'd gone, and she needed a reminder of why not to go to them. That was a bad attitude, she chided herself. She did like dancing.

Amy asked about her status with Dave. She answered, *Dave and I aren't dating exclusively, although we don't see other people often. He says he wants me to date others. He said greater commitment will come out of it, if it's meant to be. Otherwise, he'll have been blessed to have loved me and have had me in his life. I know he's e-mailing other people, too. We talk about the other people sometimes. I date and write others to keep my options open. If God wants to lead me to someone, I'm doing my part, and if not, I'm committed to healing and building a new life with my children.*

I don't see him as much as I'd like, but I'm so busy with school and kids, and he's busy with work. There's hardly any time to do anything. We talk on the phone almost every day, if only for a short time.

After writing this, it worried Charlene that Dave might not like her e-mailing others. She mentioned her concern in their next conversation and Dave said he was fine with it and that he himself was e-mailing some interesting people.

Charlene smiled as she thought about the help he had been last night. Charlene was completely lost with Sandra's math, and he had helped her for hours then patiently went over all those terms with her for her quiz. She had joked that he would make a great therapist the way he helped her study her own material too. He'd better watch it or he'd start psychoanalyzing everyone.

*

It was another Sunday without the kids. Charlene decided to use the down time to think about how being single didn't mean a person was nobody. Judy had suggested the assignment. She wrote:

1) There are really cool people who are single, like Judy.
2) A lot of unhealthy people stay in bad relationships and

therefore stay unhealthy. They aren't happy; they are just in a relationship.
3) It takes courage to stand up for yourself and declare that you deserve to be treated better.
4) Many people are single because they refuse to sell out. They know their worth and they aren't settling for less.
5) The only true validation that matters comes from God.
6) Some singles, shocking as it seems, are happy that way and don't want to get married.

After writing the list and cooking dinner for herself, she realized she had fallen into the trap of feeling inadequate because she was single. If she kept that up, the work she'd done to learn to value herself would end up being wasted.

*

The temperature had turned colder, with the hint of winter filling the air. Charlene was continuing on with school pressure, children, and trying not to think about her divorce. Her first "single" Thanksgiving was coming up, and she wasn't sure what she was going to do. She didn't know if she wanted to enjoy the holiday alone with her children or involve Dave since he was included in so many things with her family anyway. She wrote to him about possible plans.

Subject: Hypnotic Power
Date: November 18
From: "Charlene" <char@CharlenesWeb.net>
To: "Dave" <allaroundman@yesterday.com>

Baby Babe, ☺

Hello again. Thursday should work. Let me know what time so I can arrange some things here. Funny, my aunt wants me to come over to her house, which is near where you are going for Thanksgiving. Isn't that where you said you were going? I have the kids. I thought it would be a nice gesture on my part to give Brad the first Christmas. I figured God would take care of me on that day. I haven't decided about Island Park, even though it's one of my favorite places in the whole world. Yellowstone, too. I liked doing a lot of thinking and reflecting on the lake when I was younger. I hesitate to go. I don't want to be on my own with five kids.

As to your comments about love, I do feel a lot from you and your e-mails. It has a hypnotic, drawing power. I want to learn how to give more love to others. I'd like to be able to touch my children with it and heal their shattered hearts. My oldest noticed you love me, but she's not quite so happy. She says that you touch me in ways my X never did, more caring, tender, and caressing. And as I thought about it, she's right. I've been spending the past couple of days working with her and helping her get her feelings out. She's coming along. At first, she associated touch with violence. Today, as I talked to her, she acted upset about me seeing people, but that wasn't the real issue. The real issue is that I get to escape my X and she's still stuck with him every other weekend. She's mad at me for that. I can't blame her. I wish I could get her out of that predicament. All I can do is pray for the angels to protect her and for God to continue to work His miracles. I need to continue to do my part.

I've gone on too long, and I need to get back to the nagging homework. Bye. I look forward to hearing from you.

Charlene

A few hours later, right after Charlene put Lorine on the bus for school, an e-mail arrived from Dave. He suggested that they enjoy Thanksgiving together at Island Park. Charlene was torn about the idea. Traveling with him would make things a lot easier on her, but could he endure the trip with five children?

Dave assured her he could handle it. *That* Charlene would have to see.

CHAPTER 24

On November 22, Charlene stumbled down to her computer before any light had appeared outside and before any rustling from her children. It had become a habit to come see what surprises awaited her on the computer before she launched into the day. Today there was a date request from a guy named Darren she had met on the single's site.

Darren looked average with a few zits sprouting in his face and dull eyes. He was a mailman and had two children. He had one of those kind but boring appearing auras about him. Charlene sighed. She didn't want to go out with him. It was close to Thanksgiving, she had a lot to do to prepare for the holiday and to keep up with the house, children, and her schoolwork. Besides, he didn't look her type.

She thought about this throughout her routine of getting the children off to school. Once she had Lorine and Nathan busy watching an alphabet DVD, she sat at her computer to face her problem. She wrote: *Dear Darren, I'd better stay home and work on my homework. I'd rather be a friend right now. I'm still struggling with the divorce. I wish you the best.* She pushed the send button before she could think about it any further.

Afterwards she stared at the computer screen. What had she done? She didn't want to go with him. She knew it would be a waste of her time and she said, "No." Of course, doubts kept running in her head. *Maybe he would treat me like a queen, and I'm passing up the best thing in the world.* Or, *You're being so judgmental and shallow, Charlene.* Or, *What harm is there in going out with him? You're hurting his feelings.* But today, this time, she stood up for herself. She said, "*No!*" She didn't feel right about going with this person. She sensed it would never work, so she stuck with her instincts.

The people she dated needed to be a good match. She resolved that she wasn't going to be co-dependent anymore and worry about everyone else while ignoring herself. Besides, if she said yes to the guy, she was saying no to her children. She needed to weigh that consideration. It was easier to say no if she thought about it as putting her children first.

*

Charlene said no to Darren, but yes to Dave coming over two days later. He did the dishes while she tucked the kids in bed, which had been their routine. After she worked an hour on her homework with him, she set it aside and curled up in his arms.

He bent down and kissed her on her forehead. "So this Thanksgiving with your aunt, will there be any other family there?"

"No, I don't think so," Charlene said, shifting positions in his lap.

"What about your dad?"

"No."

"Isn't this his sister?"

"Yeah, but they don't speak to each other," Charlene said, sitting up.

"Why don't you call him and invite him?"

Charlene felt her eyes narrow. Was he crazy? He already knew their relationship was strained. She had explained this to him before. Why was he suggesting something like that? "I don't think so."

"That's so weird. I don't get how your family can be so…"

Charlene could no longer hear what he was saying. Her head spun. Dad. Dave wanted her to call her dad. Even the idea of talking to him made her want to retreat. It would be one thing if her father would accept her. If he would put his arm around her and say, "I'm sure proud of you, and I'm sorry for all that you had to go through," but that wasn't what he would do. No, the last time she'd spoken to him he had told her she wasn't good enough. That she was fat and needed to lose weight and she needed to work harder with Brad. Her father didn't believe anything she said about Brad. Brad was a good guy, and he didn't know why she was suddenly accusing him of being abusive.

"You don't understand," she said, pulling a pillow close to her chest.

"You're right, I don't." Dave's eyes flashed distance. "My dad has been dead for fifteen years, and I'd give anything to talk to him. Your dad is alive and you choose to ignore him. Your mom is alive and you have no relationship with her either."

"She's in the metal hospital and will start yelling and screaming if I come up to her."

"Excuses. And you left Brad after ten years. He wants the kids all the time and he takes them everywhere. Him hitting you was certainly not okay, but I can't help but wonder if you aren't contributing to the family relationship problems."

Charlene jumped to her feet. "I thought you understood, but obviously you don't." She ran upstairs to her room. David was not who she thought he was. Why did he want to hurt her all of a sudden? His spots had totally changed color. All this time he had been sympathetic, a good friend. Now he turned on her without warning. How could he suggest she deserved to be abused? How could he suggest the beatings she'd endured from her father had been okay? How could he think she should have stayed with Brad, who had nearly killed her? It probably meant that underneath his nice exterior he was an abuser as well, and his true personality was at last coming out. She buried her head into a pillow, trying to stop the spinning.

A few minutes later, she heard a knock on her bedroom door. "I'm sorry, Charlene. I said some things I shouldn't have. I didn't mean to suggest that you should have put up with abuse if that is how you took it. I am really sorry."

Charlene didn't even want to talk to him. She remained quiet.

"Okay, I guess you want to be on your own."

Charlene cried harder. Dave was leaving her. Running away. Good. She didn't want to be around him anyway.

*

The next day, Charlene was heading for the grocery store with the kids when her phone rang. It was Dave.

"Hi," she said shyly.

He cleared his throat. "Sorry if I hurt your feelings. I think there's been some misunderstanding."

"Okay," Charlene said, pulling the car to the side of the road. It was hard hearing him over the noise of her children.

"I don't get all this family contention. Life is too short. I just don't get it."

"What don't you get?" Charlene asked. "You don't talk to your youngest son. That's family contention."

"Yeah, well I don't have a choice unless I enjoy physical, mental, and spiritual abuse."

Charlene could feel her heart pound, mixing with her anger. He was being such a judgmental jerk. How could she have thought that he got what she was about? That he understood? She pressed her lips together, not knowing what to say and knowing if she did speak it would be mean words that she would regret. She needed to get control and act like a grown-up. "I'm drowning in homework. I don't think going to Idaho together is a good idea." Maybe not seeing each other would be a good thing.

"I didn't call to get into it again," Dave said.

"That's good." Charlene slipped out of the car and stepped onto the sidewalk. The kids continued to laugh and talk.

"I need to pray about this," Dave said.

"I will too."

"So since you aren't going to go to Idaho, are you going to go to the Thanksgiving Eve dance?"

"I was thinking about it," Charlene said.

"Well if you go, have fun."
"I will."

*

Charlene waited until she unloaded the groceries before she e-mailed her friend about going to the dance. Now that Dave was out of the picture, she could go back to enjoying her freedom at the dances.

Unfortunately, the dance turned out to not be as fun as she'd hoped. She danced a lot but none of the guys she spent time with were (a) interesting, or (b) good dancers, so she (c) wished things were different through the entire night and wondered what Dave was doing. Dave and she had often danced the night away, their feet stepping together in unison. She hoped he wasn't with some other girl. She didn't know why she cared, but something twisted inside her and formed a ball of anger when she realized he could be calling someone else, "Darling." That word should only be for her.

Chapter 25

The weather had sunk into the forties for Thanksgiving, but there was a lot of bright sunlight spilling to earth. Charlene, though, didn't see much of the light. Instead, she labored in the kitchen hoping to put on a nice Thanksgiving dinner for her children. Karla and Harold were coming over, bringing their famous homemade apple pie.

The kids loved the food. After they were finished, they wandered outside to play on the trampoline. The dishes still needed to be done, but Charlene smiled and let them go. This was the first holiday without their dad, and she didn't want to expect too much out of them. She wanted them to glide through the day with as much ease as possible.

Karla asked if she was going to shop on the busiest shopping day. "Naw," she said, "Dave and I plan to do that later this month. I'm going to do homework instead and try to get caught up."

"You and Dave do a lot of things together."

"We do," Charlene said, sighing. She couldn't get thoughts of their last fight out of her head. She didn't know what to make of Dave. Was he an egotist who thought men had the right to mistreat women? She hadn't thought that about him before, but she couldn't help but thinking it now because of what he'd said. He seemed so judgmental. That really shook her. He acted like she was so wrong and what he thought she should do was so right. Was he an abuser in disguise?

The phone rang. It was Brad. He had some more angry words to share with her, threats, and a desire to know how Thanksgiving was going for the children.

*

Charlene didn't get as much of her homework done on the day after Thanksgiving as she thought she would. Dave stopped by.

"I thought I'd come over and say hello," he said, standing at her doorstep wearing his long, black leather jacket. He looked nice. "And say I'm sorry. I was completely out of line. I don't know what got into me. I was being a real jerk."

Charlene nodded. He had been.

"I'm sorry. I don't want to ever treat you like that again."

"Then don't," she said.

"I am sorry. I get caught up in things, and I just really can't relate to a lot of things you've been through. It seems so unreal. Not that I don't believe you. It's just amazing that people would treat others like what you've experience."

She watched him, waiting to see what he'd do next.

"I brought flowers." He handed her a dozen red roses. "And a promise to treat you right."

Charlene thought it over. Was this the honeymoon stage? She didn't want to live that life. But then again, Brad had never accepted responsibilities for his misbehaviors. It could be true that abuse would be hard to understand. She decided that she would give him another chance.

"Want to come in?" Charlene asked.

"Sure."

Charlene made hot chocolate as he walked around the room, examining things again. He sure liked to examine things. "How was the dance?" he asked.

Charlene looked at him out of the corner of her eyes. He asked that so casually, like he really didn't care, but it could be that he did care and was trying hard not to show it. Why were men so stingy with showing feelings? Why couldn't they just be manly and say, "Hey, I like you and I hope that you haven't found anyone that you like better than me."

"The dance was kind of boring."

He nodded.

Before he could ask any more about that, she asked how his trip was. He told her about his family gathering and the latest news about people she had never met. It didn't sound like he went girl shopping while he was away. That was good.

When Dave stood to leave, he invited her to go to the Christmas concert with him on the 14th. Charlene couldn't hold back her smile when she accepted his invitation.

David looked into her face and bent to give her a long, rich kiss.

*

Subject: I never knew
Date: December 10
From: "Charlene" <char@CharlenesWeb.net>
To: "Judy" <bchcomber@yippee.com>

Judy,

I never knew I could feel so alive and happy. Who'd have thought? My doctor told me he'd kick my butt if I ever went back to Brad. He was completely amazed by my health. He has never seen me so healthy.

I cleared the walks with a snow blower today. It was a complete celebration. My father wouldn't let me drive any mechanical vehicle because I was a girl, and girls don't do those things. Brad wouldn't let me either. Ha! I showed them both, and I didn't make any huge mistakes like I did when I mowed the lawn. Paige tried to stop me from doing it. "You should let Dad do that for you. He'll take care of you." Never. I can survive by myself. I can thrive. I'm dependent on no one but God.

Dave came over and performed gymnastic tricks on a mattress in the basement. The kids followed his lead, and I did homework. They got into the silliest contest. I laughed. The kids have a lot of fun with Dave.

Brad still scares me. With his irrational behavior, there's no telling what he'll do. I'm not safe, but I'll not worry about it. God will help me.

Charlene

*

By the time the Christmas concert came around, Charlene needed the break. Tension had been growing. There was the pressure of getting ready for Christmas even though she wasn't going to have her children, the mounting schoolwork, and Brad becoming more intense and angry every time they had an exchange. The notes of Handel at the concert melted away her tension and let her spirit soar. In the middle of the climax of a one of the pieces, Dave reached over and pulled her to him. Charlene looked up at him. He bent and kissed her then smiled. She smiled too, nestled her head on his strong chest, and continued to let the music sweep her away.

At the end of the date, Dave asked her to go see his favorite play of all time, *A Christmas Carol*, or the "Scrooge re-born story" as Dave put it. Charlene couldn't wait. Thinking of going to that would help her to be able to press on, but it didn't stop her from having a nightmare that night.

She was in a car with Brad. They were on a family vacation. He was being abusive. She and the kids were scared. They finally stopped for a break. Charlene called her minister. He said, "If I were you, I would run straight down that road as hard and as fast as I could."

"Yeah, but I have five kids," she said. "I can't do that or I would."

"That's the kicker," he said.

She was depressed, scared, not wanting to get back into the car. Lorine was with her. They wandered into a grove of trees. She lay down with Lorine, trying to hide her, protect her. He was coming. They weren't safe. There was nowhere to go. She woke up praying.

That hadn't stopped her stomach from knotting or her heart pounding. She struggled to breathe.

What was she to do with this unsettled dread? Brad had controlled her for over ten years. Her father before him. Brad was capable of killing her. In the past, his rage knew no bounds.

Charlene grabbed the phone and tucked it up against her cheek. That way if Brad tried anything, she could call the cops immediately. She knew she was probably having a post-traumatic stress disorder reaction. She knew that after one left a situation, the fear that was suppressed would find ways to come out. That's all it was, she reminded herself. But that reminder didn't stop her from thinking that it sure didn't feel like a reaction. The dark and the fear seemed to be lasting forever.

*

Subject: I'm Gambling
Date: December 23
From: "Charlene" <char@CharlenesWeb.net>
To: "Dave" <allaroundman@yesterday.com>

Dear Dave,

I'm going to take another risk and tell you what's going on with me. I'm having struggles. I don't know if you know it or not, but I have attachment problems. Because my father was mean and not a person a child would choose to bond with, I didn't bond to him, and I had a difficult time bonding with my mom as well. As a result I have developed attachment problems. I'm trying to overcome them, and I know the only way I can truly become healed is through a relationship with someone who patiently helps me through it. Trust is a key foundational issue. A lot to ask of anyone, I know.

In psychology, they did an experiment called "The Still Face Game." They had a mother smiling and interacting with her three-month-old child. They videotaped each expression of the child and studied it. When the mother was attentive, the child was happy and responsive. Then they had the mother do a straight face. No matter what the child did the mother showed no emotion. The child would continuously try for interaction with the par-

ent but would get none. After the fourth or so attempt to engage the mother, the child would have extreme reactions, painful looks, desperation, and anxiety. The child would try to wrestle out of his seat and was hard to settle down. Eventually the child would sink into depression. (I wonder if those children are now in therapy—or prison! ☺

I got a lot of those straight faces as a child. This Saturday I was extremely vulnerable to you, and I felt like I really opened up and took risks, which I'm glad I did. You were so tender with me and my children, something I think I only experienced with one other person, a boy in high school. It brought up my issues and what I lacked with my dad. I rejoice in having the experience with you, but now that I haven't heard your voice or seen you for so long, my abandonment issues are rising. I'm not sure what to do with them. I don't want to be manipulative or clingy, and I don't want to run away. So I thought I'd shoot straight and tell you about it. I'm scared. I think I love you, and I don't know what to do.

Charlene

After hitting the send button, Charlene got up to check on the kids. This e-mail stuff could sure get her in a lot of trouble. Why did she have to go blab all her deep problems? She knew that if they were ever going to have a relationship and work out, he had to know. It would only be best if he found out before they got involved and made any commitments. But it was so embarrassing. Would he reject her?

She changed the laundry, helped the kids with their homework questions, then read to them and put them to bed. She could stand the tension inside no longer. She needed to talk to someone about what she had done. There was only one person who would even understand and who she knew wouldn't beat her up for taking such a risk. She e-mailed Judy.

Subject: Call me a sucker
Date: December 23
From: "Charlene" <char@CharlenesWeb.net>
To: "Judy" <bchcomber@yippee.com>

Judy,

I wrote Dave one of the most risky letters I could ever write. I included a copy of it in this e-mail for you to see. I can't believe what I told him. I think I'm really falling for this guy, but then he goes silent on me. I can't stand it. No other guy I have ever dated has ever done that to me. Do you think he's playing me?

I sent the e-mail to him about three hours ago. It's almost ten thirty here. He's probably not going to respond. I think I made a big fool of myself. I should go to bed and bury my head. I can't believe I told him those things.

Oh, that's him calling on the phone. Ah, I had better answer it. I don't know what to say.

Charlene

"Hello?"

"Hi, sweetheart, how are you?"

"Fine," Charlene said, tucking her feet behind her as she sat on the couch.

"I got your e-mail."

"You did?" Charlene knew that was a stupid thing to say, but with her heart thumping so loudly it felt like it was in her throat, and heat rushing through her as she blushed thinking about what she had written, she had no idea what else to say.

"I thought you would be okay if I called you so late."

"It's fine," Charlene said. "I was up."

"Do you mind expanding on your feelings?"

"What do you want me to say?" Charlene asked.

"Why you are so upset that you haven't heard from me for one? Why does it matter to you so much?"

"Okay," Charlene said. She thought about hanging up the phone, but running from this wouldn't get her anywhere. "Why don't you tell me what you are thinking and feeling?"

"You go first."

He spoke so absolutely Charlene knew she didn't have a choice. She was going to have to risk it. "I think I'm falling for you. We are at the point where I can back out right now and be okay, but if we pursue this relationship any further, I could get hurt." Charlene took a deep breath while she waited for him to reassure her. To tell her that it would be okay because he was falling for her too, that he loved her and there wasn't anyone else he wanted to be with. She was the one he'd been waiting for.

"Well, there're always risks in life," he said.

Charlene waited for him to say more and he didn't. Her stomach immediately felt ill. She couldn't believe he had said that. "Aren't you going to say more?" she finally asked, frustrated that he wasn't speaking.

"What else do you want me to say?" he asked, laughing.

He was enjoying this. "What do you feel?" Charlene asked.

"I'm going to have to go. I have to get this contract done tonight."

"Oh, no you don't," she said, as though she was speaking to one of her kids who was trying to do something that they knew was wrong. "You're not getting off that easy. I put myself on the line. I want to know what you are thinking."

"But—"

"Dave, please tell me."

It grew silent on the other end. Charlene could hear the ticking of her clock. She waited. She was not going to speak until he said something even if it killed her. She took a deep breath, trying to gain more patience as she waited. Finally he said, "I'm growing in love with you too."

Charlene smiled. He had said it. "Geez. You sure like to make me suffer."

He laughed. "You can't expect me to admit stuff like that all the time. That's hard."

When Charlene hung up the phone, she hoped that by risking her soul to tell him what his silence did to her would help him resist doing it again.

*

For the first Christmas after the divorce, and without her children, Charlene hung out with Dave. They met early and fed the homeless at a shelter. Charlene hadn't done that before, and she was a bit scared, but when she got over the smell and the look of some of the people, she was glad she'd done it. Of course, Dave joked with her and the people they were feeding the entire time, so it went fast.

As a Christmas gift, Charlene gave Dave the ingredients to make his favorite smoothie. He loved it when she made it for him. She thought if she got him everything he needed, he could make it himself. He thought that when Charlene came to visit him at his house she could make it for him. He was very traditional in some ways. He gave her balloons, cards, and some purified water that held the balloons down. They parted with a nice long Christmas kiss. Karla called to see how she was doing. She had decided to ditch her mother and go watch a chick flick—a romance—with Charlene. They spent the time laughing in the almost completely empty theater.

*

Charlene had hoped her vulnerability in the e-mail explaining that silence ripped into her would fix her communication problems with Dave. That hope was crushed when days and days went by after Christmas without Dave e-mailing, calling, or coming over.

Charlene had hoped he would want to take her out for a night on the town on New Years, but she heard nothing from him. Remembering her promise to herself, she planned to go to the big single's dance with friends. Maybe that was what Dave was planning on doing and why he wasn't calling.

The dance Charlene and her friend picked ended up being the Old-Timers one. The next youngest person besides her and Amy was sixty-five! It wasn't a complete waste, though. Charlene liked talking to people and hearing their stories. She flattered herself that in some small way she was helping them, making their loads lighter while developing her own therapy skills.

Tired, she struggled into her house and over to her computer to find an e-mail from Dave. He wrote that he'd been trying to reach her. He'd be on his computer studying, so if she wanted to write him back they could hook up. He also asked if she would go to the movies with him on Friday.

When Charlene read the week-in-advance invitation, she smiled. Her not being available at his beck and call was teaching him to plan ahead.

*

Charlene didn't know what woke her up at 4:30 a.m. or why she was compelled to look out her window, but she did. There, in a small, compact gray car, was someone sitting outside of her house. She kept glancing out her window, watching a person in shadows in the car. It appeared that the person was scoping her house, but she couldn't be sure. It was too dark.

Charlene bit her lip and wondered what she could do about it. She grabbed a phone and her blanket, which she wrapped herself in, and watched. The car stayed until seven in the morning, engine running, then drove away.

The next several mornings proved to her that someone was watching her house. Who was it? Did Brad rent a car so he could come and spy on her? Was he bemoaning what he didn't have by coming in the early morning because he couldn't sleep? Unfortunately it was too dark to see the license plate number, but somehow she knew that it was Brad, still unable to let go of her.

Charlene decided that although she didn't like it, she would ignore it and hope it went away. Her class was starting up again, and she needed to turn her focus to something she could control. This semester they were studying theory. Paying attention to her studies and the kids became increasingly difficult, however. Brad called daily, most days three to five times.

"Why are you calling?" Charlene snapped at him after his sixth call one day.

"What do you mean?" he asked, sounding surprised.

"What do you want?"

"What are you doing right now?"

"Brad, why does that matter?"

"I thought I'd let you know that I'm not going to wait for you any longer."

Charlene tried to quickly determine what game he was playing and how to best respond. "Okay," she said.

"You're making a big mistake. You're destroying our family. I don't worry about you now, but I worry that a year from now you're going to wake up and realize that you made a big mistake. I heard that a lot of divorced people live to regret what they did."

"Thanks for your concern," Charlene said, not knowing what to do with another one of his desperate attempts to get back together. She knew that she wouldn't regret this in a year. She might regret not leaving him earlier.

She needed to stop answering his calls. That was how he controlled her. She went outside to enjoy the sun that was spilling forth. She wanted to capture it and put it into a box to bring out when things were dismal.

Taking a deep breath, she reflected on her professor's compliment in her last class. "You have a natural knack for understanding." She had never heard her professor compliment anyone, so she figured he must have meant it. That eased Charlene's worries about making a mistake in doing all this schooling. If she was a natural, then surely she could get a job after all this. She hoped. It was at least a good sign.

*

By mid-January, Charlene was growing restless from all the gray weather, the work, kids, and everything else. She decided the best way to add spice would be to get on another singles' site and see what adventure lay in store there.

She immediately received an e-mail after posting. A young man said he could understand why she needed to get married, having so many children and all. Like she was some desperate woman waiting to be saved.

Need to get married! Charlene wanted to scream. She didn't need to get married. Then the fellow asked her to rate her spirituality by a checklist. Oh, brother. She couldn't resist giving the presumptuous fellow a piece of her mind. She wrote him:

Dear Jim,

I get a lot of e-mails asking strange questions, but you're the first one to ask what kind of husband I want. You're also the first to try to rate my spirituality with a "to do" list, right off the top.

You want to know what kind of "hubby" I want and if I read the Bible? Let me answer. I'd like an extremely smart, fearless man who knows how to love a woman and how to lead like Christ. I would like someone who's experienced with childrearing and who isn't afraid of children. It would also be nice if he could avoid being yanked around by them.

I want someone who is a Truth Seeker and who isn't afraid to have emotions and to admit to them. I want someone who's well-educated in the language of communication and who knows how to hang in there when life gets tough. I want someone who isn't afraid of a strong, educated woman and who doesn't feel threatened by her; someone who respects women and can, and often does, take counsel from them. I want someone who can handle controversy and who will stay true to his beliefs and to his lady. I want someone who lives his life by principle and has unshakable faith. Someone with maturity and experience and who isn't afraid of the reality of life and hard issues. Someone who isn't afraid to question, and someone who isn't afraid of thinking outside the box. Someone who isn't afraid that I have a crazy X-husband who stalks me and will always, to one degree or another, be in my life. Above all, I want someone who's through and through respectful and full of love.

Outward symbols can mean nothing. It's the inner conversion that's important.

Misty

*

It was Saturday. A day full of homework and housework, Charlene decided as she slipped into her sweats. She was halfway through cleaning her kitchen floor that looked like her children had thrown a New Year's Eve graffiti of crumbs all over when the doorbell rang. It was her neighbor, Alan. He'd stopped by apparently to hang out. Then Bill stopped by too and so did Dave.

Charlene looked between the men who were stiltedly talking to each other. What had happened? Oh well, if these guys had problems with each other it was their own problem. She had commitments to no one. Opening up her fridge, she said, "Anyone want a sandwich?" She smiled to herself. She might as well enjoy this.

That night she went to another dance. She was becoming so much more assertive there. "No thanks." "What? Go out? Not until I get to know you better. A girl's got to keep herself safe, you know." She actually enjoyed going now. She did note that there were a lot of men who looked only at the exterior, thinking that was all they needed. Some of these men appeared to have no concept of what it meant to have children when they proposed marriage—to a woman they hardly knew!

One guy said, "You look like my image of the perfect woman, so let's get married."

Other men had fear in their eyes if they danced more than two songs with her. "Commitment fear," her girlfriends complained. "When will they get over it?"

She danced with Charles. He was old enough to be her father but she liked talking to him. They chatted about the silliness in the singles' world. He said, "There needs to be more stability in all areas of our lives."

After coming in from a breathless dance spin, Charlene asked, "What does stability really mean? What does it look like? Is it not thinking you're going to die if you don't get married? I think unstable and unhealthy are traits that are easier to recognize."

Charles smiled. "Let's point out unhealthy."

Charlene was ready to take that on. "Okay, unhealthy is when people go to dances like this and get depressed when the dance is over and they haven't met *the one*. It's people who, after just meeting, start making out on the dance floor or in the parking lot. It's the ones who commit to someone when they have nothing in common.

It's those who change with the wind and have no center they can identify as themselves."

Charles laughed. "You do have it figured out. So how do you know when you're off balance?"

"Easy," Charlene said, putting a little distance between them so she could follow the music, which had changed from slow to fast. She started to rock out to the drums. Once she got her pattern down, she said, "One thing I've learned for sure is everyone has their own opinion, and they aren't the least bit shy about voicing it. For example, my best friend keeps harping about 'establishing a friendship' first. Friendship! It sounds good and that's smart, but is friendship enough?"

"Why don't you think that would be enough?" Charles asked.

Charlene spun around to the music. She leaned toward him so he could hear her over the beat. "I'm a romantic. I want to have passion along with friendship. But I don't want to meet someone who sweeps me off my feet to the point I'm not thinking rationally. My affection has to be earned and the person has to be trustworthy to get it."

"A romantic, huh?" Charles raised his eyebrows. "I'd better watch out."

Chapter 26

Subject: Hi, Jonathan
Date: January 28
From: "Charlene" <char@CharlenesWeb.net>
To: "Jonathan" <skipper@hotday.com>

Jonathan,

I'm sorry, but I don't think we matched very well together, so I'll have to pass on another date. Have fun at the game tonight.

Charlene

*

February had arrived and so had Charlene's third class in her master's program. Next on the agenda was Social and Multicultural Foundation. She had thought they had covered a lot of that last semester, but it looked like they were going into more depth on how to counsel to a variety of cultures, beliefs, and family systems.

Her ex was still calling. His latest reasons were to give her suggestions. "You need to work on…for your new husband."

The statement was so loaded with "you're not enough." Would there ever be a time in her life when people like parents, exes, and critical bystanders would not tear her down? What vibe was she putting out that caused others to treat her like that? There was a philosophy she had learned that said people teach others how to treat them. She wondered what she was doing or not doing? And what flaws was she instilling in her children?

Judy wrote her about it. She said that Charlene had fallen into the victim trap. She had been a victim for so long she could not expect herself to suddenly stop thinking that way. Charlene hoped someday she would be the strong woman she aspired to be and not let people stomp all over her.

Subject: I've been a stranger
Date: February 3
From: "Charlene" <char@CharlenesWeb.net>
To: "Richard" <richardb@ripples.com>

Richard,

I'm sorry I haven't responded to you in a long time. I didn't mean to put you off. I hope all finds you well. Dave is a very kind, gentle man who treats me like a queen. He's intelligent and challenges me intellectually, which I love. But now everything is starting to scare me. I have developed feelings for him, and he says he's willing to take on my five children. He's mature and has an understanding of what life with five young children means. He has excellent communication skills, and we seem to be able to work through things smoothly. He's sincerely religious. We have talked many hours about relationships. It feels natural and right to be with him.

So what's the problem? It's a little more than jitters. I've learned at school that people often marry what feels right and natural. They're trying to fix the damage done in their childhood. I definitely did that in my first marriage. I don't want to do it again. He seems charming, but my X did/does, too. I think I might be making the same mistake instead of focusing on healing myself. My heart tells me, "This relationship is good, really good. I may never be loved like this again. Go for it." My head tells me to run. I fear that if I don't get out of this relationship, I will be making a big mistake. It's okay and understandable to goof up and marry wrong once. It's not okay to do it the second time, especially because of my children.

That would mean that something was seriously wrong with me. Pray for me.

How's your dating life? Hope to hear from you soon.

Charlene

*

Some days just waking up seemed to cause attitude and grouchiness. Charlene found this to be the case one early February morning. She called her therapist and made an appointment to find out what was afflicting her.

Charlene was told by her therapist that she was having open-heart surgery, and no one would expect her to jump back into life full force. She needed to take time to care for herself. Charlene was told to work on being more grounded so she wouldn't take people's comments so personally.

"My friend Judy is getting foot surgery," she told Cindy. "She had a bunion that needs to be removed. She signed up for a trial research program where she has to call in every hour and report how she feels in order to get the surgery paid for. I guess they have to tell how the drug is working." Charlene shifted on the couch. "I wonder if there is a trial program to see if I could get my ex-husband removed, and I could call in every hour to tell them how I feel."

"That would be nice," her therapist said. "But I doubt it will be that easy for you."

"Darn."

*

Two days before Valentine's, Dave called Charlene. "Will you go to dinner and a dance on Valentine's with me?"

Charlene beamed. "Of course."

That night turned out to be a dream. Charlene decided she could stay in Dave's arms forever. They danced all night in sync.

Once he pushed her from him. "If you want to dance with other guys, feel free. I don't want you to feel obligated to have to stay with me all night. I know you have a lot of friends here."

Charlene looked at him, not sure what he meant. Why had he said that? Was he trying to get rid of her so he could go dance with some other women? Was he tired of being with her?

"I want to stay here with you," she said, honestly, not knowing if he would take that as entrapment. But why would you ask someone to be with you on Valentine's then ditch them to be with other women? She looked around the dance floor, wondering who it was he wanted to be with. Was she not good enough?

"Good, because that's what I wanted. I only didn't want you to feel obligated."

After giving Dave a long and rich kiss good night, Charlene went in her house to find the babysitter.

The sitter looked up from the TV, asked about Charlene's night then said, "Brad came over at 8:30 to give the kids their Valentines. The kids reported Brad had gone out on a date and took her to your spot in Park City, but he couldn't stop thinking of you, so he took his date home."

Charlene wondered why he would take someone to their old spot. That didn't seem wise.

The next morning she woke to the phone. "Hello."

"How was your date?" Brad asked.

Charlene rolled over to lie flat on her bed. "Fine, and yours?"

He said the same thing the babysitter had said then ended it with, "I'm not ready to date yet."

"You know it's not appropriate to talk about your dating relationships with the kids."

"They like to hear what's going on with their dad."

"Brad, why did you tell the kids last week that you wouldn't buy them something because you pay their mother child support?"

"It's true. I pay you plenty."

Grrr. "I can't buy them everything they want. I have to be careful since I'm paying for graduate school and everything."

"Whatever," he said.

After hanging up, to mentally shift from the bad mood Brad had created, Charlene listed on paper the things Dave had told her about how she blessed his life.

1. He appreciates that I don't always agree with him, and that I'm comfortable about voicing it. That's huge. He doesn't want a chameleon. Authenticity is big with him.
2. He explained he's not pushing the relationship because he's sensitive about being pushy and wants to give me space to think and feel what I want. He knows I haven't had that much freedom to choose in my life.
3. He likes the sense of family and being involved in peoples' lives and having the chance to make a difference, rather than looking after just himself and his older daughter.
4. By being with me, he's learning how to love better.
5. He enjoys my companionship.
6. He enjoys my unique personality combined with humor and charm and my ability to deal with genuine issues. He finds this complimentary to his own issues and personality.

*

Subject: Single Misery
Date: February 18
From: "Charlene" <char@CharlenesWeb.net>
To: "Judy" <bchcomber@yippee.com>

Judy,

I'm lonely, and I feel sad. I'm missing the intimacy I used to have with Brad. We were together so many years that I was used to it. I have to remind myself of all the hell I've gone through. I wish Brad could've been his "kind" self all the time or at least not abusive, but he couldn't. I wish I could be married to my children's natural father and we could raise our children as a team. That's the way it's supposed to be. Do people who have that realize how lucky they are?

A friend told me that my X husband was perfect. What a thing to say to an X-wife! I couldn't believe it.

I want to hear how the latest surgery went. Are you okay? Okay enough to listen to me whine on e-mail? If so, read on, if not, wait till later. I'm doing fine. I have so many options. I don't have much time to think about this subject with school and all, but Dave and I have talked about whether we would suit each other if we considered marriage.

No, Randal is not an option. He keeps reappearing in my life with the study groups and such. He's not capable of any relationship right now, too hurt and injured, and yet I sense there's still an attraction there.

My children need help and are suffering. So many things to sort out. My oldest daughter doesn't like me getting close to Dave—not one bit. I am making great efforts to give her extra time and attention to help our relationship. With dating, some people advise me to go slow and others to speed up. I keep asking myself, is Dave really safe, or is he pretending? Is he different than my X? I guess it'll take time to know if he'd treat me well.

I do fear I'm going to rush into another marriage—then rush right back out of one. I want to be with Dave, spend time with him, be held by him, and kiss him. Perhaps I have gotten this whole hormone thing mixed up with love.

Oh, the e-mail he sent me on Sunday! He told me he loves me. How could I not fall for him? He's driven, heaven bound, loves God, affectionate, tender, and respectful. I feel comfortable with him, praised and adored. He sees me for who I am. Could I find any of this elsewhere?

Charlene

*

"Mom, I don't want to go with him."

"I know, dear, but he's your dad," Charlene said.

"He's over an hour late, and he just wants to punish me 'cause I told him he was wrong." Sandra's face was drawn in, tight and determined.

Charlene sighed, looking out the window. When was Brad going to get here? Sandra would keep up her protests until he did.

"Mom, I hate it over there. You can't make me go."

Charlene had been told that if she didn't make her children go on their visits with their dad she could be thrown in prison. She was sure Brad would jump at that chance. She finished folding the towel in her hand and started toward the stairs to put it away. She had no idea how to answer her daughter. She wasn't supposed to get into it according to the special master, the person who had the authority of the courts to manage Brad's and her conflicts, but Sandra wasn't one of those children you put off.

In Paige's room, Charlene peered out the window and saw her ex pull in. A few minutes later, Cameron came up to her. "Mom, Dad wants to talk to you."

Her shoulders sunk with the burden of the news. "Okay."

When she greeted him at her front step, he dove into her, "Why aren't you keeping Sandra off of sugar? I said she couldn't have any for a week for calling me a jerk."

"That was at your house," Charlene said, crossing her arms. "I don't feel right enforcing your punishments. I will punish her over here for what she does over here and you can punish her over there for what she does there."

"What are you telling me? That you aren't going to support me? Are you saying it is all right for her to put her father down?"

Charlene stepped back from him. "I'm not telling you that…" On they went into the same old argument. It only changed when Charlene said, "Sandra has asked if she could come home earlier."

Brad turned to his daughter and said, "If you behave yourself, you can stay with me."

Ouch, Charlene thought, looking at the hurt covering her daughter's face. Brad was basically saying, "If you are good, I want you. If not, forget it."

"How can you say that to her?" Charlene asked, knowing that the anger she felt was coming out in her voice.

"Whatever, Char." His eyes narrowed. "Come on, kids, get in the car."

When he had driven away, Charlene shook her arms as though she could shake off the negativity that just happened. Luckily, she was going up to Dave's tonight. She often felt peace with him. He would make it better for her. If only there was something she could do for her daughter. Sandra's therapist had said there really wasn't anything.

Lately Dave and she had talked a lot about trust. Dave would probably want to discuss that again. Charlene wanted to trust him. She knew she had too many betrayals in her past to just be able to wish it and have it come true, although she was willing to work through her fear and doubt to embrace a higher light.

Dave did want to talk about trust. He sat her down on his couch in the living room. "I fear that you aren't spiritual enough. If you were, you wouldn't be so fearful."

Charlene felt her body tense. He couldn't really be saying that. Not spiritual enough? How dare he? She tried to live her whole life under God's will. That didn't mean she didn't have a lot of fear to deal with because people like Brad had tried to kill her. "What? Is my fear supposed to magically go away because I believe in God? Will that magically erase all the abuse and wrong that has happened to me? Does it mean I don't believe because I'm still afraid? How can you say that?"

Charlene glared at him, daring him to answer. He was clearly in the wrong on this one, and he needed to apologize. Instead, he said nothing. He couldn't even give her the courtesy of an answer. It was like he wasn't even acknowledging that she existed. "Aren't you going to apologize?" she asked.

"For what?"

"What do you mean for what? For calling me not spiritual."

"Sorry I called you not spiritual. Does that solve anything?"

He didn't mean a word he was saying. How dare he think those things about her? She'd thought he loved her. She'd thought he understood her. Why had she been so dumb? "I love you, Dave, but I'm not all wrong. I can't continue to see someone who can't clearly acknowledge my value and is always questioning it."

He stood. "You can't accept the truth. You can't see yourself. You always have to turn issues around to be about you personally. There is a need for principles and alignment to faith to prevail. You don't know how to do that." He left the room.

Charlene heard the noise of the television. She waited for him to come back and ask for forgiveness—he was clearly in the wrong.

He never did. She went into his living room and looked at him. He asked if she wanted to watch a show with him. It seemed he didn't want to deal with their conflict or answer for his divisive remarks. This wasn't acceptable. In a calm cool tone, she said, "Do you think we need a break from each other?"

Dave looked at her for a moment. "Okay. Do you want to go home now?"

Shocked that he'd said "okay," so easily, she said, "Yes."

He courteously but coolly escorted her to her car.

The next day she e-mailed him, too angry to want to call.

Subject: Things to Consider
Date: February 21
From: "Charlene" <char@CharlenesWeb.net>
To: "Dave" <allaroundman@yesterday.com>

Dave,

I feel bad that we got in a fight last night. I have to admit I find it surprising when everything seemed to be going so great. After reflecting, here's how I see things. I feel like neither one of us knows the other well enough. I don't know you well enough to have faith in your kindness and goodness, and you don't know me well enough to know I have faith in God. Perhaps with time this trust could be built.

As far as "there are some things that need attention," here's what I have to say. I will not change the essence of who I am for anyone. But if what needs correcting will make me a better person and more true to who I am, then I am willing to consider change. In order for me to be in a relationship, it must be a two-way street. It would not be a relationship if I were the only one willing to change. I know you have been willing to look at what I had to say and to admit a mistake when you saw yourself in error in the past. This gives me hope that you'll do it again. If partnership is not what you are looking for, then we don't belong together.

Charlene

It was noon when Dave called. "I'm sorry, Charlene," he said, "but you're too wishy-washy. I can't live like that."

"I just got divorced, less than a year ago. How am I supposed to know what's going on for me? I'm still in the middle of the grieving process."

"You have too much fear, Charlene. You let that rule you."

"Oh, I'm sorry that I don't bury my head to make everything roses when it's not. I'm a realist and can't do anything but say things the way they really are. Sorry you can't accept the truth."

"Whatever," he said, his voice sounding tired and deflated.

"Maybe we shouldn't see each other," Charlene said. "I'm sick of your self-righteousness. I'm sick of you not seeing the virtues I clearly have. All this sounds too familiar. I'm sorry. I wish you the best."

When they hung up, Charlene immediately wrote her friend about it. *I'm relieved we aren't together. Okay, I'm done venting. Dave really pushes my buttons when he acts like he thinks he knows everything. He has a lot of great qualities. I learned a lot from him and was loved by him. I enjoyed his company. He caused me to dive into myself more. He caused me to think, think hard, to learn about myself and gain more understanding. I felt loved and appreciated. Those are all nice things to experience. I feel like I contributed to his life and did what I was supposed to in that relationship. I'm sure I caused him to stop and think. Perhaps the next guy I get involved with will have his good qualities and others I desire (my list is growing).*

When the weekend arrived, Charlene had to talk about the break-up, so she called Judy even though it was going to cost money. When Judy confirmed it seemed the right thing to do and that Dave seemed very arrogant, and that Charlene wouldn't want to be involved with that, Charlene felt better. She even danced around the house singing "Breaking Up Is Hard To Do."

But the dancing didn't get her to stop thinking about Dave's accusation that she lived in her fears. He was right. She was scared. Scared about dating and getting into new relationships—scared about getting her heart broken—but the thing Dave couldn't know was that if her heart did break, the Lord would take care of her. What Dave also didn't know was Charlene was grateful to now focus her spare time on her kids. The first thing she did when they got home from school was take them to the park. She'd cooked them a big meal after they returned and read to them until they feel asleep. It was good to just focus on them. She was going to do more of that.

*

Subject: *Breakup Blues*
Date: *March 5*
From: *"Charlene"* <char@CharlenesWeb.net>
To: *"Judy"* <bchcomber@yippee.com>

Judy,

Okay, maybe you're right and I did have something to do with the breakup. I started seeing that he was taking time away from what I really should be doing—loving my children, school, work, healing, and exploring the single life. Plus, I worry about what involvement with him would do to my children. My oldest is much happier now that Dave and I are no longer seeing each other. I think she needs me to be uncommitted for now, although Dave is the type of man she needs to have around. It would be good for her to be exposed to someone who consciously lives his religion and is kind. My Lorine is flipping and won't stop crying and screaming over not seeing him any more. She wanted to know if she could still see him even if I didn't. I didn't answer. I don't want to talk to Dave about that. It would be sticky.

When the other kids realized they wouldn't be seeing Dave anymore, they joined in with Lorine's tears. Lorine became so bad I had to take her to therapy to help her cope. I've decided I'm not going to let any more boyfriends meet my children unless we're getting serious. It's too hard on them. I do want to evaluate the guy's parenting skills and their chemistry with my children. Those are all big issues for me, but I don't want my children to grow attached and feel abandoned if it doesn't work out. It's a hard thing to know the right way of going about it.

I'm so new at this. I can't commit yet. That would be wrong. If I settled down after only seriously dating one person, will I regret not having more experience? Would I wonder if I made the right decision? Would I regret giving up my freedom? Would I be disappointed that I didn't prove to myself I could make it on my own?

I need time to heal my wounds, and I don't want to bring that into a marriage. I don't want to marry out of a co-dependent need that I have yet to resolve. I want to marry on a healthier premise. I can't continue to date Dave and not get married. He's not up for that. Besides, even if he was willing to wait, there's no guarantee I would ever feel right about marrying him. I don't want to hurt him.

If I blindly overlook all the problems I have with Dave, I'd be making the same mistake I made with Brad. I don't want that end result. So overall, it is best to let him go.

I've decided I'm going to slow down and heal myself, and if I just relax for a long time, that's all right. That's what people do when someone dies. Why should I be hard on myself or expect more? I need the time, and I should go easy on myself. I'll keep up with school, but I won't put so much pressure on myself about the other stuff. Maybe when I don't have the kids on Sundays I will do absolutely nothing. I long for it, yet guilt gets the best of me. I need to figure out what is controlling me and who I am, give myself time to live at a slower speed. That will be hard, but how else am I going to become rooted in who I am and where I want to go? I need to get rid of my hurry and impatience and allow the tears, sorrow, and regret. I need to go through the cycle several times and not put time constraints on my healing journey. This would make the trip a whole lot more comfortable. I feel more at ease about it.

Lately I've been avoiding interactions with Brad. Keeping them simple.

Charlene

P.S. Can you believe in a month, I'll have been divorced for a year? Wow, time has gone by.

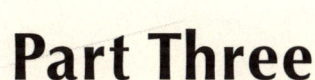

Part Three

Chapter 27

Subject: It's for good.
Date: April 13
From: "Charlene" <char@CharlenesWeb.net>
To: "Judy" <bchcomber@yippee.com>

Yes, Judy, Dave and I are still broken up. It's for good. We might as well face the fact that it isn't going to work, and move on. That's what I told him when he called and asked if we wanted to see if we could make it work. I also said that I just wasn't ready for a relationship. I want time to be on my own and to focus on the children. They need to do more healing.

I'm not as cold as I sound. I did cry about it once, okay maybe twice when I was missing his hugs, but I figure I'm in God's hands. I'm at peace. He's blessing me. Besides, my new class at school is a killer—Legal and Ethical Issues. It's very detailed, technical, and boring, but I can see how this stuff could be important in a practice, so I'm paying close attention and learning how the government is run. Besides focusing on school, I'm learning to adjust to a slower pace of life. You know, one without a husband, boyfriend, or lots of dates—one filled with homework and paying extra attention to the kids. Until I have adjusted to my situation, I'm clearly not ready to get into another serious relationship. Of course, I have to ask the question, "Why should I learn to slow down when I'm waiting for things to speed up again?" Maybe I haven't caught the whole vision of a healthy lifestyle. Of course I haven't. What am I thinking? I'm new at being single, and I'm sure that other new singles never catch the whole vision starting out. I need to develop patience.

Just a minute, I'm not being fair to myself. I do see benefits in slowing down. I'm doing more of what I like to do. I'm playing with my kids—tag, Connect Four, puzzles, reading books with them, working harder on helping them grasp new concepts in their homework, and taking time to watch shows with them.

Charlene

Judy wrote back quickly. One statement in her e-mail stuck with Charlene. *I decided that I may never get remarried. I didn't want to spend my whole life waiting for "when I get married." I choose to live my life now and stop waiting for "when."*

Each morning, as Charlene got dressed, ready for the day, she told herself that she was the creator of her future. She could have and be what she wanted. She only had to set her mind to it.

*

"I need to see the kids more."

"You already have them almost half the time." Charlene's stomach tightened. Why did Brad always have to threaten that? Why couldn't he just leave her alone? She knew it was probably an idle threat, but what if he actually did take her to court for the kids?

"I need them more. I don't do well without them. I can't stand it. I was talking to Nathan about it, and he says he would like to go to more sports games with me. He says he misses doing that with me. Paige said she dreams of becoming a professional golfer. She wants me to take her out to the course more often so she can reach her dreams. Nathan said he cries because he misses me…"

The knot in her stomach twisted as Brad went through the children and all the fun things he had promised if only their mom would let them. A total setup again. He was forcing her to fight Disneyland Dad. This was what caused the Disneyland Parent wars. She looked past him at the cars that were speeding by on the street. It was too bad she wasn't on the phone. If she was on the phone, she could hang up on him and not have to listen to this endless rattle of nonsense.

"Charlene," his voice spoke with command.

She looked back at him.

"So will you give them to me more?"

She couldn't argue that the kids wouldn't like it at his house. They probably did like it more. She had rules and enforced them. She didn't play with them as much as he did. She was too busy playing catch-up with the homework they didn't complete at his house, fighting them on the importance of good grooming they didn't have to bother with over there, plus going into long reasons why cleaning their rooms was actually necessary, even though they didn't do that at their dad's, either. Despite all that, she wouldn't give up her rights.

How was she supposed to break the chains of abuse if she hardly ever saw her children? How could they heal and learn new ways of living if she wasn't around them enough to teach them? She was sick of having this threat of losing her kids hanging over her. Same old, same old, same old.

*

On the next children-free weekend, Charlene decided to go to a raw food seminar. Totally crazy, she knew. That was what attracted her. She wanted to find out what the heck those people ate. From now on, every weekend she didn't have the kids, she resolved to do something she'd never done before. It would be an adventure. Think of what she would learn!

*

Against her better judgment, Charlene decided to attend another dance. Sometimes it was nice to be around people who were in similar situations—single. She was making friends, and they'd asked her to dance, so it was becoming fun.

Jim was way too old for her, in his fifties, so that friendship felt safe. As they walked onto the dance floor, he talked about wanting to get together with his ex-wife. "I made so many mistakes and didn't even realize it. Do you think she would ever take me back and forgive me?" He shared with Charlene how his ex-wife was dating and how she had told him that she couldn't do "the couple thing" with him anymore.

Charlene carefully encouraged him to move on, hoping that was the best advice. "I always feel so much better after talking to you," he said, giving her a fatherly squeeze on the shoulders. "Thanks. How are things going for you?"

Charlene described her latest struggles with Brad.

"Oh, you have it hard," Jim said. "I wish it didn't have to be like that for you."

Charlene liked his sympathy. It made her feel like she could survive for another week because someone listened and understood. She discussed her children with Jim too, and as he was a sixth grade teacher, he had a lot of insight. They laughed about that stage of life which Sandra was now in—self-conscious, sensitive, peer oriented. It helped Charlene to hear reassurances that Sandra's behavior was developmentally common.

After they finished their dance, Charlene danced with a new guy. He grew animated as he talked about his job working as a nurse. When he launched into a drama that happened recently, his gum flew out of his mouth and straight into her hair. He apologized as she tried to get it out and save as much of her long hair as possible. Others gathered to watch as he, too, tried to work the gum out. The more unsuccessful his attempts, the larger the crowd became. Someone fetched scissors and he ended up cutting the gum out, causing Charlene to lose two inches of hair that hung over her right shoulder. When the crowd dispersed, the gum chewer kissed her hand and said, "I promise I'll make this up to you."

Charlene thought the best way to make it up to her was to try his lines on someone else and leave her be. She smiled then left him when the music changed.

A half hour later, Bob, who was closer to her age, danced with her.

They immediately began chatting about parenting and the importance of parents setting limits. After they had danced a couple of songs, he said, "You're really different. You aren't like the rest of the women. You have more spunk."

He asked her to a football game.

A football game? Charlene wanted to say "No," because she hated sitting in the cold watching guys with tight pants run around, but she was interested in learning more about Bob, so she said, "Yes."

Brad had asked Charlene to keep the kids that night, which she had already agreed to. When Bob called to schedule the date, he suggested they meet at six.

"I have my kids this weekend," Charlene told him. "Could we wait until after eight-thirty when they go to bed?"

"We'd miss half the game," Bob said.

After going back and forth, Charlene finally said "Okay, I guess I'll have to leave them early. How about we go at seven? I'll have to have my phone with me in case they need me."

He agreed.

The night was cold. Once at the game, she hunkered down into her coat and a blanket and watched the players run back and forth. As she watched, she wondered what would happen to this world if people had this kind of enthusiasm for something that actually mattered.

Bob turned to her and smiled. "Isn't this great? I can always get good seats because my uncle is the football coach. The team is doing really well this year. I think they'll get a bowl. " And on he went about the team.

Charlene tried not to yawn. She didn't get this whole sports thing. She looked around at the roaring crowd and felt very alone. When her phone rang several times within the first two hours, she was grateful to talk to her kids. The calls were about nothing serious. Lorine didn't want to listen to Sandra, especially when it came to going to bed. Charlene sighed, wishing she was at home. She'd have to be more careful to what dates she agreed to from now on.

When the game was finally over, Bob took her for a bite to eat at a greasy pizza joint. He got an expression of longing on his face. "You know, you have the life I always wanted."

This took Charlene by surprise. "How's that?" She poked her fork at half-wilted iceberg lettuce.

His said, the dreamy expression still on his face, "With the kids and all. You have no idea how lonely it is to be by yourself."

He spoke with such intensity that Charlene wondered if he was hinting at wanting to marry her so he could have her life.

"It's not everything it's cracked up to be," she said.

"Yes, it is," he said, with finality.

*

The next week the kids were gone to their dad's house, so Charlene braved the dance floor again. She met a man who a couple of weeks before had called her "Wonder Woman." "I have something special to send you through e-mail," he had said. Charlene had forgotten about it until he came up to her at the dance. "Did you receive the e-mail I sent you?" he asked.

Charlene suddenly remembered deleting something that had seemed suspicious, like spam or a virus. "Sorry, I thought it was spam and deleted it."

He shook his head and walked away. He gave her several dirty looks that night.

Charlene didn't have time to think about it as another man asked her to dance. As they moved to the fast beat, he said, "You look so good in your black clothes against your white skin. I love your whiteness."

Charlene didn't know how to take that, or the other lines she heard.

"You look like a Russian queen."

"I've wanted to dance with you before, but you were too busy with other guys."

"A guy hardly has a chance with you. You're always dancing."

"What beautiful features."

"You move so well."

"You're a great dancer."

"I'll look you up later."

What a meat market! The comments went on and on. They

meant nothing. The men knew nothing about her. She guessed she would have to put up with the lines if she was going to have the social contact. It all seemed so shallow, which was good, she concluded, because it would keep her from getting involved with anyone.

*

Nathan woke up from his nap not feeling well. Charlene took his temperature, put Sesame Street on for him, kissed his forehead, and went into the next room to finish her homework. About a half an hour later, she heard, faintly, "Help." She hurried into the living room. She couldn't see Nathan, but heard him crying. She ran around the house searching for him, fear creeping up the back of her neck.

Finally, she ran outside, calling to him. It was a warm spring day and she had opened the living room window to let in the breezes. Her son's cries were louder outside. "Where are you?" she screamed.

"Down here, Mommy," came a sobbing, scared voice.

Charlene rushed over to the open window, noticing for the first time that the screen was gone. Inside the window well, lying against the metal, she discovered her son. He had opened the window and leaned too hard against the screen, knocked it out, and fallen before he could regain his balance.

Charlene pulled him out and looked him over. "Are you okay?" she asked, examining his head for bumps and blood.

"That was fun. I bounced like a bunny."

She put him in the car and drove to the chiropractor's. They brought him into the exam room immediately and took great pains to make sure he was okay. They found no internal injuries, but told Charlene that for the next twenty-four hours, she must watch out for dilating eyes, swelling on his head, and disorientation.

Brad had visitation on Wednesday nights while Charlene attended school. She decided it was best to call and tell him what to watch for with Nathan while it was still fresh on her mind.

"What happened?" Brad yelled.

She explained again.

"You have to take him to the emergency room."

"No," Charlene said as she stopped for a red light. "I took him to the chiropractor. They checked him completely out. He'll be all right."

"What? Those freaks? You have to take him to the emergency room."

"Brad, he's fine. You just have to look out for those signs while you have him. If anything like that happens, then he should go to the emergency room."

"Are you telling me that you won't take him?"

Charlene bit her lip. Why was he being so insistent? "The emergency room costs a lot of money, and I don't want to have to pay it if I don't have to."

"Take him. Those quack doctors don't know anything."

"They handle this kind of stuff all the time. In Europe, a chiropractor is the first person some see in the emergency room." Charlene decided she needed to calm Brad down. Sometimes he could really freak. "The chiropractor already did a very thorough exam. He'll be okay. You just need to keep an eye on him."

"Chiropractors aren't real doctors," he said. "That was a bad fall. Take him to the emergency room now."

"He's fine. Really, Brad."

"You're not taking him?"

"No."

"Where are you?"

"Why?" Charlene's heart started to thump so hard she had trouble breathing. What was he going to do?

"Tell me where you are." His voice had that ticked-off sound that she hated. He often used to sound like that right before he hit her.

"What do you want?" She stopped again for a light, her hands sweating. This wasn't going to be good. Was he going to be out searching for her? Would he force her to take Nathan to the emergency room?

"I'm calling DCFS and the cops. They're going to be out looking for you. You're not going to get away with hurting my son." He hung up.

Charlene drove two more lights. What should she do? Would the cops find her? Would she lose her children over this? Brad was such a jerk.

She couldn't think straight. She needed help. She flipped the car around and returned to the chiropractor's office. She ran in and told him what had happened. "What do I do?" she asked. "He's going to take the kids from me."

"Don't worry about that. But to be on the safe side, go to the emergency room," he said.

Charlene nodded and followed his suggestion. Her heart continued to thunder in her chest as she waited to be seen. She tugged at her shirtsleeves. How could Brad do this to her? Nathan was fine. Did he want her to spend all her money so she would be broke?

Her phone rang.

"Hello."

"DCFS said they would do nothing," Brad said. "They said chiropractors are better for that type of injury so you don't have to go to the emergency room if you don't want to."

Charlene told the attending nurse then left, her heart still pounding hard inside her chest. She couldn't help wonder if the next time something happened, he would be successful in getting the kids from her.

Chapter 28

The day was slow and rainy. Charlene spent it catching up on her studies. She had a final in two days. She worried about remembering the information on all the laws and codes. On her breaks, she read *Alexander and the Terrible, Horrible, No Good, Very Bad Day* to the kids, who were home. They laughed when Charlene put on a pouting voice and stuck out her lower lip.

The phone rang. "Your school's hurting the children. If you keep going, I'll take you to court." Brad again. Of course.

Here he went again trying to control.

"You'll lose the children because you're not paying proper attention to them. A mother should be at home and doing nothing else but taking care of her kids."

*

The final was done at last. Relief washed through Charlene. To celebrate, she stopped for an ice cream cone on the way home. She was still licking the last of it when she entered her office and checked her e-mails. Her eyes glanced over the new ones then her stomach knotted. An e-mail from Dave.

Heart thumping hard, she opened it to find a form letter inviting her to his Successful Singles group. Why would he send this to her? He wouldn't actually want her to show up, would he? That would be awkward. No way. Maybe he forgot to take her off the list, she concluded. But he sure hadn't waited very long to change his post on the Internet, not to mention he was active on the dating service.

She wrote to Judy about it. The next day, Judy pointedly asked how Charlene knew that Dave had changed his post. Also, how had she known how active he was on the dating service? Those were two questions Charlene didn't want to answer.

Subject: Checking
Date: May 13
From: "Charlene" <char@CharlenesWeb.net>
To: "Judy" <bchcomber@yippee.com>

Judy,

Fine, I'm on the Internet service daily, too, but that's just to see how he redirects his life after he broke up with me. Ok, fine, I'll admit it, I'm obsessive too. ☺

And no I'm not the one who is still interested in him. He's the one that ended it, but I'm not going to fight you about it nor waste my time checking up on him. You're right; I need to let it go.

Charlene

School became extra busy with lots of projects and papers due all at once. The individual counseling was intense, but Charlene liked it so much better than the legal class. They were now into fun stuff, actually learning how to apply what they had been learning by going over strategies and intervention methods. Soon they'd be writing up treatment plans. That was what Charlene longed to do.

*

Subject: You're turning green.
Date: May 24
From: "Charlene" <char@CharlenesWeb.net>
To: "Judy" <bchcomber@yippee.com>

Judy,

Your whole body's going to turn green from the amount of time you spend in the garden. It seems like it's a spiritual experience for you. That's cool. I'm surprised you can slip any of your day job in ☺*. I wish I had the same feeling about weeding as you. My whole yard is filled with weeds from all the rain. You're welcome to become acquainted with them anytime. I'm sure you're running out of weeds up there. Our sun is bright here. Tempted?* ☺

Charlene told her friend about the adventures she was having on the weekends, when homework wasn't overloading her. Most recently, she'd taken a CPR class. On the weekends she had the kids, she tried to do special things with them. They went to the movies, the park, the theater, and other fun things. She had to admit it, Dave had inspired her. He had often planned family trips with the kids and had made the outings fun. She was going to try to keep that tradition up, although it wasn't as easy without help.

Charlene continued the e-mail:

The other day Karla told me I have a tendency to zero right into the heart of matters. She says that threatens some guys, and she's right, it does. But I'm not going to change. I'm happy with that quality. Surely there's some self-assured man out there who would appreciate it, instead of running away in fear. If not, oh well. I'm content raising my kids and going to school.

I'm so thankful. Thankful to God, thankful to you, and thankful to the others who helped me get here—to this freedom. I'm able to explore who I am. What a great opportunity.

Charlene

It was the weekend, and Charlene needed a break from her studies. She jumped on the Internet and decided to respond to some e-mails. A guy named Todd had written her. He seemed to have a relaxed, easy-going lifestyle.

He wanted to know about Charlene's life. Feeling playful, she wrote back. *An adventure. I never know what I'm going to get myself into next. Right now I'm learning how to do "guy" things. You know, things that involve a hammer, screwdriver, or a drill. I even changed a light bulb the other day.* ☺

Todd wanted to play. He stated that he was impressed with her light bulb changing ability.

Charlene thanked him for his compliment: *It's a technical and highly difficult job, but someone has to do it. I have other abilities, too. Like I can change diapers, even deadly ones.* ☺ *Can I get a certificate for that too? If I think hard, maybe I could come up with another talent. Hmm. I'll have to give it thought and get back to you.*

Todd asked her out, but Charlene wasn't sure if she was up for *another* bad date. Even though this guy sounded funny, she wanted to be careful. She decided the best way to handle it was to write: *Lunch sounds like an adventure. Keep writing so I can learn more about you and make sure you're not an ax murderer or a polygamist.* ☺ *You know a girl's got to tend to safety first.*

Paige found Charlene on the computer. "Mom, I have an idea."

Charlene looked to her daughter. "Yes?"

"How about you date Daddy?" She then launched into a long list of the ways he had changed and why dating him would be a good idea.

"Paige, I can understand why you want me to date your dad, and you made some really good points, but your dad and I aren't going to get back together. No matter what."

Paige said with clenched jaw, "You aren't going to change what I believe."

Charlene looked at her daughter's quivering lip and wondered what Brad had done. He must have been saying something to fill the kids with false hopes. Charlene walked over to the kitchen cabinet. She needed an aspirin.

*

Charlene had written back and forth to Todd enough that she decided it was time to say yes to his invitation. There was only so much you could learn about a person through e-mail. The thing she did learn was that Todd was funny, so the date couldn't be that bad.

Charlene was wrong. He was anything but funny. Dry, non-talkative, moping about the breakup of his marriage, he even asked Charlene if she would take care of him since she was already a mother of five. Geez.

Charlene shook her head, hurrying out of the mall. He had taken her there to eat. It was going to be a long time before she would date again. She was going to be single for a very long time. There were worse things...like being married!

That night she prayed for guidance about resigning from her Internet dating service. But the next morning, she woke with a lingering impression that she should write different words in her profile instead. Why? She didn't know. Maybe she just had to get it out of her system.

After Charlene took Lorine to the school bus, she returned to her computer to find another invitation to one of Dave's groups. Charlene hated how her heart trembled every time she saw his e-mail address.

*

Saturday came along, and Charlene knew that she could no longer put off working on clearing the forest of weeds in her yard. Within the first hour of the chore, Charlene's back throbbed. As she stood to stretch, she saw Andrew, a single guy who lived in her neighborhood, coming up her walkway. He asked what he could do. Charlene immediately put him to work on fixing the smoke alarm that kept chirping as it demanded a fresh battery.

She went outside and begged her kids to help as she yanked at the weeds. Her children stood around watching her until Andrew, a thirty-five-year-old civil engineer, decided that her yard needed a rescue mission. He called his friends, who came armed with shovels and hoes. Even with the crew working full force, her yard didn't yield without a fierce battle. Andrew and friends said they'd return next week. Charlene made sure to feed them sandwiches, cookies, and lots of ice water. When they had worn themselves out working, she invited them all in to play board games. All of them played with her children, who loved it.

Charlene felt strange with them working for her and thought about not letting them, but then she'd have to do it all herself. That was just foolishness. She was extremely grateful. These were great examples of good men her children could look up to. Charlene was sure that most single mothers were not as lucky as she.

Subject: Prozac and Pretense
Date: June 16
From: "Charlene" <char@CharlenesWeb.net>
To: "Shane" <shaneb@bowers.com>

Shane,

Thanks for your note on the Internet site. All I can say is, wow! A man into deep relationships who admits he has emotions! Are you sure moving to the mountains is not in your current plans? ☺
Okay, I admit there are a lot of people here who live the "Prozac and Pretense" life, but there are others who are golden. Rare, but there are some. Where I live is really beautiful. I'm in the mountains, overlooking a distant range and lake, not far from outdoor adventures or cultural events. Feel like moving yet?

What kind of things do you like to study?

Misty

Charlene couldn't believe the guy who had starting e-mailing her. In his picture, he looked rough and handsome rugged, the outdoorsman type. He said that he wanted a deep relationship. Charlene decided that was something she could definitely go for. She had been divorced now for almost a year and a quarter. The kids had settled into their new neighborhood. They had friends, they slept well at night, and they handled the back and forth with her ex much better than in the beginning. Brad kept talking to the kids about their mommy and daddy getting back together, which really bugged her, but there was nothing she could do about it. That would probably go on happening until one of them got married. Maybe now was a good time to get into a relationship.

*

Over the next few days, she and Shane wrote back and forth in a fury. Shane asked if he could fly out and meet her in September. They figured if they were honest and open, they should have a fairly good idea about each other by then and might even come to know each other better than they would if they lived closer.

Charlene wondered what a man who wanted a deep relationship was like. She shot him a ton of questions. *What do you do in retail? How long have you been divorced? Why did your marriage break up? What are your dreams, besides meeting a soul mate who wants and treasures a deep relationship? Tell me about your eight-year-old daughter.*

Shane answered every one of her questions and showed her a picture of his girl, who was darling. Shane revealed that he sold shoes for a living. Charlene joked, *Do you have some spares? I could use some. ☺   A girl can't have too many, you know.* When she learned that his hobby was to be "Bob the Builder Fix-It-Man," she disclosed to him that since she had been single, she made it a goal to actually use a hammer, screwdriver, and drill. Who would have known that a drill was a staple in running a household? She also revealed that her biggest success so far had been putting together bookcases, and yes, thank you, they were still standing. She told him the secret she'd learned to success. Whenever she had tried to get her ex to teach her, he'd refused. Now she asked the neighbors for help. They were always willing to pass on their skills so she could become as independent as possible and not ask for help again.

When Shane asked for deeper details about her, she said, *My life circumstances aren't exactly—hum, let's say not what everyone would want to get involved in, but it makes me who I am, and God arranged it this way so I'm not complaining. I'm including my story on the events of my life in an attachment. I wrote it up once and don't want to rewrite it.*

She had to respond to his words about her touching his heart. She burned with warmth from the mere suggestion. She squirmed in her computer chair when she confessed to him, *You've also touched my heart.*

Charlene was surprised by Shane's response to her life trauma. He wanted to know whom she had dated since she'd divorced.

Hmm. She told about how early on she had met someone she liked very much, and how well they got along. She confessed that she thought they were compatible, but then she saw red flags. She didn't feel comfortable with that and called the relationship off. Since then, she went out every once in a while, but didn't want to waste her time and spent most of her time doing schoolwork and being with her kids.

Shane liked hearing her stories. He told her he felt he could tell her anything. Charlene remembered a romantic night with Dave, when he had pulled her close in front of the living room fire and said, "Who are you and why do I spill my soul to you?" She didn't know why, but she liked it, especially from him.

Now Charlene realized that Dave had been tight with his emotions. He didn't let them out like Shane did so freely. It seemed that Shane wasn't afraid to adore her, love her, and admit it. She told him of her dreams. *I'd love to get married to a man I'm passionately in love with, and I'd love to stay where I'm at. I enjoy my new house. I felt inspired to move here and so did my children. They were instrumental in the move. The transition was hard on them, but it has worked out. I felt impressed that if I moved within the shadows of the mountain, I'd be safe.*

Shane told her that he wanted her to be safe. He agreed that passion was one of the highest virtues. Charlene felt she had found a piece of paradise.

She knew better than to let herself get sucked away in this fairytale. She had made that mistake before. She needed to discover Shane's flaws. *Now I'm going to probe deeper, if that's okay. You say your marriage was rocky for the last seven years? What were the difficulties? Why were the issues irresolvable? Who decided to end the marriage? How would you describe your personality? What kinds of things do you like to think about?*

Looking forward to learning more about you, the good, the bad, and the ugly. ☺

She was in the middle of reading Shane's explanation about how he married someone he wasn't compatible with when her e-mail dinged. Charlene flipped over to see who the new message was from.

Dave.

Again.

Another invitation. Her heart in her throat, she knew it was time to stop hearing from him. She needed to move on. She wrote:

Subject: E-mail List
Date: June 21
From: "Charlene" <char@CharlenesWeb.net>
To: "Dave" <allaroundman@yesterday.com>

Dave,

I'd appreciate it if you'd take me off your e-mail list. It's too painful.

Charlene

When Charlene reviewed Shane's explanations, some things weren't making sense. She was sure that if she could talk to him it would all clear up, though. She told him that she was feeling the pains of e-mail communication. She was unsure really what the problem was. She thought from what he wrote that he was saying he felt unsupported, unappreciated, alone, and perhaps that his wife wasn't as committed to God as he was?

*

As the days went by, Charlene found herself taking more time-outs to see what Shane had to say. She reasoned that she was making a safe friend. E-mail, safe. Long distance, safe. And yet she got to throw around ideas and communicate with someone, so she didn't feel so lonely. Having a male e-mail correspondent was fun. Besides, she felt she was getting to know him really well before ever having to throw in the physical component or take time away from her kids.

Her phone rang. It was Shane.

"Hi!" she said, hoping she didn't sound stupid and would know what to say.

"I thought I'd call."

"I'm glad."

"I'd like to come out in a couple of months. What do you think?"

Charlene went instantly hot. What was she to say to that? "That would be good."

"You'd want me to?"

"Yeah," she said, hearing her voice crack.

"What's it like where you live?" he asked.

They talked about the mountain range, the weather, then eventually the conversation turned to his ex. The way Shane explained the problems, they really didn't seem to have much in common, Charlene concluded.

*

That weekend, Charlene leapt around her house as she prepared for the dance that night. She wanted to go out and just have fun. And fun she did have. She didn't meet anyone extra special, but she did have fun flirting. As she spun around doing the barn dance, one guy told her that she was trouble.

"Me, trouble?"

"Yeah, I've been watching you, and you're definitely trouble."

A guy she often danced with, Jeff, was her next partner. Jeff immediately called her "Hot Stuff" and asked, "Are you ripping up the dance floor?"

"I'm trying," she said, laughing.

After that song, she asked someone to dance! He turned out to be a lawyer. She had asked him because he was young and cute and that combination was rare at the dances. "Having fun?" she asked.

"Not really."

He looked away from her and moped.

She shrugged. She had definitely picked a lemon this time.

She walked away from him, glad the song had ended, when an older fellow she had met a few weeks before asked her to dance. Afterward the song he asked her, "Will you please ask my friend Eric to dance? He's shy and it would really help him out."

Charlene asked the bashful, dark-haired thirty-year-old.

After that dance, another guy named Owen asked her to dance, and while they waltzed he asked her to ask his friend Keith for a dance.

Charlene was wondering how long this game would go on as she went up to Keith, a tall, slender fellow. He said, "I will, but not this dance."

"See what I get for asking?" she went back and told Owen with a smile.

An older friend took Charlene on the dance floor to do a fast rendition of the swing.

Later, while Charlene was dancing with another man, Keith came up, stopped them and said, "I thought this was my dance. What are you doing with another guy?"

Charlene looked at him curiously as the fellow she was dancing with spun her away from the demanding and grouchy Keith. "Do you want to dance with him instead?" he asked.

"Are you crazy?" she said. "That was weird."

After the dance, she drove to a restaurant where many of the dancing singles liked to go. A white-haired, nice-looking man gave her grief for having so many kids. Charlene told him, "You're ancient if you have to have everything stale and quiet at home."

The table of people laughed at that and he fell silent.

A distinguished, salt-and-pepper-haired man down at the end of the table who had been staring at her blurted out, "If you marry me, next year all your kids could ski for free. I'm a children's ski instructor."

What could she say to that?

CHAPTER 29

Subject: Starting
Date: June 24
From: "Charlene" <char@CharlenesWeb.net>
To: "Shane" <shaneb@bowers.com>

Hi Shane,

I agree, starting with friendship is a great way to begin. I also believe in the hard work of communication, figuring out how the other person expresses himself, what triggers him, and being willing to look at oneself and realize why we do what we do. We have to own our own part, communicating with complete honesty, even when it's hard and embarrassing. I believe in figuring out each person's love language, and how best to be there for the other person, bringing a problem to the table instead of looking the other way and pretending that problem doesn't exist. You know, that kind of stuff. I think people can avoid getting close because at times it's painful to open up and be vulnerable. It takes commitment on each person's part to create a safe environment where that can happen. Being a person who can course-correct and admit when they're wrong is an important ingredient to a healthy relationship.

Give me your thoughts on relationship stuff, if you have anything to say. Happy trails.

Charlene

*

Charlene rolled over in her bed and stretched, enjoying sleeping in. Being divorced did come with perks. Her ex had the kids until about nine. She planned to take them on a picnic in the mountains when they arrived home. They liked to splash around in the creek.

If Shane lived near, would he want to go to the creek? Would he enjoy it as much as she did? She felt confident he would. He liked just about everything she did. It was nice to talk to him. They had chatted again last night after she came home from the dance. She told him that she would have to limit her time on the phone on weekdays because she needed to work on her school assignments. She would be freer on the weekends when she didn't have her children. She also explained that they would have to talk after the kids were read to and put to bed. She wouldn't cheat her children.

The phone rang. It was Shane. "Good morning, princess."

"Morning," Charlene said. "I was just thinking about you. I have a question for you."

"Shoot."

"You say you want a deep relationship, where you feel really connected. My question for you is, how do you plan on going about getting that kind of relationship?"

"What do you think would be the best way to go about it?" he asked. "You're the soon-to-be therapist."

Charlene sat up in bed. She had a lot to say about this.

*

The kids were watching a movie that hot Sunday, and Charlene had gone into in her office to review the e-mails she had saved from Shane. He was a kind, humble, and faithful man she decided.

She couldn't resist writing to him. *I can't wait meet you. I'd like to see what your spirit is like. It's scary to think about meeting someone away from the Internet. With my past, I'm more leery than others. But as of yet, I don't feel that with you. Hmm.*

She could picture their meeting now. He'd walk into her view, and it would be just like the movies. The music would play, and she'd go toward him as he smiled. It would be like they had known each other their whole lives and were simply reuniting after an unnecessary time apart. Charlene floated on these ideas.

Knowing that Shane would want to know more about her kids, she spent the rest of the day putting together pictures to e-mail him. She wrote him how once a lady she knew came up to her and said, "Your kids are so cute, you should have as many as you can." Charlene had laughed at the well-meaning lady. Her reaction was more welcome than the normal gruffness she received for having so many so fast.

Shane's e-mail earned him bonus points. He didn't like sports! Charlene hadn't thought that was possible to find in a man. What a great and rare attribute.

She immediately wrote him to see if he was into physical fitness. If he was, it would be another sign that theirs was a match made in heaven.

Subject: Dead phone
Date: June 30
From: "Charlene" <char@CharlenesWeb.net>
To: "Shane" <shaneb@bowers.com>

Hey Shane Babe,

I'm glad to hear you'll be able to see your daughter today and spend some unexpected time with her. I like the fact that you enjoy being with your child. Do you think you'd feel the same way with five more who aren't yours?

Also glad you're into physical fitness. It's something important in my life.

Sorry my phone went dead last night. I guess that was a signal that our time was up for that talk. ☺

May God's love pour upon you.

Charlene

P.S. My daughter loved the CD you burned for her. It's cool you can get so much music for such a little monthly fee. Sandra wants to know if you can make her another CD. If this is a problem, let me know.

*

"I'm going to take it all."

Brad was at his old games again. Would it ever end? "What are you talking about?" Charlene asked, wishing she could grab his neck and squeeze.

"You cheat me and now I am suing. There's no way you are going to get away with getting all that money from me."

Charlene had been in the living room playing with the kids. She quickly moved into her office and shut the door, not wanting her children to overhear her on the phone. "What are you talking about?"

"The taxes." Brad proceeded to trump up charges against her. "I promise I will go after you until I get it all and the kids."

When Charlene hung up, she was shaking. Could he do that to her? Would he? One of these days he would. He had hit her, spit on her, and ripped up things that mattered to her. What made her think that he would stop there? What was she going to do?

Crying, she dialed Shane's number. "Help me," she said, sobbing.

"Anything, princess," Shane said.

After hearing what ailed Charlene, he declared, "I'll keep you safe. I promise you that."

Nothing sounded better to Charlene than that. Imagine: safety. She knew that she was being silly, imagining a man could fix her problems. She had to stop getting swept away in the "prince comes to save the day" thinking. Shane's talk just tempted her to slip back to her old habits.

*

In Shane's next e-mail, he wanted to know how affectionate she was. She told him she loved to snuggle and be caressed and adored. She also explained that if she didn't feel safe, understood, listened to, or respected, she would have a hard time with affection. She thought that was about as honest as she could be.

She also warned that when it came to dating, she had certain guidelines. She did not like to be in a position where she had to be on guard and worried. She had chosen to live a virtuous life.

Shane immediately wrote back that they saw eye to eye.

*

Subject: *Neglect*
Date: *July 3*
From: *"Charlene" <char@CharlenesWeb.net>*
To: *"Judy" <bchcomber@yippee.com>*

Judy,

I'm writing Shane so much that I've been neglecting you. Sorry, I didn't mean to hurt your feelings. I'll be better about it. Promise. Forgive me? I miss hearing from you too. Are you still active with your grandkids? How's being the chorister going? How's your foot feeling? How's your boss treating you? Have you heard from your mom lately? Is she still mad about you moving away from her? Catch me up.

I'm having a lot of fun corresponding with Shane. I hope you understand. I'm developing a fondness for him, which is surprising since we haven't met yet. Maybe we're able to develop a deeper relationship because of the distance between us. I know you're going to say that writing someone is not the same as meeting them. But honestly, I feel like I know him as well as any good friend. I'm being cautious, but enjoying the ride.

My kids are enjoying the summer. Thank heavens Sandra now has a best friend who lives up the street. They like to do "late nights." Her parents won't allow sleepovers, which is probably a good rule. When her friend is here, I try to convince her that I'm weirder than her mom. So far my daughter believes I am, but Melissa still claims her mom is stranger with her vegan lifestyle and belief in no heater or air conditioner. I have to admit that's a tough one to beat.

Shane's supposed to be calling any time now. Oh, there's the phone. Till next time.

Charlene

Chapter 30

In true Fourth of July fashion, Charlene went to a romantic chick flick the night before the parade with her best friend, Karla. She had to admit she was a hopeless romantic. Plus, she liked her friendship with Karla. They got along great. She had asked her if they had ever had an argument or disagreement. Neither of them could remember one. Sometimes they "sparred," but it was always friendly. Karla didn't like Charlene's ex much, but said she figured she'd made a lot of dumb decisions in her life and so she wouldn't judge.

On the Fourth, Charlene and Karla attended the parade together. Fireworks were in the plans for later. The extra playing celebrated Charlene having taken her final in Individual Counseling. She had to live it up because next week she'd start Group Counseling.

In between the parade and the fireworks, Shane and Charlene e-mailed each other. As they corresponded, they decided to take the Color Code Personality Test. When the test results were done, they discovered they were both blue, which was supposed to be an incredibly connected, loyal, and passionate relationship.

"Well, sweet blue, looks like we have a lot to look forward to."

Charlene had to come up with a name for him back. After giving it a moment, she shot back with "true blue."

From then on, they wrote to each other every night, short e-mails ending with "have nice dreams" or a "hello" e-mail in the morning.

When Charlene wrote to Judy about him, she explained that she had never in a million years thought she would get involved in something like this. *I feel like I know him on so many levels. He's kind and genuine. He doesn't like to talk about complicated subjects like Dave did. It's a relief not to have my brain hurting from so much discussion and analysis. Although I have to admit, there was something special about those discussions with Dave…(Forget I said that!)*

*

When the kids came home, they told Charlene how much they had missed her over the Fourth. Nathan cried when the fireworks started and, according to reports, asked for his mom.

Charlene took him in her arms. "Oh," she said, kissing him on the head, feeling glad he wanted her but sad that it was hard on him. Mothers who weren't separated from their babies were so lucky. Having to send Nathan, who was only three years old, away to his father always tugged at her heart. He was too young to be away from his mom. Charlene didn't care what the law said, it was too young.

That night, Shane mentioned that he wanted to come earlier. Charlene told him to go ahead. They immediately began working out the flight times. It was cute the way he asked to come, making sure she would feel comfortable about it. He insisted that they be partners in the decision. He wouldn't run the show, and she wouldn't run it. What a new concept.

They agreed it would be best if he came when she didn't have the children. She had learned her lesson with Dave. Plus, she didn't want Brad to find out about it. It would really set him off. Charlene knew that Shane wanted to protect her, but she doubted that he could actually do it. And to add to her worries, she didn't want to see Brad and him fighting.

Time dragged as they waited for the day he would come out. They continued to e-mail. Charlene had mentioned a relationship book that she was impressed with. Shane got it and read it. That was impressive. As time went by, he opened up more about his frustrations with his former wife. She understood. Shane complained his ex was a workaholic. Brad had definitely been that. Of course she was benefiting from that now, but she'd rather that they had enjoyed being together and she had been treated well.

Shane asked her what she thought about exclusive dating. She answered, *I think most couples do it too soon. It's a mistake to date exclusively unless you are engaged. If there's no commitment, there's no commitment. If a relationship is formed, then it's top priority and other romantic relationships must fall away.*

*

The weekend came again. Charlene attended a local dance, but no one she knew was there. Then she drove to another single's social in a nearby town and there met a guy who talked about all his issues he had worked through. Charlene looked at him, listened, excused herself, and went right out of the dance hall to her car and off she drove to a different dance. She wondered about herself and the ditching she was doing.

This dance had many more people her age. She normally attended dances populated with older men. Right after she walked in someone ran up to her and said, "Hey, you look like the girl on *Seinfeld*."

Other people gathered around. "She does."

"Is that good?" Charlene asked.

"Yeah, she was cool."

As Charlene stood there listening she heard a lot of people putting others down. "Look at that geek." "Doesn't she think she's something?" Charlene frowned.

On the dance floor, the girls danced with the girls and the boys with the boys. They formed huge groups without any interaction, no social dancing, but lots of jumping up and down. A lot of boys stood around wallowing in apparent misery.

After about an hour there, she concluded that her generation had no people skills and didn't know how to interact. How were her children going to develop relationship skills in an environment like this?

She overheard conversations about who had slept with whom last night and who they wanted to make it with tonight. Her worries were usually about her children's homework and passing her own classes. It became very clear she didn't belong there. She danced, listened to the music, then left to return to her family, thinking about how superficial the younger single's world was. Older men with baggage were better any day. At least they had the ability to express themselves and interact emotionally. They could participate in the pleasure of social dancing.

Subject: Metal and Steel
Date: July 11
From: "Charlene" <char@CharlenesWeb.net>
To: "Shane" <shaneb@bowers.com>

Hi Shane,

Thank you for sharing with me. Yes, I'm feeling drawn to you as I pray. I feel a sweetness, a comfort. It's something I haven't felt in a relationship before. My logical mind says, "You haven't even met him," but that doesn't seem to play a factor.

I'm glad you're steel. I need steel. I won't hide the fact that my life has its challenges that most people do not have the strength, character, maturity, or desire to get involved with. God has made my burdens lighter, and He's blessed me to be able to handle whatever comes my way. Many times He has blessed me richly by bringing the perfect person into my life at the perfect time. Since you have come into my life, things seem to flow. You're strengthening me over the Internet. Thank you. Thank you for being faithful. Thank you for listening to God. And thank you for wanting and desiring glorious things.

Charlene

*

Another e-mail arrived from Dave. This time when Charlene opened it she found an animated music-gram of female and male stick figures dancing, then they bowed and curtsied and the curtains closed on them. He asked if she would still be his friend if they ever bumped into each other.

A yearning overcame her. He was calling her back. This was just an excuse to connect. She missed him, his laughs, their debates, his strong shoulders that used to hold her to him. But they didn't belong together. What could she say?

Subject: Friends
Date: July 12
From: "Charlene" <char@CharlenesWeb.net>
To: "Dave" <allaroundman@yesterday.com>

Dave,

Of course we can always be friends. Good luck with everything.
Charlene

Charlene found herself going through the day thinking about Dave and why they hadn't worked out. It didn't matter why, she told herself. Nothing ever completely made sense. Everyone went through life telling themselves little stories about their lives and what happened. For example, she told everyone Brad was abusive and wouldn't stop hitting her and that was why they broke up, but was that the truth? Was that really what had happened or was that the way she simply chose to relate it to make things easier? Yes, he did hit her, but could the failure of their relationship be summed up to that? It was the same with Dave. Yes, there was no doubt that he was arrogant and that he would get more swept up in his thoughts than her. She, from his point of view, feared too much, but was that the reason they weren't together? Who could really know the truth of relationships with so much room to question oneself?

She had a new love now. Shane sent her a "magnet and steel" song. He said that was what their relationship was. She wondered what exactly he meant. She wrote and asked. He said that he found her impossible to resist like a magnet does steel.

At church, Charlene thought about Shane. He worked on Sundays and said he didn't like it. If he didn't like working on the

Sabbath, why didn't he do anything about it? And he lied to his ex-wife while he was on the phone with Charlene. He told his ex that he had to work one day because he didn't want to watch his daughter. Red flag. If this was a one-time thing, then maybe it was okay, but if it happened more, it wasn't good.

That night she dreamed that Shane turned out to be a fifteen-year-old boy who lied and accused her of lying.

Charlene woke up and thought about the dream. Was she fearful of getting close to someone? Maybe she wasn't ready to settle down. Maybe he wasn't the right person for her. The night before Shane had said, "Our souls communicate." Dave had said the same kind of thing and that turned out badly. She had *really* connected with him. She felt they were going to work out, then poof. It all fell apart. How could such powerful feelings for Dave come to nothing? How was she supposed to trust herself? Perhaps her fears were bubbling up as the time drew near when Shane would be visiting in person. Psychologically, it could be her efforts to disconnect before really connecting, for safety. It was confusing.

Maybe she'd stay single and not connect. She thought about the dances she had gone to. That wasn't going to work. They weren't fun anymore. She felt like she was running from guys—sharks—the whole time. Maybe she would stay home tonight.

Subject: Swimming with a shark.
Date: July 14
From: "Charlene" <char@CharlenesWeb.net>
To: "Judy" <bchcomber@yippee.com>

Judy,

Oh my gosh, Judy. You won't believe what happened to me at the dance last night! Dave was there. Everywhere I went I saw him off to the side dancing with someone else, watching me.

About the middle of the evening, I didn't see him anywhere. Someone tapped me on the shoulder. I turned around. It was him! He asked for a fast dance. I said yes, heart thundering. It was awkward. He told me his daughter was preparing for college, sending off applications. He was so proud of her. After he made sure it was a fast number, he asked if I would dance another. We did. The song after that was slow. He bolted. I was left wishing he would have taken me in his arms just once more.

He hung around afterwards, watching as this 50+ man tried to convince me he was getting younger every year and I should give him a try on a date. The guy was persistent, which worked in my favor, because Dave grew tired of waiting for me and left. And no, before you ask, the old guy didn't convince me. I left him by laughing and saying, "I'll see you at the next dance."

In his last e-mail, Shane said he prays and his answers draw him nearer to me. I would like some spirituality in a relationship after so much superficiality at the dances.

Charlene

CHAPTER 31

Shane wanted to know about Charlene's church experience after the divorce. Charlene didn't like to think about that. She remembered praying and asking the Lord why people were treating her so badly. She suspected there was a lot of abuse taking place behind closed doors in that neighborhood, and here she was, bringing it all out in public. She had helped several abused women get help. One worked to improve her marriage and sought intervention. The other fled before her husband could kill her. She had talked with many women and with her church leader.

As Charlene wrote to Shane about what happened, she understood that she had needed that experience. She had needed to stand completely on her own. If people had been supportive and kind, as they would be in an ideal world, she would have leaned on them too much. She needed to be by herself, with no one to lean on, to know how strong she was.

Now she was in a good church, where the people were loving and supportive. Cameron's scout leader picked him up for meetings along with some of the other single-mother sons and had them stay after to help them earn their merit badges. She appreciated it.

In Shane's next e-mail, Charlene learned he was getting flack from his ex about his relationship with her. Charlene didn't know why he would tell his ex about them. It didn't seem like something the ex needed to know right now. Charlene was still trying to keep it from her kids, but they had guessed that something was up. "Who are you on the phone with and talking to after we go to bed?" they asked.

Charlene smiled but changed the subject.

That weekend, she told her friends she was staying home from dancing for a "phone date" with Shane. They teased her. "Phone date? What is that? Talk on Saturday, come to the dance with us now."

> Subject: Wondering
> Date: July 18
> From: "Charlene" <char@CharlenesWeb.net>
> To: "Shane" <shaneb@bowers.com>
>
> Shane,
>
> I'm sitting here wondering if I should tell you what's going on with me. I don't know what's happening, and I don't know how to explain it, but somehow I have connected with you to the point that I'm frightened. The logical part of me says, "No way." But I prayed and it seems all right.
>
> My past interferes with my present despite how much I work to improve. In the past, when I started feeling something for someone, it meant pain and abuse. I have abandonment issues. When I connect with someone, I immediately start fearing I'll be left. (It's nothing that can't be worked out, though.) Silly, but that's the way I am. When I do something I think a person I care about might not like, I wait for the abuse or abandonment to begin. I guess telling you I had other plans for tonight triggered my anxiety. I worry that I hurt you. I worry you'll pull away.
>
> When I make commitments, I stick by them. I know we have no commitments. It's just I feel a sense of loyalty to you, and I don't want to betray that. I can't explain why.
>
> I'm being silly. I'm making a big deal out of nothing. I'm feeling stupid right now and embarrassed.
>
> Charlene

*

A loud bang woke Charlene from a sound sleep. She sat up in her bed, gripping her blanket close to her chest. What was that? Her heart seemed to go into her throat, and she couldn't breathe. She couldn't move, but she had to. Were her children in danger?

She forced her feet off the bed and to the floor. Picking up the phone, just in case, she opened her bedroom door to investigate what had caused the noise.

She looked down and saw Lorine sleeping outside her bedroom on the floor. She had taken that up recently to be close to Charlene. Actually, so had Nathan and Paige, sometimes. Lorine must have rolled over and kicked the wall.

That knowledge didn't stop Charlene's thundering heart or the fear of what might be lurking to get her. She remembered the gray car sitting outside her house. She had never figured out what that was about. There were too many memories. Too many bad experiences.

*

When Shane talked about life, he'd say things like "It will all turn out." "Problems pass, so don't get too hung up on them." It was a calm and comforting approach. Simple, yet strong and solid.

Charlene pondered why her way had to be so complicated. Why did she have so much fear? And why did she keep trying, keep risking? At times she hurt so much she wondered if the pain would shatter her. Yet off she went to try again—risking, trying, putting her heart out. She believed if she did this what she longed for would come and everything would be worthwhile. If it didn't, God would catch her when she fell and put her back together.

She thought about this after watching the movie *My Big Fat Greek Wedding*. She hated the title, but what she liked about the movie was how the main character, a woman overwhelmed by her family's baggage, found a guy who loved her and accepted her and her family. Yes, it was difficult for him, but he willingly went the distance with her and showed her how much he loved her. She was grateful to him, and they were able to blend their lives. Charlene liked the movie's themes of compromise, love, sacrifice, and learning to accept where a person comes from but not having any of that rule or ruin the relationship.

*

For Christmas Charlene had gotten Paige a season pass to the local theater. Paige seemed to want time with her mom and this was something Charlene thought they could do together.

"It's just me and you tonight, right Mom?" Paige asked.

Charlene nodded, noting the sparkle in her daughter's eyes. This was a good idea.

When they arrived home from the play, laughing about the funny parts, Paige said, "When's the next play?"

"In a couple of months," Charlene said.

"Just you and me?"

"Yep."

"Cool."

Charlene picked up her phone to check for messages and found one from Brad. "I'm suing you for neglecting the kids by going to school."

Charlene sighed. She was going to have to get her lawyer involved again.

*

Charlene woke to a sick child. Nathan was hot and miserable, not wanting to move. Shane had complained of having the flu also. Charlene joked that maybe the virus transported over the Internet waves and Nathan caught it from him.

After she sent off her other children and made sure that Nathan was all right resting on the couch, Charlene knew she had put off playing Mr. Fix-It Man on her front door long enough. A main door that wouldn't open wasn't something she could put off.

She found her screwdriver and studied the knob. She had no idea what she was doing. She couldn't remember ever repairing anything. As she looked at it, she saw a screw poking out. That must be the reason it was getting jammed.

She pounded the screw to death and the door still stuck. She opened and closed it, watching carefully. The screw wasn't the reason the door wasn't working. As she looked, she thought it might have something with the doorknob, so she took apart the whole doorknob. Springs and other things fell off. "Ugh, how am I going to get this back together?" she muttered. "Oh, well, here goes." She struggled to figure it out.

When she put it back on, it worked. She stared at. How did she get it to work?

That night she wrote Shane of her great success and went on about her beliefs on politics and money. They were trying to get to know each other extremely well on every level before they met.

*

Subject: Soul mates?
Date: July 22
From: "Charlene" <char@CharlenesWeb.net>
To: "Shane" <shaneb@bowers.com>

Hi True Blue,

You think we might be soul mates, huh? I wonder. I'm amazed by what I feel. I must have been struck with a bolt of lightning. I'm sitting here wondering what happened. A good bolt of lightning, one sprinkled with a lot of sweet feelings. You're kind, and yet interesting.

That's cool that you bought a Bowflex. You should get a lot of use out of it. I like that you're into physical fitness. I worked out and lifted yesterday, and I think I did something wrong, because I'm sure hurting today. I'd have gone to the gym this morning and even wanted to, but my baby still had a high fever. I never want my children to be sick, but when they are I'm sure do get great snuggles! I do like that. Nathan slept with me last night and was all over my bed. That was tiring, but his fever is down. It's interesting how when the kids are sick all they want is their mom.

Have an amazing day. Do you get Alli all day again? Bye.

Charlene

*

"Do we have the tax situation figured out?"

"I think so," Brad said.

"So," Charlene said hesitantly, flipping a pen around on her desk as she spoke on the phone to her ex, "you're dropping the lawsuit?"

"Whatever. I don't know why we have to deal with all this. If you hadn't given up on us and the family so easily, we wouldn't have these problems. I can't believe you did this to the family."

"That's not the reason we got divorced and you know it."

"Charlene, I'm sick of your lies and you always trying to make yourself into a victim…" And off went their argument.

Charlene grimaced when she hung up the phone. Why did they have to talk about it? He beat her, controlled her, and emotionally and spiritually abused her. Getting a divorce *was* the only resolution. What else was there to say that they hadn't said a thousand times already?

When she called Shane to complain and for a listening ear, she found him putting together his Bowflex. She liked to hear that he was taking care of himself. He told her that when they were together he would hold her forever. Charlene liked the sound of that.

It also impressed Charlene that he took time for her no matter when she called. He made sure that she felt important. He also wanted to know about her. He asked why she had married Brad. She wrote back: *He was the first nice guy that I found interesting and who liked me. (It always seemed like all the interesting guys weren't religious.) He was funny. I believed his "perfect guy" image and didn't look any further. I was glad someone loved me and I jumped. At last, I thought. I was so desperate for love and anxious to have a man in my life who wasn't like my father. Besides that, marriage gave me an escape from my father.*

As she thought about it, since she got to do it over again, she decided this time if she ever remarried she would do it out of love for the other person. She dreamed of being her future spouse's cheerleader and experiencing unity together. She told Shane she would consider getting into another relationship. She needed an outlet for the passion and love that was bubbling up inside her. She couldn't believe she said that.

*

When Charlene took breaks and informed Judy about her relationship with Shane, she explained how much calmer their relationship was than the one she'd had with Dave. They hadn't had a single disagreement. She asked him a ton of questions on the phone and through e-mail. She couldn't think of a subject they hadn't covered. She also wrote about the good stuff, like Shane wanting to come to her rescue when she had problems with her ex. Shane had promised that Brad would never hurt her again with him in her life. She loved it that Shane said that, although she knew it wasn't true. There were some things a person couldn't be protected from.

Shane said he would accept her children as his own. He would follow her rules and support her role. He said he'd have an "easy-going" attitude toward them. He did ask a lot of questions about the kids. He wanted to know what they were like. He even asked how this or that little scenario worked out. Sometimes he overheard Charlene talking to the kids and would laugh at their explanations for why they simply couldn't clean their rooms.

She explained to Judy about how when Brad called and put her down all she had to do was call Shane and she felt better and the fear lessened. He was safe to talk to about her fears. Through Judy's encouragement, Charlene decided that she would open up even more.

Subject: Looking forward
Date: July 26
From: "Charlene" <char@CharlenesWeb.net>
To: "Shane" <shaneb@bowers.com>

Shane,

I look forward to your calls and your e-mails. You've captured me in a way I've never experienced before. It is good. Don't worry— you aren't drawing me away from things that are important. I'm becoming more involved in things that are me, like school and hanging out with my kids.

I worry that my life is too hard and no one will honestly want to take it on if they know the truth. I worried about that when I called you the night I was upset with my X. I worry about it when the kids cause stress. I think, if I don't want to handle my X and my children, why in the world would anyone else?

I also fear that what we have will end. I don't want that. Relationships either grow or die, but things are nice as they are. I don't want trouble to come. My therapist said that with complete commitment, lots of communication and total honesty, it can stay that way. I want that.

When I prayed today, I felt the impression that God was thanking me for going through all the hard things I did for Brad. I knew I had helped and Brad would soon release me. He's in the process of doing that. I also felt that I needed to learn to accept God's blessings and learn how to accept goodness.

God sent you into my life, Shane. I know that. I knew things about you before I even sent the e-mail smile on the dating site. I knew you loved God. It's amazing how life seems easy with you in it. It was so hard with others. You were right when you called yourself steel.

Your Sweet Blue, still thinking of you.

Shane's response to her vulnerability made her smile. He said he was holding her hand. When he said that, Charlene knew that she shouldn't worry. They had a great thing between them. They knew each other too well now. Their souls had connected on many levels. There was nothing to fear. When he called her "Sweet Blue" when they met in real life, she would melt like she always did, and they'd be as comfortable as though they were on the phone.

*

Charlene couldn't understand why her ex always had to intrude in her life. Since they'd divorced, he hadn't stopped calling, and almost every week he asked to have the kids during her time. She hadn't noticed this until recently.

Her therapist had advised her to stand up and say "No." She said she was afraid that Charlene was so worried about getting physically hurt by Brad that she let him take advantage of her. So Charlene started saying "No" to him taking the kids to "this incredible sports game" and "this other activity that is so important."

He responded by calling multiple times to tell Charlene how essential it was for the kids to be with him to do this and that activity. Charlene asked him if it was important for the children to be with their mother. He agreed it was, but…and he'd go on proving his point. When he wasn't phoning, he was e-mailing.

Several times he said to Charlene, "Well, I'm not going to bring the kids home. What are you going to do about that?"

The last time he said that, Charlene called her lawyer, which resulted in them going to their "special master," the court appointed expert who had the power to decide disputes over care of the children.

Charlene had heard so much about fathers, who, after their divorces, didn't pay anymore attention to their kids. She had planned on that. The fact that Brad was demanding the children was shocking. To give him credit, he spent a lot more time with them being a better dad since they divorced.

*

After the recent incident with Brad, Charlene figured she better see if she was on the same page as Shane when it came to parenting. According to her studies in school, issues regarding step-parenting led to the failure of many second marriages. She didn't want to have that fate.

Subject: Step-parenting Drama
Date: July 28
From: "Charlene" <char@CharlenesWeb.net>
To: "Shane" <shaneb@bowers.com>

Shane,

I'm striving to make my children more and more self-sufficient, so they could operate well even if I wasn't in the picture. Like this morning, I had to leave early, and I know that my children, except the youngest, will get up, eat, and go to school without a problem.

I have been training my oldest to babysit and hold down the fort. I'm grooming my second-oldest to do the same.

What I would like in a partner is someone who would support me in my parenting. "Mind your mom," kind of thing. And someone who would support me in my efforts to help heal my children, and if he has children, his too, if that's what he wants of me. I want someone who will let me crawl into his arms at the end of the day and say, "Wow, it was tough today." Then, as he holds me, I can gather strength for the next day.

In my dreams, I'd have someone who'd be willing to get an education with me on the subject of blending families, because I know blending families is a challenge. I approach difficulties by learning the most I can about how to handle them and then turn to God to hear what He has to say. I'd love to have a partner who would attend seminars with me, holding my hand or snuggling through the lecture, and then talking later.

I'm of the mindset that weekly dates are a must. And if it could be arranged, visitation with his children and time with my children would be scheduled together. First, it's good for children to be with other children. There are a lot of social skills to learn in that environment. And second, I'd love to have every other weekend alone with my partner.

I also believe that, because my children are fairly young, they are open and accepting about other people in their lives. When I have my talks with Heavenly Father, I say it the way I see it—either He needs to send the person I should be with in the next couple of years or wait for a long time. It would really be hard to bring in someone new when my children are teenagers. They are much more open-minded and accepting now. But of course everything is in His hands, and I believe He will do what's best, as long as I'm willing to follow His will.

Tell me what you think.

Charlene

*

The closer the day came for the meeting between Charlene and Shane, the more nervous she became. Her face suddenly erupted in zits. She fought frantically to get rid of those, but that wasn't her biggest concern. As she ate dinner with her kids, her fork hit her front tooth and clipped it, making her look like a chipmunk. Then her worries descended to how much weight she hadn't yet lost. She knew she was being silly, but couldn't stop herself. What if she wasn't good enough? She looked in the mirror, examining her flaws, and knew she needed to work on her self-esteem. How could she be a good therapist if she still thought her worth was based on her appearance?

Chapter 32

"**Do you worry that Brad will make** good on his threats and take off with the kids?" Shane asked over the phone.

Charlene had been telling him about another of Brad's episodes. When her ex dropped off the kids, he had said maybe next time he wouldn't bring them back.

"You jerk," Charlene had said without thinking, and slammed the front door on his face once all the kids were inside.

Later, she felt bad for what she had done, but she didn't know what else she could do about it. She thought if she brainstormed with Shane they could come up with ideas.

"He won't take off with the kids," Charlene said. "Even if he did, the kids are old enough that they would call me."

Charlene thanked him for his listening ear and told him that unfortunately homework awaited her. They didn't talk until the next day when Charlene came home from the lawyer's office.

"How did it go?" Shane asked.

"Good things. I'm glad I went. I might be able to stop Brad's harassment, keep my kids, and stay out of court. I feel the glorious Lord watching over me and my children." Then she proceeded to tell Shane about her lawyer's plan.

But the plan didn't stop Brad from entering into Charlene's house with the kids when she was gone that night. When she walked in and saw him standing in her office, she asked, trying to hold back her anger, "What are you doing here?"

"Oh, sorry. The kids needed to get their stuff."

As they stood together in the front entry, Brad put his finger to his forehead. "I've been thinking about how stupid you are for leaving me. You know, God doesn't approve of your behavior. He doesn't approve of how much you hurt the children by leaving me."

Charlene waited until Brad drove to the stop sign with the kids in the car before she speed-dialed Shane.

He said, "Hey, Babe, how are you doing?"

She started to cry.

"What's going on?"

She explained the situation.

"When I'm there by your side, nobody is going to hurt you. I'll see to that. You've been through enough pain. My Italian side will come out, and Brad won't want to mess with you. I will protect you. You're my princess, and when you stand by my side, you'll be my queen. I'll protect you so you can become strong, like you were meant to be."

She really cried then.

"There's no reason for him to be mean to you. When I'm there, he'll have to go through me."

Charlene wondered how she could not fall for this man. She knew her feelings weren't only about what he could do for her, because she knew she could fight the battles and be okay. Her feelings were more about what she could see, feel, and gain by having a relationship that she had always longed to have. He longed for the same things. She had stepped into a dream world. A dream world of happiness.

Shane said, "God has His hand in this."

She loved Shane's faith, his goodness, his manliness. He told her that his ex said his best quality was that he kept things running in the house. That was so unbelievable. He was such a team player, wanting someone by his side. He was willing to try things, explore life. She told him how incredible his faith and strength were. He said his wife never saw it. "What a shame," Charlene whispered.

*

Not until Sunday did Charlene realize that there were small things that bugged her about Shane. She knew she was being nitpicky, but she couldn't help herself. When she talked to him on the phone, he used poor grammar. She didn't want to be stuck-up or anything, but that bothered her.

When he called that afternoon, she said, "I've noticed that sometimes you use improper grammar. I was wondering if you'd like that to be corrected. If you would straighten out some of those words, you would sound much more intelligent. I know that you are intelligent, but it gets lost when you mess up your verb tenses."

He was silent for a long time. Had she hurt his feelings? Was she out of line? She began to regret what she'd said and hate herself for being so nitpicky. Then he said, "Sure. I can work on it."

Charlene breathed a sigh of relief. As they talked, Charlene couldn't get the voice of her therapist out of her head. "Be careful not to look to Shane as a 'rescuer,' someone who you depend on to get you out of all your problems."

Why had her therapist said that? She knew Shane couldn't save her from all the hardships, although she wished he could. That was normal, wasn't it?

"Charlene?"

He drew her attention back to him. "I was thinking about looking for a job when I'm up there visiting you. What do you think?"

She couldn't find words to that. What did she think about it?

After she got off the phone, she felt like she needed to smooth the waters, so to speak, so she admitted in an e-mail: *I noticed your poor grammar the first time we talked. But as I have come to know you, my worries subsided, because you're a wise man with profound insights and longings for knowledge. You aren't a showy intellectual, like Dave. You are humble about your knowledge, and at times you shock me with what you know. I accept you however you speak. That's not important; your character and heart are.*

*

Charlene could hardly wait to talk to her therapist about the most recent updates. "He wants to get a job here!" were the first words out of her mouth.

"What do you think about that?" her therapist asked.

Charlene twisted her fingers in her lap. "I have no idea."

"Do you think you might be experiencing relationship anxiety?"

"Maybe."

*

After the therapy session, Charlene listened to a message Brad had left on her cell phone. "I thought I would tell you why I won't marry you."

"Ha," Charlene said. Like she had asked him to marry her—*not*! Why wouldn't he leave her alone?

*

Subject: Wagging Tongues
Date: August 16
From: "Charlene" <char@CharlenesWeb.net>
To: "Judy" <bchcomber@yippee.com>

Judy,

On the Sunday that Shane walks into church with me, holding my hand, it won't be only the few gossips and my minister who will be alarmed. Several gentlemen have taken to calling me a lot lately. I usually miss the phone calls because I'm busy talking to Shane. One guy has come over when I'm not here. Another man has begun calling me daily and wanting to go do this and that. I think he senses that my heart is being lost to another.

On the same note, I saw Dave at a single's dance. He watched me and ended up dancing by me no matter where I was. (I had three other guys watching me all night—grr. I felt like I was playing dodgeball instead of dancing.) Dave has e-mailed several times, although he promised he wouldn't contact me again. He didn't want to be accused of being a stalker like Brad. I wrote to him last time, wishing him luck in his life and telling him graciously that I didn't want to hear from him again.

I get asked out a lot at the dances. I very, very rarely accept. I like spending most my free time with my children, playing games, taking them on walks, to the movies, or to the museum. Some of the guys I manage to make into friends, but eventually they want to change the relationship dynamics. This is so stressful. I had no idea being single would be like this.

I know you say your experience is different. Maybe you're the lucky one, because when men show an interest in you, it's not so superficial. I don't think these men see the real me. I think some of them don't even grasp the reality that I have five children. It's like they have huge blinders on and what I'm saying is just talk and wouldn't affect them if they got involved with me. All they see is that I'm funny and cute. Why bother about the other details?

Charlene

*

"Five days until I see you, my dear."

"Crazy isn't it?" Charlene asked as she washed dishes.

"We'll have a lot to talk about then," he said.

He was hinting at proposing. What was she going to do about that? Marriage? She hadn't met him yet. What should she say in response? She couldn't come up with anything. This seemed to be going too fast.

"I want to hold your hand for eternity," he continued as though she had already agreed to his hints about marriage.

Were they going too fast? Charlene didn't dare speak her worries out loud. She knew she had been guilty of encouraging it at times, but she had five kids to consider and didn't see any harm in slowing things down.

"I'd like to know where you stand," he said.

"So would I," Charlene muttered.

"What?"

"Let's talk about that after we meet," she suggested. That would give her more time.

That night, she prayed about what to feel and felt the answer back to her was "at least meet him." She thought that wise counsel. How would she ever know without meeting him? She did need to get a better sense of him as a friend, possible father—things like that. She reflected that when she was around others, she would start worrying, but when he called and she heard his voice, and he said, "Hey, baby," her heart would jump. He said he would support her career. He'd embrace her children, love them. He'd do any little or big thing she requested of him. She asked, "Why are you so good to me?"

He would say, "I'm your soul mate. You have blessed me in ways you can't even know."

"What have I done?"

"You have opened yourself up to me, accepted me like no one ever has. You have trusted me and shared yourself with me. I know your character, your goodness."

"How do you know these things?"

"I just know."

He asked her one night, "You're going to make it hard on me to leave you when I have to return home, aren't you?"

"Very difficult," she said. "I'll try my best."

"I knew that."

"How?"

"Just did. I could sense that from you. Besides, if I was in your position, I'd do the same thing, because I want to be with you."

Other things that he'd say were, "Can you imagine how wonderful it's going to be when we have three whole days together?" or "Don't leave this life without marrying me. I'd spend all my days longing for you. You're permanently in my heart. I want to make you happy, happier than you've ever been before."

Her friend Karla said this was infatuation. Perhaps. The truth was Charlene felt like they had been together for a long time. As

Charlene wrestled with what to do, her doorbell rang and there were her next door neighbors, Sue and Marsha. "We came to see how you were doing," Sue said.

"Come in and sit down," Charlene said, gesturing them to her front room.

Marsha was plump, pretty, and fifty-something. "So what's new for you?" she asked.

"Well, I met this neat guy from New Mexico—"

"Oh, no, dear, that's not healthy. You have a lot more healing that you need to do."

Charlene looked at the window. Too many voices jerking her this way and that. She was going to have to tune everyone out and let God guide.

Chapter 33

Sandra yelled, screamed, and threw things. "I don't have to listen to you," she said at the top of her lungs.

Charlene stared at her daughter. She had simply asked the child to clean her room. Why was she acting so vile?

"You can't make me do anything." Sandra pulled herself up straight, standing just inches from Charlene's face.

Brad had done that to Charlene. It was such an intimidation move, she hated that. Thankfully, Sandra wasn't tall enough to make the threat serious yet, but she was very close.

"Mom, I hate you. You ruined my life. Why did you have to get divorced? You don't care about me."

"Yes, I do, Sandra. I love you."

"You don't. If you did you wouldn't have left Dad or moved away from all my friends. You're ruining my life."

Charlene's stomach twisted, reminding her of the fear that had been so common when she was with Brad and he went into one of his rages. She knew Sandra must be repeating things her father had said. She also knew the children didn't know much of what had happened between their parents. Charlene and Brad were both legally bound not to explain, although Brad talked anyway, which amplified her struggle to manage the children's adjustments.

The fight went on for hours. Sandra refused to listen. She started hitting her siblings if they got any where near her.

"Sandra, don't," Charlene said.

"Make me," she snapped back, crossing her arms over her chest.

Charlene's head spun, and she could feel her anger rising. How dare anyone hurt her children. She needed to get away from her daughter. She called a friend for help.

"Glad to take her on and give her some jobs," Jill said.

Charlene told the kids they were going out. Sandra filed into the car along with everyone else. Pulling up to Jill's house, she said to Sandra, "Come with me." When Sandra figured out what was going on, it was too late for her to do anything else.

"Mom, don't leave me," she screamed. "I promise I'll be good."

"Great, have fun doing the chores they have waiting for you."

"We'll take great care of her," her friend said, winking.

Charlene climbed into the car and breathed a big sigh of relief, only to hear Lorine start to cry and explode. Lorine was easier to handle, though, because she was younger. When Charlene finally could focus on something other than kids, she was exhausted.

Shane called later that day. They talked. He listened. He cared. Then he said, "Maybe when I get up there we need to talk about doing something more permanent so I can be more of a help to you. Right now, I can't really do anything. What do you say?"

"We'll see," she answered.

He said, "I've prayed and gotten a green light. It's shining brighter. I want to come and protect you, strengthen you." Then he said, "If either of us are feeling love for the other, let's not say so until we meet. It wouldn't be right until we're looking each other in the eyes."

Charlene knew he told other people he had met the love of his life, his soul mate. He'd ask Charlene on the phone, "Can it be any better than to be so deeply connected with someone?"

"No," she'd say.

Chapter 34

Subject: 24 hrs.
Date: August 21
From: "Charlene" <char@CharlenesWeb.net>
To: "Shane" <shaneb@bowers.com>

Shane,

Know I'm thinking of you, and in less than twenty-four hours we'll be together. Mmm.

Sweet Blue

Charlene was a pile of nerves. The day of meeting her possible future husband was tomorrow. Would he be okay with her? Would it be the same as it had been through e-mails? Would she find the same peace with him in the flesh as she did on the Internet waves? She felt confident that she would, but doubts found a way to shoot up every once in awhile.

That night she slept restlessly. She kept replaying in her mind what their meeting would be like. He'd walk off the plane. She'd see him, the electricity would strike them, and they would smile.

When her alarm beeped, Charlene dragged herself out of bed. She was so tired. She sleepily started getting ready for the grand meeting. When she looked in the mirror, she couldn't believe it. She had to write Judy about this.

Subject: Big Zit Meeting
Date: August 22
From: "Charlene" <char@CharlenesWeb.net>
To: "Judy" <bchcomber@yippee.com>

Judy,

Today is the day I meet Shane face-to-face. I'm about to leave for the airport. I'm nervous. I admit it. I hope he's everything I think he is.

Charlene

P.S. Wouldn't it figure? I have a big zit on my cheek.

*

The instant Charlene saw Shane's face from around the escalators at the airport, her stomach twisted. It wasn't going to work. None of it. Everything had been a lie. He had lied to her.

He vaguely looked like his picture but without the rose in his hand and big smile directed at her, she wouldn't have recognized him. Shane had only sent one photo of himself, adding many descriptions through e-mails and conversations. What Charlene had been led to believe she would see in meeting Shane was abrasively striking against reality.

Rather than a rugged woodsman like the Brawny paper towel man, he appeared to be a weakly office worker. Rather than the strong healthy physique reflected in a man claiming to workout on his Bowflex, a man claiming to be fit, the real Shane appeared more like a flabby sports fan watching athletics on TV while drinking and eating armchair calories. The photo and descriptions she had received were like another person altogether. The disappointing incongruity sucked away any excitement Charlene had been feeling. In a spilt second she had slipped into sense of dread.

She forced herself to stand still and wait, though she wanted to turn and run. She had to give him more time. Maybe her first impression was way off. They had connected so much on the phone and the Internet. To be fair, she had to give this a chance. She might just be refusing a good guy because she still had an addiction to the "bad boy" persona. She needed to learn to become attracted to healthy, less-intense people. Now was her chance.

His arms wrapped around her, jerking her to him. His lips pressed down on her.

Charlene's eyes were opened wide as he kissed her. She thought about pulling away, but with all the buildup to their meeting, she worried it would be rude.

He pulled slightly from her and his fingers traced her jawbone. "Sweet Blue," he whispered. His eyes studied hers intently.

She compelled herself to look at him, resisting every urge to bolt. Things had to get better. "Should we get your suitcase?" she asked.

"I just want to stand here and look at you."

*

She had never realized how long a visit could feel until Shane kept trying to hold her and kiss her and push, push, push his love on her. She just wanted him to get off and leave her alone. "Back," she said angrily when one time he tried to kiss her too long. "We've got to go do something else," she said, and stood so he couldn't take her in his arms again.

Not only was there no spark, he had lied. She couldn't seem to get over that fact.

She wanted to shout, but hated to be so rude to the man who was supposed to be her "True Blue." Then again, she was walking arm in arm with something very different. Deceived!

His concerted efforts to be always kissing continued. He kept forcing his affection on her until she pushed him off. "Stay back," she yelled.

She felt like she was back with Brad, completely trapped. No way out. He wasn't listening to her or respecting her. It was ridiculous. She wasn't going to be a victim anymore. No matter what either of their expectations had been, he wasn't respecting her, and she didn't want to align herself with a person like that. That was not healthy.

Since she had committed to being with him for the weekend he was in town, she said, "Let's go to a dance." She hoped he would want to dance with someone else. He didn't. He kept pawing her. He never took his hands off of her for an instant.

Charlene looked around the floor, embarrassed. Once he went to the bathroom and she ran up to a man she knew, Tanner. "Help me," she pleaded. "I can't stand it."

Tanner laughed.

"Stop laughing. It's not funny."

"Yes, it is," Tanner said as he led her into a spin.

She fell back in step with him and said, "What will I do if he proposes? I'm having a hard time even holding his hand!"

That brought on greater laughter. Charlene narrowed her eyes and tried to act like she was mad, but she couldn't keep it up. This was a funny situation in some ways. "You know, it's like he's two different people. The person on the Internet and phone, and this other physical presence."

"There are huge pitfalls to Internet dating," Tanner said. "People can be dishonest or misrepresent themselves in a lot of different ways."

"Ain't that the truth," Charlene said, before Shane came to lead her back to the dance floor with him. When he asked her what was wrong, she said, "I need to be courted."

*

Subject: Thanks
Date: August 25
From: "Charlene" <char@CharlenesWeb.net>
To: "Shane" <shaneb@bowers.com>

Shane,

Thanks for coming out to meet me. It was nice getting to know you better. You might want to hold off on getting those plane tickets. I'm not so sure how I feel about that after having given it some more thought. I don't like some of the things that happened between us.

I thought I had made it very clear that I expected you to act like a gentleman. When you became carried away with the kissing and I said, "No more," I did not appreciate it that you backed away for a few minutes and then started pushing me to go further than I felt comfortable doing. I had to literally push you off and yell at you to stay away from me. I don't know how I can trust you when you promised me that you would keep your passion under control.

Shane, you're a wonderful man who has been deprived of love your whole life. You crave it so badly that it starts to rule you, and you exhibit behaviors that aren't healthy—like clinginess. Be kind to yourself. I suggest you take the money you would have used to come out here and get some therapy. Begin your healing journey. Then maybe you'll be able to get into the kind of relationship you long for and deserve.

Sorry.

Charlene

*

Charlene curled up by the fireplace and stared out over the lake and the mountain range. She thought about nothing. She was numb. She stayed that way for quite awhile before dragging herself into action. She could at least check her e-mails.

Another e-mail from Dave. He was telling her about problems he found himself in. He wanted to know what Charlene thought of him and the treatment that he had given her when they were dating. That was easy to respond to.

Subject: Blessing
Date: August 27
From: "Charlene" <char@CharlenesWeb.net>
To: "Dave" <allaroundman@yesterday.com>

Dave,

You have unwittingly offered me comfort and tenderness in a time when I was in need. I'm grateful for your kindness and how you have blessed my life. I wish you the best.

Charlene

Judy called right after she pressed the send button on the e-mail. "I have got to get more details about you and Shane."

Charlene groaned. "I don't know how it could go so wrong. I don't know what happened."

After hearing the details, Judy asked, "Do you think you might have given him the wrong impression when you were so open with your feelings? You know, like when you talked about him holding you forever and other stuff like that?"

"I hope not," Charlene said.

"You know, guys think differently than females. You might have unknowingly led him on."

"Just great," Charlene said. "I'll e-mail him and tell him I'm sorry if that's what I did. I don't see how I did that, but you just might be right."

Subject: I hope....
Date: August 27
From: "Charlene" <char@CharlenesWeb.net>
To: "Shane" <shaneb@bowers.com>

Shane,

As I reflect on our interactions, I hope I didn't give you any reason to think that being too physical with me was okay. I can see that my being so open with you could lead to a misunderstanding. If this is the case, I am truly sorry.

Charlene

The phone rang before she could send off the e-mail. She answered, pushing the send button as she did.

It was Shane. He was crying. "Please forgive me. I'm sorry. I'm so sorry. I didn't mean to scare you like that. Even if you don't give me another chance, I'll pray for you. I want to heal."

"Oh, no," Charlene thought. What was she going to do? Shane, no matter how much she wanted it to be different, was not exciting to her. He was not stupid but not really very smart, either. Plus, there were a few things they disagreed on. For instance, he let his ex-wife suffer on her own by not helping her with her mounting financial struggles. That seemed wrong when she was trying to support their daughter. Charlene didn't like the way Shane acted sometimes with his daughter, either. When the child was with him, he talked to Charlene on the phone instead of giving his daughter attention. It was Shane's only time with his child. He didn't seem to be making his child a priority. Charlene had always put Shane on hold when her children needed something. She'd tended to their need then gotten back on. But the biggest thing that bothered her was that he hadn't respected her when she said no. If he couldn't do that when they first met, that seemed to be a clear sign that there could be future problems.

"I'm praying and getting confirmation. I know it's only a matter of time, and we'll be together."

Charlene found that doubtful. "Let's try being friends for awhile," she concluded. She couldn't give him any more.

That night Sandra came home. "Oh my gosh, Mom. You dress so dumb. You are so embarrassing."

Good to see you too, Charlene thought. She hoped her daughter would grow out of the mouthy stage soon.

*

The week sped by, busy with worries of school and kids. The only thing that seemed different was the absence of phone calls and e-mails from Shane, but change was always a bit of an adjustment. By the time Friday rolled around, Charlene was more than ready for a dance.

What she wasn't ready for was Dave. He hadn't been to most of the dances since they broke up. Charlene did a double take to make sure it was really him. It was.

He came over to her and said, "Hi," when she was busy dancing.

She greeted him back.

He was hanging out with a gorgeous blonde who had strong facial features and lots of makeup. Charlene wasn't sure why she kept glancing at the blonde, or why she didn't like how pretty she was. Why did it matter?

A guy named Nicholas danced with her. He had the rugged look she liked, with a beard, strong arms, and sun colored hair. Charlene was in a funny mood when he pulled her in his arms.

"Would you like to go out sometime?" he asked.

"I'm sick of being asked to get married within the first month of meeting a guy. So if you can promise to not do that, then I'll consider it."

He said, "I won't get serious until I've dated fifty-one girls."

She nodded, not sure how to respond.

"You're number fifty-two," he said.

Too funny. Charlene liked that.

One creepy guy she danced with wanted to talk to her about marriage. "I don't think so," she said, fed up with all this relationship pressure crap.

She went up to Nicholas. "Would you mind walking me to my car?"

He smiled. "Not at all."

Charlene could feel Dave standing alone, watching her. She tried to shake off her strange feelings about it as she left the dance hall.

*

Subject: Are you okay? For sure?
Date: September 5
From: "Charlene" <char@CharlenesWeb.net>
To: "Judy" <bchcomber@yippee.com>

Dear Judy,

Sorry to hear about your car wreck. Glad you're all right. You might want to go to a chiropractor and have your back checked, in case you've injured it. Please do that for me.

Shane keeps e-mailing. I feel smothered. I'm gasping. Can't breathe. Ahh! On and on about how he loves me, at night it's "have a good night's sleep," again, "good morning," when I wake up. If I don't e-mail him back, he gets upset.

I can't do this. I have kids and school. I have a life. I want to be free, on my own, and in charge of my own life.

I'm frustrated, but so glad that you're all right.

Charlene

Charlene returned from class to find another e-mail from Dave. Her heart again fluttered in her chest when she saw his address. What was up with him? Why did she feel so awkward about the whole situation?

He wrote that he hoped all was well. He said he was having some extra hard challenges and thought about some things she had said to him when they were together. Her words really helped him. He wanted to say thank you.

Charlene knew that the e-mail was more than a friendly e-mail. He wanted to date her again. Her head spun when she thought about it. How come things were so hard to figure out?

*

Nicholas, the guy who had dated fifty-one women, asked her out to lunch. When she arrived, she was surprised that he brought his three-year-old daughter along. She was blonde, blue-eyed, and shy.

"So this is Samatha. She likes to come with me on my dates."

Charlene nodded.

"Actually I'm gone to work a lot, so I like to spend as much time as I can with my children."

Charlene nodded.

"Well, I'm sure you want to know why I'm divorced. My wife just one day decided that she would rather be without me. She was tired of the whole family thing…" He proceeded to tell her the long story, but in the middle of it he said, "I never had an affair."

Charlene almost choked on her sandwich. "Why do you say that?" *And in front of his daughter*, she thought.

"Often women wonder about it. I wanted to reassure you."

Charlene hadn't even thought about that. But there was something odd about him blurting it out like that. He was definitely friend material. Maybe kissing friend material, but nothing more. She was going into retirement from serious relationships, which of course meant she had to do something about Shane's constant e-mails.

In the last one he went on and on about how he had given her his heart. He also said how much he loved her and how he wanted to make her his queen. He signed it "Broken Hearted." Charlene felt bad about that, but what could she do? It wasn't her fault how things turned out. She hadn't meant for things to go the way they did. If only he hadn't misrepresented himself. If he had been honest, she never would have allowed things to go as far as they had.

Subject: Feel Bad
Date: September 20
From: "Charlene" <char@CharlenesWeb.net>
To: "Shane" <shaneb@bowers.com>

True Blue,

Thank you for being my friend. I feel bad that you gave me your heart. I'm not sure why I couldn't accept it. It just wasn't right. I wish it could have been.

Maybe we can make better friends than lovers?

Sweet Blue

Charlene received an immediate e-mail back wanting to know why things were the way they were. Why couldn't the relationship work?

Charlene sighed. She didn't want to be mean, but she was going to have to get into it if he kept insisting. How could she explain it kindly?

Subject: Here I go.
Date: September 22
From: "Charlene" <char@CharlenesWeb.net>
To: "Shane" <shaneb@bowers.com>

Shane,

I don't want to hurt you, but since you won't let it drop, I'll tell you what the problem was for me. Before I do, I want you to understand it doesn't mean there's something wrong with you. For another type of person, you would be perfect. It's just the way I'm wired. I'm a bit strange as it is, so here goes. Most of our problems are due to becoming acquainted over e-mails. The spark that ignites when two people connect after they meet face-to-face just wasn't there for me.

Also, I decided I want a relationship that is more balanced—more intellectual and less emotional. A relationship based only on emotion was way too much for me. I couldn't breathe. I thought I wanted emotional depth, so I wrote that in my profile. I have learned from you that I can't handle too much of that good thing. As you may have noticed, I have altered my profile to reflect things learned from "us." Sorry, but glad to find it out for both our sakes.

Charlene

Days went by and Charlene heard nothing from Shane. She wondered if he was okay. Was he mad? Had she hurt him? She decided she'd reach out to him one last time to make sure he was doing all right.

Subject: Hello
Date: September 29
From: "Charlene" <char@CharlenesWeb.net>
To: "Shane" <shaneb@bowers.com>

Shane,

Are you okay?

Charlene

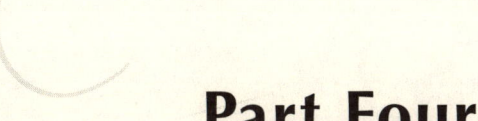

Part Four

CHAPTER 35

Subject: He's Fishing
Date: October 14
From: "Charlene" <char@CharlenesWeb.net>
To: "Judy" <bchcomber@yippee.com>

Dear Judy,

It's been a long time since I've written. I've been caught up in school. I received a letter from Dave today. Let me include some of it:

Charlene, you've been in my thoughts so many times of late that I thought I should write and share a few things.

He then goes on and explains some very personal spiritual experiences he's been having, which he claims have caused a transformation in him where he can now see how he was stuck on being right to the point of being wrong. He now sees that a better way would be to strive for unity, to live and let live, doing what is good rather than protecting himself by being right. Let the judgment be in God's hands, not his. He says he's more content and at peace, not as intense about getting people to accept his point of view.

He continues:

Why do I share these very personal things with you???? Because you have shared so many things with me, and closeness rubbed upon so many of these things. When one's views change, rising to a higher and broader vantage point than before, then past relations and experiences can be seen differently, too. It is a great thing to go through big changes. This letter is to thank you for the love you gave and the part you played in my life in the midst of great changes. This letter is to honor you for the great changes you have gone through yourself…I am humbled to reflect upon what you have so vulnerably bared about your own soul and the faith it has taken to come to where you are now. We are all little children before God, learning simple lessons in the sandbox of life, and this little boy would simply like to express loving honor and supportive blessings to a little girl, Charlene, his sister.

I'd also like to apologize for any pain or difficulty I may have caused you, especially my harsh judgments of your situation with your family and with your former husband. I have come to understand that I was so caught up in being right that I was hurting others. I am committed to pursuing a new course. For such a petite package, you sure do carry a lot of character! So, God bless you, dear Charlene. I hope my sharing with you is a blessing as it is intended. Bless you and your children. With love from your friend and brother, Dave.

Judy, Dave is fishing again. He's a good fisherman, but I'm not going to take his bait and get involved with anyone.

I'm glad to hear you have a lot of extra time to play with grandchildren. That must be rewarding. How's your diet and exercising going?

Charlene

Charlene did a lot of thinking about Dave's e-mail. What was she to make of it? It seemed he really wanted to see what the possibility was of them getting back together. She did miss his tender caresses, tingling kisses, and the laughs, but the arguments, the put-downs, the "I'm better than you" insinuations, the throwing of doubt onto her character, the questioning of her spirituality, "Are you faithful enough? Are you faithful enough?" she didn't miss at all. Neither did she miss the hyper-focused obsession on his own thoughts and his writing. She had gone through enough to get out of her last marriage that she wasn't going to settle for anything less than being completely loved and adored in a new relationship. She doubted the change he claimed included all that.

She wrote him a carefully worded response. *I do consider you a friend. I'm glad you trust me enough to share sacred things with me. I'm glad to hear you're finding peace on your journey. Congratulations on finding a better way to live life. I'm happy to hear I helped in a small way.*

She had to pause and think how to end the e-mail. She didn't want to give any suggestion that "they" were going to work, but she also didn't want to be rude. Truth be known, she did like him. He was a nice guy, and they'd had a lot of fun together, but he wasn't for her. She decided that "Best wishes" would be the most appropriate.

Once she finished that, she focused her attention on her studies. She was taking Professional Counseling Assessment Portfolio II, which meant they had to demonstrate that they knew and could apply all the information they'd learned from the other classes. It was definitely intense. It required so much attention that Charlene stayed away from the Internet and dances for a month. Life was less complicated that way, and it was easier to focus on getting her degree so she could support her family and give her children the attention they needed.

*

"Charlene, I wonder if you would be willing to visit with me. I know that I am no longer your minister, but I am Brad's, and I have some things that I'd like to discuss with you."

Strange, Charlene thought. What would Brad's minister want with her? Was Brad up to another one of his tricks? It really smelled like that could be the case. Would he stop at nothing to try to get her back? She thought about saying "No" to avoid the uncomfortable feelings that would come from the minister encouraging her to do things Brad's way. "Well, I don't know."

"It won't be any pressure, if that's what you're worrying about. I just would really like to discuss some things with you."

Had he read her mind? "All right," she agreed.

When she arrived at his office, she noticed he hadn't changed anything about the simple décor. He rose from his chair to shake her hand. "Thank you for coming," he said with a wide smile. His balding head reflected the room's overhead lights.

Charlene sat in the chair in front of his table, crossed her legs, and rested her hands in her lap.

"Thank you again for coming," the minister said, clearing his throat. "There are some things that I want you to think about and think about hard." He shifted his weight. "As you might have guessed, Brad has been in here and he wanted me to talk to you."

Charlene felt her shoulders tighten. Oh, great, she thought. Here it comes. Brad saying how sorry he was and how he would never do it again. And how much his family and wife means to him. He seemed really sincere. Couldn't you give him one more chance? God would want you to, you know.

She didn't want to hear that or anything else about how wonderful Brad was. He continued to make her life miserable even after the divorce, and the best thing she *ever* did was leave him. She was much happier now on her own, and it would be like going back to death to return to him. She liked her freedom and didn't want to lose it. Her breathing turned shallow as she waited.

"Brad has given me permission to talk to you about what he has told me. In fact, he wanted me to talk to you. He confessed everything to me. He said how sorry he was for what he had done to you and the children. It's a shame that you weren't there to hear how sincere he was." He cleared his throat. "Can't you find it in your heart to give him a chance? He has had time to change his habits. Move slow, but consider putting your marriage back together."

There it was. Charlene didn't say anything.

"I meet with a lot of couples. I interview single people, too. I have an observation about a lot of them. Many of single people have been so hurt that they end up staying away from any commitments. They refuse to continue to grow even when they get a chance. Charlene, let me promise you, if you want happiness, and you're given the chance to pursue that goal with a good partner, it would not be good for you to pass up a real opportunity because of fear. Marriage is harder than being single, but the rewards for growth are also considerably more. I feel I'm meant to tell you that you're healed enough and to follow your heart. You can have joy and happiness."

Tears washed her face. She needed to hear this. She shook his hand and said, "You don't know how much help you've been. I appreciate it."

Suddenly she felt like she had been hiding. God did want her to get married again. She knew that wasn't the answer for all singles, but it was for her.

"Charlene, are you all right?" the minister asked.

She nodded her head. "I just realized that I have been living my life in fear."

"Don't beat yourself up over it. A lot of us do that."

"Thanks. You have given me the courage to consider taking the plunge."

Chapter 36

Judy suggested that Charlene take Dave's "transformation" e-mail along with her to therapy and see what the therapist thought about it.

"Well, what do you think?" her therapist asked after reading it.

Charlene shrugged. Her therapist waited, not letting her get away with that.

"I want to hear what you have to say about it," Charlene finally said, not wanting to influence her therapist's answer.

"What do you want to do about this e-mail?" Cindy asked, glancing it over again.

Charlene looked away from her probing eyes, scooted on the edge of the couch and said, "I want to go back to him. I want to see if what he is saying is true."

Her therapist read the e-mail again, ignoring her declaration. At last she sat back in her chair, resting the printout on the armrest. "He's addressing the areas you had problems with—his self-righteousness and his rigidity on being right. He might have actually made these changes. The nice thing about this is, if he truly made these changes, he did it on his own with no influence from you. He didn't even know if you were involved with someone else or how you would respond."

"Do you think he wants to have a relationship with me?" Charlene asked.

"Most definitely, yes. He's clearly invested a lot of thought about you. I especially like the part about 'a lot of character in such a petite package.' What do you think about that?"

And off they went, talking about her self-esteem. Later Charlene asked, "Why did I get so carried away with Shane when I had signals that it wasn't right?"

"Charlene, you know that answer," Cindy said.

To which Charlene thought, if she knew the answer she wouldn't have asked the question.

"Why did you second-guess yourself?" Cindy asked.

"Because I didn't trust myself." Charlene realized she had again made that mistake.

Cindy told Charlene not to feel bad. Many, many, many abuse victims made the same mistake. She said a lot of them end up marrying people they're not well matched with and praised Charlene for recognizing there was a problem before it was too late. She explained that abuse victims often don't know themselves very well and don't know how to ask for what they want. They don't feel they have a right to ask for those things. It was a new concept for them, to think they could have control over their lives. She also praised Charlene for standing up to all his advances.

"I only wish I would have been more assertive sooner," Charlene said.

"Baby steps," Cindy said. "Give yourself a break. You're learning new skill sets."

Charlene then said, "Shane came across as a nice guy. When things bothered me, I would say to myself, 'Charlene, you're attracted to abusers, nice guys seem so boring. Don't chase away a nice guy and get stuck with an abuser because you think he's boring.' Or 'This may be your only chance to be treated like a princess. Don't throw it away because he speaks with poor grammar or he doesn't challenge you enough. It's good that he doesn't challenge you. You aren't being abused. You just need to grow accustomed to that.' And on and on."

"You were talking yourself out of your feelings and convictions," her therapist said.

Charlene laughed. She was right. "But I thought you said nice guys were boring to me."

"That's black-and-white thinking. You believe that a man is either an abuser or boring. There's an alternative to either extreme."

"Oh."

As Charlene prepared to leave the session, her therapist asked, "What are you going to do about Dave?"

Charlene pulled her purse strap up her shoulder, giving herself time to decide on an answer. "I'm going to go to the dance tomorrow. I've seen him there several times."

Cindy nodded. "Good luck."

"I'll have to see if there's anything to this 'transformation' thing," Charlene said.

*

Charlene was dancing with Tanner, breathing in his musty cologne, when she spotted Dave. It was very early in the evening. Dave was dancing with someone, but after a few songs he sat down, watching Charlene. Some women gathered around, chatting to him. Charlene tried to act like she wasn't paying attention, but couldn't stop the flutter spinning inside her stomach.

Tanner saw him and said, "You're not going to dance with him, are you? Promise me you won't. He's no good. Just temptation."

Charlene refused to promise.

"Remember how he hurt you."

Charlene kept dancing without saying anything. She wasn't going to let Tanner keep her away from what could be her happiness.

"Then promise me you'll only dance two dances." He waved two fingers in her face.

She laughed.

Tanner danced three more numbers with her, seemingly unwilling to let her go. Charlene thought that was fine. She didn't want to seem too anxious.

As she looked at Dave, huddled in the midst of a bunch of gawking women, she wondered if coming had been a good idea. Maybe Tanner was right.

Tanner said, "I need to go to the restroom. I'll be right back. Don't go anywhere." He looked hesitant to leave.

Charlene watched him go, but before Tanner had made three steps, Dave stood in front of her.

"Hi." She grinned at him.

"Hi. Want to dance?"

She nodded and found herself in his arms. The comfort, the sweetness that existed between them splashed over her again. There was a brief moment, right as he touched her, that she saw in her mind's eye them standing together in a distant place where there was no gravity. They glowed in radiant white, holding hands, both of them filled with power, both equal to one another. It was a flash of possibilities.

Charlene began telling him about her most recent troubles with Brad, bragging about how well she was doing in school, and going on and on about the smallest things her children had been up to.

He laughed at her stories, pulled her tight, and whispered, "It's so good to see you again."

After they danced a few dances, he said, "Would you like to go get something to eat?"

They went to the buffet table, filled their plates, and found a faraway spot where they could reconnect with each other. He caught her up on his business happenings, his daughter, and then he grew serious when he spoke about his "transformation." Now he saw things in a different way. He apologized for the pressure he had put on her.

He took her hand in his and stroked her fingers. Their fingers didn't intertwine. They weren't that close yet, but they were coming back together. It felt right.

Charlene looked at him as it grew late and wondered what he would do. Would he invite her out for a bite to eat? Would he escort her to her car and try to kiss her again? Would he ditch her?

At the end of the dance, he asked, "Can I call you and arrange to see you again?"

She felt embarrassed heat coming from her neck as she nodded. He smiled and took off. Charlene watched him until Tanner ran up, wanting to talk.

*

It took Dave three days to call Charlene. She wanted to strangle him. Maybe old habits die hard. When they finally reconnected, he took her to a restaurant. After the small talk, he said, "You've changed."

"Like how?" she asked. She was sitting next to him, so she pushed from his arms to look at him as he answered.

"I don't know. Let me think about it." He pulled her back into his arms and put on a reflective expression. After some time passed, he said, "You're more open, more accepting. It seems like you're more loving."

Charlene thought about it. In this area, Shane had been very good for her. He was so open, loving, and passionate that she felt safe enough to let down some of her guard. The guard must still be down, even though he was out of the picture.

"I have learned things over the past couple of months."

"Like what?" Dave looked at her lips.

She ignored that and said, "I learned I could stand on my own. It was hard and lonely, but I could do it. Before, I hadn't had enough time being single to know if I could make it. Time away from you taught me that I could stand by myself."

"Really?" he asked, his eyebrows lifting. "So you want to be alone?"

Charlene knew that she was going red. He was kidding her, but not really. She needed to be honest no matter how hard or risky. "When I saw you at the last dance, my heart told me I didn't want to be alone. I longed for companionship. I can raise my children alone, but I don't want to. If I'm not tired and stressed trying to do it all myself, I could be a much more effective mother. I could continue as I am now and be very happy, but I feel like I have a lot I could offer a man. A lot I could bless his life with. I also want to show my children a healthy relationship. They have only seen dysfunction, and if I am truly going to break the chains of abuse, I need to give them new tools.

"It took being on my own for blocks of time to realize this. It also took dating and dancing and socializing with a lot of men for me to recognize the virtues you have."

Out of all the men she had corresponded with, Dave was by far the one who had the capacity to best enhance her life. He'd been a surrogate father to lots of children her children's ages, so he realized the reality of that kind of situation much more than the other men she had dated. He seemed confident about handling it. He had been in the field and done quite well. When her oldest daughter had made rude, sarcastic comments to him, he hadn't even flinched. Charlene had asked him if it hurt his feelings. His reply had been, "I have to expect that. I'm the new kid on the block."

Charlene knew that with Dave in her kids' lives, they would be enriched more than she could do on her own. They had talked thousands of hours on parenting, and she knew that he would be a great dad to her children and that their parenting styles would compliment each other.

Dave was intellectually smart enough to challenge her and keep her on her toes. She had learned with Shane that although it was nice at times to have someone agree with her constantly, after a while it became annoying. She needed the challenge of someone not always just agreeing with or following her lead.

She felt she could have gotten Shane to do anything she wanted. There were hardly any limits. This would never be the case with Dave. Dave would be kind, but he'd stand up if he thought she took things too far. Charlene didn't want to be dominant. If she had stayed with Shane very long, that might have become tempting.

She'd been abused. It was a common pattern in human nature for people who have been victims to dominate if they got the chance. Many people tended to reenact the abuse inflicted on them, in one way or another. She didn't want that.

*

It was Thanksgiving time again, and this year, Charlene was without her children. She decided to have a quiet Thanksgiving with Dave, his daughter, his brother and wife, and their three kids. She enjoyed it. It was nice to share common, everyday things with Dave.

Judy wanted to know how Dave had changed. Charlene wrote back.

> *Date: November 19*
> *From: "Charlene" <char@CharlenesWeb.net>*
> *To: "Judy" <bchcomber@yippee.com>*
> *Dear Judy,*
>
> *Believe me, I've watched him. I would have to say he has a more humble disposition. You know how he came off arrogant before, like he had all the answers and I didn't have any? He's not that way anymore. Dave is gentler. The need to compare, compete, and the drive to doubt me is gone. He doesn't seem threatened by me, but happy about the qualities he sees in me.*
>
> *Last night Dave took me to dinner and explained that in the time we were apart he read a book that helped give him more insight into what I must be going through. The book was about Holocaust survivors who, after the war, had struggles with the simplest of things, like eating. Some survivors would eat so much it killed them.*
>
> *After telling me this, he reached across the table and put my hand in his. "Charlene, reading this book gave me compassion for the hardships you must have suffered. You were in a concentration camp of your own. It's remarkable that you're coping as well as you are. You are one courageous woman. I admire you. I'm sorry*

for how hard I was on you. I didn't understand. The fact that you were still willing to go on seeing me after I said those things to you just proves your loving, forgiving nature. I realize that now.

"You're amazing because you chose to survive. You survived your childhood and your marriage. You have deep wisdom. You not only are a survivor, but you're determined not to be limited by your past experiences. You have an eternal quality that seeks and hungers to become a glorious being."

What to make of all of this?

Charlene

Judy was still skeptical about where all this was leading. Wanting her friend onboard with such a big thing in her life, Charlene decided to share more about the "new" Dave.

Subject: Dave's words
Date: December 1
From: "Charlene" <char@CharlenesWeb.net>
To: "Judy" <bchcomber@yippee.com>

Dear Judy,

I'm including part of the letter Dave wrote to me:
Wow, Sweetheart. Thank you for your message, a real blessing to my soul. It resonates with the Spirit in me, with all I have learned and loved about serving our Father in Heaven. I can hardly express what is struck in me by your words. You sound like a soul mate.
I certainly enjoy reading whatever you write to me. Before your e-mail arrived, I had been thinking about writing what kind of love my future wife might expect from me. When I thought about this, I felt as though "you" were with me. It was a very powerful experience. I hesitate to go here…it is not meant to manipulate or proscribe any course of action, but considering how much I have elaborated my "views" to you in the past, it might be good to share some "feelings" from where I am now…

"I see you sitting there across from me in the car, and I reach out my hand for yours. It is as though the love I feel for you consumes me, radiating out from me to envelop you. I feel the precious worth of your soul, and it seems the touch of flesh is completely inad-

equate to convey the bonding I feel. It would take a thousand sparks of shared caring interactions to equal the flame of my vision of love with you. There is no measuring that which springs eternal. I want to care for what you care for, listen to your dreams and sorrows, share tears of joy and pain, take time to be with you to strengthen and be strengthened. I want to work together with you on many different projects, to support and encourage you in those projects and pursuits in which I might not personally participate. For while we are one, we are distinct, and your life is an individual gift that must flourish and experience and grow individually, as with me... our lives together are enriched, and when we are apart our lives are enhanced.

I want to patiently embrace your children and assist in giving them strong arms to trust in. I want to labor with you in providing a pattern and nourishment that can overcome any past difficulties. I also want to enable useful good to come from ongoing challenges. I also desire to love and lift you and the children to be all that you want to be, freed from the chains of spiritual starvation and confusion. In all things, I want to share our Father in Heaven's presence, so we might be raised up and drawn together.

Through faith, I'm becoming a better man. Through faith, you're becoming a better woman. My love for God is foremost in my life. I cherish the vision of us serving Him together. Whatever the Lord requires, it would be of "us." And that would be a blessing. And we could laugh. Well, dear Charlene, it is enough. If not you, then this vision will be with the woman who shall be my wife. But why not you? For I have not met a better match! The gift of love God has blessed me with is not meant to be put under a bushel, or hid away, and I seek His guidance and blessing to provide the path and the person I shall unite with. I have said enough for now, perhaps too much. Sent with love, Dave

Judy, doesn't this sound like a marriage proposal? I don't know about that. I've been praying, making lists, thinking. Like my therapist said, he is actively addressing all the problems I had with him. He did it on his own. He didn't know if I was involved with someone else.

Judy, I know I love him. I was talking to Karla the other day, and she pointed out that in my comments and assessments of every *man I dated I would always compare them with Dave. Even with Shane I would say, "Well, Dave was like this and Shane is different, he..." Karla said I rarely compared the men with Brad, it was always Dave. "He got to you good," she said.*

I can't deny that. I can't deny the spark I feel with him, but there were problems so I walked away. I have put together a list of problems we would need to work out. We'll see.

Charlene

*

As Charlene prepared to go on another date with Dave, she thought about what kind of father he would be to her children. With Shane, she knew he'd step back and let her run the show, which would definitely be easier and would prevent fights. Dave wasn't that type of person. He would be very involved in their lives. He told her once, "Children are God's children. It doesn't matter who the earthly parents are. God would want me to raise them as my own."

She and Dave had talked many hours about parenting philosophies. She told him, thinking he would disapprove but should know anyway, about the consequences she'd been giving to her oldest child in expectation of a more socially acceptable manner. Instead of thinking she was a fanatic like her ex always said, he was awed.

From that discussion and many others, she knew they agreed that a firm line needed to be drawn. It was irresponsible for a parent not to hold a child to that line. This kind of structure gave children a feeling of security. Dave explained it in his own way. "It would be wrong if we thought we could tell God what to do. That would mix the order up. We feel secure because God draws a firm line with us."

She and Dave enjoyed a stroll through her neighborhood. It was Brad's weekend with the children, so Charlene felt free to walk slowly and take in the fresh air. The sun was slipping behind the lake, sparkling gold on the water. As they returned to the house, Charlene pulled her coat tighter, for she saw that her ex's car was parked out front. She rushed up to see what the problem was. Brad's eyes widened as he took in Dave.

"What are you doing?" Charlene asked.

"The kids left some things they needed. They let themselves in through the padlock on the garage."

When Lorine saw Dave, she ran to him and threw her arms around him. "Davy, Davy."

Coming out from the house, Sandra stopped when she spotted Dave. Her eyes narrowed. "Mom, what's he doing here?"

Cameron smiled. Nathan wrapped himself around Dave's leg. Brad slumped around the front yard.

After Dave gave her a steaming passionate kiss later that night, he left, and Charlene stood in her front entryway thinking. She and Dave had more baggage than some. They both had been through marriages to other people, which in a way made it easier for them to understand each other. They had other rough difficulties; they had both cultivated a depth. There was an understanding between them.

Charlene sat on her staircase. She had been abused for many years. That was not going to go away any time soon. It was not going to vanish because she found a wonderful man, and they both wanted to build a future together. She had residual effects. Suppose she and Dave had a "normal" disagreement once they married? Suppose he was angry and an expression crossed his face similar to what Brad had before he chucked things at her? Before she could think, she'd more than likely be under the table screaming, "Don't beat me!"

Now in this scenario, a person who had good coping skills would be able to keep his cool, crawl under the table and calmly remind her he was not Brad. Maybe someone who hadn't been through his own experiences would not be able to understand what was spewing from her mouth. That person might get defensive and label her a freak.

She'd already had an episode that was similar. Dave came over to her house in the middle of an explosive encounter with Brad. Brad glared at Dave, said some words, and left. Charlene was about to faint. Dave caught her, took her in his arms and spoke calmly. "I'm not Brad. Charlene, look at me. Who are you with?" She shook in his arms. He said nothing bad about Brad, actually never did, and he didn't take anything personally, just focused on helping her. Who else would be able to respond so maturely?

*

Dave came over and helped with the kids' homework two nights later while Charlene cooked dinner. Lorine and Cameron got into a fight. Charlene put the spatula down and went to solve the argument only to be stopped because Dave got there first.

"Now, Lorine, what seems to be the problem here?"

Charlene picked up the spatula again. It was nice having him around.

That night when Charlene retired to bed, she prayed over the marriage idea that Dave kept mentioning. She wished he would just let things be as they were. She liked him around but also liked being single. She liked the dances.

As she prayed, it was as if God opened her mind, reminding her. The words spoken by Brad's minister came back to her along with the feelings of wanting to be with Dave, the connection they had felt, the image of Dave holding her hand as an equal, all flooded into her thoughts. Still, this wasn't enough to calm her doubts. Maybe she was imagining all this because it was what she wanted.

She asked God, "Should I marry Dave?"

The answer came into her head. "Be at peace, Charlene."

"What about my children? What will I do about my children?"

"He will help bring the family together with his abilities. He will serve as a strength to you and to your children."

After praying, she reflected about her past events. She felt guided to get involved with Dave, and then to back away from him, then Shane, and now Dave again. It seemed like God was giving her unstable messages, but He wasn't. She had needed to marry Brad. She didn't regret that. Brad had his agency about what he could do with their marriage. As Dave said, "If a servant is slothful, God will take away the prize and give it to another." It would appear that was what happened with Brad's marriage to Charlene.

She and Dave were meant to meet and get involved. It was under God's direction that they separated, to learn the things each of them needed to learn before they could be together. Charlene had also needed Shane. She learned many valuable lessons from him, and she wouldn't be the same because of him. She hoped she was a positive influence on his life and helped him along his journey, too.

Life was short. If her marriage with Dave didn't work out, she was smart enough to leave again. Being married or single, she was determined, wouldn't interfere with her schooling. She had another year left and with her status she knew she'd get that degree and move on to helping others. Being single was not as horrible as she once imagined. She could do it. But when a kind, loving man was at her door, wanting to share his life with her, it would be a shame to throw that opportunity away.

The next day she decided to write to Judy and sum up what she had learned for history's sake.

Subject: What I've learned…
Date: December 5
From: "Charlene" <char@CharlenesWeb.net>
To: "Judy" <bchcomber@yippee.com>

Dear Judy,

I'll tell you what I have learned about Internet dating. It's a great way to take the "meat market feeling" out of meeting people. You can get past the physical stuff and learn what people think and feel and get a general sense of who they are. But there are people who lie and others who, like Shane, really aren't being honest with themselves. Meeting people and trusting your instincts is the only way to safely guide yourself through the complex maze of single life. I thought Internet dating was an interesting adventure. I'm glad I tried it. I can see how people would experiment in cycles. Sometimes trying it out, and then other times taking a break. After I started settling down in my singleness, I wasn't as concerned with the superficial fluff and started longing for depth in my activities.

Single life with children is not what I imagined. It is hard, but not as hard as I thought. It was important for me to find support from the outside. I could raise my children alone and teach them, perhaps more easily than with a husband who constantly undermined my efforts. My greatest sorrow, which won't end just because I get married, is having to send them to their dad. I miss having them under my roof every day and night. I'm sad about the times in their growing up that I'm going to miss because they're away from me.

I learned that being single in church is uncomfortable, but a lot of the discomfort was of my own making. If others were uncomfortable with me, I did not have to take that on. I could have been a more important part of the congregation. Once I stopped seeing myself as "single," others did, too. Once I learned to participate and contribute my unique talents and skills, and forgot the labels I felt were pinned on me, I became much more unified with the whole. I would still much rather have my children gathered around me at church, than not. It doesn't feel right with them gone. I doubt it ever will or that I will grow used to it.

As far as single life, it has its interesting takes. It's not something I will forget. There are ups and downs. It was fun to get out there and spread my wings and learn more about who I really am, but if I played the game too long it would have grown into a selfish existence.

Oh, and Judy, the loneliness. I've thought of how you've lived through this for so many years. Forgive me for not realizing. Loneliness is the curse and the hardship of being single. There are a lot of great freedoms and opportunities for self-development, fun, and exploration, but none of these can cure the deep sense of loneliness, at least not for me. Sometimes I would keep myself so busy I'd almost forget about it, but the dull ache was always there—the longing for intimacy, connection, and belonging. This loneliness drove me to climb out of my shell and meet others.

I formed a lot of good friendships. They enriched my life. It's sad to think I will be moving on and, most likely, leaving them in the past. I will always remember them and the great blessings they brought to me—just like I will remember those valiant souls who supported me in getting out of hell. Some of them have continued to support me through the singles' world, and some I believe will continue on into my married life. Those like you, Judy, are my

angels. I will forever be indebted to your kindness, bravery, and support. Judy, you and many others have helped my children have a better life. My children may never know what was done for them, but I do. I weep as I contemplate how God assisted me and my children through the hands of others. Some of them no doubt will never know the goodness they brought into our lives. I plead with my Maker to bless these people.
Charlene

*

The day was surprisingly warm for the middle of December. Dave had taken Charlene on a walk in the mountains. He stopped at a ledge that peered over the snowy valley. He wrapped his arms around her and smiled down at her.

"So have you given my second proposal any thought?"

Charlene nodded, wanting to make him squirm.

"And?"

"And I will."

"Will what?" he asked, watching her closely.

"Marry you."

He bent down and kissed her hard before dipping her back in his arms until her head almost reached the dirt.

"Help me up," Charlene pleaded.

When he pulled her up, Charlene playfully tapped his arm. "You're a stinker."

"Are you scared?" he asked.

"Yes."

"Then why are you doing it?"

She had been silently crying for a long time, and she hoped that this would put an end to her tears. "'Cause," Charlene said, peering into his hazel eyes and feeling his rapid heartbeat against hers. "I can't get over you, and I see the working of God in you—and in myself. So let the adventure begin."

Also by Lisa J. Peck ....

Tired of marrying the same mistake over and over again? Sure the person may be different, but the problems are usually the same. If this is the case, or if you want to avoid future pain the book, *Stop Marrying Mistakes* is for you. *Stop Marrying Mistakes* teaches principles through using a friendly easy-to-read format, plus the book includes pertinent assignments that assist the reader to apply the information into their everyday problems and relationships.

Free download Stop Marrying Mistakes Workbook at
http://www.redemptivecommunity.com/site/?page_Id=102

Available wherever books are sold.
Trade paperback, 278 pages ISBN: 978-1-934248-06-5
For more information or to order please visit: www.redemptivecommunity.com